Beethoven Studies 3

Editorial Committee

Joseph Kerman
Lewis Lockwood
Alan Tyson

Beethoven Studies 3

Edited by
Alan Tyson

Cambridge University Press
Cambridge
London   New York   New Rochelle
Melbourne   Sydney

Published by the Press Syndicate of the University of Cambridge
The Pitt Building, Trumpington Street, Cambridge CB2 1RP
32 East 57th Street, New York, NY 10022, USA
296 Beaconsfield Parade, Middle Park, Melbourne 3206, Australia

© Cambridge University Press 1982

First published 1982

Printed in Great Britain at the University Press, Cambridge

Library of Congress catalogue card number: 77–30191

British Library Cataloguing in Publication Data
  Beethoven studies.
  3
  1. Beethoven, Ludwig van
  I. Tyson, Alan
  780'.92'4   ML410.B4
  ISBN 0 521 24131 6

Contents

	page
List of Plates	vi
Preface	vii
Abbreviations	x
1794–1795: Decisive Years in Beethoven's Early Development *Douglas Johnson*	1
Ambiguities in *La Malinconia*: What the Sketches Say *Richard Kramer*	29
Beethoven's Sketches for the Variations in E♭ Op. 35 *Christopher Reynolds*	47
'Eroica' Perspectives: Strategy and Design in the First Movement *Lewis Lockwood*	85
The 'Razumovsky' Quartets: Some Aspects of the Sources *Alan Tyson*	107
Notes on Beethoven's Codas *Joseph Kerman*	141
The Historical Background to the 'Heiliger Dankgesang' in Beethoven's A-minor Quartet Op. 132 *Sieghard Brandenburg*	161
Beethoven's Tagebuch of 1812–1818 *Maynard Solomon*	193
Index of Tagebuch Entries	286
Index of Beethoven's Compositions, Sketches, Letters, and Other Documents	289
General Index	294
Addenda and Corrigenda to *Beethoven Studies* [1] and *Beethoven Studies 2*	299

Plates

		page
I	Sketches for String Quartet in C major Op. 59 No. 3, third movement: Vienna, Gesellschaft der Musikfreunde, A 36, p. 14	119
II	Sketches for String Quartet in C major Op. 59 No. 3, first movement: Bonn, Beethovenhaus, Sammlung H. C. Bodmer, Mh 72 recto	123
III	Draft title-pages for editions of Op. 58, Op. 59, and Op. 60: Berlin, Deutsche Staatsbibliothek, Autograph 35,36, verso	136
IV	Draft title-pages for editions of Op. 61 and Op. 62: Berlin, Deutsche Staatsbibliothek, Autograph 35,36, recto	137
V	Samples of Anton Gräffer's handwriting. (*left*) From a copy made by Gräffer of the *Nachlass* auction catalogue: Bonn, Beethovenhaus, NE 79. (*right*) From his copy of Beethoven's Tagebuch of 1812–1818: Iserlohn, Stadtarchiv	201
VI	Anton Gräffer's copy of Beethoven's Tagebuch of 1812–1818, fol. 1r: Iserlohn, Stadtarchiv	213

Acknowledgment is gratefully made to: Gesellschaft der Musikfreunde, Vienna (Plate I); Beethovenhaus, Bonn (Plates II and V); Deutsche Staatsbibliothek, Berlin (Plates III and IV); Stadtarchiv, Iserlohn (Plates V and VI).

Preface

The aim of the series *Beethoven Studies*, of which this is the third volume, is to present a broad selection of current work on Beethoven. What the contributors have in common is a special interest in the sources both for Beethoven's life and for his creative activity; these sources include not merely such directly musical material as his original scores and his sketchbooks, but also the conversation books and correspondence, and other less familiar documents.

Like its predecessors,[1] the present volume includes biographical, critical, and analytical contributions, with a special emphasis on Beethoven's working methods. Several of the essays focus on different aspects of his life and work over a period of no more than twelve years, from 1794 to 1806. But that was a time of prodigious productivity for Beethoven. At the start we find him engaged among other things in the double task of consolidating what he had learned from his year of study with Haydn and of gaining his artistic independence from so powerful an influence. As Douglas Johnson explains, this led him to reserve his most original musical utterances for genres that had not hitherto been associated with Haydn at his weightiest, the piano sonata and piano trio; and one cannot help feeling sorry for the young Beethoven when Haydn returned to Vienna from London in 1795, bringing with him newly written masterpieces in both those forms.

If Beethoven for some years avoided a direct confrontation with Haydn as a symphonist, he was also wary of the medium of the string quartet, where comparisons with Mozart as well as Haydn could scarcely be avoided. A certain stiffness can be observed in those parts of the Op. 18 Quartets that were written first. But the movement that opens the Finale of Op. 18 No. 6, entitled *La Malinconia*, has been

---

[1] *Beethoven Studies* [1] (New York, 1973; London, 1974) and *Beethoven Studies 2* (London New York, 1977).

claimed as the most original of the whole set; Beethoven's voice is heard in it even more unmistakably than elsewhere in Op. 18. The elaborate sketches for this short movement – and for its reappearance within the Finale – are carefully elucidated by Richard Kramer, who is able to draw attention to the 'eloquent ambiguity' of certain notes in the context of the prevailing chromaticism.

A later essay discusses the three 'Razumovsky' Quartets. By 1806, when he wrote Op. 59, Beethoven had made the genre wholly his own (although in the C-major Quartet, it is suggested, there are retrospective elements that need to be explained). Indeed, one problem in Op. 59 Nos. 1 and 2 may have been that of scale; the presence of movement after movement in sonata form, often with massive sectional repeats, serves as a reminder that these were post-'Eroica' chamber works, surrounded by orchestral compositions on the largest scale. The 'Eroica' Symphony itself is discussed here by Lewis Lockwood, who surveys some long-established analytical perspectives on its first movement, and emphasises – partly with the help of sketches – aspects that appear to have been overlooked up to now: in particular the way in which the repetition of certain segments is used to lend coherence to a movement of unprecedented length.

The Op. 35 Variations in E♭ for piano were completed in the year before the 'Eroica' was sketched. Beethoven claimed that the Variations had been worked out in 'what is really an entirely new manner'. Christopher Reynolds's examination of the sketches for Op. 35 is the first to integrate those in the 'Kessler' and 'Wielhorsky' Sketchbooks. This has the effect not only of throwing light on the meaning of Beethoven's 'new manner', but of exposing a certain overlapping in the times at which the two sketchbooks were in use.

The other contributions to the volume survey somewhat neglected critical, historical, and biographical areas. In his study of Beethoven's codas Joseph Kerman eschews any single formulation of their role; proceeding historically – that is, via the precedents of Mozart and Haydn – he succeeds in reviewing a great many of Beethoven's codas, interpreting their different functions, and exposing their techniques. Sieghard Brandenburg takes us to what will no doubt be for many readers an unfamiliar world in discussing Beethoven's models for the 'Heiliger Dankgesang' of the A-minor Quartet Op. 132. In place of the 'Renaissance' antecedents that have often been claimed for the movement, we are introduced to several theoretical writers on church music working in the second half of the eighteenth century, whom Beethoven is known to have studied. The way in which the design for the movement gradually evolved is also illustrated by the sketches for it.

The last contribution to the book is also much the longest. It is devoted to the presentation of a complex but extremely rewarding document: the transcription, apparently made in 1827, of Beethoven's Tagebuch (diary) for the years 1812–18. The original diary was lost long ago; this copy of it, made shortly after his death, is the nearest that we can get to its text. But in spite of the obscurities caused by transcribing errors and by gaps, the message that comes through is an extremely powerful one. For, as Maynard Solomon explains, the Tagebuch served Beethoven partly as a commonplace book, partly as a 'journal intime'. In the former capacity it is a record of Beethoven's activities, plans and projects, finances, and literary and intellectual interests, many of which are not documented by any other source. In the latter capacity it is a unique exposé of his subjective feelings throughout a period of his life that saw a major personal and stylistic crisis. Such a record, which most biographers have of course seized upon, needs to be used with caution and tact; the presentation of the complete Tagebuch in the best surviving German text, along with a translation and an extensive commentary, will make this unrivalled document available on the most favourable terms.

Earlier versions of the first, second, fourth, fifth, and sixth essays were presented at a conference held at the University of North Carolina, Chapel Hill, in April 1977. The conference was in recognition of the 150th anniversary of Beethoven's death; but it served also to mark the retirement of Professor William S. Newman, author of the classic three-volume *A History of the Sonata Idea* and, among many other smaller studies, one on *Performance Practices in Beethoven's Piano Sonatas* (New York, 1971). The essays in the present volume are accordingly offered to Professor Newman as a token of respect.

Alan Tyson

Abbreviations

Anderson	Emily Anderson, ed., *The Letters of Beethoven*, 3 vols. (London, 1961)
BL	British Library, London
BN	Bibliothèque Nationale, Paris
DSB	Deutsche Staatsbibliothek, Berlin
GA	*Beethovens Werke: vollständige, kritisch durchgesehene Gesamtausgabe*, 25 vols. (Leipzig, 1862–5, 1888)
GdM	Gesellschaft der Musikfreunde, Vienna
Hess	Willy Hess, *Verzeichnis der nicht in der Gesamtausgabe veröffentlichten Werke Ludwig van Beethovens* (Wiesbaden, 1957)
Kinsky–Halm	Georg Kinsky, *Das Werk Beethovens: thematisch-bibliographisches Verzeichnis seiner sämtlichen vollendeten Kompositionen*, completed and ed. Hans Halm (Munich and Duisburg, 1955)
N I	Gustav Nottebohm, *Beethoveniana* (Leipzig and Winterthur, 1872)
N II	Gustav Nottebohm, *Zweite Beethoveniana: nachgelassene Aufsätze* (Leipzig, 1887)
N 1865	Gustav Nottebohm, *Ein Skizzenbuch von Beethoven* (Leipzig, 1865); Eng. trans. in *Two Beethoven Sketchbooks* (London, 1979), pp. 3–43
N 1880	Gustav Nottebohm, *Ein Skizzenbuch von Beethoven aus dem Jahre 1803* (Leipzig,

	1880); Eng. trans. in *Two Beethoven Sketchbooks* (London, 1979), pp. 47–125
PrStB	former Preussische Staatsbibliothek, Berlin
Schindler (1840)	Anton Schindler, *Biographie von Ludwig van Beethoven* (Münster, 1840); Eng. trans. as *The Life of Beethoven*, ed. I. Moscheles, 2 vols. (London, 1841)
Schindler (1860)	Anton Schindler, *Biographie von Ludwig van Beethoven*, 2 vols. (3rd edn, Münster, 1860); Eng. trans. as *Beethoven As I Knew Him*, ed. Donald W. MacArdle (London, 1966)
SBH	Hans Schmidt, 'Die Beethoven Handschriften des Beethovenhauses in Bonn', *Beethoven-Jahrbuch*, vii (1971), vii-xxiv, 1–443
SG	Joseph Schmidt-Görg, 'Wasserzeichen in Beethoven-Briefen', *Beethoven-Jahrbuch*, v (1966), 7–74
SPK	Staatsbibliothek Preussischer Kulturbesitz, Berlin
SV	Hans Schmidt, 'Verzeichnis der Skizzen Beethovens', *Beethoven-Jahrbuch*, vi (1969), 7–128
Thayer i (1866) ii (1872) iii (1879)	Alexander Wheelock Thayer, *Ludwig van Beethoven's Leben*, 3 vols. (Berlin, 1866, 1872, 1879)
Thayer–Deiters–Riemann i–v	Alexander Wheelock Thayer, *Ludwig van Beethovens Leben*, continued Hermann Deiters, rev. vol. i (Berlin, 1901); completed Hugo Riemann, vols. iv-v (Leipzig, 1907, 1908), rev. vols. ii-iii (Leipzig, 1910, 1911), rev. Deiters's 1901 edn of vol. i (Leipzig, 1917); vols. ii-v reissued (Leipzig, 1922–3)
Thayer–Forbes	*Thayer's Life of Beethoven*, rev. and ed. Elliot Forbes, 2 vols. (Princeton, 1964)
Thayer–Krehbiel	Alexander Wheelock Thayer, *The Life of Ludwig van Beethoven*, Eng. trans. ed.

	Henry Edward Krehbiel, 3 vols. (New York, 1921)
Thayer, *Verzeichniss*	Alexander Wheelock Thayer, *Chronologisches Verzeichniss der Werke Ludwig van Beethoven's* (Berlin, 1865)
Wegeler–Ries	Franz Gerhard Wegeler and Ferdinand Ries, *Biographische Notizen über Ludwig van Beethoven* (Coblenz, 1838), suppl. by Wegeler (Coblenz, 1845); Eng. trans. ed. Alan Tyson (in preparation)
WoO	Werk(e) ohne Opuszahl (work(s) without an opus number) in the listing of Kinsky–Halm

1794–1795: Decisive Years in Beethoven's Early Development

Douglas Johnson

It is too late to tamper with the three periods. The broad stages of Beethoven's creative life – imitative, heroic, and introspective – have been assimilated into the basic popular vocabulary from which all discussion of his music now proceeds. And not without reason, for the division does associate important changes in his style with what have been perceived as crises in his life. On another level, however, the three periods are an abstraction inevitably qualified by all concrete discussion: works that are typical at one level become atypical at another, and each period, when examined closely, reveals its own distinctive subdivisions. Beethoven developed within his creative periods as well as between them.[1]

Although it is normally risky to equate development with qualitative progress, there are obvious reasons for doing so in the twenty or so years of the first period (roughly 1782–1802). These were the years of Beethoven's adolescence and early manhood, and the achievement of technical mastery was a gradual process. It is my intention here to isolate one step in that process, a critical step involving the principal compositions of the years 1794 and 1795: the Piano Trios in G major and C minor Op. 1 Nos. 2 and 3, the Sonatas in A major and C major Op. 2 Nos. 2 and 3, the C-major Piano Concerto Op. 15, and to a lesser extent the String Quintet Op. 4, and the songs 'Adelaide' Op. 46 and 'Seufzer eines Ungeliebten' WoO 118.

Two general circumstances encourage and facilitate discussion of these works. First, they are the earliest important compositions conceived and completed after Beethoven moved from Bonn to Vienna. For reasons not yet fully explained, no substantial new works were written in 1793; during that initial year of study with Haydn,

[1] For a concise survey of the ways in which Beethoven's career has been subdivided see Maynard Solomon, 'The Creative Periods of Beethoven', *Music Review*, xxxiv (1973), 30–8.

Beethoven was content to revise several of his Bonn works.[2] Second, there are some provocative bases for stylistic comparison between the works of 1794–5 and those of a few years earlier. Op. 4 is a heavily revised arrangement of the Wind Octet Op. 103, and the first movement of Op. 2 No. 3 derives in part from a piano quartet of 1785. There is also evidence of various kinds that the first of the Op. 1 Trios and the first of the Op. 2 Sonatas belong – at least in their conception – to a somewhat earlier period than the last two works in each opus.

What are the specific musical reasons for being interested in the new works of 1794–5? To put the matter bluntly, in these works Beethoven was coming to grips for the first time systematically with the most sophisticated elements of Classical style. He had had no real difficulty with the superficial elements: the basic forms, the melodic and harmonic clichés, and conventional instrumentation. But these belonged to the common language of the time and were mastered by composers of all ranks. The new procedures that are found in the works of 1794 and 1795 were the ones that set Haydn and Mozart apart from their contemporaries and which, after he had mastered them, were to do the same for Beethoven. Here, oversimplified, are the points I consider most important:

1. The distribution of thematic material throughout the texture and the natural and easy use of polyphony anywhere in a movement;
2. control in the handling of remote key relationships, especially those of the mediant and submediant in both modes;
3. concern with the organic relationships among the parts of a movement and among the movements of a work;
4. the creation of instability within thematic statements as a way of sustaining momentum.

Some of these points are easier to illustrate than others. I shall begin with the first two. A convenient place to observe the change in Beethoven's practice with respect to texture and tonal goals is in the relationship of the String Quintet Op. 4 to the Wind Octet Op. 103, since the Octet as we know it was completed in 1793 and the quintet arrangement was probably made in 1795.[3] This comparison has done service before[4] and it is not an altogether happy one, but some of the small differences between the two works are very instructive.

[2] For example, the B♭ Concerto Op. 19, the Octet Op. 103, the song 'Feuerfarb'' Op. 52 No. 2, and the Oboe Concerto, Hess 12.

[3] The relevant sources are Berlin, SPK, Artaria 132; and SPK, Autograph 28, fols. 54–55 (both Op. 103); and Bonn, SBH 606 (Op. 4).

[4] See, for example, Alfred Orel, 'Beethovens Oktett Op. 103 und seine Bearbeitung als Quintett Op. 4', *Zeitschrift für Musikwissenschaft*, iii (1920–1), 159–79.

Example 1 shows the first half of the Andante in both versions. When Beethoven revised this movement he concentrated on two things. First he tried to enrich the texture during the thematic statements. The repetition of the opening theme by the cello (Quintet bar 9) has a new anacrusis which is taken up as a contrapuntal figure by the violins. The extension (bars 17ff) has a bass line animated by a rhythmic–melodic cell from the melody. Finally, in the new theme in F major (Quintet bar 28, Octet bar 34) the first violin has a motif mimicking the rhythm of the more important original motif in the second violin, and during the repeat there is a further bit of new dialogue between the cello and the first viola.

These textural changes were all motivated by the same basic principle. A different kind of revision occurs in the modulatory passages. There are two such passages in the example, and Beethoven made substantial changes in both of them. The first is the transition from B♭ to F. In the Octet the extension of the principal theme comes to a full cadence in bar 24; at that point a new idea in G minor begins a formal transition, reaching F through the circle of fifths. In the Quintet Beethoven interrupts the same extension with a shift to the minor mode (bar 20) and replaces the tonic cadence with an augmented-sixth progression to the dominant of F, which is then prolonged for six bars – the formal transition is omitted altogether.

The second modulatory passage is the retransition from F to B♭ after the second group. In the Octet (bars 50–5) Beethoven recalls the extension (see bar 17), now in D minor, and moves with a minimum of drama to the dominant of B♭; the harmonic reinterpretation of A in the bass localises the effect without disturbing the continuity. In the Quintet he begins with the same material (bar 43), but in D♭ major, and he expands the passage to include well-articulated arrivals in A♭ (bar 49) and A minor (bar 60), before finally reinterpreting A as the leading-note in the home tonic. The retransition takes six bars in the Octet, twenty in the Quintet.

Together with the motivic additions to the texture, this motion to remote keys increases the complexity of the movement and raises its temperature appreciably. Whether or not the movement can bear the heat is a question that need not concern us here; the important thing is that Beethoven thought it could. At the same time the pre-existent material did limit the scope and effectiveness of the changes in Op. 4. In works that were newly composed in 1794 and 1795 the same compositional goals are achieved more convincingly.

The new emphasis on polyphony within thematic statements is perhaps most easily appreciated where it is least necessary: in works

Example 1
Wind Octet Op. 103, second movement

String Quintet Op. 4, second movement

1794–1795: Decisive Years

1794–1795: Decisive Years

1794–1795: Decisive Years

for solo keyboard. One striking example is the Scherzo of Op. 2 No. 3, an extended exercise in fugato texture in which all the material is derived from the opening motif. Less obvious, and for that reason more revealing, is the first movement of the A-major Sonata Op. 2 No. 2. The first group of this movement is a pair of contrasting phrases; like a stone tossed into the water, the unison antecedent is answered by a ripple of invertible counterpoint which spills from the counter-statement into the transition, wells up again at the close of the exposition, and finally engulfs the second half of the development. Light polyphony of the same sort turns up in the first movement of Op. 2 No. 3 (see second group, bars 47ff), but the opportunities there were

1794–1795: Decisive Years

restricted by Beethoven's use of material from an earlier work (WoO 36 No. 3). What is interesting about these passages is not the mere fact of polyphonic development – more rigorous examples of that could be found – but rather that the thematic material has been conceived from the start as a contrapuntal complex. Beethoven's attempt to create the illusion of similar dialogue within the thematic statements of Op. 4 (see Example 1) shows how important that illusion had become to him by 1795.

Beethoven's use of remote tonal relationships in the new works of 1794 and 1795 takes many forms; it is seen most readily in his choice of keys for slow movements and his choice of tonal goals within the development sections of sonata-form movements. The dramatic change in his practice in these two areas is illustrated in Table 1. With the exception of the Piano Quartet WoO 36 No. 2, where the choice of the diatonic mediant was dictated by a Mozartean model,[5] all the early works have slow movements in the dominant, subdominant, relative major, or tonic minor. In the works of 1794–5, on the other hand, about half the slow movements are in the mediant or submediant (at least two of the 'conservative' works, Op. 4 and Op. 1 No. 3, can be accounted for by reference to models). The preference was so strong at this time that Beethoven even contemplated replacing the E♭-major Adagio of Op. 19 (the Concerto in B♭) with one in D major.[6]

Within movements the same distinction applies: development sections before 1794 are normally directed to the subdominant or the relative minor; those in 1794–5 move to more distantly related keys. Here the contrast between Op. 103 and Op. 4 is again symptomatic. In rewriting the development section of the first movement, Beethoven changed the central tonal goal from A♭ (IV) to D♭ (♭VII); in the Andante, as I have shown, the original retransition becomes a small development and the keys introduced are all remote from the home tonic (♭III, ♭VII, vii); and in the Minuet there is a newly composed second Trio in A♭ in which E major (enharmonic ♭VI) is a local goal after the double bar. Colourful modulation had become something of an obsession between 1793 and 1795.

The last two of my four points – organic construction and thematic instability – are a bit more difficult to demonstrate because the terms themselves are harder to define. What makes a movement or a work appear to be organically constructed? Basically the illusion that certain events have been implied by or are at least related to others. One theme may be derived from the contour, the rhythm, or the harmony of another, as in familiar examples from the Fifth Symphony or the 'Appassionata' Sonata. Or the same tonal relationships may occur repeatedly, as in the Seventh and Ninth Symphonies or, again, the 'Appassionata'. Or the choice of modulatory scheme on a large scale may be dictated by a local melodic inflection or harmonic event. Dramatic instances of this have been described in some of the best recent analytical literature.

---

[5] All three of the Piano Quartets WoO 36 were modelled on violin sonatas by Mozart; the model for WoO 36 No. 2 was the Sonata in E♭ K 380, which has a slow movement in G minor.

[6] A draft of the projected D-major movement is found on fol. 127 of the 'Kafka' Miscellany (London, BL, Add. MS 29801).

Table 1

Work	Key	Goal of the development	Key of the slow movement
Piano Sonata WoO 47 No. 1	Eb	vi	Bb (V)
Piano Sonata WoO 47 No. 2	F minor	iv	Ab (rel. major)
Piano Sonata WoO 47 No. 3	D	vi	A (V)
Piano Quartet WoO 36 No. 1	Eb minor	not articulated	Eb (I)
Piano Quartet WoO 36 No. 2	D	not articulated	F# minor (iii)*
Piano Quartet WoO 36 No. 3	C	IV	F (IV)
Piano Trio WoO 37	G	vi	G minor (i)
Piano Trio WoO 38	Eb	vi and IV	Bb (V)
Wind Octet Op. 103	Eb	vi and IV	Bb and Ab (V & IV)
String Trio Op. 3	Eb	vi, IV, and ii	
Piano Trio Op. 1 No. 1	Eb	IV	Ab (IV)
Piano Sonata Op. 2 No. 1	F minor	iv and v	F (I)
Piano Concerto Op. 19	Bb	IV	Eb (IV)
Piano Trio Op. 1 No. 2	G	bIII	E (VI)
Piano Trio Op. 1 No. 3	C minor	iv	Eb (rel. major)**
Piano Sonata Op. 2 No. 2	A	bIII and bVI	D (IV)
Piano Sonata Op. 2 No. 3	C	bIII and II	E (III)
String Quintet Op. 4	Eb	bVII	Bb (V)
Piano Concerto Op. 15	C	bIII	Ab (bVI)
Wind Trio Op. 87	C	IV	F (IV)

Groupings (left bracket labels):
- before 1794: Piano Sonata WoO 47 No. 1 through String Trio Op. 3
- ? before 1794: Piano Trio Op. 1 No. 1 through Piano Concerto Op. 19
- 1794–5: Piano Trio Op. 1 No. 2 through Wind Trio Op. 87

* modelled on a work by Mozart
** modelled on a work by Haydn

To some extent the opposite of organic in this context is chaotic, or at best capricious. This is the impression left when an adventurous modulatory scheme cannot be accounted for by any of the means just mentioned. The point is relevant here because Beethoven's obsessive exploration of remote tonal relationships in the works of 1794 and 1795 was a necessary step in the coherent expansion of his vocabulary. And although many of the choices still strike this writer, at least, as capricious, there is faint evidence of a controlling hand, a large conceptual map of each piece on which the local excursions have been plotted. Thus, for example, the choice of E♭ as the initial goal of the development section in the first movement of the C-major Piano Concerto is prepared by three references to that key in the course of the double exposition, while the larger modulatory scheme of the development (E♭ to F minor to the dominant of C) mirrors the threefold statement of the second theme in the tutti exposition. On a broader scale there are occasional attempts to exploit the same relationships in more than one movement, as, for example, in the G-major Piano Trio Op. 1 No. 2, in which G major and E major exchange roles as secondary keys in the Largo and Finale.

Such attempts to avoid 'effects without causes', as Wagner would have put it, seem to me to reflect a growth of artistic conscience on Beethoven's part in the first years in Vienna. And I suggest that the principal stimulus for this growth was his encounter with Haydn and with Haydn's music. The contrapuntal studies, which were continued with Albrechtsberger after Haydn left for London, are only a part of the story. To be sure, two full years of formal exercises in strict counterpoint should explain Beethoven's progress in the handling of polyphonic texture. But the *artistic* advantages of polyphony could not be taken for granted in a style that managed reasonably well without it. Indeed from a professional point of view any sort of complexity was apt to be more of a liability than an advantage, as Mozart had discovered. Complexity was among the intellectual challenges of symphony and quartet, the serious genres in which Beethoven had not yet tried his hand when he arrived in Vienna – and would not for another five years.[7]

Beethoven's relationship with Haydn during those early years is somewhat obscure. All the unfortunate externals are well known: Beethoven's dissatisfaction with the contrapuntal studies; his apparent duplicity in the fiasco of the works sent back to Bonn as evidence of

---

[7] The fact that string quintets were also treated seriously accounts in part for Beethoven's attempts to intensify Op. 4.

his progress, which turned out to be works already written there; Haydn's subsequent failure to take Beethoven to London as had been proposed; Beethoven's refusal to put 'pupil of Haydn' on the title-pages of his first publications; and his later assertion to Ries that he had never learned anything from Haydn. But whatever bad feelings might have existed between the two, we must be careful not to take Beethoven's disavowals at face value. Some time in 1793 or 1794 he took the trouble to copy out by hand an entire quartet from Haydn's Op. 20.[8] And of more immediate importance, I think, he did not escape the influence of Haydn's symphonic style. It is hard to see how he could have, for during those first three years in Vienna he was thoroughly exposed to the first six 'London' Symphonies. Three of them were performed for the first time in Vienna in March 1793, soon after Beethoven's arrival, and there was a performance of the other three the following December. Even in Haydn's absence, in the early months of 1795, there were three performances of the already popular 'Surprise' Symphony. Moreover during the course of 1793 Haydn was already at work on the first three symphonies of the second group, the autographs of which are partly or wholly on the Italian papers used in Vienna.[9]

What impact did these works have on Beethoven? His first response was probably frustration – at the weakness in his own technical equipment and at the lack of opportunity, at least during the first year, to get started on similar works of his own. One senses some such conflict between the professional need to master strict counterpoint and the psychological need to achieve his own style in a comment that he wrote in the margin of a sketchleaf some time in 1793: 'noch ein halbes jahr in dem C.[ontrapunkt] und er kann arbeiten was er will.'[10] This comment may be interpreted in two ways: either the completion of his studies would free him to begin composing, or it would supply him with the technique he needed to achieve new goals. Beethoven was probably thinking the former, but his own satisfaction depended ultimately on the latter.

When, some time in 1794, he began to work seriously on several new compositions, his frustration must have become a practical dilemma: how to absorb the impact of the Haydn symphonies and at the same time establish his independence of them. Whether intentionally or as a

---

[8] The Quartet in E♭ Op. 20 No. 1. The copy is in the Beethovenhaus, Bonn (SBH 600).
[9] See H. C. Robbins Landon, *The Symphonies of Joseph Haydn* (London, 1955).
[10] Vienna, GdM, A 31.

result of practical considerations, Beethoven proceeded on his own grounds – with works dominated by the piano. The symphonic model is thinly disguised, however. In the Trios and Sonatas of Op. 1 and Op. 2 the scope and variety of expression are pretentious; the pervasive harmonic complexity, the preference for sonata-form Finales in all three of the Op. 1 Trios, and the four-movement format in all six works are quite uncharacteristic of the genres involved, and it was quite uncharacteristic of Beethoven to ignore the available models in works of this type. One must conclude that he was after larger game. Especially in the Op. 1 Trios and in a contemporary work like the C-major Concerto, he was getting experience in the symphonic style without taking any of the risks – in particular, the risk of direct comparison with Haydn. There was one risk of course: the risk that the amateur public would find works like the Op. 1 Trios too difficult. This seems to have been Haydn's concern when he heard them, for he confided to Ries years later that he had not expected the third, at least, to be well received. In fact, Haydn of all people could not have failed to appreciate the nature of the artistic struggle that the pieces represented for Beethoven. He was familiar enough with the models.

There was more to Haydn's symphonic style than tonal breadth and polyphony, of course, and I think it is possible to suggest the sort of sophisticated compositional device in which Beethoven was interested. One such device, the exploitation of a local ambiguity to create a large-scale structural event, can be compared in two C-minor works, the first movements of Haydn's Symphony No. 95 and Beethoven's Piano Trio Op. 1 No. 3.

The C-minor Symphony is the only one of those written for London that does not have a slow Introduction. But Haydn conceived his first-group material so as to include an introductory gesture (Example 2a). The opening two-bar motif performs a double function. Harmonically it stands in a complementary antecedent–consequent relationship to the longer phrase that follows. But the two phrases are contrasted in every other parameter, and it is obvious that Haydn intended to isolate the first two bars from the following material. In fact the internal harmonic implications of the opening motif enhance its introductory quality and prevent it from functioning as a proper resolution when it returns jarringly in bar 10. Although the fundamental step seems to be simply tonic to dominant, the passing motion to A♭ and F♯ implies a more complex event, from an augmented sixth to the dominant, which subverts the tonic quality of the initial attack. The inherent complexity of this little motif dictates its subsequent use as a cause rather than as an effect. It initiates the motion to the second

1794–1795: Decisive Years

Example 2a. Haydn, Symphony No. 95, first movement (piano reduction)

group and the new tonal departure at the beginning of the development, and at the end of the development it is expanded into a broad embellishment of the dominant, all of its tonic quality now gone.

The ambiguous structure of the first group presented Haydn with an opportunity for a remarkable effect at the beginning of the recapitulation. Having already incorporated the opening motif into the passage of dominant preparation, he allows the recapitulation to begin timidly with the consequent phrase, which defers strong cadential motion. And whereas the cadence of this phrase had been frustrated originally by a return of the opening motif, initiating the transition to the second group, that same cadence itself now serves as the arrival at the second group, here in C major. The transition has been totally elided. In larger terms, with the opening motif supported by the dominant, the consequent phrase harmonically weak, and the transition gone, all of the first group has been effectively consumed by the development.

With Haydn's procedure in mind, let us consider Beethoven's. Beneath the fat of the first thirty-nine bars of the Trio is a skeleton provided by the first fifteen bars of the Symphony (Example 2b). Bars

Example 2b. Piano Trio Op. 1 No. 3, first movement (piano part)

1–10 present an initial unison idea moving from tonic to dominant by way of an augmented-sixth chord, bars 11–30 are a contrasting gesture which does not cadence, and in bars 31ff the opening idea returns and initiates motion to E♭. Thus Beethoven's first group, like Haydn's, is a sort of odd couple, destined for divorce in the recapitulation. But since Beethoven chose to deal with much bulkier material, he had to undermine the marriage in a different way. At the beginning of the recapitulation his opening motif returns intact, but its collapse back on to the dominant serves to prolong rather than resolve the preceding dominant preparation. In a practical sense, though not so literally, this opening gesture extends the development as Haydn's does. At this point Haydn could safely bring back his consequent phrase, which begins weakly, and proceed directly to the second group without the transition. Beethoven's consequent phrase is more stable and hence less capable of preserving the momentum. Beethoven therefore elides this phrase and leaps directly to the transition, thereby also avoiding the implication of harmonic resolution. As a result, the momentum is again sustained from the development to the second group. And whereas Haydn later returns to his elided opening motif in a new guise in the coda, bending it towards the subdominant, Beethoven returns to his elided consequent phrase for the same purpose.

A few other points of contact between these two works are worth mentioning. First, Beethoven follows Haydn in using his opening phrase to generate modulatory motion in the development and also adopts the same tonal goal, F minor (although Haydn substitutes A♭ major after reaching the dominant of F). Second, the slow movement of Op. 1 No. 3 is a set of variations on an *andante cantabile* theme in E♭ as is that of the Haydn Symphony, and the Minuets of both works have Trios in the parallel major. The choice of keys is important here. In its use of the subdominant as a goal in the first movement and the relative major as the key of the second movement, Op. 1 No. 3 appears conservative with respect to the other works of 1794–5. The Haydn model may have been responsible. Finally, and most interesting of all, Beethoven does not copy Haydn's Finale, a largely fugal treatment of a theme in C major. Instead he writes another sonata-form movement in C minor using the same devices as he had in the first movement: the introductory gesture and contrasting theme in the first group; the return of the opening gesture to start the modulation to E♭ and again to begin the development, which moves at once to F minor; and the complete elision of the opening gesture at the start of the recapitulation.

Although the relationship of the C-minor Trio to the C-minor Symphony may have been extended to include such elements as the key and the overall shape of the slow movement, it seems safe to assume that Beethoven was primarily concerned with the organisation and manipulation of material in the first movement. This view gives him credit for absorbing what was most sophisticated in the Haydn model. And there is evidence that his observations were not confined to the C-minor Symphony. In the first movement of the G-major Piano Trio Op. 1 No. 2, written at about the same time as the C-minor Trio, Beethoven experiments for the first time with a slow Introduction and with a principal theme that begins off the tonic.[11] The Introduction is interesting in any event because its symphonic breadth is quite foreign to this genre. But considering the means by which instability is created in the first group of the C-minor Trio, it may be more interesting to note something similar here. The Introduction builds to a noisy dominant-seventh chord with the seventh in the high register; the Allegro theme then begins off the tonic in the middle register, and a satisfactory resolution is put off by various means until the theme has run its course. As a result the first group is again unstable, and its subsequent reappearances are necessarily occasions for some sort of dynamic manipulation. The model for this procedure, I think, was the Introduction and the first group of the 'Surprise' Symphony, also in G major. And finally, relationships of a similar sort exist between the Symphony No. 97 in C major, also from the first 'London' group, and the extensive drafts for a C-major Symphony that Beethoven began in 1795, after the completion of Op. 1.[12] To describe them here would involve the introduction of too much unfamiliar material, but again the essence of the relationship involves the way gestures presented at the beginning of the first movement are manipulated at their reappearance so as to create the illusion of implications being realised.

At this point it may be helpful if I review the central thesis of this essay, before I proceed to qualify it. The works of 1794 and 1795 reflect an attempt on Beethoven's part to master the most sophisticated aspects of the style of Haydn and Mozart: the enrichment of texture through polyphony; the coherent assimilation of remote tonal relationships into the traditional language; and the substitution of organic procedures for mechanical ones within, and to a limited extent between, movements. The new tools he brought to the task were his own

---

[11] Two other movements with themes beginning off the tonic, the Scherzo of Op. 1 No. 1 and the Finale of Op. 3, cannot be dated with certainty, although both the works in question appear to have been conceived before 1794.

[12] Most of the drafts for the first movement of this Symphony are found in the 'Kafka' Miscellany and in the 'Fischhof' Miscellany (Berlin, SPK, Autograph 28).

mastery of strict counterpoint and his increased sensitivity to these qualities in the most advanced music of the time, especially in Haydn's 'London' Symphonies. Although the qualities themselves were primarily associated with the symphony and string quartet, Beethoven incorporated them into works dominated by the piano, in which he presumably felt most at home and in which relative failure might well be viewed as relative success. The results were the pretentious Piano Trios Op. 1 Nos. 2 and 3, the pretentious Sonatas Op. 2 Nos. 2 and 3, the pretentious Concerto Op. 15, and even pretentious songs such as 'Adelaide' and the lesser-known 'Seufzer eines Ungeliebten' (the former a large sonata form and the latter modelled on the two-tempo aria with an introductory recitative). It is commonly appreciated that Beethoven applied the heroic style of his middle-period symphonies to virtually all the genres of chamber music and to the sonata itself. I am suggesting that something similar had occurred already in the early period, except that the style was not yet heroic and the symphonies were someone else's. Paradoxically, the Op. 1 Trios mark the beginning of a series of symphonically conceived chamber works in the years 1795–1800 which culminates in the first two symphonies.[13]

Having said that much I shall now touch briefly on some of the problems in my own argument. It would be wrong, first of all, to claim that polyphony and mediant key relationships were unknown to Beethoven before 1794. I think it is true that virtually all his piano and chamber music up to that time is rather primitive in texture (perhaps 'conventional' is a more flattering word), largely diatonic in the choice of key relationships, and mechanical in the treatment of the basic forms. But in his last years in Bonn Beethoven did produce a series of works in other genres which were demonstrably more ambitious. They include the two cantatas of 1790 on the death of one emperor and the elevation of another (WoO 87 and WoO 88), the concert aria for soprano 'Primo amore' (WoO 92), and a Violin Concerto in C major which survives only as a fragment (WoO 5). All these works are for orchestra, and their public function probably accounts in great part for the very large scale on which they are constructed. Are they symphonic? I should prefer to call them monumental. Presumably the seriousness required of such works caused Beethoven to attempt liberal amounts of both polyphony and chromaticism. Some of the polyphony might also be attributed to the medium – there were traditional prescriptions for a work involving solo voices and chorus – and some of the chromaticism can be attributed to the texts. But it is clear

[13] See, for example, the slow Introductions to the Piano Quintet Op. 16, the Wind Sextet Op. 71, the String Trio Op. 9 No. 1, and both the Cello Sonatas Op. 5.

that Beethoven was in any case already trying to probe the limits of his expressive vocabulary, for the Concerto fragment is more adventurous tonally than the vocal works. And the results were apparently impressive enough to win the approval of Haydn, who accepted Beethoven as a pupil after seeing one of the cantatas. At some critical distance, however, these works now seem to fail precisely to the degree that they aspire to symphonic style and proportions. What is missing in them is the relationship between expressive detail and large-scale form, and this is what the achievement of the first Vienna years is all about.

A somewhat more difficult problem is the position occupied by the first of the Piano Trios in Op. 1 and the first of the Sonatas in Op. 2. The problem can be formulated simply. In texture and tonal shape these two pieces are less advanced than their companions, and one would gladly suggest that they were conceived no later than 1793. Their compositional history is obscure, however, and although it does not directly overlap in the sources with that of the other four works, it may well extend as far as 1794 or 1795.

Only two sources for the F-minor Sonata have survived: an early draft of the first-movement exposition which appears to have been made in 1793, and a late draft of both the exposition and the development which was probably made in late 1794 or in 1795 (these dates are based on evidence provided by handwriting and paper studies).[14] No sources are known today for the last three movements.[15] With respect to the two first-movement drafts, it may be significant that the earlier one is straightforwardly homophonic, lacking the counterstatement of the opening theme in the bass and the following play with the turn motif, while these are both present in the later draft. Since the 1793 draft is juxtaposed with some ideas that turn up in the Scherzo of Op. 2 No. 3, it is tempting to suggest that Beethoven rediscovered the draft in 1795 while at work on the C-major Sonata and that he completed the first movement and added the other three at that time. But the opposite is perhaps equally likely: work on the F-minor Sonata could have led to the discovery of material useful in Op. 2 No. 3.[16] (A

[14] The earlier draft appears on Vienna, GdM, A 31; the later draft is on a leaf in Moscow, Central (Glinka) Museum for Music Culture (SV 344).
[15] A long draft for the Finale is quoted on pp. 42–5 of J.-G. Prod'homme, *Die Klaviersonaten Beethovens* (Wiesbaden, 1948; Ger. trans. of *Les sonates pour piano de Beethoven* (Paris, 1937)), but the leaf containing the draft has apparently remained in a private collection.
[16] The genesis of these two sonatas intersects at one other point: both use material from the earlier Piano Quartet WoO 36 No. 3 (the first movement in Op. 2 No. 3, the Adagio in Op. 2 No. 1).

more remote possibility is that a completed early version of the F-minor Sonata, composed in 1793, was revised in 1795 in anticipation of the publication of Op. 2. Although this last explanation has the virtue of accommodating the conservative style of the Sonata, the former makes more sense of the sources. Moreover, it seems unlikely that Beethoven would have written a piano sonata in 1793 and not included it among the works sent back to Bonn at the end of the year or, for that matter, that such a sonata would have been in four movements.)

The Piano Trio in E♭ is more elusive. Again only two sources can be definitely associated with the work. A leaf in a Berlin miscellany contains the score of the last eight bars of the Trio of the Scherzo.[17] Since there are minor points of difference from the published score, this leaf was probably rejected from an autograph in progress. It appears to be from late 1794 or early 1795. And on a roughly contemporary sketchleaf in the 'Kafka' Miscellany there is one eight-bar entry for a passage in the exposition of the first movement.[18] These two sources are evidence that Beethoven wrote out a score of Op. 1 No. 1 at about the time that he was working on Nos. 2 and 3. But they do not prove that the work was conceived at that time. Beethoven wrote out revised scores of several of his Bonn works during the first years in Vienna, and he made sketches for some of the revisions.

There are a few scraps of evidence – all flimsy – to suggest that the Piano Trio in E♭ might also have been written in Bonn and revised in Vienna. A prominent motif from the first movement turns up in the middle of a sketch made in 1792 for a cadenza to the set of variations in E♭ later published as Op. 44. Since it is difficult to imagine why Beethoven would have composed an independent set of variations for piano trio in 1792, the possibility is perhaps worth considering that Op. 44 served originally as the Finale of Op. 1 No. 1. In fact there are aspects of the published Scherzo and Finale that invite comparison with the works of 1794–5. The Scherzo theme begins off the tonic and is subjected to some pseudo-canonic development, and the Finale contains what appears to be a stylistic fingerprint of the 1795 works – a humorous digression near the end to a remote key, followed by a rapid return.[19]

The proposed stylistic distinctions between the works of 1794–5 and those of the last Bonn years do not make much sense of the Trio in E♭ and the Sonata in F minor. Without having formulated the distinctions, however, one would probably not view these works as

[17] Fol. 38 in the 'Fischhof' Miscellany.   [18] Fol. 99.
[19] See the Finales of the Piano Concertos Op. 15 and Op. 19, and of the Sonata Op. 2 No. 3. The sketch for Op. 44 is in Vienna, GdM, A 11.

problematical at all, and that seems to me a mistake. It should be emphasised in any case that compositional goals and results are not necessarily synonymous. If my observations are correct, the new compositions of 1794 and 1795 reflect Beethoven's commitment to a new ideal, namely the power, breadth, and technical sophistication of Haydn's last symphonies. What Beethoven actually achieved in these years was something less. In the search for expression he usually admitted too much – more than could be justified by his improved control of procedure. Ironically the old man's models are lean and taut, while the young man's copies are overweight and long-winded. The criticism applies less to the sonatas than to the trios, to be sure, but in all these works one senses that Beethoven was ingesting the Haydn influence faster than he could digest it. Ultimately there was something artificial in his exploitation of new expressive and procedural devices at this time. His progress is perhaps most impressive in the transformation of the first movement of the early Piano Quartet in C major WoO 36 No. 3 into that of the C-major Sonata Op. 2 No. 3.[20] It is most embarrassing, I think, in his attempt to rewrite the Wind Octet as a string quintet. For whereas the Piano Quartet had been a very modest piece of work, completed at the age of fourteen, the Octet was much more. In spite of – or perhaps because of – its unpretentious emotional scope, the Octet may well be Beethoven's most accomplished work before 1794, enlivened by just the right amount of light polyphony and free of the ambitious chromaticism that overburdens the Bonn orchestral works mentioned earlier. The attempt to inflate its proportions and add harmonic colour in 1795 turns the slim Bonn lady into a Viennese vamp.

What the new works show, then, is a conflict between ambitious compositional technique, reflected in complex textures, wider tonal schemes, and original approaches to form, and not altogether suitable material, some of it borrowed from earlier works and some of it beefed up to approximate symphonic proportions. In varying degrees the conflicting demands of overall scope and overall control affect most of the important works of the late 1790s. The long-range manipulation of first-group material in the C-minor Trio was the sort of gimmick that could not be transplanted readily into other works;[21] thus it is most significant as an indication that Beethoven had become interested in

---

[20] An important step in this transformation is a draft found on fol. 21 of the 'Fischhof' Miscellany.

[21] There are hints of it in numerous later works in C minor, perhaps most conspicuously in the String Trio Op. 9 No. 3; the String Trios in C minor and in G Op. 9 No. 1 both return to compositional problems of the Op. 1 Trios in the same keys.

the problem itself. The analogous devices in the C-major Symphony, had he finished it, would have been more sophisticated. And in a work such as the D-major Sonata Op. 10 No. 3, completed in 1798, the same basic principle – the exploitation of an initial ambiguity to good effect later in a movement – can be seen operating with much more sophisticated material. In this case a simple chromatic inflection, A to A♯, in the consequent phrase of the opening theme returns in different guises to start the transition to the second group (as leading-note in B minor), to start the development (as B♭, approached deceptively from the dominant of D minor), to force a new modulation at the beginning of the recapitulation (as the raised fourth degree moving to the dominant in E minor), and ultimately to be resolved as a B♭ in the bass in the coda. It was this concentration of ambiguity in a single chromatic inflection that Beethoven was to develop to such striking effect in many of his most ambitious middle-period works – for example, the first movements of the 'Eroica' (raised sixth versus lowered seventh degree) or the 'Waldstein' and 'Appassionata' Sonatas (raised fifth versus lowered sixth degree).

A word, finally, on the general significance of this discussion. Beethoven's first period has quite naturally received less attention than the second or third; the music is not as good. But it is a bit too facile to characterise the early years, as I did in passing at the beginning of this essay, merely as a period of imitation. There is considerably greater stylistic distance between the piano quartets of 1785 and the Second Symphony than, say, between the 'Eroica' and the Eighth, and that distance has not yet been properly measured. In fact very little work of substance has been done on the early period since Schiedermair's *Der junge Beethoven* appeared over fifty years ago. A word of caution is necessary here, however: although the stylistic problems are not uninteresting, their solution does require that the works first be put in their proper order and assigned their proper dates. Both Thayer and Kinsky made something of a mess of this, and before there is any further speculation on the genesis of a work such as the B♭ Concerto – to mention a popular example – it would be best to make certain that its sources can be dated. Otherwise our theories are doomed to go on wagging the historical facts.

In recent years a lot of progress has been made in challenging the traditional views of Beethoven's development. But we might as well speak of clarification now with respect to the early period, since there is not very much to challenge. The sample problem discussed here is typical. By 1795 there was one living composer greater than

Beethoven. It was the mark of Beethoven's own greatness that he recognised the differences and resolved to master them. It was the mark of something else in his character that he later denied the experience. Haydn would have known better at the time; and we know better now.

Ambiguities in *La Malinconia*: What the Sketches Say

Richard Kramer

I

In its terse, almost faceless plotting of a precarious harmonic track, the melancholy Adagio in the Finale of the String Quartet in B♭ Op. 18 No. 6 has much exercised the critical mind. Two of the more recent studies of the piece – one by Joseph Kerman, the other by William Mitchell[1] – develop two critical aspects of it which, seen for the moment as two elements in a paradox, may be taken to stand for the two classic elements that rub against one another in every work: expressive, fallible substance on the one hand, and determined, inexorable structure on the other. And they may be understood to voice two extremes of criticism: the one will want to convey the sense of the piece through a visceral reaction to it; the other will want to extrapolate its system, to reduce it to a single syntactic term which, like an equation, can be said to generate all the diminutions that give it contour and articulate its *Grundgesetz*. The one approach is empirical: the meaning of the piece lies in how it is experienced. The other is intellectual, and because it places high value on the universals that govern the motion of notes under certain complex conditions, may tend towards exegeses based *a priori* on those universals appropriate to the special case.

Now neither Kerman nor Mitchell would claim that these critical processes are separable. They always interlock, in various ways, and represent two extremes of a single imponderably complex act. Criticism that responds to a play between these phenomena may bring itself close to a quality of ambiguity which, in certain kinds of works, seems born of this friction between something planned and something felt.

---

[1] Joseph Kerman, *The Beethoven Quartets* (New York and London, 1967), pp. 76–82; William J. Mitchell, 'Beethoven's La Malinconia from the String Quartet, Opus 18, No. 6: Techniques and Structure', *The Music Forum*, vol. iii, ed. William J. Mitchell and Felix Salzer (New York and London, 1973), pp. 269–80.

The fourth meaning of 'ambiguity' given by the *Oxford English Dictionary* is appropriate here: 'A word or phrase susceptible of more than one meaning; an equivocal expression.' When a note, or a group of notes occurring simultaneously or forming a phrase, is said to be ambiguous, what is meant is that it can be understood in more than one way, and that its full meaning, to the extent that it can ever be known, is greater than the sum of these single meanings, and will comprehend the intimations of paradox that reside in it.

The E♭ asserted by the second violin in bar 29, burdened with this double meaning, needs to be approached from various points of view. Initially it is enough to hear it as a simple, direct disturbance of a cadence on the dominant of F. One instinctively gives weight to that cadence, for it breaks out of the spiral that begins in bar 21 and is initiated through a discomforting $^6_4$ on F♯ in bar 12. With an effect bordering on the irrational, the E♭ in bar 29 dispels the clarity of the cadence in F. Some justification for its behaviour is needed.

II

The spiral moves in an upward circle of fifths from E, contrary to the natural tendency of the fifth to descend to its root.[2] As a raw acoustic phenomenon, leaving aside the compromise imposed by the closed, tempered scale, the sequence would accumulate tension. In effect it does not. As the initial tonic, fixed in time, grows more remote, its distance seems to grow geometrically; for with each new fifth, each addressed by its own dominant, the strength of the initial tonic fades. If there is a tension here, it is not of the acoustic, spatial sort, but of time. The opening phrase of *La Malinconia* sets up a rhythm for the normal happening of things, and one's disorientation after bar 21 is essentially an ache for a return to that rhythm.

---

[2] Kerman (*The Beethoven Quartets*, p. 79) noted the similarity here to the modulatory model that governs the passage after the first double bar in the Finale of Mozart's String Quartet in G major K 387. Moreover Beethoven copied out K 387 in score, complete; the copy is now in the Beethovenhaus, Bonn (NE 119 and SBH 602), with the exception of a single leaf from the Finale, now in the Pierpont Morgan Library in New York. Characteristics of the paper and of Beethoven's handwriting argue for a date close to the end of 1798. It is not unreasonable to imagine that the copying of K 387 was an exercise preparatory to the composition of Op. 18; sketches for Op. 18 No. 6 date from the summer of 1800.

For a study of a similar compositional problem in five works from the years 1793 to 1803, see László Somfai, 'A Bold Enharmonic Modulatory Model in Joseph Haydn's String Quartets', *Studies in Eighteenth-Century Music: a Tribute to Karl Geiringer on his Seventieth Birthday*, ed. H. C. Robbins Landon with Roger E. Chapman (London, 1970), pp. 370–81.

Ambiguities in *La Malinconia*

Consider bars 1–20 and bars 21–8 as two distinct, if deeply related, rhythmic fields. In the first of them, the opening phrase sets a simple precedent for periodicity in groups of four bars. The very definite articulation of bar 4 as a point of stress – of end-accent – is reinforced in its rhyming bars, 8 and 12. In bar 8 the bass (and the harmony) shows movement for the first time. In bar 12 the inflection is momentous, initiating an overlapping five-bar phrase which explores some of the mystery of that $^6_4$ on F♯. By the last bar of each of these phrases, meaning has shifted from end-accent to upbeat. One sense of bars 12–16 is their extension of that development to the point where bar 12 now generates its own phrase – a phrase that springs from the new and complex function of bar 12. The transference of accent is complete when this extended upbeat finds its resolution in the phrase beginning in bar 17.

This is rhythm that grows and develops, rhythm that seems organic. One knows how to respond to it. The rhythm of bars 21–8, for all its evident simplicity, does not scan so well. The reiteration of a simple intervallic pattern, and of the formula that generates it, is hypnotic. Phrasing in two-bar groups, not innate, is imposed by the play of voice entries. There is no overt rhythmic drama here. The tension is neurotic, not dramatic, for it is imposed by a distortion of the natural and not by elements in true conflict, as in the normal discourse of the Classical style.

Still, these bars belong within a context. They respond to a pressure that grows across twenty bars to the downbeat at the attack in bar 21. But arsis and thesis within bar 21 are deceptive. The inflection of the harmony on the second beat imposes an accent conflicting with the structural downbeat. That inflection is a decisive motion, the quickest change of functional root so far. Beyond this, something in the intervallic pair G–F♯ responds in concentrated diminution to the larger semitones – the stressed appoggiaturas – in the bass in bars 9–10 and 17–18. The G, of course, is not an appoggiatura. But there is a sense in which G–F♯ echoes the ponderous rhythm of bars 9–10 and 17–18, and it is this imposing background that charges the second beat in bar 21.

This conflict in quality and position of stress, small in bar 21, grows to a central issue by bar 28. Four bars of *crescendo* peak at the *sforzando* on the second beat of bar 28, where the stiff pattern of root motion is finally broken. The dominant of F, folding back to reinforce its antecedent, effects a kind of closure. The very depth of its root – and the acoustic reinforcement from open strings in both cello and viola – establishes it more firmly than any single harmony since bar 17. But dominants, after all, look forward. And it is this double rhythmic message at the *sforzando* in bar 28 that puts us at the threshold of the E♭ in question.

III

That E♭, subverting a strongly articulated dominant, making it minor (and consequently redefining the function of its root from dominant to undominant), plays out a tendency in the sequence that began in bar 21, where, as a corollary to the direction of the sequence, each dominant is presently made into a minor tonic. It heightens that action, accomplishes it directly, and affects the one dominant that has been set apart from all the others.

But what gives the E♭ strength and reason is an imperative from an altogether different source. If the motivic sequence, as it evolves from the upbeat to bar 21, is laid out in abstract through the total chromatic – or rather in two coupled runs, since the motif at its smallest comprises an interval whose elements function reciprocally – it will look like Example 1a. This comes very close to expressing what actually happens, as shown in Example 1b. That is, the total chromatic itself is not violated. But it is also clear that the memorable events in the piece – those that articulate the total chromatic at its preparation, its interruption, and its dissolution – do not speak out from the abstract.

The E♭ is especially sensitive here, for the interruption is made to fall between the pair E♭ (bar 29)–D (bar 32). And here is where I want to invoke the *O.E.D.* on 'ambiguity'. According to one set of terms, the E♭ in bar 29 blunts the dominant that precedes it; it even liquidates it. The weakening occurs on a strong beat, unexpectedly, and the rhythmic frame consequently emphasises the blunting. But according to another set of terms, E♭ in bar 29 is the inexorable next pitch in the unfolding of the total chromatic. The second meaning gives reason to the E♭. The first colours its special position in the total chromatic, and defines it as a point of interruption.

Why is the total chromatic broken between E♭ and D? When the sequence regenerates itself at bar 32 its first pitches are equivalent to those at the very beginning of the piece, and the rhythm of the opening bars is reinstated. If one function of the music beginning at bar 32 is to run through the remaining pitches in the total chromatic, just those pitches have been saved which, at the same time, essentially recapitulate the opening bars. In Example 2, graphs a and b show something of the priority of the pitches D, B♭ and A. Graph c shows the chromatic sequence projected backwards for what it suggests about the incipient stages of the central chromatic. The substitution of the pair A♭–G for

Example 1

F–E in bars 9–10 seems to touch upon the crossing of these two pairs in bar 28 at the approach to the E♭ in bar 29.

Example 2

From the point where the total chromatic resumes in bar 32 to its exhaustion in bar 36, multiplicity of meaning attaches to nearly every note, and this hinges in part on the retrospective, recapitulatory sense of the passage. The B♭ in bar 35 is merely the richest in this respect. Its impact recollects the E♭ in bar 29. Each is unexpected, and each blunts the progress of the chromatic sequence by upsetting the normal course of its harmony. The Neapolitan sixth in bar 35, no less remarkable in its context than the minor triad in bar 29, imposes itself where the total chromatic, now played out, would have reinstated the pair C–B♮. The simple logic of the piece dictates the unfolding of events along a single exposition of the set.

B♭ is crucial. Following unexpectedly from C, sustained and reharmonised, it is answered in bar 36 by a diminished seventh which is both metaphor and homonym for the diminished seventh in bar 17. The two are identical in pitch, but their meanings are contrary. (See the framed end-chords in Example 1b.) The diminished seventh in bar 17 is not ambiguous: its meaning has been prepared from as far back as the $^6_4$ in bar 12. C in the bass simply retards the arrival of the root B. And it is this gesture, C–B, that becomes the intervallic source of the music that follows. In bar 36 the diminished seventh does not presuppose a root. It is genuinely diffuse, and the delaying of the movement of the B♭ to its A emphasises this aspect of it.

One further play on that critical harmony needs comment. The final *crescendo* across bars 37–42 finds a diminished seventh which puts G♭

Ambiguities in *La Malinconia* 35

fortissimo at the highest pitch in the piece. Mutation between F♯ and G♭ has been a central problem and is a factor in the special registral connection between those two pitches in bars 23 and 26. The G♭ in bar 42 reaches back to the original F♯ in bar 12, which generated the first of the diminished sevenths. The one moves away from F; the other moves towards it in a neighbour motion exacerbated by a displacement through two octaves.

This kind of ambiguity, at the intersection of several lines of thought, recurs in the cadenza-like reappearance of the Adagio that begins at bar 195. But that is best considered in the light of the sketches for the piece.

IV

The only surviving sketches for the finale of Op. 18 No. 6 are to be found on leaves used by Beethoven during the summer of 1800. At the time they belonged to a small sketchbook which contained among other things work on the revisions of the Quartets in F major and G major Op. 18 Nos. 1 and 2, and on the B♭ Piano Sonata Op. 22, the A-minor Violin Sonata Op. 23, and the G-major Piano Variations WoO 77. Since then much of the sketchbook has been dismembered; the leaves in question belong to the remnant core of the sketchbook, now in Berlin (SPK, Autograph 19e, fols. 12–31).[3] One feature of manuscript structure is to the point here: fols. 14–17, the four leaves that contain the sketches for the Finale of Op. 18 No. 6, are the four quadrants of a single sheet of paper. The order of entries on these four leaves corresponds to the most likely sequence of the pages. Thus it is fair to assume that they represent a continuous, uninterrupted run of sketches for the Finale.

Entries on fol. 14r capture something of the struggle from inchoate idea, primitively notated, towards coherent motion. It is a page that presents the first evidence of *La Malinconia*, and testifies as well that the original concept of the Finale did not include an initial Adagio.

The key to the interrelationship of entries on fol. 14r is a draft (Draft

---

[3] See Hans-Günter Klein, *Ludwig van Beethoven: Autographe und Abschriften: Katalog*, Staatsbibliothek Preussischer Kulturbesitz, Kataloge der Musikabteilung, ser. 1: Handschriften, vol. ii (Berlin, 1975), pp. 64–70. For a preliminary study of the manuscript, see Wilhelm Virneisel, 'Aus Beethovens Skizzenbüchern', *Colloquium amicorum: Joseph Schmidt-Görg zum 70. Geburtstag*, ed. Siegfried Kross and Hans Schmidt (Bonn, 1967), pp. 428–35. An edition currently in preparation of the reconstructed sketchbook in facsimile and transcription and with commentary will appear as vol. iv in the series Skizzen und Entwürfe published by the Beethovenhaus, Bonn.

A) that begins at the start of staff 13.[4] Its troubles, from there to the end of staff 15, will be dealt with later. For now, what is significant is the manifest continuity from the end of staff 15 to staves 6/7. Sketches for an unused final movement, worked out in some detail on fols. 12v and 13v, occupied staves 1–5 and 8–9.[5] When he first began to record ideas for *La Malinconia*, Beethoven will have faced a page relatively clean beneath staff 9, with some blank space above (staves 6 and 7) which could accommodate addenda. But Draft A does not begin directly beneath staff 9, and its late continuation from staves 6/7 is clearly denied access to staff 10. Sketch A at the beginning of staff 10, Sketch B in the middle of staves 10/11, and two separate entries at the end of staves 10 and 11/12 (not shown) were surely written before Draft A had run its course.

Sketch A is the mysterious member in this group. Its time signature, an extravagance in Beethoven's economical sketch notation, hints that the entry is among the earliest ideas for the piece. Example 3 shows how Sketch A and Draft A might have touched in Beethoven's mind. To put a somewhat tighter construction on the relationship: Sketch A shows an early impulse towards E minor; in the writing of Draft A that impulse is forged into a phrase heavy with motivic meaning. The second bar on staff 15, written so intensely that the figures 4 and 2 are virtually superimposed, retards the resolution of C to B which will set the sequence in motion.

Example 3

Something about the enigmatic Sketch B, which is written down in the very middle of the page in a notation that puts it outside rhythmic context, supports what I have just suggested for Sketch A: namely that it represents a very early idea for *La Malinconia* written down before

---

[4] Transcriptions of this and the other sketches discussed below are shown in the Appendix.

[5] This unused piece was conceived in G major, probably for the Finale of Op. 18 No. 2, as early as the spring of 1799. For the sketches in facsimile and transcription, see Wilhelm Virneisel, ed., *Beethoven: ein Skizzenbuch zu Streichquartetten aus Op. 18*, SV 46, 2 vols. (Bonn, 1972–4), pp. 43, 47, 51–6, of the sketchbook. Sieghard Brandenburg has also called attention to the identity of these two sets of sketches; see 'The First Version of Beethoven's G major String Quartet, Op. 18 No. 2', *Music & Letters*, lviii (1977), 150.

continuity has been attempted. Understood in this way, the 'etc.' on staff 15 stands for material that has to some degree already been worked out. Example 1c makes this clear. What leaps out from Example 1c is that the formal areas defined in the final version are explicit even in the earliest entries. Sketch B is provocative because in its spare, schematic formulation it seizes an image that will determine a central phase in the piece: from the G♭, doubled in register, which reverses the impetus of F♯, to the pair A♭–G, whose next move – to E♭ – will be burdened with several meanings.[6] Sketch B, then, shows Beethoven poised before the critical E♭. If Sketch B was written down before Draft A – like a solitary flash that illuminates some central crisis before a context has been found – then Beethoven's 'etc.' on staff 15 evades the task of establishing a liaison between the two.

But the evasion proves enlightening. Where the draft resumes after the 'etc.', it does so at the pair B♭–A (more precisely, the counterpoint to it) which will finally articulate what I have called a recapitulation. The total chromatic runs out at the bottom of the page, with a repetition of the pair C–B♮ (again, expressed through its counterpoint). Continuity from there to the beginning of staff 6 is not explicit. The gap between these two areas on the page may even signify a break in thought. The alchemy that will convert the high B♭ at the beginning of staff 6 to an inflection affecting the final pair in the total chromatic was lost somewhere between the writing of Drafts A and B.

V

There is good reason to believe that the next work on *La Malinconia* – Draft B, beginning on fol. 15r, staff 4 – followed directly upon Draft A. On the face of it more sketches for the earlier form of the Finale intrude between them on fol. 14v and the top of fol. 15r. But a strong case can be made for the view that these entries extend in tangent from their family sketches on fols. 12v, 13v, and 14r. In other words entries for that earlier form of the Finale, single in concept, were written continuously. With the first image of *La Malinconia*, notated in the blank space left on fol. 14r, the original concept is abandoned.

In many respects the main course of Draft B is very close to the final version. The articulation of the half-cadence before the Allegretto

[6] Sketch B has an uncanny Doppelgänger, even to the barless notation in semibreves, isolated on a page of sketches that date from roughly 1795–6, unrelated to Op. 18: see Joseph Kerman, ed., *Ludwig van Beethoven: Autograph Miscellany from circa 1786 to 1799: British Museum Additional Manuscript 29801, ff. 39–162 (the 'Kafka Sketchbook')*, (London, 1970), vol. i, fol. 138v.

caused the most trouble; this, as other groups of sketches prove again and again, is the kind of problem that seems to have plagued Beethoven constantly. Other points in Draft B that stray from the final version, less spectacular perhaps, nevertheless touch upon central issues.

The sensitivity to registral connection and interruption that speaks out everywhere in the final version is largely missing here. Or rather, registral exposure puts the stress on different pitch connections, and this bears heavily on the very sense of the whole. Towards the end of staff 6 Beethoven's notation underscores the enharmonic gap in bars 24 and 25, and elevates the pair C♭–B♭. The shift of focus in the final version will develop a relationship between F♯ and G♭, and will save B♭ in that exposed register for its critical task in bar 33.

Bars 25–8 in Draft B are unsettling in another way. If there is some disguised inner complexity within them it is not detectable. In the absence of an explicit E♭ in bar 29, one looks to these bars for some symptom that would put it implicitly in its place. But the very strong A♭ at the first beat in bar 29, whether it is addressed as in model a or model b in Example 4, vitiates the potential for an expressive E♭; it is A♭ that has the harmonic strength and – as dislocated neighbour to G – the expressive value.

Example 4

The entry that begins after the double bar on staff 10 (Sketch C) is a particularly problematic corollary to this undefined E♭ in Draft B. The music on staves 8 and 9 gets very close to the final version. Sketch C, if it is right to read it as a revision linked to the cross at the end of staff 7, would repudiate that concept. The high B♭ at the beginning of staff 8, the indispensable symbol of a reprise in bar 33, is eliminated, and the new continuation embodied in Sketch C moves along a different track.

If finding a context for Sketch C is problematical, the immediate sense of the entry seems clear enough. Focus is sharp at either end: E♭ is made into a tonic; D is made into a dominant. The motivic pair E♭–D is played out in the gradual transfer of weight from the one to the other. An augmented sixth on E♭ might be inferred beneath those extended C♯s before the last D, in summary allusion to the full process.

Ambiguities in *La Malinconia* 39

A third variant for the cadence (in two versions) pursues a way to B♭ – and yields a stammered motif at the end of staff 11 which is the first trace of something like the way in which the Allegretto tune will begin.

Sketch C, then, stands amid questions provoked by these various points of cadence. Later sketches may hint at answers to them:

VI

The four remaining pages of sketches fall quite naturally into four distinct projects. What is remarkable about them is the almost unbroken concentration on a single compositional problem: the integration of Adagio and Allegretto towards the end of the movement.

Entries on fol. 16r (not shown) address first of all the opening phrase of the Allegretto: there are two attempts at it. Then, apparently without further thought to working out the Allegretto in detail, Beethoven shifted his attention to the late recurrence of the Adagio. A 'loose' entry on staves 5/6, not explicitly tied to the sense of anything else on the page, shows a conventional close in F, strikingly inflected through G♭ at the fermata (see Example 5). This corresponds to nothing in the formal design of the final version. But it is evidently the germ from which Draft C was developed. For if the music on fol. 16v appears to pick up in the middle of the late recollection of the Adagio, the fermata on staff 5 of fol. 16r argues that the return of the Adagio was to have begun with that G♭. In any case Draft C exhibits an intention to recall *La Malinconia* through its chromatic pairs, and to take up the remembrance at G♭–F, a pair that had been somewhat slighted in Draft B, the last full sketch for *La Malinconia*.

Example 5
Fol. 16r

The foci of Draft C are on pitch relationships that earlier sketches have developed. The pairs that descend from G♭ describe a half cadence around E♭ and D – a reminiscence of Sketch C, and perhaps of a context that should apply to it. And that initial G♭ comes alive in the elliptically written passage from the seventh on G♮ at the end of staff 4 to the new beginning in B minor on staff 5. The understood missing term between them is the octave F♯ to which the seventh on G, reinterpreted as an augmented sixth on G, would unfold – in something like the way shown in Example 6. Here is the very deflection that, in bars 11 and 12, sets the deep chromaticism of the piece in motion.

Example 6

In its fussy mixing of the two tempi, and its exaggerated play upon the sensitive pitch areas of the piece, Draft C misses a central rhythmic task of the cadenza: it fails to achieve a clear articulation of the final tonic cadence and to find a proper balance in the music that should come after it. Draft D, on fol. 17r, responds to this. But if it is most heavily weighted towards end matters, its fleeting synoptic vision of the cadenza brings to it a measure of coherence that gets beyond the impeded view of Draft C. A central aspect of that coherence is the half-cadence on D approached through its neighbour E♭ at the end of staves 3/4. In Draft C the half-cadence on the dominant of G came early, to punctuate the chromatic sequence with which that draft began. That gambit has been replaced now, and the half-cadence on D has been relocated and magnified.

Draft E, on fol. 17v (of which staves 1–9 are not shown), comes very close to the final version. But there is a single major difference between them. On staff 10 activity around the final tonic, sustained for some forty bars, peaks at the fermata on the dominant, roughly equivalent to the pause on the dominant in bar 270 in the final version. The fermata is elaborated through a recollection of something like the final phrase of *La Malinconia*, beginning at bar 38. Another writing of it, entered on staff 14, shows how the harmony would go, and, compressing the cadence, reduces the phrase to eight bars. Draft E has given up the half-cadence in G along with the stress on E♭–D in the bass that was central to Draft D. This late reference to Melancholy, in compensation for that loss, plays on an E♭ which, as the seventh degree of a dominant, suspends its resolution to D for the full length of the chromatic digression, and in just this way revives the emphasis on those pitches.

VII

The leap from Draft E to the final version, if it was ever caught on paper, has not been preserved. None of the later autograph material for the quartet has survived. Somewhere in the unknowable distance between Draft E and the final copy, Beethoven will have revised again the design of the closing music, now purging it of the last vestige of a stress between E♭ and D. And somewhere in that distance the special quality of the E♭ in bar 29, obscure in the sketches, will have emerged.

Sketches are private records. They leave an erratic chart to the swift processes of mind. Some relationships are exaggerated, others neglected. Ambiguities form and dissolve elusively. These entries for *La Malinconia* say something about the process, for they illuminate as well through telling acts of omission. The E♭ in bar 29 is but one instance of eloquent ambiguity conceived in the final effort to reconcile sets of ideas born in conflict.

Appendix

Sketches for the Finale of Op. 18 No. 6, Berlin, SPK, Autograph 19e

Fol. 14r
[Draft A]

[Sketch A]

[Sketch B]

Fol. 15r
[Draft B]

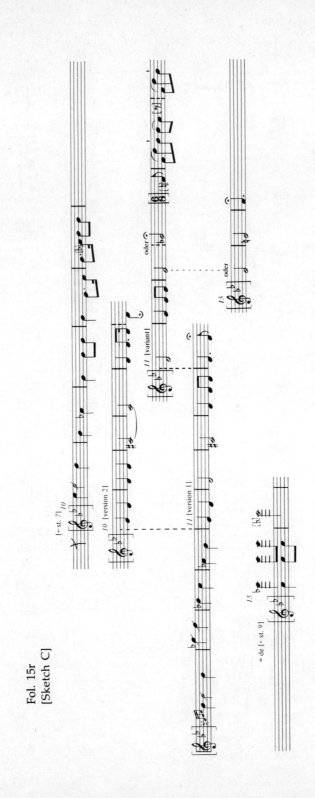

Fol. 15r
[Sketch C]

Fol. 16v
[Draft C]

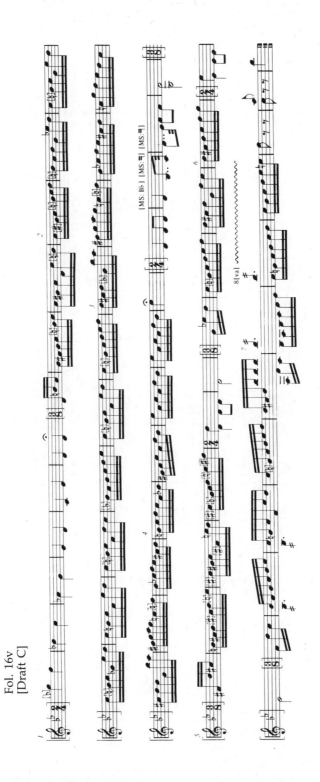

Beethoven's Sketches for the Variations in E♭ Op. 35*

Christopher Reynolds

When Beethoven began composing the Variations for Piano in E♭ Op. 35, he faced formal and contrapuntal difficulties which changed appreciably as his conception of the piece developed. The sketches that document this change reveal much about the techniques that Beethoven employed to organise a large set of variations. But it is only recently that the genesis of the Op. 35 Variations could be explored. A systematic examination was not possible even two decades ago, because for years the second of two sketchbooks containing work on this cycle could not be located. In Gustav Nottebohm's pioneering study of the 'Kessler' Sketchbook (1865) and Paul Mies's investigation of the 'Kessler' sketches for Op. 35 (1954) the inaccessibility of the 'Wielhorsky' Sketchbook posed an insuperable obstacle.[1] The meaning of the earlier 'Kessler' sketches could not be fully understood until the later sketches in 'Wielhorsky' were also available for study. This at last became possible with the publication in 1962 of Natan Fishman's three-volume edition of the 'Wielhorsky' Sketchbook (facsimile, transcription and commentary).[2] And recently Sieghard Brandenburg has

---

*An earlier version of this paper was read at the annual meeting of the American Musicological Society at Minneapolis, Minnesota, in October 1978.

[1] The 'Kessler' Sketchbook is Vienna, GdM, A 34. The studies referred to here are N 1865, p. 32; Paul Mies, 'Ludwig van Beethovens Werke über seinem Kontretanz in Es-Dur', *Beethoven-Jahrbuch*, i (1954), 80–102. Lacking the emphasis on sketches are Hugo Riemann, 'Beethovens Prometheus-Musik, ein Variationenwerk', *Die Musik*, ix (1909–10), 19–34, 107–25; Joseph Müller-Blattau, 'Beethoven und die Variation', *Neues Beethoven-Jahrbuch*, v (1933), 101–36; and Kurt von Fischer, 'Eroica-Variationen Op. 35 und Eroica-Finale', *Schweizerische Musikzeitung*, lxxxix (1949), 282–6.

[2] The 'Wielhorsky' Sketchbook is in Moscow, Central (Glinka) Museum for Music Culture (SV 343). It was edited by Natan L. Fishman as *Kniga eskizov Beethovena za 1802–1803 gody*, 3 vols. (Moscow, 1962); see also his 'Das Skizzenbuch Beethovens aus den Jahren 1802–1803 aus dem Familienarchiv Wielhorski und die ersten Skizzen zur "Eroica"', *Bericht über den Internationalen Musikwissenschaftlichen Kongress, Bonn 1970*, ed. Carl Dahlhaus and others (Kassel, 1971), pp. 104–7.

47

published the 'Kessler' Sketchbook in facsimile and transcription under the auspices of the Beethovenhaus, Bonn.[3]

Although Mies was forced to confine his attention to the sketches in 'Kessler', Fishman elected to focus his extensive remarks primarily on those in 'Wielhorsky', drawing occasionally on Mies's transcriptions when they were of interest.[4] The decision to concentrate on just one book – in one case from necessity, in the other from choice – has seriously limited the scope of both discussions. It has also encouraged arguments that were based largely on the comparison of thematic variants considered out of any developmental context and abstracted with little or no regard for the motivation behind the alterations.

This essay takes as its starting-point the task of determining the chronological order of the individual sketches in both books. By tracing the development of the variations first in 'Kessler' and then in 'Wielhorsky' it should be possible to show how the final version of these so-called 'Prometheus Variations' differs from Beethoven's initial conception. Nottebohm, by far the most astute observer of conceptual change in the sketches that were available to him, called attention to the absence of any sketches for the fugal Finale in 'Kessler', and suggested that Beethoven's original plan may have undergone substantial changes during the course of the composition. Does the fact that sketches for the fugue occur only in 'Wielhorsky' indicate that it was not part of the first plan? The answer to this question lies in a careful study of the relationship between the separate bodies of sketches.

The transition from one sketchbook to the other will therefore receive particular attention. Op. 35 is sketched in 'Kessler' on fols.

---

[3] The facsimile volume was published separately in Munich and Salzburg in 1976; the volume of transcriptions and the facsimile were published together as *Kesslerisches Skizzenbuch*, Veröffentlichungen des Beethovenhauses in Bonn, ser. 1: Skizzen und Entwürfe, vol. v/1–2 (Bonn, 1976, 1978). I am in general agreement with his transcriptions (see below, note 25, for an exception). However, with regard to the identification of individual sketches, many that he has marked 'ohne Verwendung' I believe to be early versions of variations later altered. Compare his lists on pp. 26–7 of the volume of transcriptions with my Appendix II.

[4] Fishman, ed., *Kniga eskizov Beethovena*, commentary, pp. 55–90. Taking his chapter title from Beethoven's claim that Op. 34 and Op. 35 were worked out ('bearbeitet') 'auf eine wirklich ganz neue Manier' (letter of 18 October 1802 to Breitkopf & Härtel, Anderson no. 62), Fishman directs this discussion towards the 'neue Manier' of both variation cycles. On the same track, but again without the emphasis on sketches, are Stefan Kunze, 'Die "wirklich ganz neue Manier" in Beethovens Eroica-Variationen, Op. 35', *Archiv für Musikwissenschaft*, xxix (1972), 124–49; and Carl Dahlhaus, 'Beethovens *Neuer Weg*', *Jahrbuch des Staatlichen Instituts für Musikforschung Preussischer Kulturbesitz 1974* (1975), 46–62.

82v–89v (fifteen pages) and in 'Wielhorsky' on pages 12–14 and 22–43 (twenty-five pages). No other sketches occupy a position of comparable importance in the transition between the two sketchbooks: neither the sketches for the three Op. 31 Piano Sonatas, with nine pages at the end of 'Kessler' and eleven in 'Wielhorsky', nor those for the Op. 34 Piano Variations, with seven pages in 'Wielhorsky' and only two fragments in 'Kessler'. Until now the general assumption has been that Beethoven completed the Op. 35 sketches at the end of 'Kessler' before writing those preserved in 'Wielhorsky'. Indeed the supposed continuity of this transition is one of the main premises in arguments that Fishman advanced to show that Beethoven finished with 'Kessler' shortly before his move to Heiligenstadt around May 1802.[5] As I shall show, Beethoven's path was somewhat more circuitous.

Further, musical continuity will be an issue under consideration throughout this study. With variation cycles the concepts of structural organisation and musical continuity must be approached on more than one level. On the smallest scale, the level of the single variation, structural decisions are predetermined by the melodic and harmonic organisation of the theme. Because the theme for Op. 35 is 16 bars long with a repeat at the mid-point, each variation consists of two eight-bar phrases, and the variations are faithful bar by bar to the harmonic scheme set out in the theme. Normally Beethoven's sketches for variation themes are marked by painstaking revisions – evidence of his laborious efforts to fashion a theme capable of supporting a series of variations. In Op. 35, however, Beethoven spared himself this task by varying a theme he had used twice before: once as a simple Contratanz, and once in the Finale of his music to the ballet *Prometheus* Op. 43.[6] He was to return to this theme once again, of course, and again with variations in view, in the Finale of the 'Eroica' Symphony.

But if the unit of the individual variation were the only level of organisation, the ordering of the variations might as well be random. Certainly variation cycles employ a larger scale of continuity. For cycles with a small number of variations, including variation movements within a sonata or symphony, this next level of organisation may encompass all the variations. With the fifteen variations of Op. 35,

---

[5] Fishman, ed., *Kniga eskizov Beethovena*, commentary, pp. 14–16.

[6] Alexander Ringer maintains that Beethoven originally 'borrowed' it from Clementi: see 'Clementi and the *Eroica*', *Musical Quarterly*, xlvii (1961), 454–68. On Beethoven's revisions of variation themes see Joseph Kerman's comments in 'Beethoven's Early Sketches', *Musical Quarterly*, lvi (1970), 527; and Lewis Lockwood, 'Beethoven's Sketches for *Sehnsucht* (WoO 146)', *Beethoven Studies* [1] ed. Alan Tyson (New York, 1973; London, 1974), pp. 101–2.

however, there is an intermediate level consisting of smaller groups of two, three, or more variations that have some contrapuntal, harmonic, or rhythmic device in common. Lastly, there is the overall organisation, the final ordering of the entire cycle.

Each level of organisation has its own difficulties in achieving a satisfactory musical continuity, and it is interesting to find that each set of problems is dealt with in a different sketch format. In the following discussion 'unit draft' will be used to refer to small groups of variations repeatedly sketched as a unit, and 'succession draft' to refer to the extended series in which Beethoven places single variations in a numbered order. These terms, as I shall show, recognise two distinct approaches to musical continuity among the variations. This study will begin with the most prominent example of variations sketched as a unit, the five introductory movements marked by Beethoven 'Basso del Thema', 'a due', 'a tre', 'a quattro', and 'Thema'.

BASSO DEL THEMA

From the very beginning of the sketch process the cohesive agent in these first five movements is the *Basso del Thema* (henceforth 'BdT' will be used to refer both to the opening movement and to the bass line of the theme). Beethoven required four drafts to develop a contrapuntal accompaniment around the varied registrations of the *BdT* (references are given to the folios and staves of 'Kessler' preceded by the letter K, and to the pages and staves of 'Wielhorsky' preceded by the letter W):

K84r, 9–K84v, 2
K85v, 1–K86r, 2
K89r, 1–K89v, 8
W12, 1–2, W13, 1–14

In the last draft Beethoven began numbering the movements after the *BdT*, beginning with the *a due*: 'I°', '2', '3', and '4', adding the word 'Thema' above number 4. The first movement is found on W12 with the title *Basso del Thema*.[7] The evolution of the *BdT* from one unit draft to another, and thus the chronology of the drafts themselves, can be

---

[7] This movement also begins a set continued on W12, 3–7, which is distinguished by the absence of anything but the *Basso del Thema*. The significance of this title for Beethoven bears further study. It appears to be one associated with registrally independent bass lines. In sketches for the concluding Rondo of the A-minor Violin Sonata Op. 23 Beethoven wrote above the bass 'Basso il thema': see p. 8 of Karl Mikulicz's transcription of Landsberg 7, *Ein Notierungsbuch von Beethoven* (Leipzig, 1927). For the final statement the *Basso* takes the upper and middle registers: see bars 304–11 and 312–23.

demonstrated by comparing selected points of divergence in the sixteen sketches that comprise the four drafts. The columns of Table 1 list the rhythmic patterns of the initial chord of the *BdT* and the cadential bars 8 and 16, along with the occurrence of double bars and repeat signs. The sketches are grouped by draft and the drafts in the order of their pagination, concluding with the final version as published in Op. 35.

Table 1. *Comparison of* Basso del Thema *sketches*

Folio or page and staff no.		Double bars	*BdT* chord	Bar 8	Bar 16
BdT	K84r, 9	A B ‖		♩	♩ ♪
a2	10–11	A ‖: B ‖		♪ 𝄽 𝄽 ‖:	
a3	11–14	A ‖ B ‖		♩. ‖	
a4	15–K84v, 2	‖ A ‖: B ‖		♩ ‖:	
BdT	K85v, 1–2	‖ A A B B ‖			
		‖: A :‖: B ‖	♩. 𝄽	♩. :‖ 𝄽	♩
a2	3–6	‖ A ‖ B :‖		♩. ‖	
a3	5–10	‖ A :‖ B ‖		♩. :‖ 𝄽	♩ ♪
a4	11–16	‖ A ‖ B ‖		♩. ‖ 𝄽	♩ 𝄽
a2	K89r, 1–8	‖ A ‖ B ‖		♩. ‖	
a3	5–16	‖ A ‖ B ‖		♩. ‖ 𝄽	♩
a4	13–K89v, 8	‖ A ‖ B ‖		♫♫ ‖	♩
BdT	W12, 1/2	‖ A :‖: B :‖	♩	♩ :‖	♩ 𝄽
a2	W13, 1–4	‖ A :‖: B :‖		♩ 𝄽 :‖	♩
a3	3–6	‖ A :‖: B :‖		♩ 𝄽 :‖	♩
a4	7–10	‖ A :‖: B :‖		♩. :‖	♩
Thema	11–14	‖ A :‖: B :‖		♫♫ :‖	♩
BdT	Op. 35	‖: A :‖: B :‖	♩	♩ ♪ :‖	♩ 𝄽
a2		‖: A :‖: B :‖		♩ 𝄽 :‖ 𝄽	♩ 𝄽
a3		‖: A :‖: B :‖		♩ 𝄽 :‖ 𝄽	♩ 𝄽
a4		‖: A :‖: B :‖		♩. :‖ 𝄽	♩ 𝄽
Thema		‖: A :‖: B :‖		♫♫ :‖ 𝄽	♫♫

For the purposes of this Table the relative chronology of a sketch is judged by the degree of its correspondence to the published version; for instance the presence of repeat signs in the 'Wielhorsky' draft is taken as an indication of a later stage than that shown in the drafts on K84 and K89, which lack not only repeat signs but, as in the last bars of the former, final notes (and phrases) as well. The development of the *BdT*'s initial chord follows a growth from K84r (nothing) to K85v (♩. 𝄽) to W12 (♩). The relation between K85v and W12–13 is also indicated by the shift to quarter-notes from dotted quarter-notes in bar 8. Table 1 suggests the following chronology:[8]

BdT	K84	—	K85v	W12	Op. 35
a due	K84	K89	K85v	W13	Op. 35
a tre	K84	K89	K85v	W13	Op. 35
a quattro	K84	K89	K85v	W13	Op. 35
Thema				W13	Op. 35

UNIT DRAFT 1

The similarities between Draft 1 (K84) and the opening movements of Op. 35 are many – but so are the differences. In Op. 35 the *Thema* is introduced by four statements of the theme's bass, each of which sounds an octave higher than the previous one; hence the register of the *BdT* in the *a quattro* is exactly that of the *Thema*. The *Thema* is directly adumbrated by the last phrase of its bass (Example 1). While Draft 1 does combine a registrally varied treatment of the *BdT* with a gradual increase in the number of voices, the use of register is neither so subtle nor the addition of voices so systematic as they are in Op. 35. The register of the *BdT* leaps three octaves between the *a due* and *a tre* (E♭ to e♭″), and then falls an octave to become the middle of three voices in the movement which should correspond to the *a quattro*; and for the accompaniments in all three movements Beethoven employs not contrapuntal elaborations of the theme but already the theme itself.

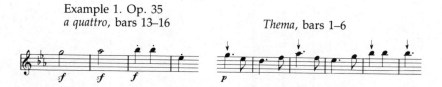

Example 1. Op. 35
a quattro, bars 13–16   *Thema*, bars 1–6

What corresponds to the *Thema* for this draft appears two pages earlier (K83r, 2/3), marked *forte*. The *BdT*, scored in octaves, lies appropriately in the bass, the *Thema* is in the uppermost voice, and the accompaniment, in the middle, uses the figuration introduced in the three-voice 'a quattro'. Above the sketch Beethoven has outlined in

---

[8] Despite its brevity a related fragment on K82v, 3/4 provides enough evidence to place it in the overall development of the *BdT*. The presence of the upper octave and the fact that the opening chord is a half-note indicate that it comes after the sketch on K85v, while the lack of the lower octave would place it before W12.

words and numbers his scheme for this entire group of movements: '2 3 4 Stimmig forte'. It would have made no sense to label these variations 'a due', 'a tre', 'a quattro', and then 'Thema', because the *Thema* had been present all along. Instead Beethoven called this last movement 'forte' both in the draft and in the inscription immediately above it, differentiating it from the preceding variations by scoring and dynamics, rather than melody. The draft does feature an octave-by-octave ascent of melodic material across movements, but it is applied to the *Thema* and not the *BdT*. Starting with its first appearance in the *a due*, a two-octave ascent leaves the Thema in the same register for the *a quattro* and the *forte*.

Yet this succession of registers does not represent Beethoven's earliest conception. At the bottom of K83r, 14 he sketched the registral layout of the *a due, a tre*, and *a quattro* (Example 2). The discrepancy between this blueprint and the full draft is telling. Whereas here the *BdT* climbs steadily from variation to variation, in the draft the order of the second and third fragments is reversed. The possibility that this 'concept sketch' is a revision can be discounted.[9] Most significant is the notational blur that begins the *a tre* (K84r, 11). On close inspection it can be seen that Beethoven first wrote an *eb'* then crossed it out and started again one octave higher. His false start is the exact pitch on which he had planned to begin the *a tre* in his concept sketch.[10]

Example 2. K83r, 14

Though in one sense the registral variation of the *BdT* in Draft 1 arose by default – perhaps Beethoven raised the *a tre* an octave to extricate it from the low range previously occupied by both the *BdT* and the *a due* – it has a precedent among Beethoven's early unpublished works. Approximately ten years before, for the Holy Week of 1790, 1791 or 1792, he devised a series of highly chromatic harmonisations to accompany the chant for the *Lamentations of Jeremiah*. With the avowed

---

[9] The term 'concept sketch' was coined by Alan Tyson to refer to just such a brief sketch of the preliminary nature: see 'The 1803 Version of Beethoven's *Christus am Oelberge*', *Musical Quarterly*, lvi (1970), 570–1.

[10] There is more evidence on K83r. Staves 9–11 contain a complete sketch of the *Thema* harmonised in sixths and thirds – the same harmonisation that appears in the *a tre*, but an octave lower. Also, the sixteenth-note figures of bars 9–11 are present in the unit draft, but, as in all succeeding versions, they are in the *a quattro* not the *a tre*.

intention of confusing the singers of the electoral Kapelle, he methodically arranged a number of eccentric 'Modulationen'. The preparations for the occasion have been preserved on fol. 96 of the 'Kafka' Miscellany.[11] Even a cursory glance at this leaf is sufficient to reveal Beethoven's concern for harmonic variety. Because of the explicit manner in which they prescribe varieties of register, texture, voicing and dynamics, these sketches should be ranked among the most important of his early variation sketches. Indeed in their reliance upon written instructions they resemble sketches for some of Beethoven's latest variation sets, more so in fact than any of the variation sketches in 'Kafka'. The greatest concentration of verbal notes is in the upper right-hand corner. Three have particular relevance to procedures employed again in Op. 35:

1 'einen ganzen Vers die melodie in basso'. Compare Example 3a with the placement of the *Thema* in the *a tre* (K84r, 11/12); in both cases the melody is in the top voice of the left hand.

Example 3. Sketches for the *Lamentations of Jeremiah*, 'Kafka' Miscellany, fol. 96

2 'einen Vers vierstimmig'. This is reflected in the '2 3 4 Stimmig forte' on K83r, and again much later in sketches for the 'Diabelli' Variations Op. 120, when Beethoven specifies 'Var. 1–4 Stimmig' and 'Var. 2 vollstimmig'.[12]

3 'in der höhe einen ganzen Vers gespielt ebenso in der Tiefe und in der mitte' (Example 3b). The relationship this and its accompanying

---

[11] This incident has been related on numerous occasions, most recently by Richard Kramer, 'Notes to Beethoven's Education', *Journal of the American Musicological Society*, xxviii (1975), 76–86; and also Joseph Schmidt-Görg, 'Ein neuer Fund in den Skizzenbüchern Beethovens: Die Lamentationen des Propheten Jeremias', *Beethoven-Jahrbuch*, iii (1959), 107–10. The 'Kafka' Miscellany is London, BL, Add MS 29801; see Joseph Kerman's two-volume edition, *Ludwig van Beethoven: Autograph Miscellany from circa 1786 to 1799: British Museum Additional Manuscript 29801, ff. 39–162* (the 'Kafka Sketchbook') (London, 1970).

[12] Paris, BN, Ms. 58, no. 2, fol. 2v. As with Op. 35 these instructions occur in what appears to be the earliest layer of sketches for Op. 120.

Beethoven's Sketches for Op. 35

chords have to the registral organisation described above is clear. The *BdT* on K84r moves from low to high to middle register – a progression closer in contour to three verses in the *Lamentations of Jeremiah* than to the introductory variations of Op. 35.

To summarise: the earliest sketches for the opening movements show that the expansion of voices was planned by Beethoven from the outset, as was the concurrent variation of register. Even though the registral variation of the *BdT* was not consistent in the unit draft, the initial plan had been to place it in a higher register in each movement. The major contribution of Draft 1 to the evolution of these variations is to be seen in the alteration of Beethoven's first thoughts and the introduction of a steady, octave-by-octave ascent. That it was the *Thema* that climbed by octaves and not its bass matters little, for the principle was then applied to the *BdT* in the second unit draft.

UNIT DRAFT 2

The extent to which compositional conceptions (whether instrumentation, register, counterpoint or some other) influence and affect the sketch format is nowhere more evident than in Draft 2 (K89r–89v). Exceptional not only for Op. 35, but also for sketches of Beethoven's piano works in general, this draft forsakes the customary single- or double-staff sketch in favour of a string quartet score – four separate staves with the appropriate clefs. The quartet influence is also present in the '2da' Beethoven wrote underneath the uppermost line of the *a tre* (K89r, 9). This may be interpreted as a direction to shift these bars down to the 'second violin' one staff below, which he proceeds to do for the second half of the *a tre*.[13] But there is an element of confusion at the top of the draft regarding the location of the 'viola' line. For the *a due*, the part to be read with the alto clef is not the third staff but the second (K89r, 2, 6). Beethoven catches the apparent error at the beginning of the *a tre*, crosses out a false start and moves the 'viola' line down to its customary staff.[14]

The new format constitutes a response to the registral difficulties encountered in the first draft by varying the register of one voice only, the *BdT*. Beethoven perhaps owed a debt to the technique of cantus firmus variation found pre-eminently in certain of Haydn's string

---

[13] Brandenburg transcribed this '[violino] 2 do': ed., *Kesslerisches Skizzenbuch*, transcription, p. 189.

[14] Mies misread this draft of the *a due* ('Beethovens Werke über seinem Kontretanz', 87). Supposing the second staff to belong to the 'second violin', he transcribed it with a treble clef.

quartets; as for example in two of the last to be published before work began on Op. 35. Both Op. 76 Nos. 3 and 6, published by Artaria in 1799, contain cantus firmus variations.[15] The first movement of No. 6 shares with Op. 35 the additional features of being in E♭ and culminating in a fugue.

Nevertheless the change of format does not imply a change from piano to string quartet.[16] Beethoven did not sketch string quartets very differently from the way in which he sketched sonatas or symphonies. The initial conception is noted sometimes on one staff, sometimes on two, according to the demands of the accompaniment, and intermediate drafts generally occupy a single staff, with the exception of contrapuntally intricate passages requiring two or more staves. When he was near the end of his compositional process Beethoven would expand the format to fit the instrumentation. After blocking off a number of empty bars on a blank page and 'entering the results of the last draft slightly in advance, he would have added the remaining parts'.[17]

But there is a fundamental difference between this process and what is going on in Draft 2. There, having blocked off the requisite number of bars and entered the *BdT*, Beethoven began to add his first rudimentary contrapuntal ideas. The careless errors, the skeletal form of the *a quattro*, and the content of the revisions are all consistent with the early stage of composition represented by this draft. Only the *a due* resembles its final form. Numerically the draft may be the second, but musically it is the first to treat the *a due*, *a tre*, and *a quattro* as contrapuntal variations of the theme. Were it in fact a draft for strings, four staves would be equally unusual at such an early stage.

The choice of format has a parallel in Beethoven's contrapuntal studies. Two-part, three-part, and four-part counterpoint on separate staves, a migratory cantus firmus, and a concern for the spacing of registers – this description is no less characteristic of Draft 2 than it is of the standard Fuxian pedagogy first expounded to Beethoven by Haydn and later by Schenk and Albrechtsberger.[18] Most important of all were his studies of double counterpoint which began in earnest

---

[15] See James Webster, 'The Chronology of Haydn's String Quartets', *Musical Quarterly*, lxi (1975), 24–6.

[16] Equally unwarranted is Mies's suggestion that the idea for the fourth movement of the 'Eroica' Symphony comes from such a draft; 'Beethovens Werke über seinem Kontretanz', 85.

[17] Douglas Johnson, 'Beethoven's Sketches for the Scherzo of the Quartet Op. 18, No. 6', *Journal of the American Musicological Society*, xxiii (1970), 403.

[18] Schenk professed to have studied with Georg Christoph Wagenseil, himself a pupil of Fux; see 'Johann Baptist Schenk: Autobiographische Skizze', *Studien zur Musikwissenschaft*, xi (1924), 77, 81–3.

under Albrechtsberger in 1794. Just as a record of Haydn's teachings is transmitted in the *Elementarbuch* of 1789, Albrechtsberger's *Anweisung zur Composition* of 1790 preserves a thorough account of the contrapuntal principles he espoused. His precepts are there organised in terms of a cumulative development, progressing from simple counterpoint (two, three, and four parts) to imitation and fugue (two, three, and more parts), double counterpoint, double fugue, and canon. Nottebohm has shown that Beethoven's lessons adhered to the same general progression.[19] With regard to double counterpoint, Albrechtsberger drilled Beethoven in inversions at the octave, tenth, and twelfth, beginning each section with an abstract taken from his *Anweisung*, stressing the rules governing each inversion. These guidelines were most extensive for double counterpoint at the tenth, because it is at this point that Albrechtsberger appended several instructions pertaining specifically to the expansion of a two-voice passage to one with three and four voices. One principle is of particular interest: 'Rule for the *a tre* and *a quattro*: here all the strings must be written in opposite or oblique motion with no dissonant suspensions – only thirds, sixths, and octaves.'[20] There is here an explicit association of strings with double counterpoint, an association for which there is a ready explanation. The connection is to be attributed not to any instrumental qualities inherent in double counterpoint itself, but to the indispensability of this technique for fugal composition, and to Albrechtsberger's well-known predilection for string quartet fugues.[21]

Once Beethoven abandoned the idea of using the theme in the movements before the *Thema*, he turned to a varied form of double counterpoint to expand the *a due*. In Draft 2 the inversion is the least strict. Avoiding dissonant suspensions and moving in opposite or oblique motion, as Albrechtsberger had prescribed, the *a tre* varies the counterpoint of the *a due* primarily through the addition of passing-notes (Example 4). More literal is the inversion of bars 13 and 14. The inversion of bar 13 is still present as late as the first stage of the fourth draft (W13, 3, 6). Through the ensuing unit drafts Beethoven focused on strengthening the invertibility of the accompaniment, especially for

---

[19] Gustav Nottebohm, *Beethovens Studien: Beethovens Unterricht bei J. Haydn, Albrechtsberger und Salieri* (Leipzig, 1873), pp. 45ff.

[20] 'Regel zum *a tre* und *a quattro*: Hier müssen alle Streiche in der Gegen- oder Seitenbewegung und keine Dissonanz-Ligaturen gemacht werden, sondern nur 3., 6., 8.' (Nottebohm, *Beethovens Studien*, p. 143.)

[21] Warren Kirkendale estimated his total output of fugues for strings to be in excess of 160; *Fuge und Fugato in der Kammermusik des Rokoko und der Klassik* (Tutzing, 1966), p. 37. In the revised Eng. trans. (Durham, N. C., 1979), the precise figure is given as '159' (p. 290).

Example 4. Sketches for bars 1–5 of the *a due* and *a tre*

bars 1–2, since in bars 3–4 the original registral pairing had to be maintained (that is, without inversion) in order not to end on a perfect fourth. The change in contour between Drafts 3 and 4 (Example 5) seems motivated by a desire to retain the opening upbeat of the *a tre*. The upbeat that begins the *a due* is not invertible; according to Fux 'it is easily understood why, in this species of counterpoint, the fifth is forbidden; by inversion it would become a dissonance, namely a fourth'.[22] More to the point are two rules Beethoven paraphrased from Kirnberger's *Kunst des reinen Satzes* while he was studying with Albrechtsberger: 'No melody to be transposed according to counterpoint at the octave can begin or end with a fifth . . . The perfect fifth can be used in ascent or descent as a passing-note.'[23] By changing the

Example 5. Sketches for bars 1–4 of the *a due* and *a tre*

[22] Fux, *Gradus ad Parnassum*, trans. and ed. Alfred Mann, *Musical Quarterly*, xxxvii (1951), 204.

[23] 'Keine in den Contrapunct der Octave zu versetzende Melodie kann mit der Quinte anfangen noch endigen . . . Die perfect Quinte kann im Auf- und Absteigen als durchgehend gebraucht werden.' (Johann Philipp Kirnberger, *Die Kunst des reinen*

Beethoven's Sketches for Op. 35

contour Beethoven manages to incorporate the upbeat *bb* into the counterpoint of the *a tre* (Draft 4). He avoids a perfect fourth on the downbeat of bar 1 by moving stepwise downward through a perfect fifth *ab* which serves as an accented passing-note to *g–f–eb* inverted from the *a due*. The *a tre* thus gains the upbeat at the expense of the suspension that characterises the *a due*, whereas in Draft 3 the *a tre* kept the suspensions intact while forgoing the upbeat.

A DUE

The development of the *a due*'s contrapuntal accompaniment within the unit drafts (Example 6) can be seen as a meticulous testing of

Example 6. Bars 1–8 of the *a due*: unit drafts and final version

Satzes in der Musik, Part ii (Berlin and Königsberg, 1776–9), pp. 12–13; Nottebohm published Beethoven's abstract, *Beethovens Studien*, pp. 126–7.)

alternatives to, and eventual modification of, Beethoven's earliest conception as recorded in Draft 2. Clearly the bars he found most troublesome were bars 5 and 6, of which Draft 4 contains what I discern to be three separate readings.[24] When these three variants are placed alongside Op. 35 one sees how thoroughly Beethoven explored every possible combination of these bars. I have labelled the Op. 35 versions of bars 5 and 6 'Y' and 'Z', the penultimate versions 'W' and 'X', and so on. For bar 6 Beethoven alternated between two possibilities, but in bar 5 he experimented with four. The difficulty has to do with the manner in which the pivotal bb', the high-point in the first half of the theme, is approached and left. Since the B♭ is heard in relation to the G and A♭ that precede it in both the *Thema* and *BdT* (Example 1), it comes as no surprise to find a correlation between the metric position of the g' and ab' and the placement of the bb'. In Draft 2 each of these notes comes on the third eighth-note of a bar. Indeed, the four versions of bar 5 at one time or another allow for bb' to fall on each of the four eighth-notes of the bar. Only the Y form (the first and final choice) remains faithful to the repetition of the bb'' in bar 5 of the *Thema*.[25]

Beethoven's first impulse in Draft 4 is to relocate the g'–ab'–bb' to the second eighth-notes of their respective bars. Perhaps because it does not retain the *Thema*'s repetition of the B♭, he strikes this variant in favour of one that does. However, the version in Draft 4b disturbs the sequence of the melodic rhythm; whatever legitimacy the Y form of bar 5 has in Draft 2 and Op. 35 is lost when it is inserted into Draft 4. The placement of the repeated bb' is no longer consistent with the metric position of the preceding g' and ab'. Beethoven is thus apparently in the position of having to settle for the lesser of two evils (W–X) so long as the *a due* begins as it does in Draft 4a. Once the g' and ab' are shifted back to the third eighth-notes (that is, once the basic shape of Draft 2 is reincorporated in Op. 35), the repeated bb' becomes possible – but not without cost. I have shown that Beethoven had been seeking a counterpoint that would serve with small modifications as a beginning for both the *a due* and *a tre*. By selecting Y–Z over W–X, he was forced to abandon the melodic bond between these variations which he had carefully worked out in Drafts 3 and 4.[26]

[24] Fishman's transcription distinguishes two: ed., *Kniga eskizov Beethovena*, transcription, p. 13.

[25] The figure X is the only variant of bar 5 to place the bb' on the fourth eighth-note. As such it is consistent with the preceding bars of Draft 3b, in which the g' and ab' of the first and third bars are placed on the same beat. Draft 3a is the first version Beethoven wrote on K85v, 3. He had previously sketched it on K83v, 15. Brandenburg gives only the revised version: ed., *Kesslerisches Skizzenbuch*, transcription, p. 183.

[26] In a paper read at the National Conference on Music Theory, in Evanston, Illinois

SUCCESSION DRAFT

Beethoven's approach to the numbered variations utilised a different sketch format from the outset. In the first sustained work that he devoted to single variations Beethoven wrote down ideas for ten separate variations on the sixteen staves of K82v. Most are no more than four to five bars long, concern only the first phrase, and employ two staves.[27] There is as yet no sense of continuity between sketches; in fact, when Beethoven later sought to impose a semblance of order by adding variation numbers to four of the first-phrase ideas, he did not see fit to assign consecutive numbers to any two adjacent sketches. At the present stage his principal aim was to set down a varied series of ideas for further expansion, a source he could tap throughout the sketch process.

Both Beethoven's methods and the format changed as these variations evolved. By the time he had come to the advanced sketches on W26–33, the progression between variations had become as important as the figuration within them, and instead of the large preponderance of sketches on two staves, single-staff sketches were favoured. Even when Beethoven did resort to two staves, it was usually to accommodate a single musical line. More important, instead of ten discontinuous fragments there were now many full-length variations, including one in which Beethoven went so far as to mark off the bar-lines of bars he left blank. Because he was at this point capable of writing out complete drafts of each variation, Beethoven was for the first time able to turn seriously to the task of establishing the sequence of all the variations.

W26 thus marks the beginning of what I am calling a 'succession draft'. Over the next few pages the variations were numbered and renumbered as Beethoven experimented with various combinations and numerical orders in search of the most convincing succession of movements. Throughout 'Kessler' and 'Wielhorsky', not only do sketches for the majority of these variations not appear in the order

(18–20 November 1977), Ellwood Derr pointed out a number of what he termed 'unwitting borrowings' between Op. 35 and C.P.E. Bach's Rondo in E♭ W 61/1 (1787). One of his strongest examples involved the *a due* from Draft 4, which, Derr note, echoes the main theme of Bach's E♭ Rondo. Whether Beethoven caught himself in an 'unconscious plagiarism', or thought better of an intentional borrowing, or was simply frustrated by the dilemma he faced in bars 5 and 6 of the *a due*, is a matter of conjecture. An abstract of Derr's paper appears in the *College Music Symposium*, xviii (1978), 230.

[27] Sieghard Brandenburg gives a similar description in 'Beethovens "Erste Entwürfe" zu Variationzyklen', *Bericht über den Internationalen Musikwissenschaftlichen Kongress, Bonn 1970*, ed. Carl Dahlhaus and others (Kassel, 1971), pp. 108–11.

that was finally fixed in Op. 35, they recur in no consistent sequential ordering whatsoever.[28]

Renumberings within the succession draft did not necessarily entail musical revisions, as can be seen at the beginning of W26, 4, where Beethoven simply wrote the number 5 over a number 3. But in a few instances a change in numerical position resulted in a complete rewriting of the variation to fit it into a new environment. Beethoven would either retain the contours of a musical line while changing the figuration – from triplets to sixteenth-notes for example – or just the reverse: he would keep the figuration and change the line. The latter occurs in the variations numbered 2 and 6 on W26. They are musical twins, not identical, but with such slight differences in contour that it is difficult to imagine Beethoven including both in the same set of variations. In fact by the time Op. 35 was published the two versions had become thoroughly integrated as Variation 4. Diverging after the second bar, the two versions contributed alternate bars to the finished variation: from W26 no. 2 came bars 5–7, 9, and 11–12; while W26 no. 6 provided bars 3–4, 8, 10, and 13–14.

The discrepancies between the final phrases of these two versions bring into focus one of the most significant means of establishing a continuity between successive variations. Example 7a gives the last three bars of the version numbered 2 as it leads into the first bars of the draft for the next variation. The arpeggiated beginning of this variation is anticipated in the concluding bars of no. 2. When Beethoven then relocated it as no. 6, he rewrote the conclusion to set up and lead into the rising sixth *g–eb'* of the new sequel, no. 7 (Example 7b). And the only two bars of the published Variation 4 not to come from either of the two drafts on W26 are the final two, for these bars had to be recomposed to lead into the new Variation 5.

Example 7

[28] For example, the sketch designated 'no. 1' on K82v was ultimately published as Variation 3, but on these pages Beethoven tried it out as no. 14, no. 7, and no. 5. For the numbers of others, see Appendix II.

Once the variations in the succession draft had been numbered, sketched, renumbered, and in some cases resketched, Beethoven himself must have had difficulty discerning the final order. Seeking to minimise the confusion that then obscured the sequence of movements, he turned to W33, the last page before the fugue sketches, and compiled a numerical list of variation incipits – just one or two bars each – culled from the succession draft.

SKETCH DUPLICATION

So far all work in the two books has followed a consistent progression – sketches in 'Kessler' have been thoroughly revised in 'Wielhorsky'. A major departure from this pattern occurs on W22–5, where Beethoven simply duplicated his previous work on fols. 82v–88v of 'Kessler'.[29] Appendix I details the correspondence of content and arrangement. Any doubt about which book preserves the original and which the copy is quickly dispelled by an examination of individual duplications and of the dimensions of the sketches as a whole. Beethoven managed to condense thirteen pages of 'Kessler' into four of 'Wielhorsky' by skipping over some sketches and abbreviating others. Omitted are all the unit drafts, all the sketches related to them (except two sketches for the *a tre* on K84v, 6/7 and K83r, 9–11), and all the sketches unrelated to Op. 35. Abbreviated are entries 18, 20, 21, 26, 28, 41, 42, 49, 50, 52, and 54. In 'Wielhorsky' these were shortened for one of two reasons: either Beethoven excised material he no longer wanted, as with entry 28 where the first half of Variation 15 was dropped because the material had been superseded, or he engaged in a musical shorthand, omitting all but a few key bars which then served as mnemonic aids for entire variations or individual phrases, as in entry 42 which transmits bars 1–2, 13–14 and a few notes of the arpeggio used in bar 12 of Variation 2. Of the fifty-seven items listed in Appendix I 'Kessler' accounts for fifty and 'Wielhorsky' for thirty-five. In his concern for weeding out the extraneous sketches cluttering each page of 'Kessler', Beethoven duplicated only twenty-nine of fifty 'Kessler' sketches.

The first four sketches on W22 are revisions, not duplications, of work in 'Kessler'. Entry 4 thus assumes a pivotal position. The double bar that separates it from entry 5 demarcates two distinct compositional objectives, one of which involves a sketch process that is essentially creative and progressive, while the other, being little more than the process of transcription, is basically recapitulatory. Ultimately the goal of both is a final version. In more immediate terms the aim of the first

[29] See Brandenburg's comments in *Kesslerisches Skizzenbuch*, transcription, pp. 33–4.

process is to refine or alter earlier sketches in order to bring each variation closer to autograph stage. For the duplications, however, the short-range purpose can be gleaned from a close look at the 'Kessler' sketches that Beethoven chose not to duplicate. As has already been mentioned, he passed over all unit drafts and their attendant fragments (entries 6, 16, 23, 30, 34, 38) and all sketches not specifically related to Op. 35 (entries 39, 47, 51, 53, 55). But this accounts for just eleven of the twenty-one items found only in 'Kessler'. The other ten are listed below:

entry 8   Xa
entry 10 Var. 2
entry 11 Xc
entry 15 Var. A
entry 25 Var. A
entry 29 Var. 14
entry 31 Var. 10
entry 35 Var. 1
entry 48 Var. 15
entry 56 Xj

Three of these may be set aside at the outset: the fragments Xa, Xc, and Xj are sufficiently dissimilar to subsequent sketches to prevent their being identified with any variation developed in either sketchbook. It is likely that a fourth, entry 48, was omitted because it had been superseded on the very next page (K87v). Rather than copying the same idea twice almost in succession, Beethoven transferred to 'Wielhorsky' a two-bar segment taken from the later version, entry 52a.

The remaining six sketches confirm Beethoven's desire to avoid unnecessary duplication, although one gets the impression that he was not always consistent about copying the latest revision. For instance bars 9–12 of Variation 15 turn up twice (entries 28 and 52b), yet Beethoven transcribed these bars only from the earlier of the two entries (28); and while it might be argued that entry 10 was omitted because it was rendered obsolete by the next sketch for Variation 2 (entry 42), the argument is incapable of explaining the absence of entries 31 (Variation 10) and 35 (Variation 1), since they are the only sketches for these phrases in 'Kessler'.

Table 2 suggests an explanation by placing the six sketches in question (designated by an 'X') on a grid containing all other sketches for the same variations (designated by an 'O') written up to the point at which Beethoven began copying: the variations represented in this

Beethoven's Sketches for Op. 35

Table 2. *Six sketches not copied into 'Wielhorsky'*

	K82v	K83r	K83v	K84r	K84v	K85r	K86v	K87r	K87v	W12	W13	W14	W22
Var. A	X	X		⌒						O	O		
Var. 1				X	X						O		
Var. 2	X						O				O		
Var. 10				X			O	⌒					O
Var. 14			X					O	O			O	

group of unduplicated material were already present in 'Wielhorsky', on W12, W13, W14 and W22. According to this analysis, the decision to copy 'Kessler' sketches into 'Wielhorsky' reflects an attempt to eliminate the inconvenience of working from two large sketchbooks by transferring to the new book all pertinent sketches not already present as a result of previous revision. A measure of corroboration is found on W22 itself, among the four sketches that precede the duplications. Their antecedents are spread throughout 'Kessler'. For entry 1, the twelve-bar sketch for Variation 10, Beethoven revised the first eight bars from K84r, 1/2 and the last four from K86v, 9/10; entries 2 and 3 are revisions of work on K88v and K84r; and the four bars of Variation 8 (entry 4) were taken from K87r. In other words, to assemble the four fragments on W22 Beethoven had to do a good deal of leafing through 'Kessler'. Five pages separated the two components of Variation 10, and then to seek out the next sketches he had to turn ahead four pages, back nine and forward six.

Yet some of the sketches in Table 2 were also reworked in 'Kessler', and Beethoven did duplicate these revisions, regardless of their 'Wielhorsky' counterparts. The reasons for this apparent redundancy become evident through an examination of the sketches for Variations 2 and 14.

VARIATIONS 2 AND 14

Variation 2: Sketches

K82v, 9/10   (1–3)
K86v, 5–10   (1–5, cadenza as 9–12, 13–15)
W14, 5/6   (1–4)
W24, 7   (1–2, cadenza, 13–14)
W26, 12–16   (1–8, 9–16)
W32, 4   (1–3)
W33, 1   (1)

66   Christopher Reynolds

A definite evolution towards the published form of Variation 2 takes place in the two 'Kessler' sketches (Example 8a). That on K86v is not only substantially larger in scope than the one on K82v, but the chordal figuration it introduces for the right hand is also fundamentally the same as that used in Op. 35. In contrast, the 'Wielhorsky' version is closer to the earlier 'Kessler' sketch in both content and form (Example 8b). Changes between the two are minimal but significant. Paul Mies, in his extensive study of the use of the upbeat in Beethoven's melodic lines, noted how 'in the sketch-books there are a large number of instances in which melodies, originally without up-beat, are given one later on'.[30] Op. 35 provides several prime examples, for although many of the variations lack an upbeat in the sketches, upbeats had been introduced by the time of publication. And I have demonstrated the struggle that Beethoven faced in the unit drafts, resolved ultimately in Draft 4 when the upbeat won acceptance at the expense of double counterpoint. Falling as they do in the shadow of Draft 4, the four bars of Variation 2 on W14 are noteworthy for the addition of an upbeat, which enables the right hand to include the opening G of the *Thema* on the downbeat of the first bar. But the real import of this upbeat derives from its status as a refinement of the sketch on K82v, and thus as an intermediate stage between the two 'Kessler' sketches.

Example 8. Bars 1–2 of Variation 2: sketches and final version

Earlier in this essay another sketch on K82v was placed vaguely in its chronological order. When it was determined that the five-bar fragment of the *BdT* on staves 3/4 belonged after Draft 3 (K85v) and before Draft 4 (W12), the conclusion was drawn that at least one sketch on

---

[30] Paul Mies, *Die Bedeutung der Skizzen Beethovens zur Erkenntnis seines Stiles* (Leipzig, 1925); Eng. trans. (London, 1929), p. 5.

Beethoven's Sketches for Op. 35

K82v followed K85v (see footnote 8). Now that a second sketch further down the page can be identified as a predecessor to material on W14, the following sequence of pages begins to emerge: Draft 3 (K85v–86r), K82v, Draft 4 (W12–13), W14, and then back to K86v.

The pattern of sketches for Variation 2 also exists among sketches for the *Minore*, Variation 14.

Variation 14: Sketches

K83v, 12/13 (1–8, 9–12 + 1)
K87r, 15/16 (1–7, 1a–8a, 9–16)
K87v, 13/14 (9a–16a)
W12, 11/12 (9–16)
W14, 9/10 (1–8, 9–12 + 1, 13–16)
W25, 3–6   (1–4, 1a–8a, 9–16, 9a–16a)
W28, 7–10 (1–8, 1a–8a, 9–16, 9a–16a)
W29, 1–3   (1–8, 1a–8a, 9–16)
W31, 14/15 (9–12)

Once again the chain of development separates the two 'Kessler' sketches with intervening work in 'Wielhorsky'. In this case they are mediated by two 'Wielhorsky' sketches, one on W14 and a revision of it on W12. That K83v and W14 are consecutive links in this developmental chain is verified by a quirk common to each: the third phrase (bars 9–12 of the final version) is five bars long in these two sketches (Example 9). Beethoven's next step is to isolate this irregular passage (W12) and trim the extra measure off the beginning of the phrase, an operation accompanied by a general rewriting that anchors these bars more securely to the dominant of E♭ by resolving the cb'' twice (bars 10 and 12) to a root-position dominant seventh, rather than once (as on

Example 9. Sketches for bars 9–12 of Variation 14

W14). For the sketch on K87r–87v, Beethoven's whole conception of the variation has been greatly expanded. No longer merely a single *Minore*, Variation 14 has grown into a double variation, a hybrid alternately major and minor in mode, unison and polyphonic in texture, and high and low in register. Bars 9–12 first elaborate the *BdT*'s repeated Bbs by juxtaposing the registral extremes established in the first half of the variation. In the varied repetition Beethoven intensifies the emphasis on the Bb, employing it in each of the four bars as the resolution of Cb. Thus the progressions from W14 to W12 and from W12 to K87r are both marked by a doubling of the previous number of resolutions in these bars.

THE TRANSITION FROM 'KESSLER' TO 'WIELHORSKY'

Tracing the circuitous evolutions of Variations 2 and 14 is the key to recognising the extraordinary extent of the interaction between 'Kessler' and 'Wielhorsky'. While the six sketches featured in Table 2 were not copied into 'Wielhorsky' because subsequent sketches for those variations were already present there, Beethoven did duplicate the later 'Kessler' sketches for the same variations because they postdate the first work in the new book.

The questions raised by this interaction probe what has in general been a little-examined facet of Beethoven's compositional process: the transition from one sketchbook to another. When the end of a sketchbook was reached, were the compositions still in progress affected by the interruption? Is it even proper to speak of an 'interruption'? Did he proceed automatically to a new sketchbook or loose leaves, or was it necessary to plan his sketches around the transition? Beethoven's procedural response may have varied from composition to composition and according to the stage that a composition had reached at the time of the switch. Op. 34, for example, has only two early fragments in 'Kessler', a two-bar incipit of the theme and four bars of Variation 6 (K88v and K90r). Yet in 'Wielhorsky' the sketches (W16–22) are at a late and highly developed stage. Most of the early and all the intermediate sketching must have been done on loose leaves. The same conclusion is warranted for the three Op. 31 Piano Sonatas: they account for little or no overlap between the two sketchbooks – 'Kessler' has several folios of early work on the first Sonata, and 'Wielhorsky' begins with eleven pages devoted to the third of the set.

Beethoven followed a different procedure in the sketches for Op. 35. There is no evidence that sketches were written between books, although loose leaves may have been utilised at a later time (for example for the canonic Variation 7, for which no sketches are known). It is also clear from their placement in 'Kessler' and 'Wielhorsky' that the transition from one book to the other was not abrupt. Beethoven did not fill the pages of 'Kessler' and then put it away as he began work in 'Wielhorsky'. On the contrary, the two must have lain side by side for the duration of the period of transition. At the very latest the conclusion of this period would coincide with the completion of work on the variations in 'Wielhorsky', at the point at which Beethoven turned his efforts to the fugue that begins the Finale.

But some questions remain. The second move to 'Wielhorsky', to write the last variations and the fugue, can safely be attributed to a lack of space in 'Kessler'. But what was the impetus for the first move? And why after having left the old sketchbook did he return? When Beethoven turned to 'Wielhorsky' to write out Draft 4 of the introductory variations, there were enough blank pages in 'Kessler' to accommodate them with room to spare. In that sense, it is true, limitations of space were not a factor. However, the imminent presence of sketches for Op. 31 No. 1 (K91v–96v) placed a considerable constraint on any other sketches Beethoven intended to write for Op. 35. Sooner or later the shortage of space would force a move to a new sketchbook. For that reason, I interpret the timing of the original move as a reflection first of a confidence on Beethoven's part that he was now in a position to complete the introductory unit draft, and second of a desire to use the new sketchbook primarily as a final proving-ground in which the variations could be sketched in full and ordered numerically.

Of these criteria the last – the numerical ordering – deserves emphasis. According to Beethoven's initial plan, the succession draft began as an extension of Draft 4 of the *BdT* variations. His intent emerges from the common numbering system that the two shared from the beginning – a system obscured by subsequent revisions. In its present form the unit draft on W12–13 carries a curious mixture of labels and numerals. The *BdT* is unnumbered, the next three movements are unnamed, and the *Thema* is both named and numbered:

BdT	Basso del Thema
a due	1°
a tre	2
a quattro	3
Thema	4 Thema

Then on W26 Beethoven started the succession draft with the number 2, skipped ahead to number 5, and continued until he reached '17'. Originally the second sketch on W26 had been assigned the number 3, and as such it flowed easily out of the arpeggiation that concluded sketch no. 2. But before proceeding to sketch no. 4, he changed the '3' to a '5' and went on to no. 6, which, as noted above, is the musical double of sketch no. 2. The source of the confusion must lie in an alteration in Beethoven's method of reckoning the introductory variations. His first designations would be 'Basso del Thema', 'I°', and 'Thema', with the 'I°' encompassing the *a due, a tre,* and *a quattro*. By this reasoning Beethoven would quite naturally have begun W26 with no. 2 and followed it with no. 3. But when he then renumbered the sketches on W13 from 'I°' to 'I°', '2', '3', '4', he returned to W26 and changed no. 3 to no. 5, rewrote no. 2 as no. 6, and proceeded from there.

Exactly why Beethoven renumbered Draft 4 is uncertain. Maybe he wanted to indicate the individuality of each introductory variation, rather than subsume them all under a single numeral. Perhaps it should be interpreted as nothing more than a ruse to inflate the total number of variations as much as possible, in accord with the letter to Breitkopf & Härtel of 18 October 1802 (Anderson no. 62) which boasted that this opus contained thirty variations. But the numerical connection with W26 has unmistakable implications. If the timing of the first transition to 'Wielhorsky' reflects an awareness that the opening movements were ready for their final draft, it is doubtful that the move was ever anything more than a temporary foray, conceived to free the available pages in 'Kessler' for the preparatory work which remained a necessity before continuing to the succession draft.

The decision to begin the Finale with a fugue further contributed to the inevitability of a move to a new book. Nottebohm, observing the absence of sketches for a fugue in 'Kessler', commented: 'the impression is that Beethoven had at first wanted to write variations in a traditional manner'.[31] In fact, there is no sign of the fugue until W12, 16, written about the same time as Draft 4, while among the earliest sketches for Op. 35 there are several staves labelled 'Finale presto' (K83r, 6–8) which are contemporaneous with the first draft of the introductory group. The character of the early Finale is entirely in keeping with the rousing conclusions Beethoven had written for most of his previous variation sets. Certainly Beethoven changed his plans for the Finale before the first fugal jottings on W12. By the time he wrote the third draft of the introductory variations, he had begun dismembering the Finale presto and attaching segments of it to selected variations by means of 'Vi=de's.

But I think it is possible to push the change in Beethoven's conception back still further. In Draft 3 Beethoven strove for an accompaniment unified by double counterpoint; but, as shown above, this idea arose in Draft 2. A logical time for the inception of the fugal Finale would be the second draft of the introductory variations, when a structural counterbalance to the newly conceived contrapuntal beginning was first appropriate. Some time later, after completing his sketches in the two books, Beethoven decided to inject another form of strict counterpoint into the middle of this opus, adding a canonic number as Variation 7.

Finally, Beethoven's manipulation of the 'Kessler' and 'Wielhorsky' Sketchbooks throughout work on Op. 35 has implications for dating his completion of 'Kessler'. Brandenburg argues for a completion date some time between July and August 1802, based on his dating of works sketched on either side of Op. 35. He has shown that the three Violin Sonatas Op. 30, sketched in 'Kessler' on fols. 37v–38r and 43v–81r, were ready for Breitkopf & Härtel by 22 April 1802. But for the Piano Sonatas Op. 31 there is no clear evidence for determining either when Beethoven began or finished his work in 'Kessler', only that the beginning of work could have come no later than August.[32] Beethoven apparently completed his variation cycles Op. 34 and Op. 35 by mid-October, for on 18 October 1802 he wrote to Breitkopf & Härtel offering the new pieces, both worked out 'auf eine wirklich ganz *neue Manier*'. If his E♭ Variations stood ready to be published in mid-October, then the sketches for them probably were concluded not long before. Yet in assessing 'Kessler''s dates on the basis of the sketches for Op. 35, one variable that cannot be gauged is the amount

[31] N 1865, p. 32.
[32] Brandenburg, ed., *Kesslerisches Skizzenbuch*, transcription, pp. 16 and 34.

of time that elapsed between the three blocks of Op. 35 sketches while Beethoven devoted himself to Op. 31 and Op. 34. Nevertheless, since activity in 'Kessler' continued for some time after Beethoven inaugurated 'Wielhorsky', it would appear that he utilised the 'Kessler' Sketchbook through the summer, and only laid it aside permanently in the late summer or early autumn of 1802.[33] However, if the fact that Beethoven did not send the autographs of Op. 34 and Op. 35 to the publisher before early December means that the sketches were not finished before the end of November (as Brandenburg believes),[34] then 'Kessler' probably remained in use further into the autumn. In that case the moves between 'Kessler' and 'Wielhorsky' may have received impetus from Beethoven's mid-October return to Vienna, following six months in Heiligenstadt.

CONCLUSION

A few summary observations on Beethoven's compositional process for variation cycles are in order. According to Louis Schlösser's recollections, Beethoven prided himself on his ability to work on more than one composition at the same time: 'sometimes I have several compositions in labour at once, though I am sure never to confuse one with the other'.[35] While the remark was intended as a testament to his mental capacities, this talent was obviously dependent on the sketchbooks. But if the sketchbooks were necessary to keep individual works separate and distinct, they also made possible the transfer of ideas from one composition to another.[36] These functions are mirrored in the two activities central to the sketches for Op. 35. On the one hand Beethoven sought to cultivate the autonomy of individual variations as well as the differences between these variations and the theme; but

---

[33] In the course of his dissertation, 'The Sketches for Beethoven's Violin Sonatas, Opus 30: History, Transcription, Analysis' (Ph.D., Princeton University, 1973), Richard A. Kramer reached a similar conclusion: 'Beethoven may even have worked in them alternately during the spring and summer months of 1802' (vol. i, pp. 243–4).

[34] 'Die Skizzen zu op. 34 und op. 35 in Wielhorski sind mit Ende Oktober/Anfang November bis vielleicht Anfang Dezember 1802 zu datieren' (Brandenburg, ed., *Kesslerisches Skizzenbuch*, transcription, p. 34).

[35] Recounted in Thayer–Forbes, p. 851, from Schlösser's 'Persönliche Erinnerungen an Beethoven', *Hallelujah*, vi (1885), nos. 20, 21.

[36] Fishman, for example, has credited certain passages in the Piano Sonata Op. 31 No. 3 to various sketches for Op. 35: ed., *Kniga eskizov Beethovena*, commentary, pp. 147–8. Also worth mentioning is a connection between the theme that begins the *Minore* (Variation 14) and the E-minor subject that appears in the development section of the first movement of the 'Eroica' Symphony.

on the other hand, he also strove to co-ordinate and refine the subtle connections between variations.

The latter concern is most visible in the unit drafts. The bond between the physical contiguity of sketches and the musical continuity of variations is strongest for the introductory movements, and – although their relationship to each other has not been discussed in this study – for the *Minore, Maggiore* and Coda. For the *BdT* variations Beethoven imposed a numerical and musical order on the variations before beginning to sketch. He decided first on the number of voices ('2 3 4 Stimig forte') and then the ascending register of the *BdT*. Thus the continuity of contrapuntal detail had to be tailored to fit the specifications of the predetermined sequence of movements. For the *Minore, Maggiore* and Coda the controlling factors were tonality – tonic minor, tonic major, and for the Coda first submediant major and later submediant minor – and metre – 2/4, 3/4 then 6/8, 2/4 then 6/8. Again, the problem lay not in the ordering but in the unifying fabric of musical detail.

Yet the ordering of the remaining variations was highly uncertain. Between the early numbering of the amorphous collection of fragments on K82v and the first extended attempt to order the sketches on W26–31, Beethoven began to organise his ideas around the elaboration of a particular detail, such as the use of a C♯ in bar 2 of sketches on K84r (leading to the *a due* counterpoint of W13), the manipulation of a C♭ in sketches on W14, W12, and K87r–88v, and the integration of a pedal point in the first four sketches on W22 (coming from the sketch for Variation 9 on K88v).[37] On W26–31 and W33 Beethoven arranged groups of sketches, experimenting with various combinations in search of the most convincing succession of variations. Continuity is thus approached from two different directions, one in which work on a cohesive musical progression from variation to variation is fitted into a preordained sequence of movements, and the other in which the sequence of movements is arrived at through an aesthetic appraisal of the wide range of possible successions.

It is, I think, safe to tie Beethoven's self-professed 'entirely new manner' of composing variations to the change in his first conception of these E♭ Piano Variations. He had written sixteen sets of variation cycles for piano before Op. 34 and Op. 35. Very few sketches survive for them, and those that do are perfunctory.[38] Yet this scarcity may owe more to the improvisatory character of the early cycles than to the loss

---

[37] The four sketches on W22 remained a unit all the way into Op. 35 where they settled as Variations 8, 9, 10, and 13.

[38] Of the five sets of piano variations with sketches in the 'Kafka' Miscellany, three consist of one page or less, one requires two pages, and another three.

of their sketches. Beethoven's prowess as a concert extemporiser of variations was well known to his Viennese public. With the Op. 35 sketches the original allotment of space in the 'Kessler' sketchbook may have been entirely adequate for the old manner of writing variations, but for the series of unit drafts and the succession draft in which Beethoven worked out his 'new manner', a new sketchbook was necessary.

Appendix I

Duplication of K28v–88v on W22–5

Sketches are listed consecutively by page or folio and staff number, with the bar numbers in parentheses. The bar numbers are those of the final version and the letter 'a' following a bar number signifies the written-out varied repeat of a double variation. '+' or 'minus' indicates that a sketch has more or fewer bars than the finished variation (e.g. entry 29 is a thirteen-bar sketch for what became the first twelve bars of Variation 14). Entries for sketches requiring separate staves for the treble and bass lines list both staff numbers separated by a solidus (e.g. entry 11); when a single sketch continues from one staff to the next the staff numbers are separated by a dash (e.g. entry 9 in 'Wielhorsky'); when a sketch occurs on two staves interrupted by other material the staff numbers are separated by a comma (e.g. entry 12 in Wielhorsky). A single entry written on two pages is indicated by number and letter; for example entries 50a and 50b are a sketch for Variation 14 written across the bottom of K87r and K87v. Isolated fragments are designated 'Xa', 'Xb', 'Xc', etc. Variation A is a complete variation that was eventually discarded after much sketching. All sketches are listed by Variation in Appendix II.

Entry	Sketches	'Kessler'	'Wielhorsky'	Changes
1	Var. 10 (1–3, 13–16)	—	22, 7/8	
2	Var. 9 (1–2)	—	22, 9	
3	Var. 13 (1–8)	—	22, 9	
4	Var. 8 (1–4)	—	22, 10/11	
5	Var. 3 (1–4)	82v, 1/2	22, 10/11	b. 1: K has correction in RH b. 2: W has bass clef b. 3: K has correction in LH
6	BdT (0–4)	3/4	—	
7	Var. 5 (1–5)	5/6	22, 12	no LH in W b. 2, 4: K has revisions in RH 'Vi=de' to K83r, 7/8; see no. 20 below

Entry	Sketches	'Kessler'	'Wielhorsky'	Changes
8	Xa (13–14)	7/8	—	
9	Xb (10–14)	7–9	22, 12–13	W adds bar-lines between b. 9–10 and 13–14 b. 11–12: W alters to put fermata on beat 1 of b. 12 b. 12: W adds clef
10	Var. 2 (1–3)	9/10	—	
11	Xc (10–12)	11/12	—	
12	Xd (1–8)	11, 12	22, 13, 15	W has 'Vi=de' and adds bar-line between b. 7–8
13	Var. 5a (1–8)	13/14	22, 14	Originally a complete variation with no. 14 W drops LH and b. 6–8
14	Var. 11 (9–16)	13–16	22, 14–16	Originally a complete variation with no. 13 W changes b. 11–12
15	Var. A (9–10, 1–2, 5)	15/16	—	
16	U.D. 1 Thema (1–4) 83r,	2/3	—	
17	Fugue (4–8)	—	23, 1	
18	Xe (1–8)	5/6	23, 2	W drops b. 5–8, and condenses b. 1–4 to single staff Eventually in *a tre* of Op. 55/IV
19	Xf (9–11)	6	23, 2	W drops 'Finale presto'
20	Xg (1–4, 12–16)	7/8	23, 2–4	b. 1: W adds trill b. 4: W drops 'f' b. 12: W abbreviates the arpeggio b. 13: K has revisions, W adds trills 'Vi=de' is from 82v, 5/6; see no. 7 above
21	*a tre* (1–16)	9–11	23, 4	W adds clef; gives first 2 bars only, then 'etc.'
22	Var. 13 (1–8)	12/13	23, 5/6	b. 1–2: W adds parallel 6ths in RH, perhaps influenced by no. 33 below
23	BdT (1–4)	14–15	—	
24	Var. 13 (1–4)	15	23, 5	b. 2: W changes note values b. 4: W drops last note This is the LH of no. 22 raised 2 octaves
25	Var. A (9–10)	15/16	—	
26	Coda + Finale	83v, 1–6	23, 6–7	W adds 'Fine', and duplicates the last 3 bars of K83v, 5 and all of staff 6
27	Xh (1–4)	7/8	23, 7/8	K has time signature b. 3–4: W drops LH

Entry	Sketches	'Kessler'	'Wielhorsky'	Changes
28	Var. 15 (1–6, 9–16)	9–13	23, 9–10	W gives b. 10–16 b. 12: W extends register of the figuration and abbreviates it with 'etc.' b. 15–16: W omits chords b. 16: W omits 32nd-notes
29	Var. 14 (1–12 + 1)	12/13	—	
30	*a due* (1–2, 9–14)	14–15	—	
31	Var. 10 (1–2, 5–6)	84r, 1/2	—	
32	Var. 8 (1–8)	4/5	23, 10/11	b. 1: W alters RH; LH spills into b. 2 b. 5: K has correction K calls for 'pedal'
33	Var. 13 (1–8)	7/8	23, 12/13	b. 1: K has correction b. 1–4: W omits LH after barring for it b. 2: W adds upbeat to b. 3 in RH
34a	U.D. 1	9–16	—	
34b	U.D. 1	84v, 1/2	—	
35a	Var. 1 (1–6, 9–12)	3–5	—	
36	*a tre* (9–12)	6/7	23, 12/13	b. 10: W writes out 8th-notes in LH
37	Var. 11 (9–12, 1–4)	8/9	23, 14/15	b. 9: W has cancellation in LH b. 10: W omits *bb* in LH b. 11: W omits first chord in LH b. 12: W adds LH and fermata b. 2–4: W uses ℵ b. 2: W omits grace-note b. 4: W adds resolution in RH and chord in LH
35b	Var. 1 (13–16)	85r, 1	—	
38a	U.D. 3	85v, 1–16	—	
38b	U.D. 3	86r, 1/2	—	
39	Unrelated frag.	4/5	—	
40	Tedesco	—	24, 1–4	
41	Var. 3ª (1–2, 9–14)	86v, 1–4	24, 5/6	b. 2: K follows with a double bar, W with an 'etc.' b. 9–12: W omits LH chords b. 10: W omits repeat sign that creates b. 11–12 in K b. 13: K has a correction b. 14: W omits LH
42	Var. 2 (1–5, 9–15)	5–10	24, 7	W omits b. 3–5, 9–11, 15, and abbreviates the arpeggio in b. 12 b. 13: W has correction W adds bar-line between b. 1–2, omits bar-line between b. 13–14

Entry	Sketches	'Kessler'	'Wielhorsky'	Changes
43	Xi (9–16, minus 1)	9/10	24, 7–9	b. 9–10, 12: W has quarter-notes in LH b. 11: W omits LH b. 14–15: LH altered in W b. 15: RH altered in W Final phrase is 1 bar short because b. 13–14 condensed into 1 bar
44	Var. 3b (1–8, 9–18)	11–14	24, 8–11	b. 3–4: W omits rests in LH b. 10: W alters RH K puts repeat signs around b. 11–12 while W puts them only around b. 11, having '4 mal' W omits bar-lines between b. 3–4, 16–17
45	Var. 4 (1–2)	15/16	24, 10/11	W omits bar-line K has 'etc.' after b. 2
46	Var. 6 (9–12)	—	24, 12/13	
47	Unrelated sketch	87r, 1–12	—	
48	Var. 15 (1–4)	13	—	
49	Var. 8 (1–5, 9–16)	14–15	25, 1/2	W bars 2 staves b. 1: W omits clefs and LH b. 5: W replaces with 'etc.' b. 9: W omits LH
50a	Var. 14 (1–7, 1a–8a, 9–10)	15/16	25, 3/4	b. 3–4: W adds octaves in LH b. 5–7: W omits b. 7a–8a: W adds alto part b. 9: W has 'dur'
51	Unrelated sketch	87v, 1–12	—	
50b	Var. 14 (9a–16a)	13/14	25, 5/6	b. 11a: K has cancellations K follows with 'dopo largo $\frac{6}{8}$'
52a	Var. 15 (1–8 + 1, 1a–4a)	15–16	25, 5/6	W has only b. 1a–2a and expands to 2 staves
53	Unrelated sketch	88r, 1–4	—	
54a	Finale	6–9	—	
54b	BdT (1–4)	5/6	25, 7	In K the inversion appears to have been added after no. 54a
52b	Var. 15 (5a–8a, 9–16, 9a–16a, Coda)	11–16	—	
55	Sketch for Op. 34	88v, 1	—	
52c	Coda + Finale	3–5	—	
56	Xj (1–4)	5–6	—	? Continues from no. 52c

Entry	Sketches	'Kessler'	'Wielhorsky'	Changes
57	Var. 9 (1–16)	7–10	25, 7–10	b. 7: W omits LH and alters RH
				b. 11: W. omits LH
				b. 12: K has correction
				b. 13: W alters LH
				b. 14: K has correction

Appendix II
List of sketches for the Variations in Eb Op. 35

The purpose of this Appendix is to list together all the sketches Beethoven made for each variation as he composed Op. 35. Sketches leading directly to one of the published variations are grouped under the number assigned to that variation in Op. 35. Sketches that did not lead directly to a published, final version are accounted for in one of three ways:

1 ideas completely discarded after a few, brief sketches had been made are listed together at the end of the Appendix as 'unidentified';
2 ideas completely discarded after extensive sketching are labelled with letters – the one example is Variation A;
3 ideas partly discarded but partly incorporated into the sketches for a variation are listed alongside the variations they influenced (e.g. Variations 3a and 3b) with arrows indicating points of influence: in some cases the influence appears limited to a type of figuration (e.g. triplets or arpeggiation); in other cases whole melodic lines or phrases were transferred from work on one variation to work on another; in still other cases the discarded sketches may have been more of a redundancy than an influence, and may have been abandoned because they were too similar to another set of sketches.

Sketches are listed by page, staff and bar, and are preceded by a number indicating chronological order. Numbers Beethoven assigned to sketches are listed on the left in parentheses. An asterisk signifies 'Kessler' material copied into 'Wielhorsky'. Duplicate listings of the same bar numbers (as in Variation 8) indicate multiple sketches of a single phrase. (For other abbreviations and signs, see the introductory note to Appendix I.)

Beethoven's Sketches for Op. 35   81

		Variation 1
	1	{ K84v, 3–5 (1–6, 9–12)
		{ K85r, 1 (13–16)
	2	W14, 3–5 (all)
(3/5)	3	W26, 4–5 (all)
(2)	4	W33, 1 (1–2)

		Variation 2
(2)	1	K82v, 9/10 (1–3)
	3	K86v, 5–10 (1–5, cadenza as 9–12, 13–15)
	2	W14, 5/6 (1–4)
	*3	W24, 7 (1–2, cadenza, 13–14)
(8)	4	W26, 12–16 (all)
	6	W32, 4 (1–3)
(3)	5	W33, 1 (1)

                  Variation 3   a   b
(1)   1   K82v, 1/2 (1–4)   2 K86v, 1–4 (1–2,   1 K86v, 11–14
                                              9–14)   (1–8, 9–18)
                                       1 W14, 1/2 (1–8)
        *1   W22, 10/11 (1–4)   *2 W24, 5/6 (1–2,   *1 W24, 8–11
                                              9–14)   (1–8, 9–18)
                                       3 W27, 1/2 (13–16)
                                 (10) 4 W27, 5–8 (1–8,
                                              9–21)
(14/7) 2   W29, 9–14 (1–8, 9–12)   2 W29, 13/14
        3   W32, 1/2 (9–10)   (1–8) (see
        5   W32, 13/14 (5–8, 9–16)   Variation
                                                                 13)
(5)   4   W33, 2 (1)   ? W33, 13

                  Variation 4   a
        2   K86v, 15/16 (1–2)
        1   W14, 5/6 (1–2)
        *2   W24, 10/11 (1–2)
(2/6)   3   W26, 6–8 (all)   1 W26, 1–3 (all)
        4   W33, 9 (1–2)   (6)   2 W33, 2 (1–2)

                  Variation 5   a (see Variation 11)
        1   { K82v, 5/6 (1–5) vi=   1 K82v, 13/14 (1–8)
              { K83r, 7/8 (12–16)=de   *1 W22, 14 (1–5)
        *1   W22, 12 (1–5)
(9)   2   { W27, 2–5 (all)
              { W27, 13/14 (9–16)
        3   W33, 2 (1–3)
(7)   4   W33, 6/7 (1–4)

Variation 6

	1 or 2	W24, 12/13 (9–12)
(17)	2 or 1	W31, 1–6 (1–8, 9–16, 9a–16a)

Variation 7

none

Variation 8

	1	K84r 4/5 (1–8)
	2	K87r 14–15 (1–5, 9–16)
	3	W22 10/11 (1–4)
	*1	W23 10/11 (1–8)
	*2	W25 1/2 (1–4, 9–16)
(15/12)	4	W30 1–5 (1–8, 9–16, 9–16)
(11)	5	W33 4 (1–4)

Variation 9

	1	K88v, 7–10 (all)
	2	W22, 9 (1–2)
	*1	W25, 7–10 (all)
(16)	3	W30, 6–14 (1–4, 1–4, 1–8, 9–16)
(13)	4	W33, 4 (1–2)

Variation 10

	1	K84r 1/2 (1–2, 5–6)
	2	K86v 9/10 (9–16, minus 1)
	3	W22, 7–8 (1–8, 13–16)
	*2	W24, 7/9 (9–16, minus 1)
(13)	4	W29, 5–8 (all)
(8)	5	W33, 3 (1–2)
	6	W33, 13/14 (9–12)

Variation 11   *a* (from Variation 5a)

	1	K84v 8/9 (9–12, 1–4)	1	K82v, 13–16 (9–16)
	*1	W23, 14/15 (9–12, 1–4)	*1	W22, 14–16 (9–16)
(14)	2	W33, 5 (1–2)		
	3 or 4	W33, 9 (1–2)		
	4 or 5	W33, 11/12 (9–16)		
	5 or 3	W33, 16 (1–2)		

Variation 12

(7)	1	W26, 9–11 (all)
(100)	2	W31, 11–12 (1–2, 1–2)
	6	W32, 6/7 (5–6)

Beethoven's Sketches for Op. 35

(10)	3	W33, 3 (1–2)
	4	W33, 8 (4–5)
	5	W33, 11/12 (3, 5, 13–14)

Variation 13   *a* (from Variation 3b)

	1 or 2	K83r, 12/13 (1–8)
	2 or 1	K83r, 15 (1–4)
	3	K84r, 7/8 (1–8)
	4	W22, 9 (1–8)
	*1	W23, 5/6 (1–8)
	*2	W23, 5 (1–4)
	*3	W23, 12/13 (1–8)
(13)	5	W33, 4 (1–2) ◄─────── W29, 13/14 (1–8)

Variation 14

	1	K83v, 12/13 (1–8, 9–12 + 1)
	4	K87r, 15/16 (1–7, 1a–8a, 9–16)
		K87r, 13/14 (9a–16a)
	3	W12, 11/12 (9–16)
	2	W14, 9/10 (1–8, 9–12 + 1, 13–16)
	*4	W25, 3–6 (1–4, 1a–8a, 9–16, 9a–16a)
(12)	6	W28, 7–10 (all)
	5	W29, 1–3 (1–8, 1a–8a, 9–16)
	7	W31, 14/15 (9–12)
(15)	8	W33, 5 (Minore)

Variation 15

	1	K83v, 9–13 (1–6, 9–16)
	3	K87r, 13 (1–4)
	4	K87v, 15–16 to K88r/11–16 (1–8 + 1, 1a–8a, 9–16, 9a–16a)
	2	W14, 11–14 (all)
	*1	W23, 9–10 (9–16)
	*4	W25, 5/6 (1a–2a)
	5	W28, 9–11 (1–8, 1a–4a)
	6	W33, 13/14 (1–4)

Variation A

(4)	1	K82v, 15/16 (9–10, 1–2, 5)
	?2	K83r, 15/16 (9–10)
	4	W13, 15 (9–12)
	3	W14, 7/8 (9–16)
(11/10)	5	W27, 9–11 (all)
(8)	6	W29, 15 (1–2)
(4)	7	W33, 1 (1)
	8	W32, 4 (1–2)

	Coda
1	K83v, 1–6
4	K88r, 15/16 to K88v, 3–5
2	W12, 15/16
3	W14, 13–16
*1	W23, 6–7
5	W28, 12–13

Unidentified

K82v, 7/8 (13–14)
K82v, 7/9 (10–14)   *W22, 12–13 (10–14)
K82v, 11/12 (10–12)
K82v, 11, 12 (1–8)   *W22, 13, 15 (1–8)
K83r, 5/6 (1–8)   *W23, 2 (1–4)
K83v, 7/8 (1–4)   *W23, 7/8 (1–4)
K88v, 5–6 (1–4)

                                  W28, 5/6 (1–3)
                                  W29, 15 (1–8 + 1)
                                  W31, 7/8 (1–4)
                                  W33, 3 (1–4)
                                  W33, 6/7 (1–2, 1–2)

'Eroica' Perspectives: Strategy and Design in the First Movement

Lewis Lockwood

A new paper on the 'Eroica' calls for justification. Surely no other Beethoven symphony – not even the Fifth or the Ninth – has evoked a wider flood of commentary, whether historical, analytical, or broadly interpretative. In the vein of biography one could fill an anthology with variants on the thesis, by now the most obvious of commonplaces, that this Symphony marks a decisive turning-point in Beethoven's development. Wagner, whose published remarks on the 'Eroica' are only outnumbered by his writings on the Ninth, regarded the 'Eroica' as the first work in which Beethoven thrust forward in what was to be his own fully individual direction.[1] Equally canonic by now is the famous episode in which Beethoven abandoned the dedication of the Symphony on receiving news of Napoleon's imperial ascendancy; the testimony for this effectively began with Ferdinand Ries, was picked up by Schindler and by Thayer, and in the wake of Thayer reappears in one book after another.[2] Recently a valuable and dispassionate review of the matter was provided by Maynard Solomon, who persuasively demonstrates the ambivalence of Beethoven's attitude towards Napoleon.[3] Approaching from another direction Alan Tyson suggests that the work forms part of a crucially important, and

---

[1] Wagner's published comments on the 'Eroica' are found in the following writings (references to volume and page numbers are those of *Richard Wagner: Gesammelte Schriften und Dichtungen*, ed. Julius Kapp, 12 vols. (Leipzig, 1914)): 'Ein glücklicher Abend', vol. vii, pp. 154–6; 'Ueber das Dirigieren', vol. viii, p. 182; 'Beethoven', vol. ix, pp. 110–14; 'Ueber die Anwendung der Musik auf das Drama', vol. xiii, pp. 284–6. Wagner's programme note for the Symphony is in vol. ix, pp. 110–12, written for his performance of the work at a subscription concert in Zurich on 25 February 1851.
[2] Wegeler–Ries, pp. 77–9; Schindler (1840), pp. 55–7; Thayer–Deiters–Riemann ii, pp. 418–19. For a sample of more recent biography in which the older evidence is repeated uncritically, see George R. Marek, *Beethoven: Biography of a Genius* (New York, 1969), p. 343.
[3] Maynard Solomon, 'Beethoven and Bonaparte', *Music Review*, xxix (1968), 96–105.

definable segment of Beethoven's creative growth, from about 1801 (and his first accommodation to his growing deafness) to the completion of the first *Leonore* in 1805. In this 'heroic phase', as Tyson calls it, Beethoven finds his way to the realisation of heroic themes in oratorio and opera, with the 'Eroica' as a monumental mid-point in this tremendous development. *Prometheus* and *Christus am Oelberge* lie before it; the explicit affirmation of personal redemption and political freedom in *Leonore* come directly after it.[4]

But the purpose of this paper is not to explore primarily the personal or evolutionary significance of the Symphony. It is rather to focus attention on certain well-known and long-established analytic perspectives upon it (restricted here to its first movement), to sum up current patterns of thought about the work, and to bring out some aspects that seem to me to have been neglected. This too is certainly not owing to any lack of published commentary; the literature is large and sprawls over many different avenues of approach. Inevitably it partly divides along lines of intellectual prejudice, partly along linguistic and national boundaries.

In the nineteenth century vast battles were waged over the programmatic interpretation of the 'Eroica', not without overtones of Franco-German rivalries in the post-Napoleonic and post-Beethovenian era. On the French side are the programmes of Berlioz and Oulibicheff; on the German side, among others the far less pictorial and more abstract programme note by Wagner (1851).[5] In 1859 A. B. Marx reviewed the entire matter in a separate chapter in his book on Beethoven. He abruptly dismisses what he calls the 'French hypothesis' but quotes Wagner and insists on a purely musical interpretation.[6] A late example of programmatic and hermeneutic exegesis is that of Paul Bekker (1911).[7] It was Bekker who made the truly remarkable suggestion that Beethoven's revelation of his heroic subject would have been improved if only the slow movement and Scherzo had been reversed in order. Bekker explains that Beethoven must really have intended such an ordering, but 'did not dare' to use it, 'having offered his contemporaries enough innovation for one occasion'.

---

[4] Alan Tyson, 'Beethoven's Heroic Phase', *Musical Times*, cx (1969), 139–41.

[5] See Berlioz's discussion in his *À travers chants* (2nd edn, Paris, 1872), pp. 22–9; Alexandre Oulibicheff, *Beethoven, ses critiques et ses glossateurs* (Leipzig and Paris, 1875), pp. 173–87; on Wagner's programme note see footnote 1 above.

[6] Adolph Bernhard Marx, 'Die Sinfonia eroica und die Idealmusik', *Ludwig van Beethoven: Leben und Schaffen* (6th edn, Leipzig, 1902), vol. i, pp. 203–18.

[7] Paul Bekker, *Beethoven* (2nd edn, Berlin, 1912), p. 223; Eng. trans. (London, 1925), p. 163.

In a different and more responsible quarter stands Nottebohm's presentation of the sketches for the Symphony in his monograph *Ein Skizzenbuch von Beethoven aus dem Jahre 1803*, issued in 1880.[8] However limited Nottebohm's transcriptions and commentary are they opened up a larger body of genetic material for the 'Eroica' than anyone could have anticipated, and laid a basis that has yet to be seriously challenged or drastically modified – although the eventual publication of the full contents of the sketchbook may afford new perspectives. I shall return later to some issues posed by the sketches, or what is now known of them, but it should be said that the rich material presented by Nottebohm has still been only sparsely cultivated by his successors, and is explicitly neglected by his normally enthusiastic supporter Heinrich Schenker, who usually spares Nottebohm the scorn with which he treats most other earlier writers.

To the turn of the century belongs the chapter by Grove in his book on the symphonies, a mild and gentle exegesis that was followed more brilliantly and incisively by Tovey in various writings.[9] Then, from Germany in the 1920s and 1930s came a succession of 'Eroica' commentaries, most of them analytical essays of one type or another. This series began with the highly portentous analysis by Fritz Cassirer in his book *Beethoven und die Gestalt* (1925), which employed what were then quite new approaches to the perception of formal structures, developed by the pioneers of Gestalt psychology.[10] In contrast is a pair of essays by the Wagnerian Alfred Lorenz, who found in the middle section of the 'Eroica' first movement the same formal–periodic symmetries he was then seeking to reveal as the 'secret of form' in Wagner's *Ring*, and which he would later claim to find as well in Wagner's other late major works. The second of Lorenz's essays is a sensitive discussion of the first-movement sketches as published by Nottebohm.[11] The same year saw the publication of a striking article by August Halm, on the so-called 'new episode' in the middle section, which Halm was apparently the first (in print) to associate with the

---

[8] N 1880; the most recent reprint was issued by Johnson Reprint Corp. (New York, 1970).

[9] George Grove, *Beethoven and his Nine Symphonies* (3rd edn, London, 1898; reprinted New York, 1962), pp. 49–95. Donald Francis Tovey, *Essays in Musical Analysis*, vol. i (London, 1935), pp. 29–33; 'Sonata Forms', *Musical Articles from the Encyclopaedia Britannica* (London, 1944), pp. 221–8; *Beethoven* (London, 1944), *passim*.

[10] Fritz Cassirer, *Beethoven und die Gestalt* (Stuttgart, 1925); the first chapter had been issued separately in *Der Dreiklang*, iv (1922), 192ff.

[11] Alfred Lorenz, 'Worauf beruht die bekannte Wirkung der Durchführung im I. Eroicasatze?', *Neues Beethoven-Jahrbuch*, i (1924), 159–83; 'Betrachtungen über Beethovens Eroica-Skizzen', *Zeitschrift für Musikwissenschaft*, vii (1924–5), 409–22.

contour of the main motif of the opening of the movement.[12] And in 1930 there appeared the most detailed and far-reaching analytic study of the Symphony yet published: Schenker's tract on the 'Eroica' as issued in volume iii of his yearbook *Das Meisterwerk in der Musik* (1930).[13] I shall come back to the Schenker essay shortly; for now it suffices to mention briefly a few later commentaries of different kinds: one is Walter Engelsmann's article of 1940 on the organic unity of the motivic material of all four movements of the Symphony.[14] Another is the lengthy analysis of the first movement, primarily on motivic lines, by Walter Riezler, issued as an appendix to his book on Beethoven and thus the only one of these contributions available also in English.[15]

If the Lorenz and Schenker analyses are exempted, there emerges a by now familiar underlying concept, or *Grundgestalt*, which pervades these essays in one form or another. They embody the view that the 'Eroica' (and especially the first movement) is not only a landmark in the entire development of the symphony, but that its immensity of scope is correlative to its presentation of an unusually large number of musical ideas, and that it reveals an exceptionally high degree of interrelationship among these ideas – whether themes, motifs, or rhythmic units. For some writers this is especially true of the first movement; for others, of the whole work. Along with this expansion of the formal structure goes its transformation, in the first movement, into a vast four-section structure, with greatly extended coda and middle section balancing the exposition and recapitulation.

One could write a brief history of the idea of motivic interconnection from 'Eroica' commentaries alone, so pervasive is the concept in writings on the Symphony's first movement. An early exponent of the idea of motivic interconnection in a Beethoven symphony was E. T. A. Hoffmann in his essay on the Fifth Symphony (1810).[16] And its most

---

[12] August Halm, 'Der Fremdkörper im ersten Satz der Eroica', *Die Musik*, xxi (1928–9), 481–4.

[13] 'Beethovens Dritte Sinfonie zum erstenmal in ihrem wahren Inhalt dargestellt', *Das Meisterwerk in der Musik: ein Jahrbuch von Heinrich Schenker*, vol. iii (Munich, 1930), pp. 25–101; the three volumes of this yearbook were reprinted in one volume by Georg Olms Verlag (Hildesheim and New York, 1974).

[14] Walter Engelsmann, 'Beethovens Werkthematik, dargestellt an der "Eroica"', *Archiv für Musikforschung*, v (1940), 104–13.

[15] Walter Riezler, *Beethoven* (8th edn, rev. Zurich, 1962), pp. 289–324; Eng. trans. (New York, 1938; reprinted 1962), pp. 247–81.

[16] Hoffmann's essay appeared in *Allgemeine musikalische Zeitung*, xii (1810), cols. 630–42, 652–9; it is conveniently available in English translation in *Beethoven, Symphony No. 5 in C Minor*, ed. Elliot Forbes, Norton Critical Scores (New York, 1971), pp. 150–63.

relentless twentieth-century advocate, Walter Engelsmann, not only proposed the close motivic linking of all movements, but perhaps knowingly distorted for his own purposes a valuable anecdote which reveals something of the mature Richard Wagner's view of the material of the first movement. Since this anecdote does not seem to have been available hitherto in English it is worth quoting here. It stems from a young and enthusiastic admirer of Wagner, the budding composer Felix Draeseke, who visited him at Lucerne in 1859 and later reported the following episode to a biographer:

> Finally he gave me an explanation of melody that totally altered my musical outlook and has been more useful to me than the entire course of studies that I took at the Leipzig Conservatory. In a quite unexpected way – I am not sure how it came about – on a very hot August afternoon he began to sing the first movement of the 'Eroica'. He fell into a violent passion, sang on and on, became very overheated, quite beside himself, and did not stop until he had come to the end of the exposition. 'What is that ?', he cried out to me. To which I naturally replied, 'The "Eroica"'. 'Now then, isn't pure melody enough? Must you always have your crazy harmonies along with it?' – At first I didn't understand what he meant by that. When he later calmed down he explained to me that the melodic flow in the Beethoven symphonies streams forth inexhaustibly, and that by means of these melodies one can clearly recall to memory the whole symphony. This gave me a spur to later consideration that has had a deep effect on my own production.[17]

It is of the highest interest to realise that at Lucerne in 1859 Wagner had just finished the gigantic third act and thus the whole of *Tristan*, which is manifestly the quintessence in his own work of wide-spanned and continually resurgent melodic flow, as well as of complex developmental processes within the musico-dramatic scheme. Draeseke's report is also consistent with Wagner's programme note for the 'Eroica', written eight years earlier, and his later declaration, in an essay of 1879, that the great achievement of his dramatic music lay in its attaining the

---

[17] Erich Roeder, *Felix Draeseke, Der Lebens- und Leidensweg eines deutschen Meisters*, vol. i (Dresden and Berlin, 1932), p. 106; Roeder quotes Draeseke's words from the latter's essay, 'Was tut der heutigen musikalischen Produktion not?', *Signale*, lxv (1907), 1–12. The episode is also described in Otto zur Nedden, *Felix Draeseke* (Pforzheim, 1952), p. 7, and mentioned in Fritz Reckow, 'Zur Wagners Begriff der unendlichen Melodie', *Das Drama Richard Wagners als musikalische Kunstwerk*, ed. Carl Dahlhaus (Regensburg, 1970), pp. 87f. As cited by Engelsmann in 'Beethovens Werkthematik', 112, the story was given a different twist of meaning: according to Engelsmann, 'Richard Wagner . . . zeigte Felix Draeseke bei einer Zusammenkunft in Luzern, dass im Werk-Anfang der Eroica die Melodie der ganzen Sinfonie enthalten ist.'

unity of a symphonic composition: 'the whole artwork is a thorough web of basic themes, which, as in a symphonic movement, relate to one another through contrast, mutual complementation, formation of new shapes, articulation, and connection'.[18] In such discussions he often invokes the name of Beethoven: 'If there had not been a Beethoven, I could never have composed as I have.'[19]

This approach, which seems to me inescapable in some degree, finds its way into the most diverse 'Eroica' writings; even Grove, who is scarcely a transcendental motif-hunter, writes as follows: 'The Eroica first shows us the methods which were so completely to revolutionise that department of music – the continuous and organic mode of connecting the second subject with the first, the introduction of episodes into the working-out, the extraordinary importance of the *Coda*.'[20] Fifty years later Walter Engelsmann was at pains to derive all four movements from the same basic *Werkthema*, which in turn can be reduced to three basic *Urmotiven*. Engelsmann traces the transformation of this material through all four movements, and for him it collectively forms an 'artistic law of the symphony'.[21] This is said to be a musical equivalent of Goethe's concept, which Engelsmann quotes, that all organic life consists of transformations of a single basic substance (*Urstoff*) through procedures that can be called 'metamorphosis', 'evolution', 'variation', and 'osmosis'. Goethe himself had originally developed these views in connection with his early botanical studies on the growth of plants from seeds, and it comes as something of a shock to realise that his first publication on this subject appeared as early as 1790.[22] In 1940 Engelsmann not only explicitly quoted Goethe's

---

[18] 'Ueber die Anwendung der Musik auf das Drama', *Richard Wagner: Gesammelte Schriften*, ed. Kapp, vol. xiii, pp. 290f, cited in *Die Musik in Geschichte und Gegenwart* [*MGG*], ed. Friedrich Blume, vol. xiv (Kassel, 1968), col. 113.
[19] Cited in *MGG*, vol. xiv col. 113.
[20] Grove, *Beethoven and his Nine Symphonies*, p. 50.
[21] Engelsmann, 'Beethovens Werkthematik', p. 112.
[22] The central early writing by Goethe on this subject is his *Versuch die Metamorphose der Pflanzen zu erklären* (Gotha, 1790). Further on Goethe's views on organic form, in relation to German scientific thought of his time, see Hugh Barr Nisbet, *Goethe and the Scientific Tradition* (London, 1972); for an attempt to apply the same views to analysis of Goethe's *Faust*, see Peter Salm, *The Poem as Plant: a biological View of Goethe's Faust* (Cleveland, 1971). And for a wide-ranging study of the entire concept of organic form in literature and in the history of ideas, see the essays by G. N. Giordano Orsini, Philip C. Ritterbush, and William K. Wimsatt collected in G. S. Rousseau, ed., *Organic Form: the Life of an Idea* (London, 1972); the volume has an extended bibliography of writings on the subject, but lacks all reference to publications of any kind on music. Although the issue has yet to be seriously studied by musicologists, it would be extremely profitable to trace the ways in which this idea, gathering force in the nineteenth

'Gesetz des Lebens' but claimed to find musical counterparts for each of these means of transformation, including 'osmosis'. The later approach of Rudolph Réti is fully prefigured in this study. And Engelsmann's invocation of Goethe shows that the quasi-biological cast of much thinking along these lines is, if I may use the expression, rooted in German traditions of science and aesthetics characteristic of the late eighteenth and early nineteenth centuries, in particular the fusion of scientific observation with German philosophical idealism, which Goethe proudly espoused and which found in him its most eloquent and, for later generations, its most authoritative spokesman.

In turning to the published analysis by Schenker one enters a different world. By 1930 Schenker's views had totally departed from what then seemed to be firmly settled traditions of harmonic analysis as expounded by Riemann, and of motivic analysis as expounded by Engelsmann and others. Schenker's monograph on the Ninth Symphony had been published in 1912, before his analytic views had crystallised in the concept of the *Ursatz* and its ramifications; and his essay of 1925 on the Fifth Symphony had elucidated background features but had also included much discussion of motivic details, sketches, and other aspects of the foreground.[23] The 'Eroica' analysis, on the other hand, is conceived uncompromisingly from the standpoint of his later concepts of tonal structure and syntax. Even though these views have spread, more through Schenkerians than through Schenker's own writings, at a rate that would be envied by an evangelical missionary, it may not be useless to review once more some aspects of the approach.

Although the Schenkerian method is popularly believed to consist in the search for a supposedly single *Urlinie* and *Ursatz* that underlies each tonal composition, it appears that it is more adequately perceived as proceeding from the concept of 'levels' or 'layers' (*Schichten*), co-existing planes of organisation of musical content in tonal music.[24] The

century following Goethe, Coleridge, and other writers, found its way readily into writings on music and became deeply embedded in analytic procedures.

[23] Heinrich Schenker, *Beethovens Neunte Sinfonie: eine Darstellung des musikalischen Inhalts unter fortlaufender Berücksichtigung auch des Vortrags und der Literatur* (Vienna, 1912; reprinted, 1969). 'Beethovens Fünfte Sinfonie', *Der Tonwille*, i (1922), 27–37; ii (1923), no. 5, pp. 10–42, no. 6, pp. 9–35; this was separately published (Vienna, 1925; reprinted 1969) and is partly available in English translation in Forbes's edition of the Symphony for the Norton Critical Scores, pp. 164–82. *Der freie Satz* (Vienna, 1935), ed. Oswald Jonas (2nd edn, rev., Vienna, 1956); Ernst Oser's complete translation of Schenker's *Der freie Satz* was issued in two volumes under the title *Free Composition* (New York and London, 1979).

[24] From the large recent literature pursuing, explicating, or developing the Schenkerian approach, at times in ways that would not be likely to have met with Schenker's

layers are seen as being connected and related to one another as if they were closer and more distant perspectives upon the same phenomena; Schenker applies to the *Schichten* the familiar spatial terms 'foreground', 'middleground', and 'background' (without claiming that there are only three), and uses them as analytic constructs or frameworks for the diverse types and forms of prolongation of musical units (linear, contrapuntal, and harmonic, of various durations and directions) which emerge as basic components of the tonal language. Again, to put something complex very simply, the so-called 'reduction' procedure appears to consist in using the traditional concepts of tonal species counterpoint as analytic tools, in order to reformulate or reconceive a given passage according to voice-leading rules and to produce distinctions between its more essential and less essential members. The application of the rules of tonal species counterpoint makes the reduction procedure less arbitrary than it might seem otherwise, and has seemed to many of Schenker's critics. It also reinforces the sense that one of the strengths of Schenker's later theory of tonal music is not merely its comprehensive attempt to formulate a grammar of tonality, but its attachment to the traditions of tonal counterpoint as descended from Fux and as utilised in tonal music.

Closely related to the reduction procedure is Schenker's concept of 'diminution', which is explored at length in *Der freie Satz*, published five years after the 'Eroica' analysis.[25] Here Schenker seems to reach a partial rapprochement with motivic analysis; 'diminution' designates a complex of linear details visible at the foreground level, small-scale 'figurations' that are susceptible of reduction to their basic decorative elements; Schenker accepted that such diminution techniques were connected historically to diminution and ornamentation procedures of late Renaissance and Baroque vocal music, which were later developed in instrumental as well as vocal music in the tonal era.[26]

---

approval, I should mention the following, which seem to me especially significant: Felix Salzer, *Structural Hearing*, 2 vols. (New York, 1952; reprinted, 1962); the immensely important review of Salzer's work by Milton Babbitt, *Journal of the American Musicological Society*, v (1952), 260–5; and the yearbook *The Music Forum*, ed. William J. Mitchell and Felix Salzer (New York and London, 1967–), of which five volumes have so far appeared, and which contains a number of important articles written along Schenkerian lines. For a convenient and extensive listing of writings by Heinrich Schenker and of works written about him and his theoretical views, up to 1969, see David Beach, 'A Schenker Bibliography', *Journal of Music Theory*, xiii (1969), 2–37.

[25] 'Diminution', *Der freie Satz*, Part iii, chapter 3, no. 7.

[26] Schenker himself contributed to the literature on this enormous field in his early study, *Ein Beitrag zur Ornamentik* (Vienna, c. 1902), recently translated into English by Hedi Siegel as 'A Contribution to the Study of Ornamentation', in *The Music Forum*,

In his 'Eroica' analysis Schenker provides a massive foreground 'picture' (*Bild*) of each movement of the Symphony, and follows these with 'figures' (*Figuren*) that represent closer and more distant perspectives upon segments of varying length, ranging from short passages to entire movements; they show the foreshortened and synthesised representations used to delineate the more background layers. His *Bild* no. 1 represents the first 399 bars of the first movement. Some essential features of the opening are these: the upper-line $\hat{3}$ (g'') of the very opening sonority is seen as the primary initial triad member of the upper line and is prolonged by various means in the first violin part through the passing-note $\hat{2}$ (f'') in bar 12 to $\hat{1}$ (eb) in bar 15; all this forms a *Terzzug* (a prolongation of the interval of a third, with the two triad members connected by the passing-note) in the upper line; it is supported in a complex way by the bass, which grafts its chromatic motion of bars 6–11 into a supporting bass for the upper-line motion. This bass support is displaced, however, at its beginning, through the chromatic descent to d and $c\sharp$, returning through d to eb. Simultaneously *Bild* no. 1 shows many other prolongation-units of various lengths and registers, interlocking with one another, and all potentially to be subsumed into a larger and more sweeping structural motion in the upper line, consisting in a long-range rise through members of the tonic triad; this begins from g'' in bar 1, proceeds to bb'' in bar 23, and to the still higher eb''' in bar 37; then in its turn it will move upwards through the crucially important rising semitone motion to f''' at the moment of achieving the first motion by step to the dominant key area, at bar 45. This larger motion forms part of another layer at a somewhat more background level, but not far behind the foreground; and this is essentially what Schenker shows in his *Figur* no. 6.

Despite the brevity of this glimpse of Schenker's treatment of one aspect of the first movement, I want to linger a moment more over some details of his *Bild* no. 1 to consider what sorts of detail Schenker's approach tends to bring out and what it tends to minimise or suppress. Let it be said first, however, that the collection of analytic tools at his disposal for conceptualising the smaller- and larger-scale procedures of tonal music must be impressive to anyone, whether one is inclined to love or to leave it, whether one is prepared or not to follow him from foreground to more background layers, and whether or not his

vol. iv (1976), pp. 1–40. Only after the completion of this article, in the spring of 1977, did I become aware of David Epstein's recent analytic discussion of the 'Eroica' in his book *Beyond Orpheus* (Cambridge, Mass., 1979), pp. 111–38. Epstein attempts to utilise Schenker's analytic views of various portions of the work and to relate them to aspects of the motivic structure.

particular analyses seem convincing. My own respect for the scope of his achievement in this analysis, though I shall try to signal its limitations with regard to certain musical events, even suffices to excuse, in my mind, the title of his essay, 'Beethoven's Third Symphony, presented for the first time in its true content'.[27]

To return to Schenker's 'picture' of the opening of the first movement. In addition to the larger framework he is at pains to establish several smaller segments as well: the upper-line g'' generates several prolongations of different lengths, while the bass eb in bar 3 expands to the g'' in the upper line in bar 7; then there is the chromatic motion in the bass (indicated by the arrow in bar 8), which he calls in the prose commentary the 'first breath' of the piece. What is obliterated from view is at least one small-scale, but to my mind vital, harmonic implication that arises early in the piece: this is the momentary inflection of G minor that emerges in bars 7–9, as the bass reaches its lower chromatic neighbour, $c\sharp$, and proceeds to d while the upper line holds g''; the second violin in bar 9 deftly converts its repeated g' into a new figure that alternates g' and bb. Thus in bar 9 the entire texture lightly touches upon a I_4^6 of G minor before the immediate reassertion of Eb major by means of the upper-line motion to ab''.[28] But this implication of G minor has considerable importance for later aspects of the Symphony: not merely those significant uses of G minor in the first three movements, but the striking use of a descending G-minor scale to open the Finale and the same choice of tonality for the powerful dance episode that stands at the centre of the movement. Similarly, in Schenker's picture of the opening, his insistence in bars 12–14 on small-scale prolongation-units of a third (*Terzzugen*) seems to me to involve rather arbitrary choices in the upper line, which may be interpreted quite differently and, to my mind, more convincingly.

One more instance will show even more strikingly Schenker's divergence from the viewpoint of motivic analysis: this is his treatment of the transition passage in bars 23–36, which separates the second and third statements of the opening subject. In *Bild* no. 1 Schenker's analysis discloses the following features: in the bass the progression by step downwards from the bass Bb achieved in bar 23 through Ab in bar 29

---

[27] Schenker's essay not only provides a thorough-going analysis but also a partial *Revisionbericht* for the Symphony, offering some comparisons of readings between the earliest surviving sources (the corrected copy of the full score and the first edition of the performing parts); there is, as well, a very brief discussion of the literature, mentioning only Halm and Nottebohm.

[28] An example of an earlier commentary that does take note of the G-minor implication at the beginning is Marx, *Ludwig van Beethoven*, vol. i, p. 189.

and G in bar 31; then the repetition of those pitches in quarter-note diminution in bars 34–5, reaching the cadential F and B♭ in bars 35 and 36 and aiming at resolution to the tonic E♭ in bar 37. In the upper line he presents in bars 29–35 the continuation of a bb'' prolongation from bar 23, which is fundamentally maintained all the way to the rising cadence in bars 36–7; in bars 29–32 he sees small-scale realisations of the harmony V_2^4 moving to I_3^6, first in half-notes, then in quarters. All this is conceptualised in such a way as to make the most of the large-scale prolongation of the pitch $\hat{5}$ (B♭) and the dominant harmony it expresses, from bar 23 to bar 36.

But another way of looking at the material of bars 29–35 is hinted at darkly by Riezler, was later mentioned by Philip Downs, and is said by Charles Rosen to be obvious to everyone; I have noticed it myself and so, no doubt, have many others.[29] The point is that the means by which this transition is made not only prolongs the dominant but does so in such a way as to repeat the basic triadic interval succession established at the opening of the movement by the triadic subjects – now, however, with the pitches transferred to other registers. Thus the first violin in bars 29–30 rises through members of the dominant triad in the same order in which the cellos at the opening rose through members of the tonic triad 1–3–1–5–1 (adding triad members to the root but returning to the root before moving to the next new triad member). The effect of the interval succession here is to infuse this transition passage with obvious motivic importance and give it a close (may I say 'organic'?) connection to the primary thematic statements that stand before and after it. It is especially striking that in the recapitulation, in which the descending chromatic motion of the opening is entirely reinterpreted and leads to new elaborations, this transition passage is cut out. Its important uses lie elsewhere: it reappears in the middle section in bars 250–71 as a component of the vast motion towards E minor that is to bring about the famous 'new episode', beginning at bar 284. It then reappears at the end of the middle section, in bars 338–64, in a new form, as the first segment of the extended retransition and dominant preparation for the return at bar 397. Later it makes two further appearances, both in the coda: in bars 603–31, following the return of the 'new episode', and finally in bars 685–9, at the very end, to reinforce thematically the final assertion of the dominant harmony before the last chords. In each case it functions as a dominant transition

---

[29] Riezler, *Beethoven*, Eng. trans., p. 251; Philip Downs, 'Beethoven's "New Way" and the *Eroica*', *Musical Quarterly*, lvi (1970), 598–9 (especially Example 8), reprinted in *The Creative World of Beethoven*, ed. Paul Henry Lang, (New York, 1970), pp. 96–7; Charles Rosen, *The Classical Style* (New York and London, 1971), p. 393.

or retransition, and typically in the role of prolonging an unstable phrase segment on its way towards resolution.

From here on my aim in this paper will be to focus on the kinds of structural purpose indicated by the uses of the figure that I have just discussed – purposes that I believe are inadequately reflected by traditional motivic analysis on the one hand, and by the Schenker analysis on the other. The category that I have in mind can be characterised as 'compositional strategy'. By this I refer to Beethoven's deployment, as part of the design of this movement, of certain small-scale foreground units of musical structure in such a way as to shape the larger conformation of the movement, using them as widely separated points of connection and association that are outside the sequential norms of exposition and recapitulation. Thus the importance of a particular musical idea may be projected over long time-spans and over the boundaries of the familiar large-scale divisions of the movement.

I now return to the age-old but essential observation that the first movement of the 'Eroica' is of a length unprecedented in the symphonic tradition. A defensive-sounding note was included in the first edition of 1806, referring to the Symphony's having been 'deliberately written at greater length than is usual'.[30] In certain early works Beethoven had written first movements of great length, by contemporary standards, even some in the less frequent 3/4. Among these are the first movements of the Eb-major Piano Quintet Op. 16, which runs to 395 bars, and the still longer opening Allegro of the G-minor Cello Sonata Op. 5 No.2, of 509 bars (not including the slow Introductions). These are still short of the immense 691 of the 'Eroica', but of course neither movement possesses the rich profusion of ideas, the complexity of content, or the capacity for integration that is found here.[31] To

---

[30] See Kinsky–Halm, pp. 129–30. There is also the testimony of Carl van Beethoven that 'my brother at first believed, before he had heard the Symphony, that it would be too long if the first part of the first movement were repeated, but after frequent performances he found that it is detrimental if the first part is not repeated'. See Carl's letter of 12 February 1805, in Thayer–Deiters–Riemann ii, pp. 625f.

[31] In Op. 16 the formal structure of the first movement is unexceptional in its thematic and harmonic design. The middle section employs as a central articulation merely a restatement of the opening theme on the subdominant (Ab major) in bars 175–86, and in much of the middle section the piano routinely hammers out eighth-note triplets against arpeggiated quarter-note figures in the winds; the whole is entirely within the scope established by the first movement of the Clarinet Trio Op. 11, and consolidated in the Septet Op. 20. The Cello Sonata Op. 5 No. 2, on the other hand, has always been recognised as a much more ambitious work, and comparison of some features with the Quintet shows why: the segments of its first movement are much larger than

lead up to the main point I now need to focus attention particularly on the exposition of the 'Eroica'.

Not only does the dominant section of the exposition consist of a long thematic chain, but it subdivides into six clearly formed segments, each possessing highly individual melodic, motivic, harmonic, and rhythmic features. Of these one of the most important, as Tovey points out, is the unit in bars 57–64, which emerges *piano* from a *fortissimo* cadential figure. This passage brings in contrary motion a diatonic, ascending upper line and a partly chromatic, descending lower line. The upper line appears to have the particular function of transporting scale-degree $\hat{3}$ (now D in the key of B♭) from a middle-range octave to a higher one; then an elaborated repetition in the next two bars moves this scale-degree still another octave higher, while the bass expands to the lower octave. I shall designate this entire phrase, bars 57–64, 'Unit C' of the exposition.

Now another necessity for the coherence of this complex exposition is the use of decisive cadential passages to introduce each of the six thematic segments; and for this purpose Beethoven furnishes a chain of articulative figures which are shown in short score in Example 1. The first one sets a pattern, in bars 35–6, within the tonic section of the exposition, by preparing the arrival at E♭ for the final statement of the opening subject; it is characterised by eighth-note motion in all voices and contrary motion in the upper lines, arriving at the tonic through rising and falling scale patterns.

With one exception each of these strongly articulated cadential figures lands firmly on a downbeat and on a contextually stable harmony, normally the tonicised B♭ major. An apparent exception is the unit that arrives at bar 123 on a D-major chord, which is to function as local dominant of a G-minor harmony; but this D-major chord has at least the relative stability possessed by a major triad in root position. The only genuine exception, therefore strikingly anomalous, occurs in bar 65 (see Example 1c). Here the cadence arrives on a diminished-seventh chord with F♯ in the bass, which fortifies the chain of descending sequential figures in the upper line; these develop with increasing power over the next eighteen bars and lead to a new climax in bar 83 with a firm cadential motion to B♭ once more, introducing the next new segment.

those of Op. 16 not merely in length but in material; the typical piano triplet figurations are here vastly richer and more linear in character; and the middle section even has room for a new subject, presented in D minor, G minor, and E♭ major (bars 264–94). This last may be unique in early works before the 'Eroica' first movement, which in a formal sense the Cello Sonata foreshadows.

Example 1. Cadential figures in the exposition

The entire passage in bars 57–64 recurs in the same form in the recapitulation as part of the full and literal return of all the material of the dominant section of the exposition. The *coup de théâtre* is reserved for much later, in the enormous coda of the movement. The coda encompasses five segments in all: first a restatement of the opening subject with new counterpoint, then the return of the 'new episode' of the middle section; then in bars 603–31 a return of that version of the syncopated transition figure, originally from bars 25–36, in the form that had animated the immense retransition at the end of the middle section. The next, central, event in the coda is the climactic peroration on the opening triadic theme, now in a form that makes possible powerful and simple alternations of tonic and dominant harmonies, covering bars 631–72. At bar 673 the last great cadence could end the movement, but there is one more stroke to be accomplished: there returns, in sudden *piano*, the contrary motion subject, Unit C, of the exposition and recapitulation, in virtually literal form, only slightly retouched in orchestration owing to the voice-leading in the violin parts. In both its earlier uses this passage led to a diminished seventh. Now as it moves to its destination in bar 681, the goal is converted to a *forte* attack on a full-range dominant seventh, and from here on the dominant is held steady for eight more bars, rising to a peak ab''' in the first violins at bar 684 and driving home the conclusion in the two final tonic chords. In this view, bar 681 is a 'resolution' of the moment of instability established in bar 64 and reiterated in bar 468 in the recapitulation. That this point of resolution comes so late only serves to reinforce one's awareness of the magnitude of the span over which this connection is extended, by means of which Beethoven is able to hold the coiled spring of this passage at maximum tension before releasing it at the last possible moment. This event confers on the end of the coda a function parallel to, but different from, the transformation that takes place at the opening of the recapitulation; what is parallel is the dramatic change that coincides with the articulation of a major structural boundary.

The point of view espoused by motivic analysis has long since contributed to the characterisation of the first movement as a congeries of intricately linked musical ideas. The point of view of reduction analysis has shown, or has the potential to show, a deeper skeletal structure that gives shape and foundation to the myriad of details of the movement. The kind of strategy operating here is of a type unlikely to be apprehended by purely motivic analysis, since what is important in the long term is not the complex derivation of one figure from another but the significant location of similar or associated events over long time-spans; and these events are more likely to consist in literal or nearly literal repetition than in subtle thematic transformations. Such strategies may also fail to emerge from reduction analysis, (though this depends on the particulars of the analysis), for the elements are all units of the foreground and their points of articulation may not coincide with those more background shapes of the basic prolongations which it is the purpose of the reduction procedure to elucidate. Schenker's analytic discussion of the coda contains a number of very subtle observations on voice-leading, as one might expect, and on motivic transformation, or 'diminution' procedures as he prefers to call it; but according to his analysis the crucial events of the coda are the prolongations that bring the upper line down eventually from scale-degree 5̂ in bar 595 to its eventual resolution to Eb in 631. He comments briefly on the choice of foreground upper-line pitches in bars 668 to the end, but has nothing at all to say on the recurrence of Unit C in bar 673. In Schenker's layered analysis the fundamental issue is the final achievement of tonal closure in bar 631 (and perhaps the further close in bar 673, though he does not say so).

Even more remarkable, in my view, is the discussion of this passage by Philip Downs, whose concern (similarly to mine in this paper) is with motivic relationships within the formal structure of the movement. Downs recognises the reappearance of Unit C in bars 673–81, but for him the essential point is that 'this material stands as representative of the second group in its unchangeability . . . that is, it stands for the necessary formality of the sonata principle'.[32] In my view this is somewhat like noticing that the concluding lines of Keats's *Ode on a Grecian Urn*, ' "Beauty is truth, truth beauty . . ." ' occur at the end of the poem and are therefore part of its culmination, but not noticing that they are given in quotation marks and are therefore qualitatively and rhetorically different from all other utterances in the poem.[33] It is not merely that the coda bears a far-flung relationship to two earlier moments but that the coda version differs in its kinetic force from the antecedents that give its recurrence associative meaning.

That analogies to such procedures may be found in other works by Beethoven, certainly of the great middle period and perhaps of other periods as well, seems to me rather more than likely. One, surely, is to be found in the first movement of the so-called 'Ghost' Trio Op. 70 No. 1, which employs near the beginning a chromatic motion that is drastically reinterpreted harmonically at the point of recapitulation, and in which, too, the strong implications of a harmonic motion to the subdominant, G major, are utilised early in the movement and receive their final confirmation in the motion to the subdominant at the beginning of the coda.[34] Another parallel of a different kind is the dramatic

---

[32] Downs, 'Beethoven's "New Way"', *The Creative World of Beethoven*, ed. Lang, p. 100; Downs further says of three appearances of this subject that Beethoven uses them in the same form, 'nowhere modifying a note and only slightly strengthening the color in the final appearance'. He makes no reference to the alteration of the harmonic goal that occurs in bar 681.

[33] See Leo Spitzer, *Studies in English and American Literature* (Princeton, 1962).

[34] I refer here to bars 5–7, 161–3, and 251–8.

postponement of a crucial formal element in the first movement of the 'Appassionata' Sonata Op. 57. Here the first attempt at a cadence (bars 3–4) stops unfulfilled on a weak dominant; this is left unresolved while the harmony moves to the distant Neapolitan G♭ that follows, and it is n used again and again in the movement without resolution to the tonic. Then at the end of the movement the coda consists of nothing else than the powerful repetition of a full cadence in which the dominant is driven down to its tonic again and again.[35] I am certain that other similar cases of various types can be found.

To conclude this paper, one more, larger, question remains to be dealt with. The kind of question that I am projecting into the foreground – that of long-range planning and compositional strategy – is manifestly the kind of issue that might be illuminated by study of surviving sketches, above all, of course, those wide-spanning sketches that encompass entire large formal divisions of a movement, and which evidently have the function of laying out, in rapidly written one-line drafts, the basic direction of whole sections. From such 'continuity drafts', notably those for the Second Symphony and other works of the same period, it appears that Beethoven's characteristic size of framework for a draft of this kind was the single large section – an exposition, a middle section, or a coda. The sketches for the 'Eroica' first movement follow this procedure through the first 41 pages of the 'Eroica' Sketchbook (Kraków, Bibliotéka Jagiellońska, Landsberg 6). Earlier than this, on two pages of the 'Wielhorsky' Sketchbook, there is, as Fishman has shown, a 'concept sketch' for a work in E♭ major, which appears to be the earliest jotting of ideas for what later became the 'Eroica'; this concept sketch appears to include the following: a triadic opening section, which was probably a slow Introduction as in the Second Symphony, followed by a 3/4 Allegro in E♭; then an idea for a slow movement, marked 'Adagio C dur' (C major, 6/8), and having, remarkably, the theme that was later to be used for the slow movement of the Quartet Op. 135; then a Minuet and Trio.[36] That these ideas crop

---

[35] For aspects of this view of the first movement of Op. 57 I am indebted in a very long-range sense to the teachings, years ago, of Edward Lowinsky and of the late composer and teacher Hugo Kauder.

[36] The 'Wielhorsky' Sketchbook (Moscow, Central (Glinka) Museum for Music Culture (SV 343)) was edited by Natan L. Fishman as *Kniga eskizov Beethovena za 1802–1803 gody*, 3 vols. (Moscow, 1962); the two pages referred to here are pp. 44–5 of the sketchbook (see facsimile and transcription volumes). See also Natan L. Fishman, 'Das Skizzenbuch Beethovens aus den Jahren 1802–1803 aus dem Familienarchiv Wielhorski und die ersten Skizzen zur "Eroica"', *Bericht über den Internationalen Musikwissenschaftlichen Kongress, Bonn 1970*, ed. Carl Dahlhaus and others (Kassel, 1971), pp. 104–7.

up directly following the end of his sketch work on the so-called 'Prometheus' Variations Op. 35, suggests that at that moment Beethoven foresaw the possibility of another large-scale work in E♭ major, for which the 'Prometheus' theme might also serve as Finale. At least one is free so to speculate.[37]

The 'Eroica' Sketchbook contains a large body of sketches covering all parts of the Symphony, and for the first movement exposition there are four large continuity drafts, plus extensive supplementary drafts of portions.[38] For the moment I shall focus only on certain aspects of these exposition drafts, all of which were published by Nottebohm but which have been carefully and closely studied with a view to improving his readings if possible. Again, Tovey's view, based on Nottebohm, is striking; he sees them as evidence of Beethoven's working at top speed, putting down 'any cliché that would mark the place where an idea ought to be . . . when he had advanced to sketching whole sections of a work . . . he often found it easier to begin again from the beginning and copy out the unaltered parts of the sketch, so that the act of writing had the same continuity as the flow of his thoughts, rather than tinker at isolated passages'.[39]

The first three of these continuity drafts are on consecutive pages in the sketchbook, while the fourth, after some complications, begins five pages after the end of the third.[40] Taken in their order of redaction, as a working hypothesis, they show a substantial evolution of procedures and ideas, though not without puzzling elements. For example, three of them display a feature that was to become untenable in the final version: namely, the appearance of the main theme in literal form in the dominant directly after the opening statements of the main theme in the tonic. And the one draft that lacks this feature is not no. 4 but

[37] That Beethoven's intended title for Opus 35 was 'Prometheus' Variations is shown by his correspondence with Breitkopf & Härtel over their first edition of the work: 'For the big set of variations it has been forgotten that the theme is taken from an allegorical ballet of mine, namely *Prometheus* . . . which should have appeared on the title-page; if this can be done, I beg you to see to it. If the title-page must be altered, let it be done at my own expense.' This letter is undated but is generally assigned to mid-June 1803; see Anderson no. 79. For a recent discussion of the 'Eroica' Symphony that seeks to link its movements to the dramatic and aesthetic categories found in the *Prometheus* ballet, see Constantin Floros, *Beethoven's Eroica- und Prometheus-Musik* (Wilhelmshaven, 1978).

[38] The background of this discussion is a seminar on the sketches for the first movement of the 'Eroica' which I conducted at Princeton University in the autumn of 1975; to the careful and assiduous work of the graduate students in that seminar I am indebted in ways that go far beyond the present paper.

[39] Donald Francis Tovey, *The Integrity of Music* (London, 1941), pp. 79–81.

[40] The four exposition continuity drafts are on these pages in Landsberg 6: no. 1, pp. 10, 11; no. 2, pp. 12–13; no. 3, pp. 14–15; no. 4, pp. 20–1.

no. 2. But in numerous other ways these drafts show a steady tendency towards the sharpening of rhythmic and linear profile of the individual motivic ideas, and a growing individualisation of the successive motivic units. For present purposes one feature is particularly striking. The passage that I am calling 'Unit C' in the exposition, the one that moves linearly up a sixth from $\hat{3}$ to $\hat{1}$ with contrary motion in the bass, is – apart from the triadic opening subject and its chromatic continuation – the only one that is present in essentially fixed form in all these drafts (Example 2). It maintains basically the same contour that it is to

Example 2. Sketches for the exposition, 'Eroica' Sketchbook (Landsberg 6)
a) Continuity Draft 1, bars 55–63 (p. 11)

* The repeat signs for these four bars are found in the sketchbook for this draft only.

b) Continuity Draft 1, variant version of bars 59–71 (p. 10)

c) Continuity Draft 2, bars 57–66 (p. 12)

have in the final version, undergoing some refinement in rhythmic continuation and in its registral position, but remaining fundamentally a fixed element in the web of transformations. Around it are shaped thematic units that have much further to go before they reach their final linear and harmonic form. Although the fourth continuity draft possesses a number of these units in shapes close to their final ones, it still would have required some important elaborative changes before it could have been used in a final version. In the absence of the autograph, and of any drafts in reduced-score form, one can only speculate about where this later phase may have taken place.

The fixed and significant position of Unit C vividly supports the presentiment that its role in the larger strategy may have emerged at a relatively early stage of planning. Yet there were steps to be taken: the drafts also show that the sequential figure that follows it (the material of bars 65–6 of the final version) was not always intended to open in a G-minor context. In Continuity Draft (CD) 1 plus its variant, and in CD 2, these bars express either a B♭-major context or the dominant of B♭, with a conspicuous F♮. Thus there was no very early thought of arriving on an F♯ diminished seventh. But by CD 3 and CD 4 the final form of the upper line is given, allowing for at least the possibility of the diminished seventh as local harmonic framework for both measures (Example 3). And then, later, in the sketches for the coda, for which Beethoven made at least one continuity draft and some preliminary patches, the flow of ideas is once again absolutely clear.[41] The

Example 3. Sketches for the exposition, 'Eroica' Sketchbook (Landsberg 6)
a) Continuity Draft 3 (p. 14)

b) Continuity Draft 4 (p. 20)

[41] For a study of the sketches of the coda and middle section I am especially indebted to Lawrence Earp, who took part in the seminar mentioned in footnote 38. In a paper written after the present one but published before it, I have attempted to expand the ideas suggested above in the footnotes 36 and 37, on the first known sketches for the Symphony and its earliest phases of planning. See my 'Beethoven's Earliest Sketches for the *Eroica* Symphony', *Musical Quarterly*, lxvii (1981), 457–78.

coda continuity draft shows that certain problems in this final section could only be worked out, for obvious reasons, in conjunction with Beethoven's plans for the middle section. And this essential draft for the coda already contains a statement of Unit C as the closing thematic material in an upper line, implying its long-range 'resolution' to a dominant harmony before the final tonic (Example 4). It is hardly

Example 4. Sketch for the coda, 'Eroica' Sketchbook (Landsberg 6, p. 37)

surprising that even if Beethoven was putting down on paper as fast as possible his flow of thoughts for a given section, he should have been aware of the implications of certain ideas for another, partly analogous formal division of the same movement. And in fact this is exactly the feeling that he confesses in a famous letter to Treitschke, in connection with the revision of *Fidelio*, in 1814:

> I could compose something new far more quickly than patch up the old with something new, as I am now doing. For my custom when I am composing even instrumental music is always to keep the whole in view. (Anderson no. 479)

The 'Razumovsky' Quartets: Some Aspects of the Sources

Alan Tyson

I

Unlike the Op. 18 quartets, the composition of which was evidently both arduous and prolonged, the three Op. 59 Quartets dedicated to Count Razumovsky appear to have been completed by Beethoven in a mood of self-confidence within a comparatively short period of time. That was the late spring, summer, and autumn of 1806. For much of the two preceding years his chief musical preoccupation had been his opera *Leonore*. After long delays it had reached the stage for three performances in November 1805, and – following its revision that winter in response to criticisms – the drastically cut second version had been given twice, on 29 March and 10 April 1806. No further performance in Vienna was likely, and whatever the nature of Beethoven's regrets there, no doubt he felt himself freed to turn once more to instrumental music.

There had not been much of that in the previous two years. Apart from the completion of the Triple Concerto Op. 56 and two Piano Sonatas (Op. 54 and Op. 57), and work on the Fourth Piano Concerto Op. 58, the opera had engaged him fully, and it may be that he had been impatient for some while to return to quartet writing. A hint that even during the early work on the opera his mind might be turning to quartets for the first time since around 1800 comes in a letter from his brother Carl to the publisher Härtel, dated 10 October 1804. After reviewing other compositions that were under offer, Carl added that if Härtel were to choose to order two or three string quartets they could be produced.[1] But a second letter to Härtel from Carl some six weeks later was less forthcoming; by that time Beethoven was again deeply engaged in the opera. It was only when *Leonore* had been put behind

---

[1] One stimulus, no doubt, was the series of quartet evenings initiated by Ignaz Schuppanzigh in the winter season of 1804–5.

him in the spring of 1806 that he could concentrate on the quartets. Beethoven inscribed the first page of the F-major Quartet with the words 'angefangen am 26ten Maj – 1806'; and this date for the time at which he started to write out this autograph – for that is what the phrase must mean – is confirmed by passages in two of his letters to Breitkopf & Härtel:

> You may discuss [with my brother] the question of new violin quartets, one of which I have already finished; and indeed I am thinking of devoting myself almost entirely to this type of composition. (5 July 1806, Anderson no. 132)

> As soon as I have been informed of your views on this matter – I can then send you immediately three violin quartets, a new piano concerto, a new symphony. (3 September 1806, Anderson no. 134)

No one familiar with Beethoven's approaches to publishers will assume that all three Quartets were ready for dispatch at the beginning of September. And evidence will be presented later to suggest that as late as the end of October no more than the first Quartet and the first two movements of the second were in score, though other movements had already been sketched. Probably, then, it was not till November 1806 that all three Quartets were ready. The earliest reports of performances, which record the dismay that the Quartets produced in their first audiences, date from three months later, the end of February 1807. But the Quartets must have been finished much earlier than that, for it is necessary to find some time in Beethoven's life for the other great works of 1806 and the beginning of 1807 that were probably completed together with the Quartets or after them: the Fourth Symphony (summer or autumn of 1806: autograph dated '1806'), the Violin Concerto (performed on 23 December 1806), the *Coriolan* Overture (beginning of 1807: autograph dated '1807'), as well as the Fourth Piano Concerto, most of which seems to have been written *before* the Quartets.[2] The

---

[2] It is not in fact at all clear when the main work on the Fourth Concerto was carried out. Few sketches survive: some 'concept' sketches for the first movement (Kraków, Biblioteka Jagiellońska, Landsberg 6, p. 148; and Berlin, SPK, Autograph 19e, fols. 96r and v) come from the early months of 1804, but a sketch for the second movement, on a bifolium (collection of Mrs Friskin, New York (SV 350)) that also contains sketches for the first movement of Op. 67 can be dated no more precisely than 'around 1806'. On 27 March 1806 Carl offered the Concerto to Hoffmeister & Kühnel of Leipzig, and on 5 July 1806 Beethoven informed Breitkopf & Härtel, to whom the Concerto was also offered, that Carl was travelling to Leipzig with the score. Neither firm bought the work, which was ultimately published by a Viennese firm. Fair copies of certain passages in the piano part (first and last movements) are to be found in Berlin, SPK, Landsberg 10, pp. 1–4 and 13–16; these probably date from around the time of the

Symphony, Piano Concerto, and Overture were all performed in March 1807, and I believe that the series of opus numbers – 58 for the Fourth Piano Concerto, 59 for the Quartets, 60 for the Fourth Symphony, 61 for the Violin Concerto, and 62 for *Coriolan* – represents the order in which the pieces were completed. All in all, it seems logical to place the substance of Beethoven's work on the Quartets in the time from April to November 1806 – that is, in the period between the unsatisfactory revival of *Leonore* in March and April, and the weeks following Beethoven's trip to Prince Karl Lichnowsky's country seat at Grätz, near Troppau (Silesia) in the autumn. One may make what one likes – some of course have made a good deal – of the fact that their composition was almost wholly surrounded by the creation of orchestral works on the largest scale.

II

Having established the context and overall date for the Quartets, it is possible to go on and ask in which order the three Quartets, and the various movements that make them up, were written. The answer is clear and contains no surprises. The evidence on which it is based comes both from the autograph scores, all three of which have been preserved, and from the surviving sketches. The former is perhaps the easier to summarise. For writing out the autographs – the F-major and E-minor are now in the Staatsbibliothek Preussischer Kulturbesitz, Berlin,[3] the C-major in the Beethovenhaus, Bonn[4] – Beethoven used paper of four different types which are easily differentiated by their watermarks (see Figures 1–4), as well as by the number of staves and the total span of the staves:

Paper 1   FS and three moons (twelve staves, with total span of 185 mm)
Paper 2   FS with G.A.EMERICH and three moons (twelve staves, with total span of 185 mm)
Paper 3   GA/F in an apple and a single moon (sixteen staves, with total span of 195 mm)

Concerto's first performance (March 1807): see my article, 'The Problem of Beethoven's "First" *Leonore* Overture', *Journal of the American Musicological Society*, xxviii (1975), 313–14.

[3] They are catalogued as Mendelssohn 10 and as Autograph 21: see Hans-Günter Klein, *Ludwig van Beethoven: Autographe und Abschriften: Katalog*, Staatsbibliothek Preussischer Kulturbesitz, Kataloge der Musikabteilung, ser. 1: Handschriften, vol. ii (Berlin, 1975), pp. 228, 73–4. Facsimiles of these two autograph scores, with introductions by the present writer, have been published by the Scolar Press (London, 1981).

[4] Catalogued as BH 62 (SBH 544).

Figure 1. Watermark of Paper 1

Figure 2. Watermark of Paper 2

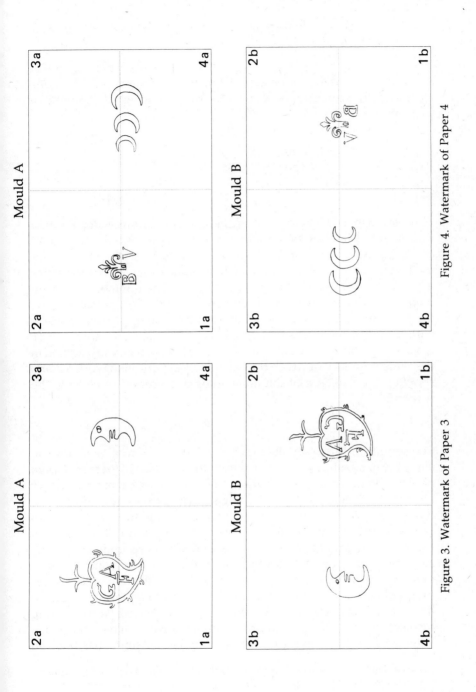

Figure 3. Watermark of Paper 3

Figure 4. Watermark of Paper 4

Paper 4   BV under a fleur-de-lis and three moons (sixteen staves, with total span of 190 mm)

It is possible, even probable, that the first two papers are variants of each other, but they can be kept distinct for the moment. When one examines the autographs, one finds the following distribution of papers:

	F-major	E-minor	C-major
Paper 1	I, II, IV (pp. 79–86 only)	I	
Paper 2	III, IV (pp. 69–78, 87–94)		
Paper 3		II, III	
Paper 4		IV	I, II, III, IV

Thus the paper used for most of the F-major continues for the first movement of the E-minor; another paper is used for only the second and third movements of the E-minor; and a further paper is used for the Finale of the E-minor and the whole of the C-major. The inference is that the F-major and the first movement of the E-minor were completed first; then the two middle movements of the E-minor; and lastly, the E-minor's Finale and the whole of the C-major. This inference is entirely confirmed by the sketches, which show that not only the three Quartets but the individual movements in them as well were written in the same sequence in which they stand in the published work. Charts showing the make-up of the three autograph scores are given in the Appendix.

III

The subtitle of this essay, 'Some Aspects of the Sources', will, I hope, allow me to be selective and to focus on those details in them that seem particularly to require examination. In fact the sources for Op. 59 have been largely neglected by musicologists. The three autograph scores, though they contain many features of interest, and though they are all accessible, have never been the subject of a major study. The neglect of the sketches, though regrettable, is perhaps more understandable, since they present some formidable difficulties to anyone trying to organise them. This was a task that Nottebohm, the only writer so far to give them serious attention, did not attempt to undertake. Instead, he very skilfully selected interesting but unconnected passages from the sketches for citation and brief comments which have been much quoted.[5] Today sketch research has a number of techniques that can

---

[5] Gustav Nottebohm in *Musikalisches Wochenblatt*, vi (1875), 649–52, 665–7; reprinted with minor alterations in N II, pp. 79–90.

hope to take things a little further – for instance, by offering criteria for determining the original order of the sketches. And since the problems posed by sources such as the Op. 59 sketches arise again and again in Beethoven scholarship, this may justify the space I propose to devote to them now.

The sketches for the Quartets are scattered today, but by far the largest number of them are in one place, the Gesellschaft der Musikfreunde, Vienna. These are unbound, and are kept in a single folder catalogued as A 36. Later I shall scrutinise the bibliographical status of this collection, but it is clear at least that it is a mixed bag. Of the thirty-two leaves that go to make it up, twenty-five relate directly or indirectly to the Op. 59 Quartets; the rest are single leaves or bifolia of various dates – such as 1808, 1810, and 1814. In fact A 36 would automatically be classified as a *Konvolut* or miscellany if it did not give some impression of being a genuine collection of Op. 59 leaves diluted by the inclusion of extraneous sketchleaves.

The origins of the collection are obscure, but it seems to have been together for at least a century. For in the 1860s both Thayer and Nohl reported that there were twenty-one leaves in the Gesellschaft der Musikfreunde with Op. 59 sketches, and this figure corresponds very closely to the present number (twenty-five) if leaves blank on both sides are excluded from the roll-call.[6] Most of Nottebohm's examples are drawn from A 36, and the fact that all the leaves that he cites are still there is extra evidence of a sort that the collection has stayed intact.

But the other sketchleaves for Op. 59 are widely scattered. There is one other sketch in the Gesellschaft der Musikfreunde, on the first of two leaves now catalogued as A 60; these are filled mainly with sketches for the C-minor Piano Variations WoO 80 but also include a sketch for a new *Leonore* Overture and for the Finale of the C-major Quartet.[7] The first movement of the same Quartet is sketched on two leaves now in Bonn,[8] and its second movement, again with a new *Leonore* Overture, in a fragment in the Royal College of Music, London.[9] A further sketchleaf for the second movement turned up at

---

[6] Thayer, *Verzeichniss*, p. 69; Ludwig Nohl, *Beethoven's Leben*, ii (Leipzig, 1867), p. 496, note 135. In addition to pp. 15/16, 17/18, and 37/38 (leaves that are completely blank), pp. 43/44 with minimal entries on only one side may have been omitted by Thayer and Nohl.

[7] This page is illustrated in Tyson, 'The Problem of Beethoven's "First" *Leonore* Overture', p. 301.

[8] Beethovenhaus, BH 100 (SBH 616) and Mh 72 (SBH 617).

[9] MS 2175, illustrated in Tyson, 'The Problem of Beethoven's "First" *Leonore* Overture', p. 300.

auction in London recently.¹⁰ Two Berlin miscellanies include sketches for the E-minor Quartet: Landsberg 10 has four leaves, and Grasnick 20b in the Deutsche Staatsbibliothek has two leaves, one of which also contains a sketch for a setting of Klopstock's poem 'Das Rosenband'.¹¹ And finally the great *Leonore* Sketchbook (Mendelssohn 15) in the Staatsbibliothek Preussischer Kulturbesitz now contains some leaves with sketches for the second and third movements of the F-major Quartet – though it was recognised long ago by Nottebohm that the leaves in question did not truly form part of the sketchbook but had somehow been interpolated.¹²

Some means must be found of sorting out these scattered leaves and ordering them. And one means – it is not the only one – is the watermarks. With the exception of the leaves interpolated into Mendelssohn 15, which have the same watermark as that sketchbook, all the sketches for Op. 59 are on sixteen-stave paper with one of two watermarks: either GA/F in an apple and a single moon, or BV under a fleur-de-lis and three moons. These are, it will be recalled, the third and fourth of the papers found in the autograph scores of the Quartets; I shall refer to them for brevity as the 'Apple' and the 'BV' papers. Of the surviving sketchleaves about half have the Apple watermark and half the BV watermark, and since there is evidence that the Apple paper is earlier, one may start by dividing the sketches into an earlier group and a later group.

Are these two groups remnants of a sketchbook? Or of two sketchbooks? Or how are they to be classified? Since 1972 there has been some agreement that the volumes that have been preserved under the description 'sketchbooks' can be divided into three types.¹³ First, there are the integral sketchbooks that consist of one or perhaps two paper-

---

[10] One side is illustrated in the auction catalogue of Bonham's, London (23 February 1977, no. 56), and in Catalogue no. 206 (May 1977) of Hans Schneider, Tutzing (no. 3). This leaf, like the fragment in the Royal College of Music, was once owned by J. B. Cramer.

[11] For Landsberg 10, pp. 39–46, see Klein, *Beethoven: Autographe und Abschriften*, p. 134. The Grasnick 20b leaves are fols. 18–19.

[12] Nottebohm in *Musikalisches Wochenblatt*, vi (1875), 649; reprinted in N II, p. 79 (and compare pp. 409–10). I have discussed this point in 'Das Leonoreskizzenbuch (Mendelssohn 15): Probleme der Rekonstruktion und der Chronologie', *Beethoven-Jahrbuch*, ix (1977), 481–2; Eng. version 'The Leonore Sketchbook (Mendelssohn 15): Problems of Reconstruction and of Chronology', *Paper Analysis*, ed. Stephen Spector (New York, forthcoming).

[13] For an examination of the different types of sketchbook, see Douglas Johnson and Alan Tyson, 'Reconstructing Beethoven's Sketchbooks', *Journal of the American Musicological Society*, xxv (1972), 138–56.

types and have a regular gathering-structure. These were evidently put together by a bookbinder. Second, there are the integral sketchbooks that have a sequence of miscellaneous papers and no regular gathering-structure. These were no doubt assembled by Beethoven himself, and can be described as 'home-made' sketchbooks; the leaves were held together not by professional sewing along the central folds of the gatherings (as in the first type) but by threads passed through two or three crude stab-holes made in or near the inner margin of each leaf. The third type consists of the miscellanies: volumes made up of sketchleaves for compositions of widely differing dates, and containing heterogeneous paper-types. Most of these can be shown to have been compiled by collectors or dealers in the two or three decades after 1827;[14] the volumes have no genuine unity and the leaves were not in their present positions when they were sketched on by Beethoven.

Sketchbooks of the first of these three types are usually easy to identify, even when they have lost a good number of their leaves. But volumes of the second and third types can sometimes be confused, especially in cases where a genuine home-made sketchbook (or part of one) has been contaminated by extraneous leaves. For a sequence of sketchleaves to be recognised as belonging to a home-made sketchbook, three criteria must be satisfied:

1 The leaves – as in all the integral sketchbooks – must have been used for sketching by Beethoven within a comparatively narrow time-span. It is this criterion that differentiates the integral books from almost all the miscellanies.
2 All the leaves must contain the same stab-holes, identified by the gaps that separate them (which must not vary very much within the sketchbook).
3 Continuity of sketching between leaves of different paper-types, or ink-blots and their offsets linking leaves of different paper-types, must be demonstrated; for such sketch continuity and ink-blot links are always to be found in the integral sketchbooks.

Two good examples of home-made sketchbooks that satisfy these three criteria are Landsberg 7 (Staatsbibliothek Preussischer Kulturbesitz, Berlin) and the Mass in C Sketchbook (Bibliothèque Nationale, Paris). In each case the leaves have stayed together. But in other books the amateur binding has not succeeded in preventing rearrangement

---

[14] An exception to this is the portfolio that Beethoven himself kept of his early papers, and probably discontinued around the year 1799. This now survives in two sections: London, BL, Add. MS 29801, fols. 39–162 (the 'Kafka' Miscellany), and Berlin, SPK, Autograph 28 (the 'Fischhof' Miscellany).

or even dispersal of the leaves, and extraneous leaves have further confused the overall picture. Landsberg 9 (Deutsche Staatsbibliothek, Berlin), for instance, is now classed as a miscellany, since it contains three groups of sketchleaves from widely differing periods: sketches for the 'Hammerklavier' Sonata Op. 106, sketches for the 1814 revision of *Fidelio*, and sketches for the first movement of the Fifth Symphony. Yet the *Fidelio* leaves (pp. 17–68) can probably be detected as having been part of a home-made sketchbook. For though they are of a wide variety of paper-types, there are ink-blot connections between adjacent leaves of different papers, and there are stab-holes close to the inner margin in a consistent pattern: three holes, with a gap gradually widening from 81 mm to 90 mm between the upper two holes, and with a gap of 80 to 83 mm between the lower two.[15]

The criteria may even be satisfied in cases where there is no recognisable book or torso of a book; one must then suppose that the leaves of a home-made sketchbook have been completely dispersed. A large number of scattered leaves, for instance, have survived with sketches for *König Stephan* (Op. 117), written with the incidental music to *Die Ruinen von Athen* (Op. 113) in the summer of 1811. These leaves are of a variety of papers, but all of them have three stab-holes near the inner margin with gaps of 93 mm and 85 mm, and it is possible to see that some of them are connected by ink-blots.[16] So one can talk of a home-made sketchbook of 1811; and since some gathered pairs of bifolia with sketches for the F-minor Quartet Op. 95 and the 'Archduke' Trio Op. 97 also display the same triad of holes, the sketchbook should probably be regarded as having been started at the end of 1810.[17] One must be alert, then, to the possibility that the components of a home-made sketchbook may no longer be in one place, and that no central core may have survived.

---

[15] A leaf now in the Beethovenhaus, Bonn, Mh 88 (SBH 623), with the same sketch content and the same holes, was evidently once part of the same collection. At some time the *Fidelio* leaves in Landsberg 9 appear to have been rearranged: the original sequence was probably pp. 41–68, followed by the Bonn leaf, and then by pp. 17–40.

[16] Among the leaves are: Bonn, Beethovenhaus, Mh 81 (SBH 657 – two leaves), Mh 82 (SBH 658 – lower nine staves of a leaf), Mh 83 (SBH 659), Mh 84 (SBH 656), BSk 2 (SBH 660), BSk 3 (SBH 661), and BSk 4 (SBH 662 – two leaves); Paris, BN, Ms. 86, Ms. 88, Ms. 91, and Ms. 92; Cambridge, Fitzwilliam Museum, Mus. ms. 287. The ink-blot connections are between Mh 83 and Mh 82 in Bonn and Ms. 91 in Paris.

[17] Bonn, Beethovenhaus, BSk 18 (SBH 646), and New York Public Library, JOD 71-2 (both Op. 97); New York, Pierpont Morgan Library, *Catalogue of the Mary Flagler Cary Music Collection* (New York, 1970), no. 72 (Op. 95). Four further leaves with sketches for the last movement of Op. 95, recently auctioned in Paris (catalogue of Drouot Rive Gauche, 20 June 1977, no. 5), have the same stitch-holes.

IV

It seems most unlikely that anyone who has examined the surviving sketchleaves for Op. 59 would claim them as the fragments of an integral sketchbook (or two of them) of the type that was made by a bookbinder. But what of a home-made sketchbook? How far do the leaves satisfy the criteria that have been laid down here? That they virtually all date from the same year, 1806, is not in question. And there is the evidence of stab-holes: most of the Op. 59 leaves in A 36 – though not some of those for the F-major Quartet – have a pair of stab-holes about 94 mm apart in one margin, and similarly-spaced holes are found in the Op. 59 leaves in Landsberg 10 and Grasnick 20b in Berlin, and in the two Bonn leaves. But there is a strong case against accepting the majority of these leaves as being the remnant of a home-made sketchbook. It rests on a number of considerations:

1. The third of the criteria for a home-made sketchbook is not met: no convincing ink-blot connections between separate gatherings of leaves – even ones of identical paper-types – have been demonstrated.[18] (It may of course be argued against this that a great many leaves that would have provided this evidence had been lost, but its absence is nevertheless impressive.)

2. There is no reason to expect that the different papers used in making a home-made sketchbook would be arranged in chronological order, with the earliest paper at the beginning and the later papers following in strict sequence of purchase. Indeed, with a home-made book such as Landsberg 7 one can see that it is far from being the case; although the sketches are sequential, the paper-types are in no sort of order. Yet when one examines the sketches for Op. 59 that are preserved in A 36 and elsewhere one finds that all those for the last movement of the F-major, for the whole of the E-minor, and for the first movement of the C-major are on the Apple paper, the earlier of the two types I have been discussing, and that all those for the last three movements of the C-major are on the later, BV paper. This does not suggest anything like a random arrangement or use of papers.

3. One leaf in A 36 (pp. 13/14), which has the pair of stab-holes already discussed, was at one time used as a pocket-sketchleaf. Half of one

---

[18] It has been claimed that there is an ink-blot connection between staff 13 on the verso of the Bonn leaf BH 100 and staves 12–13 on p. 4 of A 36 in Vienna. I am by no means convinced that the blots do in fact match; but in any case, since both pages are versos, such blotting could only have occurred at a time when the leaves concerned were loose and did not form part of a home-made sketchbook.

side (p. 14) is filled with pencil sketches. These are upside-down in relation to the rest of the sketches on both sides, which are in ink; and it is clear from the lay-out that the pencil sketches were entered first (see Plate I). All of them are for the same movement, the third movement of the C-major Quartet (the main ones are quoted by Nottebohm in N II, p. 86 and top of p. 87). The important point is that the watermark is the later one – the BV watermark. This shows that even by the time at which Beethoven had moved on to the later paper-type and was working on the third movement of the third Quartet, the leaf was still available as a pocket sketchleaf and was not yet part of a home-made sketchbook.

4   There is a considerable number of blank pages and leaves in A 36: pp. 10 and 11, for instance, are blank, and so are pp. 15–18, a bifolium. It seems likely that pp. 15–18 were once gathered inside pp. 9–12, the other bifolium from the same sheet of paper. Thus of the gathered sheet pp. 9–12 and 15–18 only the two outside pages, pp. 9 and 12, were actually written on. The converse is also found: p. 45 and p. 52, the outside pages of another gathered sheet (pair of gathered bifolia), are blank. All this suggests that Beethoven was working with loose gathered sheets, sometimes filling only the outside leaves and sometimes only the inside ones, rather than turning from one page to the next in a continuous expanse of paper such as a home-made sketchbook would provide.

5   Lastly, there is the evidence of water-stains, which is discussed below. To anticipate the argument: if the clues have been interpreted correctly, they indicate that several of the Op. 59 sketchleaves were rearranged but were nevertheless kept together from some time after they had been used. Thus they might well have been stitched together at that later date.

The conclusion seems inescapable. The Op. 59 leaves that contain a pair of stab-holes 94 mm apart – the great majority – are not the survivors from a home-made sketchbook, but were put together as a collection at some time (perhaps a very considerable time) after they had been used. And this in turn may explain why there are almost no sketches for any other compositions of the summer of 1806 among the Op. 59 leaves. Whoever it was that made the collection may have rejected everything that was not identifiably a sketch for the Quartets.

V

We are freed, then, from an obligation to reconstruct the original sequence of the sketchleaves. At the same time we forfeit the hope of

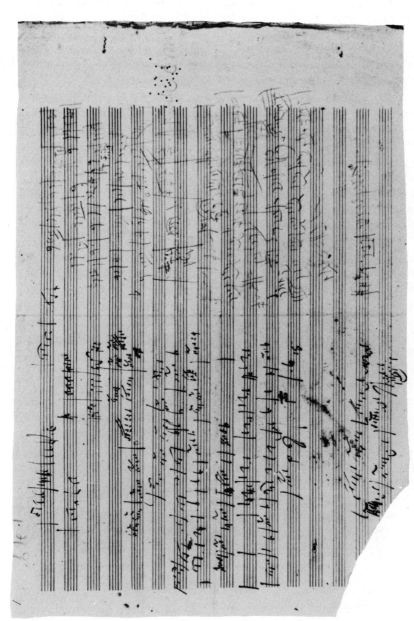

Plate I. Sketches for Op. 59 No.3, third movement: Vienna, GdM, A 36, p. 14

finding any definite structure governing the survivors; the largest unit proves to be the single-sheet gathering of four leaves. This in turn may sharpen our perception of the individual musical entries – as, ruefully, we recognise that we have not advanced so far from Nottebohm's position after all. Two things are immediately striking. First, it is clear that a large number of sketches have been lost; and second, the three Quartets are represented somewhat unequally in the surviving leaves. The F-major Quartet has suffered the worst here. Nothing at all has come down for the long first movement, and the second movement is represented only by the sketches on the bifolium interpolated into Mendelssohn 15, transcribed in detail by Nottebohm (N II, pp. 79–81). The third movement sketches, too, survive on only one bifolium (A 36, pp. 41–4), again quoted by Nottebohm (N II, p. 82), and there are only some scraps for the Finale. Clearly nothing much can be learned from these about the genesis of the F-major Quartet.

Though rather more of the sketches for the E-minor Quartet have survived, they still give a very incomplete picture. Several are for the first movement, but none seems to be continuous with any other, and they represent rather different compositional stages. For the slow movement, apart from an early concept sketch cited by Nottebohm (N II, p. 84), there is only one page – a rather curious one (Landsberg 10, p. 40), since it appears to place on record certain choice passages. Staves 1/2, for instance, have bars 37–40; staff 3 has bars 52–9; staff 4 has bars 62ff.; staff 7 has bars 16ff; and so on. This was not the way in which Beethoven customarily sketched, so perhaps these were purple passages copied from a messy sketchleaf of a more familiar type. But the lack of any other slow-movement sketches makes them hard to evaluate. The third movement is represented by one developed sketch (Landsberg 10, pp. 41–2) and one shorter one (A 36, p. 40); but the sketches for the Finale – apart from a few preparatory ideas – have in the main disappeared (there are a few in Landsberg 10, pp. 43–6). Once again, one cannot help admiring Nottebohm's skill in seizing on the scattered early sketches for a main theme to the Finale, all of which, though otherwise rather different, begin the movement in C major and settle into E minor only after some bars (N II, pp. 84–5).

VI

Over half the sketchleaves for Op. 59 that have been preserved relate to the C-major Quartet. And for the first time one finds a movement represented by a series of sketches that are not merely purposeful but even appear (as I shall show) to be nearly complete. This is the first movement. There are also a fair number of sketches for the third movement (Minuet and Trio). The slow movement is poorly represented, however, and of the Finale there is almost nothing more than ideas for the fugal beginning. So it seems sensible to restrict a discussion of the sketches to the ones for the first and third movements.

First-movement sketches are found on five leaves. The chief point of interest in the earliest of them (p. 27 of the bifolium pp. 27–30 in A 36) lies in its neat indication of the chronological relations between the three Quartets of Op. 59. The bifolium was originally used for writing out a fair copy of a short but problematical passage in the Finale of the F-major Quartet (bars 165–79), in which Beethoven had made changes in the distribution of the parts. (In the autograph score bars 173–7 had been rendered almost illegible by corrections.) It was then used for sketches for the first and last movements of the E-minor Quartet – advanced sketches for the first movement, and draft ideas for the main theme of the Finale. And subsequently Beethoven entered at the top of p. 27 an eight-bar theme in C major, marking it '3tes quartett'. This is quoted by Nottebohm (N II, p. 86), and leads one to suppose – not for the last time in the sketches for this movement – that Mozart's chamber music was at that point close to Beethoven's mind. For the phrase recalls figures in the first movements of several works by Mozart: the D-major Quartet K 575 and the Clarinet Quintet K 581, for instance, and above all the C-major Quartet K 465, which was evidently to serve to some degree as a model. But this particular idea was not taken any further.

The other four sketchleaves for the first movement are a bifolium in Vienna, A 36, pp. 1–4, and the two Bonn leaves, Mh 72 (SBH 617) and BH 100 (SBH 616). Though one of these Bonn leaves was acquired in 1899 and the other came with the Bodmer Collection in 1956, it can be shown that they were once a bifolium. Thus there are two bifolia, and it is pretty clear that they were once the two halves of the same sheet of paper. All four leaves have conspicuous water-stains on the upper edges, and when these are compared it can be seen that there are striking matches between the stains on each page. At one time, as the water-stains make clear, the leaves stood in the following sequence:

Leaf	*Watermark quadrant*
⎡ Bonn, Mh 72	4a
⎢ ⎡ Vienna, GdM A 36, pp. 3/4	3a
⎣ Vienna, GdM A 36, pp. 1/2	2a
⎣ Bonn, BH 100	1a

There is perhaps nothing so surprising in this sequence, for it is also the order (as the watermarks show) of a gathered sheet. If Beethoven were sketching on four leaves from a single sheet of paper without first separating the two bifolia, he might well have found the leaves in this order. But is it in fact the order in which the leaves were sketched on? That is something that can only be decided when the contents have been examined.

There is no doubt where these sketches begin: on the recto of Mh 72 (see Plate II). This side is marked 'quartett 3', a pretty sure sign that they are early sketches. And the first staff begins with what will become a familiar feature: a crotchet e' and a dotted minim f', marked 'sf'. This rising semitone is followed by a predominantly rising two-bar motif, making a three-bar phrase, and the whole is repeated a step higher. Finally there are the notes a', bb', $b\natural'$ – again, rising semitones; the dominant-7th harmonies of the last two are indicated by figures (Example 1). At this point there is a slight break, and then a passage

Example 1

marked 'E dur' with an accompaniment of semiquavers in thirds. Evidently this is a sketch for an Introduction; a slow tempo is indicated by the accompaniment. The sketch leads from E major through E minor in an ascending scale of minims that pauses on a dotted minim d''. This is followed immediately by the rising-semitone motif with which the sketchleaf began: e', f', now significantly marked 'i ma parte', that is, the opening of the Allegro (Example 2).

Example 2

Something of what is happening is already clear: these are early ideas for the Allegro and for a slow Introduction to it. Since slow Introductions were at this time something of a rarity in string quartets,

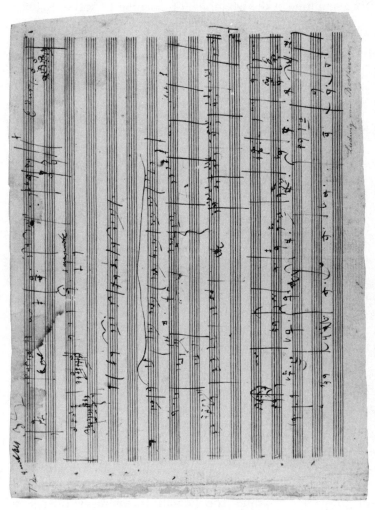

Plate II. Sketches for Op. 59 No. 3, first movement: Bonn, Beethovenhaus, Sammlung H. C. Bodmer, Mh 72 recto

one must again suspect the influence of Mozart's C-major Quartet K 465. This influence extends to some details, for what Beethoven is doing here is attempting to draw a thematic link, based on an ascending figure, between the Allegro and the preceding Introduction; the rising scale itself can be viewed as an augmentation and extension of the rising semitone at the beginning of Example 1. And in K 465 it is again an ascending figure that links the Introduction with the following Allegro. These relationships, and a further parallel to be referred to shortly, can be set out as in Example 3. At this stage both Introduction

Example 3

and Allegro were in 4/4 time. The thematic fragments on the next few staves are somewhat indistinct, or perhaps undistinctive, suggesting an Introduction rather than a main Allegro (Example 4); they are not unlike the *andante con moto* opening of the *Leonore* Overture No. 1 which was drafted shortly after this. But in retrospect one can see that they are the precursors of the unaccompanied first-violin passages at

Example 4

the start of the Allegro of the Quartet. A mild climax is suggested at staves 8/9, with two-part writing and octave doubling, and a possible modulation to the sharp side (Example 5). There is also an effort to construct a two-bar phrase out of the rising-semitone motif (compare bars 65–6 etc. of the finished Quartet).

Example 5

None of this gives any warning of what follows. On staves 12–15, and on the top two staves of the verso, there comes notated in short score the whole of the Introduction almost exactly as it appears in the finished version (which is in 3/4 time), followed by the first five bars of the Allegro (Example 6 shows the first twenty-two bars). So elaborate a construction must surely have been worked out elsewhere. There is at any rate no sign of its composition on these pages; a couple of changes made in writing it out suggest that it was still in a plastic form when it was entered here. It is followed on this verso by a coherent draft of the first part of the Allegro down to about bar 82, with very few gaps. (The reference to the first movement of Mozart's C-major Quartet becomes more or less explicit at bar 59, where – as has often been pointed out – Beethoven employs a motif from the earlier work: see Example 3 above). The recto of the other Bonn leaf (BH 100) continues the Allegro for a few more bars; but the last 20 bars or so of the exposition are missing here. Then follow two versions of the beginning of the development, the second and longer one extending on to the verso of the leaf. There is a rather simple version of the retransition, with a section

Example 6

that is barred to indicate the intended length but not otherwise filled out. The recapitulation follows, but at bar 211, at the end of a staff, there is a cross to indicate a continuation elsewhere. The remaining staves have a short sketch for the coda and an improved version of part of the retransition.

On these two leaves, therefore, it is already possible to identify sketches for virtually every part of this first movement, whether they are in more or less definitive or only in tentative shape. What is the contribution of the other two leaves, the Vienna bifolium? Here Beethoven worked over several passages more than once, so that it is not always easy to see what was written first. But the first page (A 36, p. 3 – the bifolium has been folded the wrong way in its present pagination) contains bar 81 and a reworking of the imitative passage – this time in score to exhibit more clearly the various entries of the figure. It is followed by a new, longer coda sketch. On the other side of this first leaf there is what is probably the continuation of the recapitulation sketch on the second Bonn leaf that ended with a cross – only (as sometimes happens) there is no corresponding cross here. This recapitulation sketch extends to the end of the movement – that is, it turns into a sketch for the relatively concise coda.

Finally I pass to the second leaf of the Vienna bifolium (pp. 1/2). This begins with a short E♭ passage in 3/4 time, and then the jotting down of the theme of the third-movement Minuet (first 2 bars only and 'etc.') and what is perhaps an idea for the Trio. Then comes a theme that one recognises with some surprise as that of the Allegretto of the Seventh Symphony, immediately followed by three early sketches for the present slow movement of the Quartet. The theme of this slow movement has impressed some listeners as having a 'Russian' flavour; that it cannot be a true 'thème russe', however, is shown by the fact that it evolves here only after a certain amount of sketching. A further sketch for the slow movement on the other side of the leaf is more developed, and places more emphasis on the dominant pedal.[19] All the other sketches on this last leaf are for the first movement, and take up sections that have not been previously worked out: the second part of the development and retransition, and the end of the recapitulation and coda.

Such a summary of the distribution of sketches for this first movement, though it can give little notion of their quality, allows certain observations to be made.

The vast majority of the bars that go to make up the movement are to be found on one or other of these four leaves in something close to their final form – if one is thinking not texturally but thematically. In fact the movement is really roughed out on the first (Bonn) bifolium; the second (Vienna) bifolium takes up the tricky passages in more detail, and broaches ideas for the second and third movements as well. The only passage from the first movement that seems not to be present here is the end of the exposition, bars 93–105. But the parallel passage from the recapitulation, bars 238–51, is to be found not once but twice: in an early draft on the verso of the first leaf of the Vienna bifolium, and again in what amounts to its final form on the verso of the second leaf (the last page under consideration here). These passages are of course in the tonic; all that is lacking is a version of them in the key of the second part of the exposition, which is – somewhat unusually in a post-1800 C-major work by Beethoven! – the dominant. In the light of what is known of Beethoven's usual sketching procedure, it seems certain that the sketches for these bars in G major are lost. With the exception, then, of these end-of-exposition sketches, one can say that thematically the sketches for the first movement are to all intents and purposes complete.

But are they complete texturally? One cannot help being struck by the paucity of evidence that these are *quartet* sketches. In fact there is only one passage – bars 77 and following and its various repetitions – that is regularly written out in a way that separates the voices. The question must arise whether Beethoven made a practice in these years of sketching quartets in score, and arriving by that means at the best textural solutions. If he did so, such score sketches from his middle

[19] A dominant pedal is also emphasised in the Allegretto of the Seventh Symphony. It is the location of that theme in this place (first noted by Nottebohm) that indicates that it was Beethoven's first idea for the slow movement of the C-major Quartet.

period have not been preserved in any quantity; and in fact the few specimens of short passages laid out in score that are found among the Op. 59 sketches – passages which are often mixed up (as here) with unilinear sketches – suggest that at this time Beethoven was no more in the habit of sketching his quartets in score than he was in the case of his other chamber music or his orchestral works. On the contrary: it seems that he customarily proceeded directly from unilinear sketches to the writing out of a 'final' autograph score. Of course such scores were often heavily corrected as passages were changed again and again to attain a satisfactory form, and pages that became too badly disfigured could be pasted over (or stitched over) with a fair version, or the leaf discarded.[20] Thus the absence of score sketches or textural sketches for the first movement of the C-major Quartet does not mean that anything has been lost: at the end of the sketches on the fourth leaf discussed above (A 36, pp. 1/2) Beethoven could have proceeded directly to the writing out of the autograph score of this movement.

There remains a puzzle concerning the relation between the two bifolia. The water-stains show that the Vienna bifolium was at one time gathered within the Bonn bifolium. But the sequence of sketches indicates beyond all reasonable doubt that the leaves were not in that order when Beethoven came to use them; instead, the Bonn bifolium was filled up with sketches *before* the Vienna bifolium was used. And since the damp that produced the water-stains appears to have caused the ink to run in a few passages, it looks as though the leaves had already been used for sketching before the water-staining took place. So the placing of one bifolium within the other, to which the water-stains bear witness, must also have occurred after the leaves had been used. The sequence of leaves established by the water-stains – which is not confined to these four leaves, since a water-stain on the last page (p. 46) of a bifolium in Berlin, SPK, Landsberg 10, pp. 43–6, with sketches for the Scherzo and Finale of the E-minor Quartet, exactly matches the stain on the recto of the first Bonn leaf, Mh 72 – must be rejected. For the water-stains, it seems clear, were caused only *after* the leaves had been used, and are not a reliable indication of the order in which the leaves stood when they were written on by Beethoven.

At what time, then, did the water-stains appear on the leaves? Here it is tempting to pursue a line of argument which, although speculative, helps towards a rather precise dating of the sketches and the autograph scores of Op. 59. The only sketchleaves that are water-

---

[20] In the autograph of the F-major Quartet pp. 14 and 70 were pasted or stitched over in this way, and in the E-minor Quartet fols. 20v and 32v.

stained are the ones that have already been described: those in Landsberg 10 (pp. 43–6) with sketches for the last two movements of the E-minor Quartet, and the four leaves in Bonn and Vienna with sketches for the first movement of the C-major. But parts of the autograph of the E-minor Quartet are also water-stained.[21] The first eleven leaves, which contain the first movement, are severely stained, and fols. 12–17 (second movement) also have some staining. On the other hand, fols. 18–22 (third movement) and 23–35 (Finale) are unstained, and there is also no water-staining in the autograph of the C-major Quartet. To put it another way, the only movements that show water-staining are:

E-minor Quartet	I	(autograph)
	II	(autograph)
	III	(sketches)
	IV	(sketches)
C-major Quartet	I	(sketches)

This certainly suggests some watery cataclysm at a time when the E-minor was half in score and half in sketches. And in fact there is independent evidence of a most timely deluge. The autograph score of the 'Appassionata' Sonata Op. 57, which was once owned by the pianist Marie Bigot and is now in the Bibliothèque Nationale, Paris, shows plentiful signs of having been injured by water; and Marie's husband has provided an account of the way in which the damage was sustained. Beethoven had taken the score of the Sonata with him to Lichnowsky's country seat at Grätz, near Troppau; but after a quarrel he left suddenly for Vienna:

> During the journey he encountered a storm and pouring rain which penetrated the trunk into which he had put the F-minor sonata . . . After reaching Vienna, he came to see us and laughingly showed the work, which was still wet, to my wife, who began to look at it. Finding the opening striking, she sat down at the pianoforte and started playing it . . . When Mme Bigot finished playing she begged him to make her a present of it; he consented, and faithfully brought it to her after it had been engraved.[22]

The date of this stormy journey can be fixed approximately to the

---

[21] This can be seen in the facsimile of the E-minor Quartet referred to in footnote 3. The autograph of the F-major Quartet shows no sign of water-staining today. But many of the leaves have been cleaned and repaired, so it is possible that water-stains that were once present have been removed.

[22] Thayer–Deiters–Riemann ii, pp. 455–6; Thayer–Forbes, p. 407. A copy of Bigot's account of the incident is included with the facsimile of the Op. 57 autograph (Paris, 1927).

second half of October. In that month Breuning informed Wegeler that Beethoven would remain with Lichnowsky till the end of October; but he left Grätz prematurely, and he was already back in Vienna by 1 November.[23] There are grounds, then, for concluding that by the second half of October Beethoven had the first two movements of the E-minor Quartet in score, and had sketched the other two movements of the E-minor and the first movement of the C-major Quartet.

VII

Sketches for the third movement of the C-major Quartet have been preserved on a number of leaves in A 36 (pp. 1, 14, 20–4, 26, 47, 50). Once again the more significant ones have been cited by Nottebohm (N II, pp. 86–9): he describes them as 'interessant'. Interesting they certainly are, not least for a reason unsuspected by Nottebohm: they show Beethoven returning to a thematic idea that he had abandoned some five years earlier.

It is probably this fact, the fact that he is here reworking older material, that makes it hard to be sure of the original sequence of these third-movement sketches. But the pocket sketchleaf already referred to (A 36, p. 14: see Plate I) contains what is no doubt the earliest of them. Beethoven's first idea was for a Minuet in F major (Example 7).

Example 7

This, and its somewhat bland continuation which is quoted by Nottebohm, are then immediately abandoned for something more familiar (Example 8). The opening bars of the finished Minuet and Trio are clearly recognisable, but not the sequence of keys suggested here. Further sketches, however, confirm that for a time Beethoven considered a Minuet not in the tonic but in the subdominant, F major, complemented by a Trio in D♭ and followed by a Finale starting in C minor. Only in later sketches was C major adopted as the key of the Minuet, and F major as that of the Trio.

The second part of the Minuet underwent successive alterations, but the eight bars of the first part remained unchanged. There is an unexpected reason for this, which was discovered by Richard Kramer:

[23] Thayer–Deiters–Riemann ii, pp. 518, 523; Thayer–Forbes, pp. 402, 405; letter to George Thomson of 1 November 1806 (Anderson no. 136).

Example 8

the first eight bars had been devised by Beethoven in 1801 as a theme for a set of variations in C major. These variations were evidently intended to form the second part of a Fantasia in C minor for piano. The work was never completed, but its rough outlines can be gauged from the surviving sketches (Landsberg 10 in Berlin, pp. 125–7, A 33 in the Gesellschaft der Musikfreunde, Vienna).[24] They show that the variations were planned to lead into an extended coda, with imitative passages built from the first bar (or first two bars) of the theme. And that is indeed 'interessant', since the idea was evidently a tenacious one – Beethoven decided to end the Minuet of the Quartet too with a coda, and used precisely the same kind of imitative figures there; they wander from the tonic and could be said to make the tonality and modality of the coda ambiguous. I have suggested elsewhere that this coda was originally intended to lead to a C-minor Finale,[25] and some sketches for it in A 36, as well as early ideas there for a minor-mode Finale, seem to bear this out.

VIII

Modern critical judgment has largely reversed the opinion of the 'Razumovskys'' first audiences, who found only the third Quartet acceptable. Today it is the first two Quartets, with their use of sonata form in so many movements, their vast expressive range, and above all their symphonic strivings and scale, that come in for admiration; the C-major Quartet is viewed not merely as being smaller in scale (which

---

[24] See Richard A. Kramer, 'The Sketches for Beethoven's Violin Sonatas, Opus 30: History, Transcription, Analysis' (Ph.D. dissertation, Princeton University, 1973), pp. 166–73. The sketches are transcribed there in Appendix II.

[25] Tyson, 'The Problem of Beethoven's "First" *Leonore* Overture', p. 326. See also remarks in Ludwig Finscher, 'Beethovens Streichquartett Opus 59, 3: Versuch einer Interpretation', *Zur musikalischen Analyse*, ed. Gerhard Schuhmacher (Darmstadt, 1974), pp. 150–1.

is undeniable), but as more conventional, in certain passages perfunctory, less convincing as a whole, perhaps even a little dissociated.[26] It is only the slow movement that regularly comes in for commendation, even if its integration into the Quartet is not clear to everyone.

The weighing of such matters falls of course within the province of musical aesthetics. But it cannot be denied that the sources that I have described, fragmentary as they are, are of a nature to lend some fuel to these charges. Since he had completed the 'Eroica' Symphony more than two years earlier, Beethoven's dependence, in the C-major's first movement, on a Quartet that Mozart had written twenty-one years before is a bit puzzling. If he was not merely short of time – and there *is* some evidence that the C-major Quartet was put together rather quickly – Beethoven must really have been aiming at something smaller in scale than in the other two Quartets. The absence of a genuine 'thème russe' in the third Quartet has never been explained. Perhaps it needs no explanation; but it is also possible that Beethoven, under pressure of time, lacked the inclination to search once more in Ivan Prach's 1790 collection of Russian folk melodies. The use of an old melody in the Minuet, uncertainty about the right key for it and for the Trio, and hesitation over the modality of the Finale – all these can be taken as further hints of a greater-than-usual infirmity of purpose and a readiness to settle for quick solutions. The Finale, too, has been generally acclaimed at the same time as a *tour de force* and as a slightly disappointing conclusion to the work. Clearly victories are not always to be snatched lightly from the jaws of defeat.

If the sources, then, have something to contribute to our understanding of the C-major Quartet's limitations – limitations of imagination or vision, limitations of time – they can also throw some light on the dizzy sense of scale that accompanied the writing of the F-major. In the first movement Beethoven did not mark the exposition to be repeated; the development began with the opening theme in the tonic, and to avoid all possible confusion he wrote at the head of the score: 'la prima parte solamente una volta'. Instead, he planned something more outrageous (at any rate in 1806): a repeat of the *second* part, the development and recapitulation, beginning at bar 112. There are repeat marks in the autograph score at bar 112 and the words 'la seconda parte due volte', and after bar 342 there stand six 'first-time' bars (Example 9). Such a repeat, if observed, would have made the movement very long indeed – far longer than it would have been if the

---

[26] Many of these points can be found in the literature; for a forceful expression of some of them, see Joseph Kerman, *The Beethoven Quartets* (New York and London, 1967), especially pp. 151–4.

Example 9

exposition had been repeated instead. Only after the movement had been completed in score did Beethoven change his mind and delete the repeat signs and the first-time bars.

The autograph score of the F-major Quartet shows that at one time Beethoven contemplated making repeats in the second and last movements as well. That in the second movement would have been a massive one, for after bar 393 of the autograph there once stood two 'first-time' bars; these led back to a repeat sign before bar 155. Again, in the last movement there were once three 'first-time' bars after bar 324 (Example 10). These led back to a repeat sign before bar 286. Before publication Beethoven decided to delete both these repeats, in the same way as he removed that in the first movement.

What can be seen in all these instances is a tendency on Beethoven's

Example 10

part to expand the movements of the Quartet to enormous lengths: a tendency of which he seems to have become aware and to have taken steps to curb.[27]

IX

The name of Count Razumovsky has been immortalised by the dedication to him of these Quartets. So it is entertaining to discover that for at least a short time Beethoven considered transferring the dedication to someone else. Among the papers that came to the Königliche Bibliothek in Berlin in 1880 as part of Anton Schindler's *Nachlass* there is a leaf (Deutsche Staatsbibliothek, Autograph 35,36) that records what are evidently drafts for the title-pages of seven Beethoven editions (see Plates III and IV); all the editions were subsequently published by the Bureau des Arts et d'Industrie in Vienna. These title-page drafts are not in Beethoven's own handwriting; they relate to the following works:

Fourth Piano Concerto, Op. 58 (dedicated to the Archduke Rudolph)
Three Quartets, Op. 59 (dedicated to Count Razumovsky)
Fourth Symphony, Op. 60 (dedicated to Count Oppersdorff)
Violin Concerto, Op. 61 (dedicated to 'son ami Monsieur de Breuning')
Piano Concerto arranged from the Violin Concerto (dedicated to 'Madame de Breuning')
Overture to *Coriolan*, Op. 62 (dedicated to Collin)
the same Overture arranged for the pianoforte (dedicated to Collin)

At some point Beethoven decided to revise a number of the title-pages. He crossed out the whole of the Op. 58 entry, which had been in German, and rewrote it in French, at the same time changing the dedicatee of the Concerto from Archduke Rudolph to 'son ami Gleichenstein'. He changed the dedicatee of the Quartets from 'son Excellence Monseigneur le Comte de Rasoumoffsky' to 'son Altesse Monseigneur le Prince Charles de Lichnowsky'. He also crossed out the dedication of the Violin Concerto arrangement, and he deleted the whole of the final entry.

When did Beethoven decide on these changes? The summer of 1807 is the most likely time. On 20 April Beethoven had concluded a contract with Muzio Clementi for the publication in London of the first six of these works, and Ignaz von Gleichenstein had acted as a witness.

---

[27] A similar expansiveness is to be found in the first movement of the E-minor Quartet, where both sections, the exposition and the development plus recapitulation, were marked to be repeated. But in this case the repeat marks were allowed to stand.

Some two months later the same works were sold to the Bureau des Arts et d'Industrie; in these negotiations, too, Gleichenstein lent his assistance, as is clear from Beethoven's letters to him of June 1807 (Anderson nos. 145, 146, 148, 149). No doubt the alteration in the dedication of the Fourth Concerto reflected Beethoven's gratitude. But soon after this Beethoven must have changed his mind once more, for when the works were published by the Bureau at the end of 1807[28] and in the course of 1808, they bore their original dedications.

The short-lived change in the dedication of the Op. 59 Quartets still needs to be explained. There is no doubt that Razumovsky had paid for the Quartets, and his involvement is in any case indicated by the 'thèmes russes' in the first two. But Beethoven, as we have seen, had quarrelled with his old patron Lichnowsky at Grätz in October 1806. Perhaps by the summer of 1807 he desired to make amends to him; if so, he may well have tried to persuade Razumovsky to surrender the dedication of the Quartets to Lichnowsky, the count's relative (the two men were married to sisters), and to receive another work – the latest symphony, perhaps – in exchange. In the event Razumovsky shared with Prince Lobkowitz the dedications of both the Fifth and Sixth Symphonies, and retained the dedication of Op. 59 as well – and we are spared the necessity of speaking of the three Quartets as 'the Lichnowskys'.

[28] Although the advertisements for Op. 58, 59, 61, and 62 in the *Wiener Zeitung* all appeared in 1808 (Op. 60 was not advertised), it is probable that some of the editions – Op. 62, for instance – were already available by the end of 1807. On this point, see some comments of mine in *Music & Letters*, lviii (1977), 243–4.

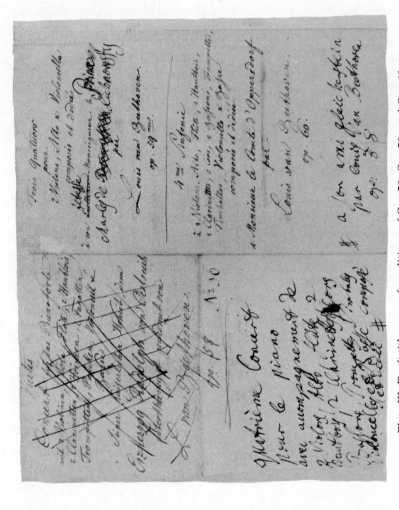

Plate III. Draft title-pages for editions of Op. 58, Op. 59, and Op. 60: Berlin, DSB, Autograph 35, 36, verso

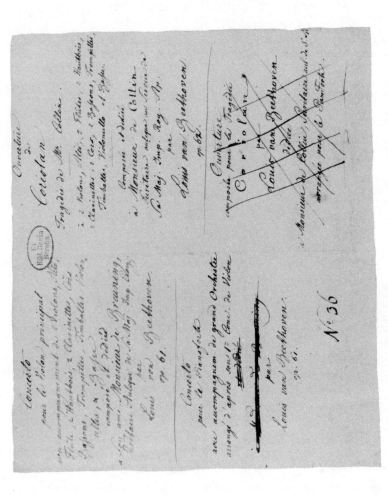

Plate IV. Draft title-pages for editions of Op. 61 and Op. 62: Berlin, DSB, Autograph 35, 36, recto

Appendix

Autograph score of the F-major Quartet
(47 leaves, paginated)

Movement	Pages	Paper	Quadrant	Movement	Pages	Paper	Quadrant
I	1/2	1	2a		49/50	1	1b
	3/4	1	1a		51/52	1	2b
	5/6	1	4a		53/54	1	3b
	7/8	1	3a		55/56	1	4b
	9/10	1	3a	III	57/58	2	3a
	11/12	1	4a		59/60	2	4a
	13/14	1	1a		61/62	2	1a
	-15/16	1	4b		63/64	2	2a
	17/18	1	2a				
	19/20	1	1b		65/66	2	2a
	21/22	1	2b		67/68	2	1a
	23/24	1	3b	IV (p. 69,	69/70	2	4a
	Stub			2nd system)			
	25/26	1	3a		71/72	2	3b
	27/28	1	4a		73/74	2	4b
	29/30	1	1a		75/76	2	1b
	31/32	1	2a		77/78	2	2b
II	33/34	1	1a		79/80	1	2b
	35/36	1	2a		81/82	1	1b
	37/38	1	3a		83/84	1	4b
	39/40	1	4a		85/86	1	3b
	41/42	1	4a		87/88	2	3a
	43/44	1	3a		89/90	2	4a
	45/46	1	2a		91/92	2	1a
	47/48	1	1a		93/94	2	2a

Pp. 15/16 were once stitched down over p. 14, since p. 16 was a replacement for p. 14. (P. 15 had originally followed p. 24, and was an earlier draft of p. 25.)
Pp. 71/72 were once stitched down over p. 70, since p. 72 was a replacement for p. 70.

Autograph score of the E-minor Quartet
(36 leaves, foliated)

Movement	Folios	Paper	Quadrant	Movement	Folios	Paper	Quadrant
I	⌈ 1	1	3b	III	⌈18	3	1b
	⌈2	1	4b		⌊19	3	4b
	⌊3	1	1b		⌈ 20	3	2a
	⌊ 4	1	2b		⌈–21	3	4b
	5	1	3b		⌊ 22	3	3a
	⌈6	1	4b	IV	⌈ 23	4	4a
	⌊7	1	1b		⌈24	4	3a
	–7a	1	?4b		⌊25	4	2a
	⌊ 8	1	2b		⌊ 26	4	1a
	–9	1	?4b		⌈ 27	4	1b
	⌈10	1	3b		⌈28	4	2b
	⌊11	1	2b		⌊29	4	3b
	⌈ 12	3	3a		⌊ 30	4	4b
II	⌈13	3	4a		–31	4	2a
	⌊14	3	1a		–32	4	1a
	⌊ 15	3	2a		–33	4	4a
	⌈ 16	3	1b		⌈34	4	3a
	⌊17	3	4b		⌊35	4	2a

Fol. 7a is stuck on the outer margin of fol. 7, and contains five bars that replace three deleted bars on fol. 7r.

Fol. 21 is an inserted leaf, intended to cover (and to replace) fol. 20v; it was once stitched down over it.

Fol. 33 is another inserted leaf, being intended to cover (and to replace) fol. 32v; it was once stuck down on it by sealing wax.

Autograph score of the C-major Quartet
(28 leaves, paginated)

Movement	Pages	Paper	Quadrant
I	⌈ 1/2	4	4b
	⌈ 3/4	4	3b
	⌊ 5/6	4	2b
	⌊ 7/8	4	1b
II	⌈ 9/10	4	2a
	⌈ 11/12	4	1a
	⌊ 13/14	4	4a
	⌊ 15/16	4	3a
	⌈ 17/18	4	1b
	⌈ 19/20	4	2b
	⌊ 21/22	4	3b
	⌊ 23/24	4	4b
III (p. 27, 2nd system)	⌈ 25/26	4	3b
	⌈ 27/28	4	4b
	⌊ 29/30	4	1b
	⌊ 31/32	4	2b
IV	⌈ 33/34	4	2a
	⌊ 35/36	4	3a
	−37/38	4	1a
	−39/40	4	2b
	⌈ 41/42	4	1b
	⌈ 43/44	4	2b
	⌊ 45/46	4	3b
	⌊ 47/48	4	4b
	⌈ 49/50	4	1b
	⌈ 51/52	4	2b
	⌊ 53/54	4	3b
	⌊ 55/56	4	4b

Notes on Beethoven's Codas*

Joseph Kerman

I

Musical analysts who deal with Beethoven's sonata-form movements generally do rather poorly by the codas – do less well, that is, in accounting for actual musical experience when dealing with codas than with other sections of the form. All over bar the shouting is the impression one is often left with when the analytical account reaches the end of the recapitulation, though as a listener one knows perfectly well that an important part of the movement, perhaps the most exciting part, is still to come. This shortcoming on the part of many analysts is only partly to be explained by the more exposed inadequacy of the theorists in this area. In fact that notoriously imperfect instrument, sonata-form theory, breaks down completely at the coda. A general theory depends upon generalisation, and one simply cannot find a common function for codas, as one can for expositions, developments, and recapitulations, over the 150-year history of sonata form. That is why in the technical language of sonata form 'coda' is the one term that does not refer (however imperfectly) to a musical function, but merely to a position. Viewing Beethoven's total output, theorists seem to feel thwarted by the variation in length and weight of his codas – if indeed a coda is present at all – and by their wide variety of function. Among the commonest statements made about Beethoven's treatment of sonata form is that he expanded the coda greatly, even decisively. But one searches far in the literature for any sustained treatment of this seemingly important matter.[1]

---

*This paper has been rewritten since its oral presentation, which was accompanied by a tape illustrating most of the codas discussed. I am especially grateful to William Newman for his thoughtful comments on this material.

[1] A conspicuous disappointment as regards the coda in sonata form is Charles Rosen's *Sonata Forms* (New York, 1980). The Polish scholar Andrzej Chodkowski has written a

There seems to be a problem here – a problem with the composer's critics, one might suppose, rather than with the composer himself. Approaching it, I have had two convictions or cautions in mind. First, whatever general principles anyone may formulate for codas, there will almost certainly be some exceptional works that will not hold to the norm – and indeed these will probably be among Beethoven's most compelling and visionary masterpieces. For such is the case with other formal principles of this kind in Beethoven. Second, it is very unlikely that a *single* principle will hold good, considering how much this composer developed and changed over the course of his career. In short, one must proceed historically, and one must anticipate that any conclusions arrived at will be normative but not binding. In accordance with what may be called the Waldstein hypothesis ('you shall receive *Mozart's spirit from Haydn's hands* . . .'), I shall begin the inquiry with Mozart and Haydn.

II

Mozart often works without a coda; this is the case in about half the sonata-form movements of his Vienna period. When he does have a coda it is short and carefully kept subsidiary to the rest of the movement. And it is likely to echo the beginning of the development section. The exceptions are impressive, but they are few and always or nearly always inspired by the same special technical concern: formal counterpoint (Finale of the 'Jupiter' Symphony K 551, first movement of the 'Hunt' Quartet K 458). The typical process in Mozart's more typical codas is the construction of new cadential phrases out of the previous thematic material. These phrases are generally two or four bars long and they are generally repeated.

They may draw on any of the previous material; Mozart ranges much more widely in this respect than Beethoven, at least before the third period. In addition to the obvious candidate, the first theme, other possibilities are the second theme (Piano Quartet in E♭ K 493), a secondary theme originally heard in the tonic (G-minor Quintet K 516), the transition to the development ('Linz' Symphony K 425), or an episode from within the development (Quartet in F major K 590, 'Hunt' Quartet). Although in these cadential phrases Mozart refers to

---

dissertation and several articles on Beethoven's codas, but his interest seems to be almost exclusively taxonomic: see 'Die Koda in der Sonatenform Beethovens', *Bericht von der Internationalen Beethoven-Kongress 10.–12. Dezember 1970 in Berlin*, ed. Heinz Alfred Brockhaus and Konrad Niemann (Berlin, 1971), pp. 391–4; and 'Problem kody w formie sonatowej Beethovena', *Muzyka*, ser. 2, xv (1970), 67–88.

the theme, whichever it is, he does not actually cite it; the listener is left not with a clear impression of the theme but with a somewhat fragmentary and ambiguous memory of its motivic content. This same technical device can cause strikingly different effects, extending from pathos in the minor mode to paradox, charm, or humour in the major. But whatever the effect, these codas generally give the impression of adding a little extra commentary upon a movement that is to all intents and purposes complete. It is as though after having left the party Mozart has a final remark to make *sur l'escalier* – a grieving remark or a wary one, a witticism, a compliment, or a retort.

Mozart's long contrapuntal codas were not imitated by the young Beethoven, who when he had serious contrapuntal business to transact preferred to use the recapitulation.[2] Nor was he really at ease with Mozart's essentially quiet device of centring his codas on new cadential phrases. One of the few examples of such a coda from Beethoven's early period comes from the Finale of the Quartet in A major Op. 18 No. 5, which is modelled on the Quartet in the same key by the older composer, K 464. Thanks to an anecdote stemming from J. B. Cramer, Beethoven is known to have admired the coda in the Finale of Mozart's C-minor Concerto K 491.[3] The first-movement coda too, I believe, must have struck him very forcibly (Example 1). The characteristic *calando* effect at the end appears to have haunted him as much as Mozart's affective cadential harmonies, which here as in other similar cases are drawn from a rich stock of dominant and diminished-seventh forms over a tonic pedal, ambiguous *tierces de Picardie*, and major and minor subdominant $^6_4$ chords. Beethoven adopted both the *calando* effect and the idea of cadential phrases in the Finale of the C-minor Sonata Op. 10 No. 1.

In other early works in the minor mode one can detect a rather amusing tug-of-war between the seduction exerted by these passive endings of Mozart's and Beethoven's own more robust personal inclinations. Mozart's strangely unquiet octaves in the last measures of the passage quoted in Example 1 proved particularly difficult to hold down; in the first movements of the Piano Concerto No. 3 and the Violin Sonata Op. 30 No. 2 – both in C minor, once again – they erupt into gestures of Beethovenian defiance. Throughout the first period, in fact, Beethoven's standard solution for a minor-mode sonata-form coda involves a pathetic *calando* followed by some sort of *furioso* conclusion, ranging in extent from just a few notes ('Pathétique' Sonata

---

[2] See Joseph Kerman, *The Beethoven Quartets* (New York and London, 1967), pp. 68, 144.
[3] Thayer–Forbes, p. 209. Cramer visited Vienna and met Beethoven in 1799.

Example 1. Mozart, Piano Concerto in C minor K 491, first movement, coda

Op. 13, third movement) to a few bars (String Trio in C minor Op. 9 No. 3, first movement) or a sizable section (Cello Sonata in G minor Op. 5 No. 2, first movement). Later he seems to have felt more comfortable ending minor-mode movements quietly, as in the first movements of the 'Appassionata' Sonata Op. 57,[4] the Quartets in E minor Op. 59 No. 2 and F minor Op. 95, and later still the C-minor Sonata Op. 111. The coda in the Finale of the Quartet in C♯ minor Op. 131, which practically quotes from the C-minor String Trio, also recalls that early work and others of its time by turning the *calando* conclusion

---

[4] Here Beethoven's idea may owe something to the coda in the first movement of Mozart's Sonata in C minor K 457.

in the nick of time into something more affirmative: in emotional terms, a curiously retrospective gesture.

What is quite rare in Mozart is a coda containing a strong return of the movement's first theme. He sometimes makes reference to the first theme in the cadential phrases, of course, but the effect of this is quite different from that of a full-scale return. The G-minor Piano Quartet K 478, where the body of the main theme returns formally after the recapitulation and gives the first movement a rounded feeling, is almost unique in Mozart's mature output. An analogous effect is achieved by the 'Jupiter' Finale, and there is a typically malicious example in the first movement of the 'Musical Joke' K 522, from which one gathers that Mozart regarded strong returns of this kind as a blunt or even a crude formal feature. One gets a startling vision from the 'Musical Joke', in fact, of Mozart's spirit engaged in a proleptic parody of middle-period Beethoven.

III

> Haydn's practice in his later works differs from Mozart's in almost every particular [writes Tovey] . . . as to recapitulation, the term is seldom applicable at all. The first theme, indeed, returns, but it is followed by a brilliant peroration full of new developments and giving the repose of recapitulation only in the fact that it remains firmly in the tonic. If after such a peroration Haydn chooses to end quietly and abruptly with his cadence-theme, the effect is witty. But it does not make him a formalist. He is a master not only of form but of spaciousness in the smallest possible compass. One main theme for both groups gives him more room for expansion than two; and instead of saying that his recapitulations are free we ought to say that he invented the most brilliant type of Beethoven coda.[5]

Strana ingiunzion! As Charles Rosen observes,

> This is only to substitute one injudicious term for another in the hope of correcting an abuse: if 'coda' is to have any meaning for audible experience, then it is not possible to use the word for everything that comes in Haydn after the return to the tonic. Although Haydn's music is too dramatic in conception for an exact repeat transposed to the tonic, he never neglected the function of 'recapitulation' as 're-solution.' By this I mean not merely a firm re-establishment and concluding reassertion of the tonic – a 'coda' could indeed do that, as in Chopin's G minor Ballade – but a 'resolution' of material, that is, of

---

[5] Donald Francis Tovey, *Musical Articles from the Encyclopaedia Britannica* (London, 1944), p. 217; compare his *Beethoven* (London, 1944), p. 107.

the 'exposition' as well as of the 'development' . . . 'Recapitulation' may be a poor term, but we still need it to describe the resolution of the exposition, of which a literal repeat at the tonic is only a limiting form.[6]

The dispute is instructive both because it brings Rosen about as close as he ever gets to defining the 'meaning for audible experience' of a coda and because it shows how little Tovey cared for consistency when he was carried away by a genuine insight. By saying that Haydn's recapitulations are like Beethoven's codas, Tovey knew he was bringing up the biggest possible gun in his battle for the recognition of Haydn's genius. But, indirectly, by saying that Beethoven's codas are like Haydn's recapitulations, Tovey was also saying that they are not like Haydn's or anyone else's developments.

I shall return to this point a little later. Beethoven's recapitulations, of course, are never like Haydn's, though there are a few early pieces in which a regular recapitulation is cut off before the cadence theme, and fresh matter is added before the movement ends with that cadence theme. This might be regarded as a somewhat stiff adaptation of Haydn's method. Elsewhere in this volume Douglas Johnson discusses Beethoven's attempt to stalk Haydn in the compositions of 1794–5, and recapitulations of this kind occur in the first movement of the Sonata in C major Op. 2 No. 3, and the first and fourth of the Piano Trio in C minor Op. 1 No. 3 (compare also Op. 1 No. 1). A later example, in the String Quintet in C Op. 29 (1800–1), is interesting because here Beethoven must have been following Haydn by way of Mozart, whose Quintet in C major K 515 is one of very few of his works to construct the recapitulation in this fashion. Neither this Quintet nor any of the pieces by Beethoven, incidentally, ends in a way that could be described as 'witty'.

In a number of Haydn's sonata-form movements – in the first movements of four of the 'London' Symphonies and a like number of late quartets – there is a strong return of the first theme at or near the end. The theme is usually varied in some imaginative way and usually shortened, but it always gives the definite sense of a return, not of a mere recollection or reference. Symphony No. 97 in C, a work that, as Johnson has shown,[7] influenced the abortive C-major Symphony

---

[6] Charles Rosen, *The Classical Style* (New York and London, 1971), p. 76.

[7] Johnson discusses this connection in Chapter 4 of his dissertation, 'Beethoven's Early Sketches in the "Fischhof" Miscellany (Berlin Aut. 28)' (Ph.D., University of California at Berkeley, 1977). Johnson's remarks on the coda sketches for this Symphony are very much to the point. (This section is omitted from the published version of the dissertation, 2 vols. (Ann Arbor, 1980).)

sketched by Beethoven in 1795 and 1796, provides an especially blunt example. This piece has a relatively regular recapitulation, by Haydn's standards, lasting seventy-eight bars compared to ninety-four in the exposition, and ending with the cadence theme – which, however, is curtailed. In place of this theme's livelier second part (which never returns after the exposition) there follows a thirty-four-bar passage in which its more mysterious first part is led through some quite remote keys. As a stabilising measure, presumably, when Haydn brings back the main theme after this he brings it in a more emphatic version (Example 2).

Example 2. Haydn, Symphony No. 97, first movement

Expanding the first theme in this way is not usual in Haydn, but it soon became very characteristic of Beethoven. The most prominent early case is in the First Symphony, written in 1800 partly on the basis of rejected sketches for the abortive Symphony of the mid-1790s (Example 3). Here the effect may be felt to be not so much blunt as overblown. But however this may be, Beethoven's triumphant C-major arpeggios have a function for the movement as a whole beyond those of the Haydn example. In Beethoven the original theme hinges on the sequence C–D, an upward thrust which provides the movement with much of its propulsive energy. What the coda provides is an expansion, and in a sense a normalisation and resolution, of this diatonic thrust into a series of simple steps up the tonic triad arpeggio, C–E–G. The first movement of the String Quintet Op. 29 has a first theme belonging to the same family, and here the theme is expanded in the coda in two distinct stages, separated by a small cadenza. The

Example 3. Symphony No. 1, first movement, bars 277–88

sequence moves up the scale C–D–E–F–G–A–C (bars 263–72) and then up the tonic arpeggio C–E–G (bars 285–97), as in the Symphony.

The Second Symphony has a first theme that follows a much more subtle rising dynamic; this is resolved in the coda by a two-stage expansion (bars 310–16, 350–4) much like that in the Quintet. The triumphant D-major arpeggio at the end of this movement (bars 350–4) finds a rather clear echo at the end of the Symphony's last movement, where a similar climactic arpeggio is built on the opening motifs of the Finale theme (bars 424–34). With this theme, of course, there is no question of any upward thrust that requires (or at least receives) 'normalisation' or 'resolution'. The theme does, however, contain anomalies of other kinds, with its acciaccatura attack on the high seventh of the dominant-seventh chord and its astonishing downward leap of a diminished twelfth. These are ironed out by the climactic arpeggio in the coda.

At this point, perhaps, a general principle behind Beethoven's codas at this period of his life begins to suggest itself. Again and again there seems to be some kind of instability, discontinuity, or thrust in the first theme which is removed in the coda. The aberration may be linear, harmonic, rhythmic, registral, or textural, but in any case the coda has a function over and above that of 'saturating the ear with the tonic chord', in Rosen's phrase.[8] In addition to this harmonic function it has a thematic function that can be described or, rather, suggested by words such as 'normalisation', 'resolution', 'expansion', 'release', 'completion', and 'fulfilment'. Everyone accepts that sonata form depends essentially on the balance and resolution of tonal forces. But

[8] Rosen, *The Classical Style*, p. 394.

with Beethoven a sonata-form movement is also 'the story of a theme' – the first theme – and the exciting last chapter of that story is told in the coda.

Let me rapidly survey a number of Beethoven codas, mostly of the second period, with this dynamic in mind. The first theme of the 'Eroica' Symphony, which in the exposition and recapitulation suffers from harmonic, rhythmic, and registral uncertainties, celebrates its release in the coda by the simplest of upward arpeggio fanfares. The mysterious low flattened seventh degree (C♯ or D♭) in bar 7 gives way to a high fifth repeated eight times in a quasi-canon at an ever-increasing dynamic level and, it seems, with ever-increasing satisfaction. 'Heroic' was Beethoven's adjective for this effect. In the 'Waldstein' Sonata Op. 53 the real (modulating) sequence at the opening is normalised in the first part of the coda as a tonal sequence;[9] then the coda ends with a compressed version of the theme, dashing upwards and clarifying the original registral discontinuity between its two components. The lively first theme of the 'Ghost' Trio Op. 70 No. 1 stops suddenly on the high flattened third degree (bar 4). The coda does not so much resolve this as side-step it, in Beethoven's most jocular spirit: when the theme stops it simply stops on the tonic – and early. Themes containing fermate often draw attention to them by means of flourishes or little cadenzas at various later points in the movement, but in the coda these themes move right along in tempo (first movements of the 'Kreutzer' Sonata Op. 47, the Cello Sonata in A Op. 69, and the Sixth Symphony – and this applies also to the third fermata in the Fifth Symphony). The tune with which the 'Archduke' Trio Op. 97 begins might be said to contain a 'fermata in tempo' at bars 8–13, duly ornamented at bars 198–204; but all traces of a slowing down are eliminated from the coda, a particularly single-minded linear ascent which gives the tune a grand sense of fulfilment. The ascent is half comical in the flute passage at the end of the first movement of the 'Pastoral' Symphony, dizzy in the 'Kreutzer', mysterious in the D-major Cello Sonata Op. 102 No. 2. Earlier in the 'Pastoral' coda Beethoven seems to have felt that the original hollow texture of the first theme required filling out, and what is more at a healthy *forte* (bars 422–6) – an effect anticipated at the analogous point in the Quartet in F Op. 59 No. 1 (bars 348–55). In the first movement of the Fourth Symphony the arpeggio expansion of the first theme in the coda (bars 467–75) is one of Beethoven's most delightful *jeux d'esprit*. The equally

---

[9] Tovey makes this point in *Beethoven's Pianoforte Sonatas* (London, 1931), pp. 160–1. The sequence I–V$_3^6$/♭VII–IV$_3^6$ in bars 1–8 becomes V$_3^6$–ii/IV$_3^6$–I in bars 261–7.

delightful but less earthy case in the 'Harp' Quartet Op. 74 (bars 251–62) serves also to resolve the registral difference between the two parts of the original Allegro theme. Canons drive up the arpeggios at the end of the *Fidelio* Overture and the Fifth Symphony Finale.

A beautiful case of linear expansion, simple and almost timid in character, occurs in the Finale of the 'Pastoral'. The hymn-like melody introduced very near the end of the piece (bar 237) moves *sotto voce* up from F to a *subito piano* D; the rondo tune itself, which the *sotto voce* melody resembles, has never ventured past C. The *sotto voce* melody resembles the rondo tune, certainly, and also the introductory shepherds' piping, but it is experienced as something essentially new – as the true 'ausdrucks des Danks . . . oherr wir danken dir' to which Beethoven refers on a leaf once in the sketchbook.[10] This is by no means the only case of a Beethoven coda introducing essentially new material.

In the middle works Beethoven becomes so fond of the feeling of consummation achieved by upward linear motion in his codas that he sometimes applies the effect indiscriminately, in such a way that it can hardly be said to emerge organically from the themes themselves (first movements of the Quartet in C major Op. 59 No. 3, and the Violin Sonata in G major Op. 96). And in the rare cases where the impetus of a primary theme is downward, not upward, he is ready to consider carrying it even further down in the coda. The first movement of the 'Lebewohl' Sonata Op. 81a contains what is probably to be reckoned as his longest sonata-form coda, in relation to the other sections of the form. The 'Lebewohl' whole-notes (G–F–Eb) finally sink down a sixth in the left hand (Eb–D–C–Bb–Ab–G) while the right hand soars up to the highest octave with new scale figures. Something similar is perhaps to be detected in an unusually extended coda from the first period, that in the first movement of the Sonata in D major Op. 10 No. 3.

Readers will doubtless find some of these capsule interpretations more convincing than others; it would of course be foolish to try to insist on all particular cases. But I hope a sufficient number of them will seem obvious enough to suggest that thematic 'completion' – to pick what is perhaps the most convenient term – should be regarded as the centrally important feature in Beethoven's codas of the second period.

IV

This central contention, in turn, suggests two fairly extended glosses. The first concerns the familiar concept of the 'terminal development'.

---

[10] N II, p. 375. The leaf is actually in Berlin, SPK, Landsberg 10, pp. 163–4.

Vincent d'Indy seems to have introduced this term, and one feels some marginal sympathy for the many theorists who have adopted it in preference to the all-inclusive and therefore virtually meaningless term 'coda'. But the use of the terms 'terminal development' or 'second development' for Beethoven's codas seems to me as injudicious as Tovey's proposed use of 'coda' for Haydn's recapitulations. For if the main function of these codas is completion, their main function is not development, and therefore they should not be called any kind of 'development'. This is not to deny that Beethoven's codas incorporate development of thematic material; of course they do, and so do his expositions and recapitulations, and so most particularly do Haydn's recapitulations. The latter should not be called 'second developments' either (any more than they should be called 'codas'), even though they contain some development, since development is not their main function. Nor should Beethoven's codas, for the same reason, be called 'second' or 'terminal' developments.

In any case, the actual extent of the development process in so-called 'terminal developments' is often overstated. Consider the first movement of the 'Eroica', whose coda is often considered prototypical in this regard. It consists of four main parts: (1) preparatory moves from E♭ via D♭ and C to F minor, articulated by the opening motif; (2) the reappearance of the development theme, first in the supertonic and then at once in the tonic minor; (3) a twenty-eight-bar passage of dominant preparation, employing the opening motif; and (4) the climactic treatment of the main theme in fourfold repetition, mentioned above. Which of these counts as 'development'? Playing a melody through twice and bringing it to rest in the tonic feels more like recapitulation, or 'symmetrical resolution' in Rosen's sense. And when Beethoven fashions a characteristic, joyous litany-cum-*crescendo* out of his main theme he is no more 'developing' it than he would be if he were to make cadential phrases out of it in Mozart's manner. As for the passage of dominant preparation, here the essential point is that instead of treating the opening motif in a new, exploratory way, Beethoven repeats a previous process, that of the retransition in the development section itself. Though there is an added melodic idea, in respect to the original thematic material the passage sounds retrospective rather than innovative and therefore sounds not like a second development but like a recollection of the first – a recollection that is, again, in some sense recapitulatory. This distinction seems to me crucial. When Beethoven really writes a second development, in the Finale of the Eighth Symphony, he unveils a striking new thematic process which has not been exposed in the first development – and finds he has to add something very much like a second recapitulation to balance it out.[11]

Of course the propriety of the term 'terminal development' depends on how broadly one wishes to define the process of development. Calling every kind of thematic manipulation 'development' is, in my view, as unilluminating as lumping all codas under a single definition; one needs to distinguish concepts such as completion, transformation, liquidation, cadential treatment, and so on. But perhaps this will lead to argument. In today's analytical climate it may be easier to agree on a critique of the 'terminal development' idea from the standpoint of tonality. Almost always in Beethoven's codas – I can think of only two exceptions[12] – the harmony is guided to the tonic with absolute clarity. There is no sense of real harmonic digression. This was perfectly well understood by d'Indy, who introduced the concept of terminal development as follows:

> Beethoven voulut ajouter encore une sorte de coronnement, véritable *développement terminal* participant des états successifs de *translation* et *d'immobilité*, mais différant du *développement central* par l'orientation des modulations: ici, en effet, la tendance *conclusive* domine toutes les harmonies, subordonées à la grande cadence tonale dont elles ne sont que l'extension.[13]

But since, for his generation, thematic work was primary – d'Indy himself conceived of the sonata under the headings 'La Sonate Pré-Beethovénienne', 'La Sonate de Beethoven', and 'La Sonate Cyclique' – he was still prepared to call his crowning section a *'véritable* développement terminal'.

This cannot be the emphasis of theorists who have pondered the Mozart concertos, for example, and whose definition of a development section is based first and foremost on harmonic factors. Both Tovey and Rosen speak freely about the development process in certain Beethoven codas. But, whether by instinct or by design, they never once call a Beethoven coda a 'terminal development' or a 'second development' – and they are right.

---

[11] This way of viewing the movement has some currency – see, for example, Rudolf Kloiber, *Handbuch der klassischen und romantischen Symphonie* (Wiesbaden, 1964), p. 100; Leonard G. Ratner, 'Key Definition – A Structural Issue in Beethoven's Music', *Journal of the American Musicological Society*, xxiii (1970), 482; Robert Simpson, *Beethoven's Symphonies*, BBC Music Guides (London, 1970), p. 52 – though most commentators consider everything after bar 267 or bar 282 to be an unusually long coda.
[12] 'Appassionata' Sonata, first movement, and Quartet in Bb Op. 130, third movement.
[13] Vincent d'Indy, *Cours de composition musicale*, vol. ii/1 (Paris, n.p. [1909]), p. 283.

V

The second gloss concerns Beethoven's use in codas of themes other than the first theme, in particular the second (that is, the main lyric theme of the second key-area). More consistently than with Mozart and Haydn – almost invariably, in fact – Beethoven's codas deal with the first theme. In the few cases where he introduces the second theme he generally does so in a special way which mutes its possible functional role and subordinates it to the first.

Codas as a matter of course draw upon all the resources available to their composers for the purpose of strengthening large-scale cadences. Mention has been made of Mozart's cadential phrases, and Beethoven not infrequently begins his codas by presenting a good section of the main theme in one of the subdominant-area keys (subdominant, supertonic, flattened supertonic, even flattened submediant) before bringing it round to the tonic. Another powerful cadential device, the cadenza, was often imported from the concerto into other genres of Classical music. Explicit cadenzas are written into the codas of several early works by Beethoven (first and last movements of the Sonata in C major Op. 2 No. 3, first movement of the Cello Sonata in F major Op. 5 No. 1, first movement of the Quintet for Piano and Winds Op. 16), and theorists have pointed out less explicit cadenzas in others.

> The coda of the first movement of the 'Waldstein' Sonata contains a typical short cadenza, which is in strict time except for the pauses which lead to one of Beethoven's most beautiful strokes of genius, the cantabile theme of the second group with its cadence twice interrupted. The notorious octave glissando in the prestissimo coda to the finale is the beginning of another cadenza, which, though without definite theme, is rhythmically unbroken. In the interesting and perhaps unconscious study for the 'Waldstein' Sonata, the G major Sonata, op. 31, no. 1, there is a highly organized quasi-fugal cadenza towards the end of the finale, bar 206 onwards . . . The final presto of the Finale of the C minor Symphony is the outcome of a grand contrapuntal cadenza for the full orchestra.[14]

All this requires a certain liberality of definition, obviously. One must accept that cadenzas may move in strict time, as Tovey says, rather than employing tempo changes and fermate, and may also skip other stereotyped features such as the closing trill ('Waldstein' Sonata, first movement), closing fermata ('Waldstein', third movement), and perhaps even the opening $^6_4$ chord, so long as they maintain 'the

[14] Tovey, *Beethoven*, p. 113.

manner of an improvisation' and also the sense of a prolonged dominant resolving with special solidity after the improvisatory digression. The cadenza that Beethoven wrote in 1809 for the Second Piano Concerto even skips the final dominant chord, ending instead with an extended tonic pedal. Also irregular is the brilliant abortive cadenza for the Fifth Piano Concerto of the same year. After only twelve bars of scales and trills, the soloist plays the second theme in the tonic in its original *minore* form – an event that one would think to be a continuation of the cadenza if the horns did not enter softly with their own *maggiore* statement.

One would think so because another stereotyped feature of Beethoven's longer cadenzas is a recollection of the second theme – a *recollection* rather than its full-scale *return* or a mere *reference* to it, because the feeling is of a distant, nostalgic memory rather than of a firm restatement of reinterpretation. Generally (though not in the Fifth Piano Concerto) this feeling is enhanced initially by the use of a remote key and then dispelled by development. For examples see the first and third cadenzas to Piano Concerto No. 1, the cadenza to No. 3 (in the major dominant), the first cadenza to No. 4, and his first-movement cadenza to Mozart's D-minor Concerto.

'Distant recollection', I believe, describes the quality of the 'beautiful stroke of genius' that Tovey mentions in the 'cadenza' of the 'Waldstein' Sonata, first movement.[15] This quality contrasts with the immediacy and presence of the 'completed' statement of the first theme in the very last bars. A similar if somewhat more problematic case occurs in the Finale of the C-minor Sonata Op. 10 No. 1. Here the cadenza-like recollection of the second subject is indeed in a remote key, the Neapolitan (Example 4). Perhaps another sonata of the same period can also be brought into this picture. The 'Grande Sonate' in E♭ Op. 7 is a work in which some commentators have recognised Beethoven's first 'masterwork', also his first 'terminal development'. But again, what happens in the coda of the first movement here is not much like a development, even by the standards of the development section of this same piece. After a large-scale vi–ii–v progression (the development section also starts with a move to vi) the dominant is extended for thirty-two bars (bars 319–50), and over this lengthy extension phrases from the lyric second theme and the cadence group are recollected. Beethoven does not mark any fermata or *rallentando* and he writes neither a trill at the end of the dominant nor a $^6_4$ chord at

---

[15] For a related phenomenon in several works of the period 1815–16, see my remarks in 'An die ferne Geliebte', *Beethoven Studies* [1], ed. Alan Tyson (New York, 1973; London, 1974), pp. 137–8.

Example 4. Piano Sonata in C minor Op. 10 No. 1, Finale

the beginning – only a strange, weak I$^6_3$ chord (Example 5). Yet this passage too has the 'manner of an improvisation', at least to my ear, and the presentation of the second theme sounds much less emphatic than that of the first theme at the very end, after the dominant has finally resolved. The main theme is run curtly up the tonic arpeggio with a striking reversal of accent, a forecast of the 'completion' technique that has been traced in works of a later period.

The second theme near the end of the Finale of the 'Moonlight' Sonata Op. 27 No. 2 can also be heard as a recollection in this sense. Again, this theme comes in the middle of a sort of cadenza.

Example 5. Piano Sonata in E♭ Op. 7, first movement, coda

The outstanding exception to everything that has been said about the use of second themes in codas is the 'Appassionata' Sonata. In the coda of the opening movement the second theme comes not within the quasi-cadenza but before it, and then again after it. Another exceptional feature of the 'Appassionata' is the introductory quality of the first theme and the unusually close derivation of the second theme from the first; no doubt these local thematic features were bound to be reflected on a larger level in the form itself. Let us by all means acknowledge – nay, celebrate – masterworks that do not fit anyone's generalisations and make compelling artistic gestures unlike any others. Beethoven wrote many such works. But let us also be clear that as a general thing the role of the second (or third, or fourth) theme in Beethoven's codas is markedly subsidiary to that of the first. To speak of a category of 'polythematic coda', as Chodkowski does,[16] while taxonomically correct, seems to me to put exactly the wrong emphasis on the matter.

VI

It is known that the first movement of the Eighth Symphony originally had a much shorter coda than the one it has now; Hess gives two versions in his *Gesamtausgabe* supplement (Example 6).[17] Something had gone badly wrong with the idea of thematic 'completion', and Beethoven was able to right things only by taking strong diversionary measures. It would be pleasant to see this coda as the turning-point in his practice, but probably the change had already set in with the Seventh Symphony. Neither of the codas in the outer movements of that work, immensely powerful as they are, depends on or involves thematic 'completion'.

This technique is intimately bound up with the enthusiastic, affirmative moods of Beethoven's so-called 'heroic phase', expressed typically in orchestral works, and non-orchestral works conceived according to the symphonic ideal. That the first prominent example of it occurs in a symphony – in the very first symphony – hardly seems fortuitous. These moods seemed blatant enough to many musicians and listeners nurtured in *fin-de-siècle* elegance, pre-war *Angst*, and post-war sophistication – a circumstance that may help explain the prim response of some theorists of those periods to Beethoven's codas. However this

---

[16] Chodkowski, 'Problem kody w formie sonatowej Beethovena', pp. 86–8.
[17] Unfortunately it is not known what happened exactly: see *Werke für Orchester*, Ludwig van Beethoven: Sämtliche Werke: Supplemente zur Gesamtausgabe, ed. Willy Hess, vol. iv (Wiesbaden, 1961), pp. 70, 102, and bibliography given on p. [i].

Example 6. Symphony No. 8, first movement: original versions of the coda, bars 301ff

may be, even before the two symphonies of 1812 Beethoven began reinterpreting the symphonic ideal and transferring portions of his interest elsewhere. The process continued to the end of his life. The techniques associated with the heroic style naturally proved less and less useful to him. In the third period, codas of the kind I have been discussing become less frequent; Beethoven was now working with a new profundity, and this is reflected in his codas as much as in his expositions, developments, fugues, variations, and everything else. The study of Beethoven's third-period codas becomes a study of fascinating special cases, and to pursue it here would extend this essay beyond reasonable or at least appropriate limits.

Two comments only, then, by way of conclusion. First, in the codas as in other sections of his later works Beethoven sometimes returns with new appreciation to the methods of Mozart and Haydn. Mozartean cadential phrases turn up again in certain codas (first movements of the Quartets in Eb Op. 127, A minor Op. 132, and Bb Op. 130). He also remembered at least one bit of sleight-of-hand he had learned from Haydn in the 1790s. This was the trick of showing how the main theme (or the first cut or segment of it) can, all by itself, and with no extensions whatsoever, make a paradoxical but plausible conclusion for the entire movement (Quartet in F Op. 135, first movement).[18] He had used this device in the first movement of the Quartet in G Op. 18 No. 2, and more recently in the new Eighth Symphony coda.

Second, the techniques and moods of the 1800s were never entirely forgotten in the more rarefied atmosphere of the 1820s. One can see this from the Finale of the last quartet, Op. 135, which ends with what must surely be Beethoven's most unexpected coda. After a *si placet* repetition of the entire development and recapitulation (complete with the second slow 'Muss es sein?' section), and then three incredulous queries of 'Es muss sein?', Beethoven makes his coda by simply repeating the last twenty-eight bars of that same recapitulation. The passage is wonderfully rescored and graced by a new eight-bar obbligato in the first violin, but in all essentials it goes just as it has twice before. So the piece ends with the four-bar cadence theme; yet of course the cadence theme in this movement is simply a cheerful, uncomplicated completion of the 'Es muss sein!' theme, reaching up to the high octave. Thus in a very new context, both technical and emotional, the old technique can still be discerned in the most visionary works of Beethoven's last period.

---

[18] I have pointed to this device previously in *Beethoven Studies* [1], pp. 139–40, and *The Beethoven Quartets*, pp. 46, 48, 355. For another type of coda developed by Beethoven in the later quartets, see *The Beethoven Quartets*, pp. 182–4.

The Historical Background to the 'Heiliger Dankgesang' in Beethoven's A-minor Quartet Op. 132

Sieghard Brandenburg

The 'Heiliger Dankgesang eines Genesenen an die Gottheit' (Hymn of thanksgiving to the deity from a convalescent), which forms the third movement of the A-minor quartet Op. 132, is probably the composition that displays most clearly the interest of the ageing Beethoven in archaic musical forms. The additional label at the head of the movement, 'In the Lydian Mode', has certainly not been overlooked by music critics and the chorale-like character of the Molto adagio sections has also not gone unrecognised. Both features seem to be clear indications that in this quartet movement Beethoven wished to breathe new life into a kind of music that belonged to past history. In spite of what is known of this supposed or actual historicising intention, there has to date, surprisingly enough, been no serious attempt to describe the notions, ideas, or even possible models that Beethoven had in mind during the composition of this highly unusual movement.

Not that there is any lack of hints and suggestions. Many authors, for instance, recall Bach's chorale arrangements, the chorale preludes and chorale partitas, without at the same time feeling obliged to reinforce their associations by more precise comparative analyses, let alone to investigate Beethoven's knowledge of Bach.[1] The great majority of critics, however, refer to the music and music theory of the

---

[1] In *The Quartets of Beethoven* (New York, 1947), p. 196, Daniel Gregory Mason writes that Beethoven 'adventures in the taking over into the string quartet of the chorale-prelude of Bach, in which the phrases are separated . . . by brief contrapuntal interludes, often in Bach's case founded on the chorale melody itself . . . The three Molto adagios are three chorale-preludes on a single chorale.' Perhaps the unfortunate comparison with Bach's chorale preludes is the reason why Mason classifies the quartet movement as one of Beethoven's 'noble failures'. In *Beethoven's Late String Quartets* (London, 1968), p. 78, Harold Truscott describes the form of the 'Dankgesang' as 'chorale variation or chorale partita, coupled with a rondo shape'. In *Beethoven: i Quartetti Galitzine e la Grande Fuga* (Turin, 1969), Massimo Mila lists – mainly on the basis of secondary

sixteenth century. Beethoven could have instructed himself on the nature and laws of the Lydian mode (or fifth mode) from the treatises of Glarean and Zarlino,[2] and he could have studied the style and spirit of genuine church music from the practical example of Palestrina's works and those of other earlier composers.[3] Kerman, too, who has provided what is no doubt the subtlest and most balanced critique of the A-minor Quartet, sees Beethoven in the grip of the 'vogue for medieval Catholicism expressed by Romantic poets like Brentano and Novalis', and in his opinion the 'Heiliger Dankgesang' 'seems to anticipate the nineteenth-century Palestrina revival in the way that *Pulcinella* anticipated the current Vivaldi fashion'.[4] But in fact those authors who suppose that Beethoven was looking back to the Middle Ages or (what is almost the same thing) to the Renaissance, whether for Romantic or for other motives, overlook certain important questions, no matter how self-evident their views may seem to be. If Beethoven did not merely have a kind of antiquarian interest in older theoretical writers, but also in fact read Glarean's *Dodecachordon* and Zarlino's *Le istitutioni harmoniche* for his own further education, one needs to investigate what he hoped to find there and what he possibly did find. Was it merely the bare characteristic features (borrowed from writers of antiquity) of the old church modes, as Kirkendale would have us believe? And, again, does a stylistic analysis confirm Palestrina as a prototype? Surely not.

Only recently the thesis has been advanced that Palestrina's Gloria from the *Magnificat tertii toni* provided Beethoven with a direct model

literature – the most diverse historical prototypes for the 'Dankgesang', the variation technique of which he compares with the chorale arrangements by German organists of the time of Bach: 'si tratta della tecnica del "corale figurato", cara agli antichi organisti tedeschi del tempo di Bach, cioè del corale trattato non già con mere figure d'accompagnamento, ma con l'aggiunta di altre voci dotate d'autonomo contenuto e significato musicale' (p. 80).

[2] See Martin Cooper, *Beethoven: the Last Decade* (London, 1970), pp. 127 and 245, and Warren Kirkendale, 'Beethovens Missa solemnis und die rhetorische Tradition', in *Beethoven-Symposion Wien 1970: Bericht* (Vienna, 1971), p. 132, make a plausible case (on the basis of entries in two conversation books of 1819 and 1820) that Beethoven became interested in theoretical writings of the sixteenth century and that he possibly borrowed for study purposes the *Dodecachordon* of Glarean and an unidentified work by Zarlino (*Le istitutioni harmoniche*?) from the library of Prince Lobkowitz.

[3] In the opinion of Basil Lam (*Beethoven String Quartets*, BBC Music Guides, (London, 1975), vol. ii, p. 27) 'Each of the five phrases is harmonised in the purest ancient style.' In *Beethoven's Last Quartets* (3rd edn, London, 1948), p. 64, Roger Fiske writes: 'This Canzona has something of the timeless spirit of Palestrina, and must be listened to in the same spirit.'

[4] Joseph Kerman, *The Beethoven Quartets* (New York and London, 1967), p. 254.

The Historical Background to the 'Heiliger Dankgesang'   163

for the 'Heiliger Dankgesang'.[5] The supporting arguments are, however, so weak that they will probably persuade no one apart from their author – although the fact that at some time in the 1820s Beethoven copied this Gloria from an unknown source with the evident aim of studying modal harmony is undoubtedly noteworthy.[6] The question of the possible models and of the historically datable ideals in the sphere of church music that may have influenced the composition of the 'Heiliger Dankgesang' must therefore still be considered as unanswered. They will be the theme of the following essay, in which the sketches for this movement will be treated particularly fully; for if there is any source that can give us unbiased information about Beethoven's compositional plans and aims, it is surely the sketches.

The first sketches that clearly relate to the third movement of Op. 132 are found on fols. 2v and 3r of the 'de Roda' Sketchbook.[7] They can

[5] Abraham Klimowitsky, 'Ein "Gloria" von Palestrina als Modell des "Heiligen Dankgesanges" aus Beethovens Streichquartett op. 132', in *Bericht über den Internationalen Beethoven-Kongress, Berlin 1977*, ed. Harry Goldschmidt, Karl-Heinz Köhler, and Konrad Niemann (Leipzig, 1978), pp. 513–17 (pp. 223–9 in the original Russian text). The *Magnificat tertii toni* appears in the first book of the *Magnificat octo tonum*, which was published simultaneously in Rome and Venice in two editions of 1591.
[6] The manuscript – a single leaf of *Hochformat* paper, with twenty staves – is in the State Conservatory, Leningrad. It is not possible at present to date it more exactly. Klimowitsky makes the unintelligible statement that Beethoven changed the accidentals that were in the (unknown) source that he followed and added new ones of his own, so as to bring the harmony into line with modern usage. Apart from the fact that there is no evidence for this in the manuscript, it would mean that Beethoven had undermined his own attempt at studying modal harmony in an original source. That he was in fact interested in the harmony of the Gloria is no doubt indicated by the characteristically unorthodox figuring of the bass, which he certainly did not take over from his source but added himself. (There is evidence for this in the manuscript.) Some time in 1826 – to judge from the paper-type – Beethoven also copied a four-part *Pueri Hebraeorum* (Vienna, GdM, A 80) from a source that might well have been the *Stichvorlage* to Gottlieb von Tucher's collection of old church music, of which the first part, with a dedication to Beethoven, was published early in 1827 (*Kirchengesänge der berühmtesten älteren italiänischen Meister gesammelt und dem Herrn Ludwig van Beethoven gewidmet . . . 1te Lieferung* (Vienna, 1827)). The motet (no. 4 on pp. 7–10) is here ascribed to Palestrina. On Tucher's relationship with Beethoven see Johannes Zahn, 'Tucher, Gottlieb von', *Allgemeine Deutsche Biographie*, vol. xxxviii (Leipzig, 1894), p. 768. The second part of Tucher's collection (1828) is dedicated to A. F. J. Thibaut of Heidelberg, not (as Zahn and several other authors state) to Beethoven. The above-mentioned Gloria is not contained in either part of the collection.
[7] The surviving sketch material for the third movement of Op. 132 is as follows: Bonn, Beethovenhaus, NE 47 (SBH 680) (the large-format 'de Roda' Sketchbook); Berlin, DSB, Artaria 205, bundle 7 (a pocket sketchbook which was originally unbound); Moscow, Central (Glinka) Museum for Music Culture (the so-called 'Moscow' Pocket

probably be dated to the beginning of May 1825, for they are directly preceded by some sketches (on fol. lv) for the canon 'Das Schöne zu dem Guten' WoO 203, which Beethoven enclosed as a parting present to Ludwig Rellstab in his letter of 3 May 1825 (Anderson no. 1366b). The key of these 'concept' sketches is clearly F major. There are no suggestions of modal harmony or melody. But at the same time it is clear that Beethoven already had the intention here of writing a kind of chorale. He obviously adhered to the current type of 'modern' church hymn that was in use in the eighteenth century and the beginning of the nineteenth in both Protestant and Catholic churches, predominantly in extra-liturgical contexts. Beethoven's plan can be made out: between the individual lines of the hymn there were to be extended interludes (each roughly twice as long as a line of the hymn), in a style that was partly one of lyrical narrative, partly one of innocent humour (Example 1).

At the end of the chorale, the melody of which was drafted in a series of separate stages, Beethoven planned to have an extended free postlude. This was to end in F minor (fol. 2v: 'in F mol aufhör[en]'), and after a bold chromatic progression to F♯ minor was to lead, via a 'Recitativ' marked 'Eingang zum Al[legr]o', to a fairly lightweight Finale in A major (Example 2). On the next two pages of the sketchbook (fol. 4r, and then fol. 3v) Beethoven experimented with a harmonically less remote transition: the postlude to the chorale section (in 3/4 time) ends much more modestly, in F major; a recitative follows in which the tempo accelerates and which leads via D minor to a *presto* Finale in A minor, having the theme of the final version (Example 3).

Beethoven soon abandoned this first plan for a chorale movement. The following pages of the 'de Roda' Sketchbook show that he was able to envisage quite different forms and ones characterised by a totally different expressive intent for the slow movement of his already half-completed A-minor Quartet. Any notions about a preconceived extra-musical programme for the Quartet as a whole can accordingly be dismissed as irrelevant.[8] There is, for instance, a draft for an 'Andante

Sketchbook); Berlin, SPK, Artaria 213, Parts 1 and 2 (score sketches); Vienna, GdM, A 58 (score sketch); Koblenz, Wegeler Collection (score sketch). While still at work on the first movement Beethoven planned a slow third movement in F major, but one that shows no resemblance to the 'Dankgesang'. See N II, p. 549, where Nottebohm cites a draft in Berlin, SPK, Autograph 11, Part 2, fols. 25v–26r.

[8] Kerman (*The Beethoven Quartets*, p. 262) claims to find the following programme: 'a violent short-circuit to the world of pain that was opened up in the first movement and turned away from in the interim'. But the sketches in 'de Roda' described above (fols. 3r–2v), with a far less dramatic recitative and a Finale in A major, show clearly enough that there was no plan of this sort to portray pain.

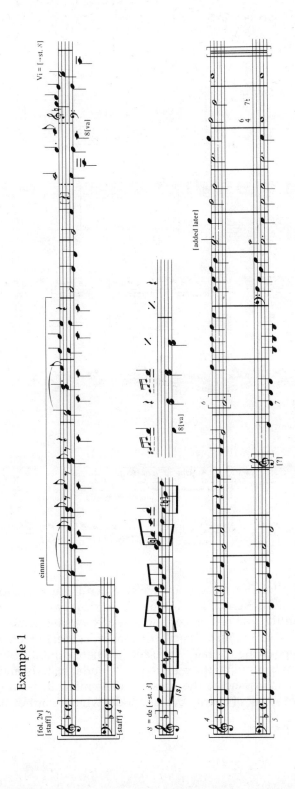

Example 1

Example 2

Example 3

scherzoso' (fol. 5v), for a 'Romanze erzählend' (fol. 6r), and a musical portrayal of 'Lachen' (fol. 4v). What these ideas have in common is no more than the key of F major and a relatively slow tempo.

Then on fols. 6r, 5v, 6v, and 7r (in that order) Beethoven returned to the concept of the chorale. The sketches here exhibit from the start, quite unambiguously, the adherence to modal melody and harmony that is characteristic of the finished movement. It is true that one cannot yet speak of a strict Lydian mode, whether or not at this stage anything of the sort was intended. The B♭ sign still makes its appearance both at the system-brace (accolade) and before individual notes; and at the same time the notes G and C are occasionally altered to G♯ and C♯. Thus the sketches on these leaves show merely an attempt at modal harmony centred on F (Example 4). No doubt the mode is defined more and more strictly in the subsequent sketches; yet the term 'Lydian' appears first in the inscription over the movement in the autograph. This inscription, it is perfectly clear, was added at a late stage, after the completion of the quartet as a whole and after the first manuscript parts of it were made by Joseph Linke and Karl Holz in the middle of August 1825. Cassiodorus's characterisation of the Lydian mode (as found in Zarlino) will have played no role in the movement's origins.[9]

One further fact can be gleaned directly from the sketches on these pages. The trenchant alterations to which Beethoven subjected the individual lines of the chorale show that he did not deal with it as a cantus prius factus – not even one serving as a model for imitation. For the same reason the melody of the 'Dankgesang' cannot be a compilation of quotations from a number of chants or other tunes, in the manner of a quodlibet.[10] It is only in a very abstract way and with the aim of stylistic assimilation that Beethoven could have taken a variety of chants as his models. The changes in the melody, as Example 4 shows, are linked with fundamental changes in the harmony. There are only a few chord sequences that Beethoven retained right through to the final version. Hence the possibility of a particular polyphonic model can be ruled out in just the same way as the possibility of a pre-existent cantus firmus. It is true that, in order to understand the peculiarities of modal harmony, Beethoven may have studied a number of sixteenth-century polyphonic compositions. But the intention of imitating this style, scarcely an end in itself, is (as will be shown in

---

[9] Kirkendale ('Beethovens Missa solemnis', p. 132) claims that Beethoven chose the Lydian mode because of the characterisation of it that he found in Zarlino's *Le istitutioni harmoniche*: 'Vuole Cassiodoro . . . che 'l Lidio sia remedio contra le fatiche dell'animo, & similmente contra quelle del corpo.' ((Venice, 1558), p. 303) Strictly speaking, this characterisation does not fit the movement, which is a 'Hymn of thanksgiving' from someone who is already a 'convalescent'.

[10] In his article 'Gregorianischer Stil in Beethovens Streichquartett op. 132', *Bericht über den Internationalen Musikwissenschaftlichen Kongress, Berlin 1974*, ed. Hellmut Kühn and Peter Nitsche (Kassel, 1980), pp. 373–6, Warren Kirkendale presents fragments of four different Gregorian chants which he claims served as models for Beethoven's chorale. But in the second part of his paper he is forced to refute his argument on the evidence of the sketches. He also later points out that Beethoven probably never had access to any of those melodies.

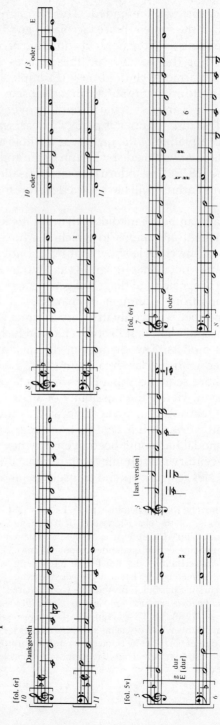

Example 4

what follows) accompanied by other ideas that likewise contributed to the composition of the 'Dankgesang' and prevented a stylistic copy. According to the account of the Silesian organist Karl Gottlieb Freudenberg (1797–1869), Beethoven expressly declared himself against imitating Palestrina. And this statement is all the more interesting as it was made shortly after the completion of the 'Heiliger Dankgesang'.[11]

It is not known how much time intervened between the first chorale concept on fols. 2v–3r of the 'de Roda' Sketchbook and the sketches on fols. 6r–5v–6v. Possibly it was two or three weeks, for his attack of jaundice, which lasted from the middle of April to the beginning of May 1825, left Beethoven very weak, and according to his own testimony it was only after the middle of May that he began normal working once more.[12] But even if he put down nothing in writing during these weeks, he must nevertheless have carried out intensive work on the chorale in his head; otherwise the progress seen on fols. 5, 6, and 7 is scarcely explicable.

What were the impulses that directed Beethoven's gaze so decisively towards the music of the past – if it was in fact 'the past' that he was intending to represent? It may well be that he recalled to mind some earlier plans. Nottebohm was the first writer to draw attention to a sketchleaf of the year 1818 on which Beethoven declared his intention of introducing an 'Adagio Cantique' or 'Cantique Eclesiastique' into a symphony 'in the old modes' that he was planning at that time.[13] In almost the whole of the later literature this remark is linked with the third movement of Op. 132, as if the 'Dankgesang' were nothing other than a subsequent realisation of that idea of 1818. Although I do not intend to deny that there may be some link, closer examination will show that the plan conceived in 1818 does not match the movement brought to fruition in Op. 132. In the former Beethoven had in mind a kind of *Te Deum* ('Herr Gott dich loben wir – alleluja'), and he was also considering a 'griechische Mithos' (Greek myth) as a text to be sung in the 'Adagio Cantique'. The third movement of the A-minor String Quartet, however, is given the description 'Dankgebeth' (Prayer of

---

[11] Freudenberg is known to have met Beethoven one afternoon in July 1825; see Thayer–Deiters–Riemann v, pp. 223–4.

[12] See Beethoven's letter of 17 May 1825 to his nephew (Anderson no. 1372): 'I am beginning to compose a fair amount again, but in this extremely gloomy, cold weather it is almost impossible to achieve anything.'

[13] Gustav Nottebohm, 'Skizzen zur neunten Symphonie', *Musikalisches Wochenblatt*, vii (1876), 185; reprinted in N II, p. 163. The sketchleaf is now in the Beethovenhaus, Bonn (BSk 8 (SBH 652)).

thanksgiving) early on in the sketches – as early as the first appearance of modal harmony on fol. 6r of 'de Roda'. In 1818 the form of the movement was still quite undecided: 'either an independent piece', wrote Beethoven at the time, 'or an introduction to a fugue'. The characteristic five-section structure of the 'Heiliger Dankgesang', with the alternation of Lydian F and D major in their respective tempi of Molto adagio and Andante, and the characteristic shape of the sections built round the chorale, are not accounted for by the jottings of 1818. Thus, like many another remark of Beethoven's quoted in this context,[14] these jottings are no more than evidence of his continuing interest in church music (especially that of earlier times), independent of his own work on settings of the Mass. But the clear difference between the drafts on fols. 2–3 and those on fols. 5–6 in 'de Roda', as well as the further development in the sketches up to the final version, permit the conclusion that Beethoven made a new (and no doubt more purposeful) attempt to come to terms with the subject of chorales, modes, and ancient and modern church music, either by recalling to mind what he had read or heard earlier, or by embarking on a new study of the relevant literature.

What writings on church music can Beethoven have known and read? The question is unavoidable; and the books that were in his *Nachlass* in 1827 naturally come under consideration first. These were:

Georg Joseph Vogler
Abt Vogler's Choral-System (Copenhagen and Stockholm, 1800; another edition was published in Offenbach by J. André, without date)[15]

Justin Heinrich Knecht
Vollständige Orgelschule für Anfänger und Geübtere, 3 vols. (Leipzig, 1795, 1796, 1798)

Daniel Gottlob Türk
Von den wichtigsten Pflichten eines Organisten: ein Beytrag zur Verbesserung der Musikalischen Liturgie (Halle, 1787)

Daniel Gottlob Türk
Kurze Anweisung zum Generalbasspielen (Halle and Leipzig, 1791)[16]

---

[14] These utterances of Beethoven's are collected in Warren Kirkendale, *Fuge und Fugato in der Kammermusik des Rokoko und der Klassik* (Tutzing, 1966), pp. 287–8; Eng. trans., rev. (Durham, N.C., 1979), pp. 249–50.

[15] It is not known which of the two editions was owned by Beethoven.

[16] In fact Beethoven owned two copies of this book, one of which is now in the Gesellschaft der Musikfreunde in Vienna. An inscription by Beethoven on the inside of the front cover states that it had once belonged to his brother Carl.

Apart from these books devoted to church music Beethoven may well have studied the relevant passages in the more comprehensive writings of Kirnberger, Koch, and many other theoreticians. He may also have known a variety of articles in periodicals. There is plenty of evidence that he read the *Musikalische Zeitungen* not only of Leipzig but of Vienna and Berlin as well; a number of copies of them were in his *Nachlass*. He informed the publishing house of Schott that the periodical *Caecilia*, which had been coming out since 1824, needed to 'pass his censorship', [17] and from then on all copies of it were sent to him gratis. All four magazines contain a wealth of information on historical matters. The Leipzig *Allgemeine musikalische Zeitung* in particular, the most important of the four, published a considerable number of very thorough articles on church music, as well as reviews of theoretical writings and performing editions, some of them very detailed. Among these may be mentioned E. T. A. Hoffmann's essay 'Alte und neue Kirchenmusik' (1814)[18] and the subjectively religious article by the Würzburg professor C. W. Fröhlich, 'Ueber die musikalische Feyer des katholischen Gottesdienstes überhaupt, und die Art einer dem Zeitbedürfnisse gemässen Einrichtung und Verbesserung derselben' (1820).[19]

In spite of some controversies on points of detail – for instance, on the need or otherwise for preludes and interludes – the accounts in the books and periodicals just mentioned show a remarkable uniformity in their approach to the nature and true aims of church music, and especially of the chorale. This uniformity extends beyond denominational bounds,[20] at any rate at the theoretical level, and Enlightenment-inspired views, orientated towards contemporary practice, are distinguishable from Romantic, historicising views more by language than by content. The broad agreement between the two may have made it easier for Beethoven, the one-time assistant organist at the electoral court in Bonn, to blend Enlightenment ideas with historicising ideas. Although there may have been changes in the practice of church music over the period that had elapsed since the appearance of Türk's

---

[17] See Beethoven's letter to Bernhard Schotts Söhne of 20 May 1824 (Anderson no. 1290).
[18] *Allgemeine musikalische Zeitung*, xvi (1814), cols. 577–84, 593–603, 611–19.
[19] *Allgemeine musikalische Zeitung*, xxii (1820), cols. 369–80, 389–96, 405–13, 421–30.
[20] The *Vollständige Orgelschule* of J. H. Knecht, a writer from the south-west corner of the Holy Roman Empire, an area deeply divided in both politics and religion, addresses itself to Protestant and Catholic organists in equal measure. In the third volume, which is especially relevant to the present inquiry (and which is subtitled: 'A theoretical and practical treatise on playing chorales on the organ, with reference to both Protestant and Catholic services'), examples are chosen from Protestant and Catholic hymnbooks in almost equal numbers.

fundamental essay on 'an organist's principal duties', the essential theoretical demands nevertheless remained the same, as is indicated by the concise summary by the Altenburg cantor 'F.S.D.' (Johann Friedrich Samuel Döring), 'Einiges über die Behandlung des Chorals beym Kirchengesange' in the Leipzig *Allgemeine musikalische Zeitung* of 1823.[21] In what follows I shall accordingly take Türk's statements as my starting-point, so as to demonstrate how strongly Beethoven was bound to contemporary thinking in the 'Heiliger Dankgesang' – even where he was apparently imitating earlier music in a historicising way – and how he converted it to his own purposes.

What distinguishes Türk's book *Von den wichtigsten Pflichten eines Organisten* from Knecht's *Vollständige Orgelschule* and Vogler's *Choral-System* is its clear exposition of the ideals of church music, behind which technical details recede and are treated merely as side-issues. It is this concentration on a few basic principles that guaranteed the work over the decades an enduring contemporary quality; this enabled it to appear at Halle in a second edition (revised by Friedrich Naue) as late as 1838. By contrast Knecht's *Vollständige Orgelschule*, because it was tied too closely to the practices of organists at the end of the eighteenth century, was quickly overtaken by the taste of the times and became out of date – even though it is one of the most comprehensive works of its kind. Knecht's later publications on church music in the *Allgemeine musikalische Zeitung* are evidence of a change in his attitudes in the direction of stricter north German ideals. In his *Vollständige Orgelschule* there is no clear distinction drawn between the secular and the sacred styles; this is an important matter for Türk (and for Johann Adam Hiller before him), and later became a generally accepted tenet of church music theory.

Vogler's *Choral-System*, which received its most favourable assessment from Knecht,[22] is a curious mixture of idiosyncratic sectarianism, expertise in music history and ethnology, and the ideas of the Enlightenment. Its aims, 'the most scrupulous preservation of genuine melodies, the strictest cleansing of them from all dross and unclean accretions',[23] may well have found general acceptance among his contemporaries; but his simplifying reconstructions of old melodies – above all his pedantic correcting of J. S. Bach's four-part chorales (edited by C. P. E. Bach and J. P. Kirnberger, Leipzig, 1784–7) – and his outbursts against Carl Heinrich Graun, Kirnberger, and Kühnau will

---

[21] *Allgemeine musikalische Zeitung*, xxv (1823), cols. 661–5, signed 'F.S.D.'.
[22] See his review in the *Allgemeine musikalische Zeitung*, iii (1801), cols. 264–9, 286–9, 315–18.
[23] Vogler, *Choral-System*, p. 38.

have won him as little sympathy as his altercation with Forkel.[24] Even in his lifetime he was suspected of an owlish dilettantism, to which criticism he reacted sharply though also with self-irony. I can hardly believe that Beethoven found much to his taste in Vogler's *Choral-System*; Türk must have been of greater importance to him, and to a lesser degree Knecht and the numerous articles on church music in the *Allgemeine musikalische Zeitung*.

As an art form the chorale presents a double aspect. As the property of school-teachers and village organists, it was commonly regarded as primitive, inartistic, and provincial, and it held little attraction for most composers and virtuosi. But from another point of view it corresponded precisely in its artlessness to the ideal of simplicity, naturalness, and closeness to the people, and this always guaranteed it a certain dutiful respect. So when criticism was directed at the chorale, it was not at the chorale itself but principally at the way it was executed. Türk and other choir-masters who wielded the pen describe the chorale somewhat defensively as one of the most important musical genres: 'Perhaps there is nothing in music to surpass the chorale melody, which if it is properly treated contains so much that is noble, sublime, solemn, touching, and reverent, that anyone who is not entirely insensitive must be filled with emotion.'[25]

Although the chorale can have a variety of contents and can express a whole range of feelings, its collective tone is one of dignified solemnity and its purpose is to induce reverence. So an especially slow tempo is appropriate. 'Too slow' is always better, according to Türk's teaching, than 'the opposite'. 'The chorale should never be taken fast; for it loses its whole dignity as soon as one adopts a somewhat rapid tempo.'[26] An anonymous author in the *Allgemeine musikalische Zeitung* fixes the tempo of the chorale as *adagio molto*;[27] this was precisely the tempo marking that Beethoven chose for the 'Dankgesang', and in a score-sketch[28] he added to it the inscription 'Mit Andacht' (with reverence). Georg Feder reports some contemporary tempo markings for the chorale in his astute essay on the decay and the subsequent restoration of Protestant church music during the eighteenth and

---

[24] See for instance the critical marginal notes of Georg Poelchau in his copy of Vogler's *Choral-System* (Berlin, DSB, G v 153).
[25] Türk, *Von den wichtigsten Pflichten eines Organisten*, pp. 44–5.
[26] *Ibid.*, p. 83.
[27] 'Ein Wort über Zwischenspiele beym Choral', *Allgemeine musikalische Zeitung*, v (1803), col. 814.
[28] Berlin, SPK, Artaria 213, Part 1, p. 37.

nineteenth centuries.[29] According to him the schoolmaster Johann Ernst Häuser in 1834 proposed an 'acceleration' to ♩ = 30 with the chorale notated in minims. This tempo approximately equals the duration of two pulse-beats per minim, as is confirmed by several other authors. As Feder points out, in practice the tempo of the chorale was even slower. As a striking example he quotes from a certain Johann Daniel von der Heydt, who stated that a duration of four pulse-beats per syllable (= 1 minim; or c. ♩ = 15) and a duration of eight to twelve pulse-beats for the fermata at the end of a line (about eight to twelve seconds) were employed in Baden in south Germany. To judge from this, the extremely slow tempo of the 'Heiliger Dankgesang' fully corresponds to contemporary chorale singing. It would be anachronistic either to suppose that Beethoven intended to imitate in a historicising way the slow tempo of Renaissance music (as it was understood by the Romantics) or to speculate that, for some strange aesthetic effect, he wanted to write against the instruments like certain twentieth-century composers.

Along with the slow, 'pathetic' tempo goes the notation of the melody in uniform minims, which are used by almost all these authors. The 4/4 notation that came to predominate in the later part of the nineteenth century is tolerated only for reasons of economy of space. According to Türk, the normal metre indication in bars in duple time is C but in his book of four-part chorales, which has survived in a manuscript copy,[30] the *alla breve* ₡ is used exclusively, as it is in the third volume of Knecht's *Vollständige Orgelschule*. Other authors give no metre indication and make no strict division into bars of equal length by means of bar-lines. Beethoven obviously had difficulty in finding the appropriate metre indication for the 'Dankgesang'. The first sketches on fols. 2–3 of 'de Roda' and the much more advanced ones on fol. 7r show that he experimented with a 4/4 notation in common time. The sketches on fols. 5–6 have the notation of two minims to the bar that is typical of the final version, but they are in *alla breve* metre. In theory C with four crotchets and ₡ with two minims represent the same tempo. The common-time signature in combination with a notation of two minims in the final version might have meant a slowing of the tempo to half its speed, had Beethoven not merely been adapting a notational practice that appeared to him to be correct.

Contemporary theory devotes considerable space to the harmonic

---

[29] Georg Feder, 'Verfall und Restauration', *Geschichte der evangelischen Kirchenmusik*, ed. Friedrich Blume, Georg Feder and others (2nd edn, Kassel, 1965), p. 232.
[30] Berlin, SPK, Mus. ms. 22079.

and polyphonic treatment of the chorale. There is general agreement that the melody should not be altered by passing-notes, ornamentation, or accidentals. This stipulation is a reaction to the fussy practice of the *galant* style, under which not even the chorale was spared. The accompanying parts are to be simple, in strict style, chiefly note against note, largely without dissonances, and as singable as possible. Beethoven obviously felt himself bound by this rule.[31] In order to make the harmony 'strong' and richly varied, secondary triads should be used liberally. Modulations into especially remote keys, for many organists (including the young Beethoven) a demonstration of their virtuosity, are to be avoided in the interests of preserving simplicity and naturalness. Four-part writing is the rule, although exceptions are permitted for the sake of variety or with the aim of creating dynamic effects. An unnamed author in the *Allgemeine musikalische Zeitung* of 1804 recommends producing a *crescendo* or *diminuendo* by gradually increasing or decreasing the number of voices 'in accordance with the mood of the chorale', in a manner corresponding to the dynamic possibilities of the Vogler organs fitted with a swell.[32] These instructions readily call to mind the *crescendo* and *decrescendo* signs in Beethoven's 'Dankgesang' and the occasional doubling of parts in open chord positions and at the dynamic climaxes.

In the interests of a greater diversity and with the representation of the text in mind, Türk and other authors ask for the accompaniment of the chorale to be varied from verse to verse.[33] Beethoven was aware of this requirement from his youthful days, as the sketches for the *Lamentations of Jeremiah* make clear.[34] A whole range of variation tech-

---

[31] In the first verse of the chorale, bars 1–30, Beethoven is remarkably sparing of dissonances.

[32] 'It is well known that Vogler builds and restores organs that are fitted with wind-swells for producing *crescendi* and *diminuendi*. Should there not be some way of partially imitating such effects in organs that do not enjoy that improvement? – Perhaps it could be done in this way: where the mood of the chorale suggests a *crescendo* the parts could gradually be doubled in both hands; a *diminuendo* could be made by gradually reducing them.' ('Aphorismen über Orgelspiel, Choralgesang und Kirchenmusik', *Allgemeine musikalische Zeitung*, vi (1804), col. 439.)

[33] Knecht discusses this subject in very great detail. His treatment of it is a kind of compendium of all the ways of handling a chorale, and by including melodic figuration, canonic variations, and chorale fugues, he ranges far beyond the liturgical use of chorales.

[34] See Joseph Kerman, ed., *Ludwig van Beethoven: Autograph Miscellany from circa 1786 to 1799: British Museum Additional Manuscript 29801, ff. 39–162 (the 'Kafka Sketchbook')* (London, 1970), vol. i (facsimile), fol. 96r; vol. ii (transcription), p. 131. For a detailed discussion see Richard Kramer, 'Notes to Beethoven's Education', *Journal of the American Musicological Society*, xxviii (1975), 72–101 (especially 76–86).

niques is available to an organist: he can ring changes on the registration and harmony, and the accompanying parts can provide an independent counterpoint. This last possibility is discussed by Türk in some detail: 'the cantus firmus can be played on another keyboard, while the organist weaves small contrapuntal subjects into the other, accompanying parts and develops them, etc., but in the process the melody must continue its simple pace quite undisturbed and be spared from any additions'.[35] The second strophe of the 'Heilige Dankgesang' obviously exemplifies this contrapuntal variation technique: the three lower parts proceed in a kind of stylised, very free counterpoint of the fourth species (over which Albrechtsberger would probably merely have shaken his head), while the cantus firmus, unaltered melodically, is displaced an octave higher as if to another register, another 'manual'. This is not an idea that Beethoven reached slowly, only in the course of sketching: it is found fully developed in the sketches when the second strophe of the chorale makes its first appearance. It seems to me highly probable that Beethoven adopted it as a current *topos* in the setting of chorales. Not that I wish to claim that Beethoven must have lifted it directly from Türk's book: since Türk's teaching was a widely shared intellectual property and broadly corresponds to the practice of organists at the time, Beethoven could have received this hint from other texts. And in any case contrapuntal variations are to be found as early as the sketches for the *Lamentations of Jeremiah*.

Türk, Knecht, Vogler, the historian E. L. Gerber, and most other authors clearly prefer the old modal melodies to the modern ones in major and minor keys. This is an attitude which in the eighteenth century already had a long tradition, but which hardened significantly in the first decades of the nineteenth century and finally led to the great church-music reforms of the two denominations. In 1819 and 1821 there appeared in the *Allgemeine musikalische Zeitung* two series of articles by the English organist Peter Mortimer, then living in Germany, in which the ancient melodies from the period of the Reformation were discussed in the same revivalist spirit and furnished with numerous examples.[36]

---

[35] Türk, *Von den wichtigsten Pflichten eines Organisten*, pp. 103–4.

[36] 'Der Choralgesang zur Zeit der Reformation, oder: Versuch, die Frage zu beantworten: Woher kommt es, dass in den Choral-Melodien der Alten etwas ist, das heut zu Tage nicht mehr erreicht wird?', *Allgemeine musikalische Zeitung*, xxi (1819), cols. 277–82, 293–9. The article is a preliminary announcement and description of Mortimer's collection of chorales, which has the same name and which was published in Berlin in 1821. 'Über Kirchentonarten', *Allgemeine musikalische Zeitung*, xxiii (1821), cols. 33–9, 49–54, 65–74 appeared as a postscript to it.

The motives for having recourse to the hymns of the sixteenth and seventeenth centuries were of many kinds, and it would be misleading to attribute them all to a historicising, Romantic enthusiasm. Since time immemorial the ancient modal chorales had been a touchstone of an organist's skill in harmony; accordingly they became a requirement of his education. For the north German advocates of *Empfindsamkeit* and the Enlightenment the preference for ancient melodies represents primarily a reaction against the *galant* style. It is true that they reject the newer church hymns on the same grounds as the Romantics – for being insipid and profane – but they are less rigorous, and above all they are no party to the value judgment that represents as church music's historical summit the compositions of the (Italian) Renaissance. Thus their recommendations for the 'improvement' (not the renovation) of church music are not aimed at stylistic copying but at the formulation of ideals: ideals which because of their abstract nature leave great freedom for realisation in practice. As a result the Protestant organists Türk, Knecht, and Rinck, and the Catholic Abbé Vogler enjoy the freedom of offering their own works and those of their established contemporaries as typical patterns (not as models); Romanticism on the other hand provides anthologies of older music.

As a creative artist Beethoven inclined somewhat to the position of the Enlightenment. This is shown especially by the way in which he treated modal harmony. Strictly speaking, according to the theorists, in a modal chorale no accidentals are permissible either in the melody or in the accompanying parts, since they would destroy the particular character of the mode. But, except for the part with the melody, Türk and many other authors do not call for so strict a rule.[37] In the accompanying parts they follow a *Baroque* tradition and make fairly liberal use of accidentals, in order to introduce secondary triads via passing dominants (Example 5).

Thus the demands of theory are not automatically adopted in a practice in which tradition proves overwhelming. Least of all was an obligation to complete strictness felt in relation to the Lydian mode, since it had been regarded as extinct since the days of Luther. Although Beethoven certainly did not take the chorale movements of Türk, Knecht, and Vogler as his prototypes, he nevertheless started from the contemporary pseudo-modal harmony. As has already been

[37] 'If these modes were to be treated with complete strictness, no G♯s, C♯s, B♭s, etc. would be allowed even in the harmony; but today the other parts are not treated so strictly, provided that the melody stays unchanged.' (Türk, *Von den wichtigsten Pflichten eines Organisten*, pp. 80–1.)

Example 5. Türk, *Von den wichtigsten Pflichten eines Organisten*, pp. 80–1

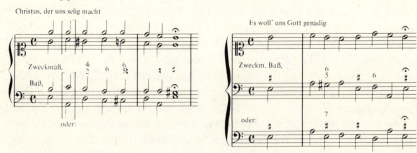

mentioned, the B♭ sign is not at first consistently eliminated in the sketches; example 4 still shows even a B♭ chord. The Phrygian half-close to the second line of the chorale in a sketch on fol. 7r of the 'de Roda' Sketchbook likewise implies a B♭ in the bass, though it is not explicitly notated. The ⁶₄ chord in the sketch shown in Example 6, which can be justified as a passing chord, is also an ingredient of contemporary chorale writing – one, moreover, that would scarcely have been tolerated by Türk and others, who would have rejected it as too bland. The consistent avoidance of the flattened fourth degree, and the harmony and melody that in the course of sketching point more firmly to a particular mode – the Lydian – make it clear that Beethoven only gradually became aware of that rather strict principle which the theoretical writers appeal to yet do not for the most part apply in their own practice.

Example 6

Beethoven's procedure, it is fair to say, was not wholly without precedents. Although, like Türk and others, Knecht held to the view that the Lydian mode had long fallen into disuse and was not to be found in any chorale melody, he was methodical enough to provide at least a prelude in that mode, 'true Lydian, in F major without B♭', as he expressly emphasises[38] (Example 7). For an example of the Lydian

---

[38] Knecht, *Orgelschule*, p. 136.

The Historical Background to the 'Heiliger Dankgesang' 179

Example 7. Knecht, *Vollständige Orgelschule*, pp. 134–5

mode Vogler chose a melody allegedly from an ancient Swedish chorale book; but it could only be made to illustrate his point if he 'purified' it in accordance with his notions. He cunningly changed the falling steps in the melody's second bar, C–B♭–A, to C–C–A; elsewhere B♭ is consistently avoided, as already indicated by the conspicuous natural sign at the beginning of the staves. At the same time Vogler did not shrink from using other alien notes (C♯, G♯) in the accompanying parts (Example 8). Even the obscure Hessian Kapellmeister Carl Guhr, in the course of his thorough 1819 review of the chorale book adopted by the Reformed Church in the Electorate of Hesse, produced instruc-

Example 8. Vogler, *Choral-System*, music appendix, Table III

tions on how the Lydian mode, with its characteristic augmented fourth, was to be used.[39]

No doubt a historicising trend can be detected in Beethoven's reconstruction of this ideal, pure Lydian mode. Perhaps, too, the part-writing of the chorale's second verse and especially the coda – a part-writing that is 'irregular' and full of dissonances – can be understood as an attempt to imitate a fictional ancient style of writing, as Kerman supposes.[40] But in spite of its strong modal aspect, the first strophe of the chorale remains, even in its final version, indebted to contemporary choral writing. The passing $^6_4$ chord already referred to is carried into the final version with little change. The unprepared seventh produced by crossing parts in bar 27 (to enliven the parts with deceptive polyphony) and the cadences in bars 11–12 and 23–4 – and even in bars 5–6 – are characteristic of late-Baroque chorale writing, unmistakable in spite of their modal disguise (Example 9).

Example 9

It may be that in the course of composition Beethoven turned to the older books of instruction for information on the cadences that were customary in the fifth mode. Like Kirkendale, Kerman – who was the

---

[39] *Allgemeine musikalische Zeitung*, xxi (1819), cols. 645–53, 661–7.
[40] Kerman (*The Beethoven Quartets*, p. 260) is no doubt alluding to a remark of Beethoven's concerning an opera based on a theme from antiquity (perhaps *Bacchus*): 'Throughout the opera, perhaps, dissonances are to be left unresolved or else are resolved in a completely different way, for our refined music is inconceivable in those barbarous times.' See N II, p. 329 (the 'Scheide' Sketchbook, Library of William Scheide, Princeton, N. J., p. 52). Did Beethoven, one wonders, know anything of the early Baroque *durezze e ligature*?

first to voice this suspicion – was probably thinking of the *Istitutioni harmoniche* of Zarlino and other writings of the sixteenth century.[41] Still, Beethoven could have instructed himself more easily in Kirnberger and Knecht, who provide extensive tables with cadences and modulations in all the modes, including the 'Lydian' modulation shown in Example 10. In spite of the possible prototypes in the theoretical writings, it seems to me more probable that Beethoven arrived at the final plan of the chorale, with closes in D minor, C, G, and F, as the result of a very innocent reflection: namely, that in the pure Lydian mode all inflected notes, and accordingly major triads on the third, flattened fourth, sixth, and seventh degrees, must be avoided, as well as the minor triad on the second degree (that is, the triads of A major, B♭ major, D major, E major, and G minor). However, in the final version there is, at the end of the chorale (as is well known), a half-cadence on A major. This must presumably be seen as a musically necessary compromise with the concept of a pure mode. Beethoven originally planned for the chorale to end in F major, or on (Phrygian) E major, so as to be able to follow with an interlude in F major or A major (Example 11). It was probably the need for harmonic diversity that made him decide to introduce the interlude not in the previously considered keys of F major or A major, but in the as yet unused key of D major.

Example 10
Knecht, *Vollständige Orgelschule*, p. 50

Beethoven

If the peculiar modal harmony of the 'Heiliger Dankgesang' is from a general point of view a result of Beethoven's own speculations and not an imitation of a specific model, there is nevertheless one passage in which a more direct external influence may be suspected: namely, the

---

[41] 'The move to the A-major triad [at the end of the chorale] sounds "right" for a number of reasons . . . It is also a fact that Palestrinian orthodoxy, as hardened in the textbooks, prescribes A as the cadence for the Lydian mode on F. The old familiar smell of classroom counterpoint emanates from this movement.' (Kerman, *The Beethoven Quartets*, p. 257)

Example 11

powerful cadence on D minor with the bare fifth in the coda (bars 180–1). Türk discusses very fully the question whether at the final cadence in the Dorian, Phrygian, or Aeolian mode the third in the tonic triad may be raised.[42] He points out that in ancient music F♯, G♯, C♯, and so on were still unknown. Because of the system of temperament at that time it was also impossible to use the minor third belonging to the scale in final cadences, and thus the third was left out altogether and only the root, the octave, and the fifth were used at the end. Even more recent composers, according to Türk, held the view that the minor third was unsuitable at the end and therefore they preferred the fifth. In evidence he quotes a passage from *Gradus ad Parnassum* by Fux (in the German translation of L. Mizler), in which the author discusses the same problem in relation to an example in the Dorian mode, permitting neither the major nor the minor third but only the fifth. Türk, who himself adopts a more liberal standpoint in the light of 'the temperament that is usual today', refers in addition to other authors such as Mattheson, Riepel, Mizler, and Adlung who agreed with Fux. He adds: 'in this piece anyone who wanted to imitate the figures of the past could leave out the minor third at the end, but in doing so he would have no right to use the major third instead'.[43] It is interesting that what Türk propounds here in such a fundamental way is in Fux only a small episode.

Beethoven had already become familiar with cadences with the bare fifth in the course of his instruction from Albrechtsberger, and later he had even copied out two four-part Dorian fugues from *Gradus ad Parnassum* that contain the same ending.[44] Thus the possibility of an ending of this sort had long been known to him. But his attention may have been drawn to its archaic quality only as a result of his later reading of Türk. From a small sketch in a conversation book of the end of May 1825 it is clear that at that time – that is, during the composition of the 'Heiliger Dankgesang' – he was also preoccupied with the Dorian mode.[45] If Beethoven really had the intention of realising in practice the notions of the theoretical writers then it was only in the coda of the Lydian 'Dankgesang' that an opportunity offered itself. Only in this

---

[42] Türk, *Von den wichtigsten Pflichten eines Organisten*, pp. 62–6.
[43] Ibid., p. 64.
[44] The autograph is in the Beethovenhaus, Bonn (Sammlung H. C. Bodmer, Mh 45 (SBH 599)).
[45] Berlin, DSB, Autograph 51, Book no. 85, fol. 23r: see *Ludwig van Beethovens Konversationshefte*, vol. vii, ed. Karl-Heinz Köhler and Grita Herre (Leipzig, 1978), p. 287. On the same page (fol. 23r), and on fols. 24v and 25r there are also sketches for the coda of the 'Heiliger Dankgesang'.

freer (two-section) chorale postlude was he able to risk introducing a Dorian final cadence (in the first section).

The influence of contemporary church-music practice and theory is in evidence not only in the harmony but in the formal plan of the movement. This is most easily recognised in the two chorale strophes of the 'Dankgesang'. The short sections before and between the lines of Beethoven's chorale correspond to the so-called 'interludes' provided by the organist accompanying a chorale in church. Originally these were a kind of cadenza and were improvised. This practice survived long after Beethoven's time but then fell more and more into disuse. The evidence is plain enough that many organists took advantage of the interludes to compensate for the dull playing of the chorale, and attempted to display here their imagination and virtuosity.

In the third volume of his *Vollständige Orgelschule* Knecht discusses this practice in great detail and devotes to it a lengthy section in which the chorale interlude is treated systematically. He distinguishes two principal kinds (the easy, simple interlude, and the more difficult and elaborate interlude), each of which is then subdivided into four types. For each type he provides an example from the Protestant and Catholic chorale books. A closer examination of Knecht's account is not necessary to the present subject, and the suspicion arises that his systematisation of the interlude serves a didactic rather than a practical need. Nevertheless, since the practices of church music at that time are now extremely remote (possibly more remote than those of the Renaissance and the Baroque), an example may be given here to illustrate the third type of the second principal kind – arpeggios (Example 12). Although Knecht already represents a moderate point of view, it is clear from his account how extensive the organist's chorale interludes were and what demands they made on his artistic skill.

The theologians of the Enlightenment, of course, could not accept this sort of independence in something that was conceived of merely as an accompaniment. The chorale had to be the principal feature, and its task of arousing devotion and religious sentiments was not to be disturbed by anything else. Throughout the course of the eighteenth century and far into the nineteenth voices were frequently raised, at time in strongly polemical tones, in an attempt to have the interludes restricted or even totally abolished.[46] The topic was pursued in many articles in the *Allgemeine musikalische Zeitung*, and Türk too discusses it

---

[46] This in fact happened in the succeeding period, and the practice, once so widely followed, fell into total oblivion.

at length;[47] the practice, once allowed to creep in, was apparently not so easily changed. Türk himself was not among the theological zealots and certainly did not regard the interlude as impermissible, but he wanted to see it used 'appropriately'. His views (which were obviously shared by many other writers) can be summed up in the following three principles:

> The interlude must preserve the unity of the chorale's character and express the sentiments contained in it;[48]
>
> it should briefly and with little display or virtuosity prepare the first note of the following chorale line and lead directly into it;[49]
>
> all the interludes should be of similar lengths, so that no disproportion results.[50]

What Türk conceived as an 'appropriate' interlude was demonstrated by him in his *Kurze Anweisung zum Generalbasspielen*:

> 'The chorale player should . . . in no way – or at least not without many restrictions – display the facility of his fingers (or feet), but should merely lead into the following note a) b) c) and – so long as the clumsily and obtrusively descriptive can be avoided – express at the same time the content of the words, or else introduce solemn interludes suitable to their place and subject. In this respect only single notes a) c) or chords b) are satisfactory and appropriate, especially in hymns with sentiments that are tender, sad, etc. However, in hymns or verses with joyful content more or less cheerful interludes, running passages and the like can of course be introduced d) e).'[51] (Example 13)

The recommendations of later authors are in essentials no different from those of Türk; they are merely formulated more categorically and place greater restrictions on the organist's freedom to improvise. In his 1823 essay already referred to, 'Einiges über die Behandlung des Chorals beym Kirchengesange', the organist Döring writes:

> The purpose of an interlude (or of an introduction) is to create a harmonic and melodic link between the last note in one line and the first note in the line that follows it . . . In the interludes it would be most inept to depart from the measured, serious pace of the chorale,

---

[47] See Türk, *Von den wichtigsten Pflichten eines Organisten*, pp. 104–9, for the fullest discussion; the matter is also referred to by him in a number of other passages. See also his *Kurze Anweisung zum Generalbasspielen*, pp. 275–9.

[48] Türk, *Von den wichtigsten Pflichten eines Organisten*, pp. 107–8.

[50] *Ibid.*, pp. 17–18.   [50] *Ibid.*, pp. 14–18.

[51] Türk, *Kurze Anweisung zum Generalbasspielen*, pp. 275–6.

Example 12. Knecht, *Vollständige Orgelschule*, p. 166

Example 13. Türk, *Kurze Anweisung zum Generalbasspielen*, pp. 277–8

and to break into a rapid pace; quick runs introduced here would contrast as sharply with the slow, dignified pace of the chorale as would be the case if the congregation chose at the end of each line to break into a Viennese Waltz.[52]

From here it seems but a short step to the unattractive, standardised, sentimental verse-transitions, modulations, and chorale endings so typical of church music in the later nineteenth century, especially if the following restrictive recommendations of Döring are taken to heart:

> The more directly and closely the introduction is linked with the chorale, in melody, harmony, and rhythm, the more effective it will be.
>
> It is best for the first note of the melody to follow in a natural way the last note of the interlude.
>
> It will be enough if, after the last note has sounded, the introduction lasts as long as three or four syllables of the hymn.

The parallel with the 'Heiliger Dankgesang' is plain enough and requires no special emphasis: the interludes are all of the same length and each one lasts for four minims, corresponding in this way to four syllables in the text of a chorale.

Judging from the sketches it seems that, as in the composition of the chorale itself, Beethoven was guided at first by less strict, contemporary organ practice. Only gradually did he become fully aware of the church musicians' ideal for an interlude; he then tried to realise it in his own uncompromising fashion. In the sketches the last notes of each line of the chorale are repeatedly marked with fermate, the sign for a cadenza to be improvised. In the cases where the interlude was sketched, it clearly displays its improvisatory character: it is metrically free, consists of 'passage-work' (partial scales, broken chords), and lacks consistent thematic definition (Example 14). In the later sketches the interludes are metrically stabilised, thematically articulated, and given a more uniform character. It is above all the demand for unity between chorale and interlude that is satisfied in this way.

Beethoven fulfils the requirement that the interlude should have a preparatory or introductory function by making the phrases of the interludes overlap those of the following lines of the chorale, and by arranging for the first note of each line of the chorale to be anticipated each time (with one exception) by the last note of the interlude. (The interlude before the fifth line of the chorale ends on the leading-note

---

[52] This and the following quotations are taken from *Allgemeine musikalische Zeitung*, xxv (1823), cols. 662–3.

Example 14

b', and prepares the following note of the chorale, c'', just as powerfully as do the other interludes.) The improvisatory aspect is completely eliminated. In this manner the cadential link with the last note of the preceding chorale line is dropped and is replaced by a new link with the beginning of the next line. The interlude has turned completely into an introduction, and one can safely say that in this respect Beethoven realised in an ideal manner the aim of church music in his day.

It is time finally to examine the other parts of this quartet movement: the two D-major sections that are independent of the chorale, and the coda that is built round it. From the point of view of the present inquiry is there any prototype for them in the history of church music? This question cannot be answered with any certainty; but it should be added that the less clearly it can be answered, the less relevant is it, in fact, to an understanding of the music.

The clearest parallels to ideas from the world of church music are to be found in the coda (which uses the chorale). Here, again, the same harmonies are found as in the verses of the chorale, only Beethoven treats dissonances with far greater freedom. The beginning of the coda, as has often been pointed out, is a sort of chorale fugue.[53] Thereafter freer elaborative devices, typical of the end of sonata movements and variation sets, conclude the piece. Here, in a way that corresponds to the formal principles of Classical instrumental music, the thematic substance is dissolved and the movement brought to rest. If one wishes to find a prototype in church music, the coda can most readily be compared to the organist's postlude. The place of the postlude is at the end of divine service, and so it has no direct connection with any preceding hymn. For this reason Türk counts it among the free fantasias; it is therefore thematically independent of a chorale

[53] The term 'chorale fugue' is a general description for fugues of various types, none of them characterised at all exactly. The sole criterion is the use of thematic material from the chorale melody. So there is little point in measuring the chorale fugue in the coda of the 'Dankgesang' against one of the examples given by the theoretical writers, in order to establish departures from a norm of some sort. Even Albrechtsberger's definition is by no means as strict as Kirkendale declares (*Fuge und Fugato*, p. 291; Eng. trans., p. 254). Türk discusses the chorale fugue in connection with the 'carefully wrought' prelude (as contrasted with free fantasia), and emphasises that in this form one is not obliged to adopt strict fugal style: 'The first line of the chorale melody can be taken as the subject. The fugue can be worked out strictly, or the prelude can merely be treated in a fugal manner; for it is not necessary, and sometimes not even appropriate, always to select a formal fugue for a prelude. Here, too, one has to look for variety. The chorale can be developed now in this and now in that part, now in canon, in augmentation, in diminution, in stretto or all'rovescio.' (*Von den wichtigsten Pflichten eines Organisten*, pp. 130–1)

cantus firmus. Apart from the free postlude, however, a chorale-linked postlude was also found. This term does not refer to the bombastic form of chorale endings, which last for only a few bars and amount to no more than an expanded final cadence. Chorale-linked postludes take the same basic forms as preludes: chorale arrangements, and especially (because of their greater effect of finality) chorale fugues. However, Beethoven's coda in the 'Heiliger Dankgesang' falls only incompletely into the category of a chorale fugue; as has been said above, that term can be applied only to the first section. So a comparison with the organist's postlude does not lead to any especially illuminating conclusions.

Much the same applies to the two D-major sections ('Neue Kraft fühlend'). Although they do not lie entirely outside a tradition of alternatim performance in church music, it has to be accepted that the introduction of a free and livelier interlude between the extremely slow lines of the chorale is a musical and psychological necessity that carries its own justification.

The results of this inquiry can be summarised as follows. The influence of church music is seen most clearly in the first chorale verse of the 'Heiliger Dankgesang'. The archaising harmony and melody are inspired by contemporary theories, and they exhibit the realisation of one of its ideals, of which however there is no example in ancient church music. In the alternating, five-section plan of the movement and especially in the coda, the part on which Beethoven no doubt spent most time, the elements adopted from church music are integrated with the language of Classical form. This can be seen as Beethoven's most important compositional achievement in the movement. From this point of view one can agree wholeheartedly with the opinion of his younger contemporary A. B. Marx: according to him, in the 'Dankgesang' Beethoven 'had not been aiming at antiquarianism or bookish learning, but had been led merely by the intuition of the artist'.[54]

[54] Adolph Bernhard Marx, *Ludwig van Beethoven: Leben und Schaffen* (Berlin, 1859), vol. ii, p. 307.

Beethoven's Tagebuch of 1812–1818

Maynard Solomon

I

During the years 1812 to 1818 Beethoven kept a Tagebuch (diary) in which he made occasional entries; although unsystematic and sometimes obscure, these illuminate many aspects of his life, personality, and creativity. After his death the Tagebuch passed, along with those personal papers that had not been appropriated by Anton Schindler, to Stephan von Breuning, the executor of Beethoven's estate. Following Breuning's own death on 4 June 1827 it came to Jacob Hotschevar, who had previously served as Johanna van Beethoven's lawyer in the litigation over the guardianship of Beethoven's nephew Karl and who now replaced Breuning as executor and guardian. Hotschevar, for reasons that will soon become apparent, left Beethoven's papers in the custody of Artaria & Co. for a brief time; then, according to Thayer,[1] whose authority was Karl's wife, Caroline, Hotschevar delivered them to Karl 'upon the attainment of his majority', which occurred on 4 September 1827. Thayer took for granted, and apparently knew as a fact, that these papers included the Tagebuch. One may infer this to have been the case inasmuch as similar documents, notably the Heiligenstadt Testament and Beethoven's 1792 *Stammbuch*, did pass to Beethoven's family around this time. But one must allow some latitude concerning the precise date and recipient, for a note on the verso of the Heiligenstadt Testament indicates that Hotschevar received it from Artaria & Co. on 21 November 1827 and transmitted it to Karl's mother rather than to Karl himself. Clearly this required Karl's approval, for he was Beethoven's sole legatee.

The original manuscript of the Tagebuch has unfortunately been lost. After Karl's death in 1858 Beethoven's papers remained for a time in his widow's possession. She appears to have been the source for the

[1] Thayer i (1866), p. x.

statement in the first volume of Thayer's biography that 'a large part of them were borrowed from her . . . and sold by the borrower for his own profit!'[2] The identity of the mysterious 'borrower' – if he indeed existed – is unknown; but there is evidence that Caroline van Beethoven disposed of some of the documents she had inherited. The *Stammbuch* was purchased by the Österreichische Nationalbibliothek from Gustav Nottebohm early in 1871.[3] Nottebohm probably was acting on Caroline van Beethoven's behalf; and it seems reasonable to assume that she sold off other Beethoven autographs – perhaps including the Tagebuch – to interested collectors, just as Karl's mother had earlier disposed of the Heiligenstadt Testament.

In any event, because the original manuscript of the Tagebuch has not been found, the present edition must be based on the surviving copies of it. Four of these are known at present. One forms part of the well-known 'Fischhof' Manuscript in the Deutsche Staatsbibliothek in Berlin (catalogued as Mus. ms. theor. 285). A second is in the Stadtarchiv at Iserlohn (*Nachlass* of Ludwig Nohl) in north-west Germany. A third is in the Universitätsbibliothek, Bonn (Sammelband Velten, catalogued as S 1665). A fourth copy, in the Deutsche Staatsbibliothek, is part of Otto Jahn's *Nachlass*. All four contain essentially the same material, presented in the same order. There are, however, numerous differences in orthography, punctuation, paragraphing, and (occasionally) in wording and content, which make it important to establish the chronology of each and their textual relationship.

All the copies owe their existence, directly or indirectly, to a projected but abortive 'Viennese biography' of Beethoven. Writing from Vienna on 14 September 1827 to Ignaz Moscheles in London, Schindler referred to the plan: 'In Prague Herr Schlosser has published a most wretched biography of Beethoven. Here, too, a subscription is circulating for another "life", which, I hear, will be compiled by Herr Gräffer . . . The newly appointed guardian of Beethoven's nephew has handed over Breuning's papers to Herr Gräffer.'[4] This last was Anton

---

[2] *Ibid.*

[3] According to the accession book of the manuscript collection (vol. i, fol. 71b) the *Stammbuch* was received on 11 March 1871: 'Von Herrn Gust. Nottebohm in Wien gekauft um 20 fl. ö. Wo. Suppl. 2816': see Hans Gerstinger, *Beethovens Stammbuch* (Bielefeld and Leipzig, 1927), pp. 25–6. See also N I, pp. 138–44; *Allgemeine musikalische Zeitung* (1871), cols. 65–8, 266. There is no basis for the belief that Anton Gräffer's brother, Franz Gräffer, ever owned the *Stammbuch*; so far as is known he had only a copy of Waldstein's entry, which he believed to be a letter rather than part of an album.

[4] Charlotte Moscheles, ed., *Aus Moscheles' Leben* (Leipzig, 1872), vol. i, p. 168; Eng.

Gräffer (1784–?1849), a musician, essayist, and engraver, who worked for Artaria & Co. from 1815 as a clerk, auctioneer, and cataloguer.[5] He was a specialist in matters pertaining to Beethoven's works, having in 1827 prepared the *Nachlass* auction catalogue, and in 1844 a further catalogue of Beethoven manuscripts then in the possession of Artaria & Co. He also compiled the second edition of the *Catalogue des oeuvres de Louis van Beethoven*, published by Artaria & Co. after the composer's death, and probably its first edition (1819) as well. It seems very likely that Karl Holz was Gräffer's collaborator and even a prime mover in the projected 'Viennese biography'; at all events he possessed the sole legal authority from Beethoven to write his life.

Invitations to subscribe to the biography, dated 'September 1827', were circulated individually and were also published in several Viennese newspapers at the time. The announcement read in part: 'With the co-operation of the guardian of Beethoven's nephew, the editors have succeeded in examining and making use of all those interesting writings of the great composer that are in his *Nachlass*. Among them are a Tagebuch and a *Stammbuch* of Beethoven's, with important chronological and other information; several documents, diplomas, manuscript letters, reviews of his most important works, etc. etc.'[6] This is the first published reference to Beethoven's Tagebuch. The (anonymous) announcement continued, optimistically: 'Thus, from

---

trans. as *The Life of Moscheles* (London, 1873), vol. i, p. 181. The reference is to Johann Aloys Schlosser, *Ludwig van Beethoven's Biographie* (Prague, 1828 [published summer 1827]).

[5] Anton Gräffer was identified, and his role in the projected 'Viennese biography' established, by Clemens Brenneis: see his articles 'Zum Fischhof-Manuskript', *Bericht über den Internationalen Beethoven-Kongress, Berlin 1977*, ed. Harry Goldschmidt, Karl-Heinz Köhler, and Konrad Niemann (Leipzig, 1978), pp. 299–306, and (with further details) 'Das Fischhof-Manuskript: zur Frühgeschichte der Beethoven-Biographik', *Zu Beethoven*, ed. Harry Goldschmidt (Berlin, 1979), pp. 90–116. For further information on Anton Gräffer, see Franz Gräffer and J. J. Czikann, eds., *Oesterreichische National-Encyklopädie*, vi (Vienna, 1837), p. 462; Georg Kinsky, 'Zur Versteigerung von Beethovens musikalischem Nachlass', *Neues Beethoven-Jahrbuch*, vi (1936), 66–86; Douglas Johnson, 'The Artaria Collection of Beethoven Manuscripts: a New Source', *Beethoven Studies* [1], ed. Alan Tyson (New York 1973; London, 1974), pp. 179–80.

[6] A copy of the announcement, as published in the *Oesterreichische Beobachter*, is to be found with the 'Fischhof' Manuscript. (It also appeared in the *Wiener Sammler*.) Clemens Brenneis has furnished me with a variant copy, lacking the final paragraph of the Fischhof copy. Further copies are in Berlin, DSB, Autograph 47b. Hotschevar's 'Nachricht an Ludwig van Beethovens Gönner, Freunde und Verehrer' (Report to Beethoven's patrons, friends, and admirers), with its promise that a 'worthy biography' would soon be forthcoming, appeared in Bäuerle's *Theaterzeitung* for 6 October 1827, p. 492 (partly reprinted in Thayer–Deiters–Riemann v, p. 500). It too exists as a separate, variant offprint (Berlin, DSB, Jahn *Nachlass*).

genuine original sources carrying the stamp of authenticity will be created the whole life history of our artistic hero.'

But the biography, the publication of which had been promised for March 1828, presumably by Artaria & Co., was soon cancelled for lack of an adequate response from subscribers and memoirists. With its cancellation, Gräffer was left with his copy of a Beethoven miscellany that included transcripts of letters to and from Beethoven, of Beethoven's baptismal certificate, of his annuity contract of 1809, of the Heiligenstadt Testament, and of the Tagebuch (though not, strangely enough, of the *Stammbuch*). It also eventually included a few original documents: one autograph letter and several autograph sketches, as well as three first editions (of WoO 47, WoO 63, and Op. 88). Some time between 1832 and June 1835 Gräffer composed a brief history of the project and a draft biographical sketch for possible future use, woven in large part from previously published materials but also drawing on the memoirs and documents supplied by Zmeskall, Simrock, Bertolini, Mosel, and J. B. Bach, now added to the miscellany.

The next stage in the history of Gräffer's Beethoven miscellany has been lucidly chronicled by Brenneis and may be briefly summarised. Gräffer prepared an inventory of the papers and offered them for sale: 'Verzeichniss einer Sammlung von merkwürdigen Stüken, Notizen, etc., welche auf . . . L. v Beethoven Bezug haben, und welche um den festgesetzten Preis von 50 fl. C.M. zu haben sind bei Hrn G * * * r in Wien' (List of a remarkable collection of memoranda, etc., concerning L. van Beethoven, which may be obtained from Herr G[räffe]r in Vienna for the firm price of 50 florins C.M.). Two slightly different copies of the list are in existence, one in the hand of Aloys Fuchs from Vienna and the other in the hand of Friedrich August Grasnick from Berlin, both assiduous collectors of musical autographs.[7] The surviving copies of the list were prepared in 1841 or 1842, but Fuchs, in a note appended to his copy and in a letter to Schindler of 9 September 1852, relates that the collection had been offered to him as early as 1828 or 1829. Apparently Gräffer was then unable to find a buyer, probably because the miscellany consisted almost entirely of transcripts, at a time when Beethoven autographs were in plentiful supply.

---

[7] For Fuchs's copy see Georg Kinsky, ed., *Manuskripte, Briefe, Dokumente von Scarlatti bis Stravinsky: Katalog der Musikautographen-Sammlung Louis Koch* (Stuttgart, 1953), p. 137; for Grasnick's see Hans-Günter Klein, *Ludwig van Beethoven: Autographe und Abschriften: Katalog*, Staatsbibliothek Preussischer Kulturbesitz, Kataloge der Musikabteilung, ser. 1: Handschriften, vol. ii (Berlin, 1975), p. 308. Fuchs also copied eighteen entries from Gräffer's Tagebuch copy – Nos. 18, 25, 26, 27, 31, 35, 36, 39, 40, 43, 85, 98, 116, 135, 151, 153, 155–6, and 161.

In 1842 Karl Holz, angered by the falsifications and personal attacks in Schindler's *Biographie von Ludwig van Beethoven* (1840), persuaded the Karlsruhe Kapellmeister Ferdinand Simon Gassner (1798–1851) to undertake to write Beethoven's biography. In September Gassner came to Vienna to gather documentary materials with Holz's assistance. His most important acquisition was the Gräffer miscellany, which he received from Gräffer along with the 'Pastoral' Symphony Sketchbook and several other sketchleaves.[8] Simultaneously Holz gave to Gassner his own collection of Beethoven materials and soon he formally transferred to Gassner his authorisation to write Beethoven's biography.[9] Although few details are known, Holz's collection apparently included several items which had been in the fund of documents and memoirs accumulated for the 'Viennese biography' and which had been withdrawn by Holz after the abandonment of the project.[10]

Perhaps in anticipation of the transfer to Gassner, Gräffer permitted Joseph Fischhof (1804–57), a prominent Viennese pianist, music teacher, and collector,[11] to make a copy of the entire miscellany, including the Tagebuch. The date of the Fischhof copy cannot be definitely fixed. The *terminus ante quem* is September 1842, when Gassner received Gräffer's collection. A marginal reference to 'Schilling Lexikon' on fol. 1r of the 'Fischhof' Manuscript implies a *terminus post quem* of May 1835, for the first volume of Gustav Schilling's *Encyclopädie der gesammten musikalischen Wissenschaften oder Universal Lexikon der Ton-*

---

[8] See Dagmar Weise, ed., *Beethoven: ein Skizzenbuch zur Pastoralsymphonie . . . Erster Teil* (Bonn, 1961), pp. 7–8; Alan Tyson, 'A Reconstruction of the Pastoral Symphony Sketchbook', *Beethoven Studies [1]*, ed. Tyson (New York, 1973; London, 1974), pp. 66, 88. The transfer of Gräffer's Beethoven collection to Gassner is confirmed by Aloys Fuchs (see Kinsky, ed., *Manuskripte, Briefe, Dokumente*, p. 137) and by a letter from Gassner to Fuchs of 23 December 1842: see Brenneis, 'Zum Fischhof-Manuskript', p. 301 and note 30, and 'Das Fischhof-Manuskript', p. 101. According to Fuchs's letter to Schindler of 9 September 1852, Gräffer gave Gassner, who was related to him, 'the whole package as a present': cited in Martin Staehelin, 'Aus der Welt der frühen Beethoven-"Forschung"', *Musik, Edition, Interpretation: Gedenkschrift Günter Henle*, ed. Martin Bente (Munich, 1980), p. 440.

[9] Letter of 4 November 1843 from Holz to Gassner, in Ludwig Nohl, ed., *Briefe Beethovens* (Stuttgart, 1865), p. 324; see also Alfred Christlieb Kalischer, ed., *The Letters of Ludwig van Beethoven*, ed. and trans. J. S. Shedlock (London, 1909), vol. ii, pp. 438–9. Holz set a deadline of August 1844, which he subsequently extended (Thayer–Deiters–Riemann v, p. 190).

[10] See Martin Staehelin, 'Die Beethoven-Materialien im Nachlass von Ludwig Nohl', *Beethoven-Jahrbuch*, x (forthcoming).

[11] See Richard Schaal, 'Fischhof, Joseph', *Die Musik in Geschichte und Gegenwart*, ed. Friedrich Blume, vol. iv (Kassel, 1955), cols. 276–7.

kunst (containing an entry on Beethoven) was published in that month. However, it is conceivable that Fischhof added the marginal reference only after he had copied Gräffer's miscellany; in that case a reference in the text to 'Schindler in Münster' proves that the transcript could not have been made earlier than 1832, for Schindler lived in Münster between the end of December 1831 and 1 June 1835.[12]

As Viennese specialists in music manuscripts Fischhof and Gräffer were well acquainted. Fischhof owned the catalogue of the Artaria Collection of Beethoven manuscripts which is in Gräffer's hand;[13] indeed, at Artaria's request, he collaborated with Gräffer in its preparation.[14] There is no doubt that the 'Fischhof' Manuscript actually derives from Gräffer's miscellany (although it may contain some additional material as well), for Brenneis has shown that the major portions of the manuscript correspond almost exactly to items 2–9 in Gräffer's sales list.[15] It is apparent from the modernisation of the spelling in Fischhof's copy of the Tagebuch that it postdates Gräffer's copy, which retains, for example, Beethoven's habitual use of 'y' instead of 'i' in such words as 'bei', 'beide', and 'sein', and the use of 'ui' in such words as 'über' and 'übel'. That the Fischhof Tagebuch was transcribed from Gräffer's copy rather than from the original is proved by Fischhof's adherence to almost all of Gräffer's obvious misreadings of, and omissions from, Beethoven's original. Furthermore, several of Beethoven's phrases that appear in Gräffer as cancellations are lacking altogether in Fischhof. For example, in entry No. 37, Fischhof's copy lacks the words 'in Canons', which in Gräffer's copy are crossed out with dots underneath to signify 'stet'; similarly, in entry No. 54, the word 'Akustik', which is cancelled but clearly legible in Gräffer, does not appear at all in Fischhof.

In 1859 Fischhof's collection became the property of the Königliche Bibliothek in Berlin; it is now in that library's successor, the Deutsche Staatsbibliothek. Both Nohl and Thayer made use of the 'Fischhof' Manuscript in their Beethoven biographies, and Nohl described it in some detail in an article of 1878.[16] Albert Leitzmann published an

---

[12] Eduard Hüffer, *Anton Felix Schindler* (Münster, 1909), pp. 20, 25.
[13] Berlin, DSB, Autograph 47a: see Douglas Johnson, 'The Artaria Collection', p. 179.
[14] For Fischhof's participation in the preparation of the catalogue, see his 'Einige Gedanken über die Auffassung von Instrumentalkompositionen in Hinsicht des Zeitmasses, namentlich bei Beethoven'schen Werke', *Caecilia*, xxvi (1847), 94, quoted in Brenneis, 'Das Fischhof-Manuskript', p. 92.
[15] Brenneis, 'Das Fischhof-Manuskript', pp. 103–8.
[16] Ludwig Nohl, 'Die Fischhofsche Handschrift: ein Beitrag zu Beethoven's Leben', *Im neuen Reich*, ix (1878), 313–30. The article makes no reference to the Gräffer/Gassner copy.

annotated transcription of Fischhof's copy of the Tagebuch in 1918,[17] which has often been reprinted and extensively used in the biographical literature.

However, the first nearly complete publication of the Tagebuch was by Nohl in 1871; for it he utilised the copy made by Gräffer, which, despite his ignorance of its origin and earlier history, he recognised as a better source for his text than the version in the 'Fischhof' Manuscript. He found the Gräffer copy in the possession of Gassner's widow (Gassner had died in 1851, his biography of Beethoven unwritten), whom he visited in Baden-Baden on several occasions. At first he assumed that she had a copy derived from Fischhof;[18] but on closer examination and comparison of the two documents he understood that Gassner's copy predated the transcript of the Tagebuch included in the 'Fischhof' Manuscript. Accordingly he borrowed it and used it as the basis for his annotated transcription of the bulk of the document, published in *Die Beethoven-Feier und die Kunst der Gegenwart* (Vienna, 1871). There he wrote: 'it is published here . . . according to an old Viennese copy which, although it contains minor errors, represents in the main a reliable source'.[19] In the final volume of *Beethoven's Leben* (1877) he specified that source:

> The Tagebuch of 1812-18 is published in my book *Die Beethoven-Feier und die Kunst der Gegenwart* . . . after an old Viennese copy which came from the estate of Court Kapellmeister Gassner, and which deviates from the Berlin copy [that is, the version in the 'Fischhof' Manuscript] in several details. Unfortunately, the publication is not free of mistakes, and where there are deviations the present final publication [that is, the extracts in *Beethoven's Leben*] is decisive.[20]

Nohl never returned the Tagebuch transcript to Frau Gassner, and it was presumed lost until 1978, when it was 'rediscovered' among Nohl's *Nachlass* at the Stadtarchiv, Iserlohn, (where it had been deposited in 1965) through the efforts of Martin Staehelin. The clearly traceable sequence of ownership of Gräffer's Tagebuch – from Gräffer to Gassner to Nohl to Nohl's *Nachlass* – makes it certain that the manuscript now in the Stadtarchiv, Iserlohn, is the copy that Gräffer

---

[17] Albert Leitzmann, ed., *Beethovens persönliche Aufzeichnungen* (Leipzig, n.d. [1918]), pp. 9–39, 49–59; Leitzmann, ed., *Ludwig van Beethoven: Berichte der Zeitgenossen, Briefe und persönliche Aufzeichnungen* (Leipzig, 1921), vol. ii, pp. 241–66, 365–74.
[18] Nohl, *Briefe Beethovens*, p. 325, note.
[19] Nohl, *Die Beethoven-Feier*, p. 52.
[20] Ludwig Nohl, *Beethoven's Leben*, vol. iii (Leipzig, 1877), p. 814, note 12; but Tagebuch material cited in vols. i and ii derives from the 'Fischhof' Manuscript (see vol. ii (Leipzig, 1867), p. 555).

made from Beethoven's original. The handwriting of the Iserlohn manuscript is without question that of Anton Gräffer[21] (see Plate V). The dates and derivation of the two remaining copies of the Tagebuch can easily be determined. Otto Jahn obtained a copy of it, transcribed from the 'Fischhof' Manuscript, along with other portions of the same document, for use in his projected, but never written, biography of Beethoven. Dated 22 September 1852, his copy bears the legend: 'From Beethoven's Tagebuch, according to the copy of Prof. Fischhof', and contains on its last page a citation of material paralleling entry No. 93 derived from the *Berlin Musik-Zeitung Echo* of 4 October 1857. The fourth copy belonged to Andreas Velten, a collector of materials pertaining to Bonn history. Velten's copy was made from Jahn's: the copyist obligingly copied Jahn's date as well as the 1857 entry; on the title-page he noted that it was made from a manuscript 'in the possession of Herr Joseph von Fischhof in Vienna'. In 1864 Velten's collection, including his Tagebuch, was acquired by the Universitätsbibliothek, Bonn.

Thus a direct sequence can be established for the four extant copies of Beethoven's Tagebuch:

Beethoven's original (1812–18; lost) ⟶

Gräffer's copy (summer 1827; Iserlohn, Stadtarchiv) ⟶

Fischhof's copy (1832–42; Berlin, DSB) ⟶

Otto Jahn's copy (1852; Berlin, DSB) ⟶

Velten's copy (1857–64; Bonn, Universitätsbibliothek)

In the absence of the original manuscript, the transcription and translation of the document that follow are based on the Gräffer copy.

II

The edition that follows consists of a transcription of the German manuscript, an English translation, and a commentary. My aim has been to provide a complete and correct transcription, one that preserves the manuscript's idiosyncrasies of spelling, capitalisation, punctuation, and paragraphing. Cancelled words and passages are identified either by a footnote or by a line through the text. Words underlined in the manuscript are underlined in the transcription and italicised in the translation. Marginal notations on the manuscript are printed in the footnotes. Editorial corrections and alternative readings

[21] I owe this identification to Sieghard Brandenburg.

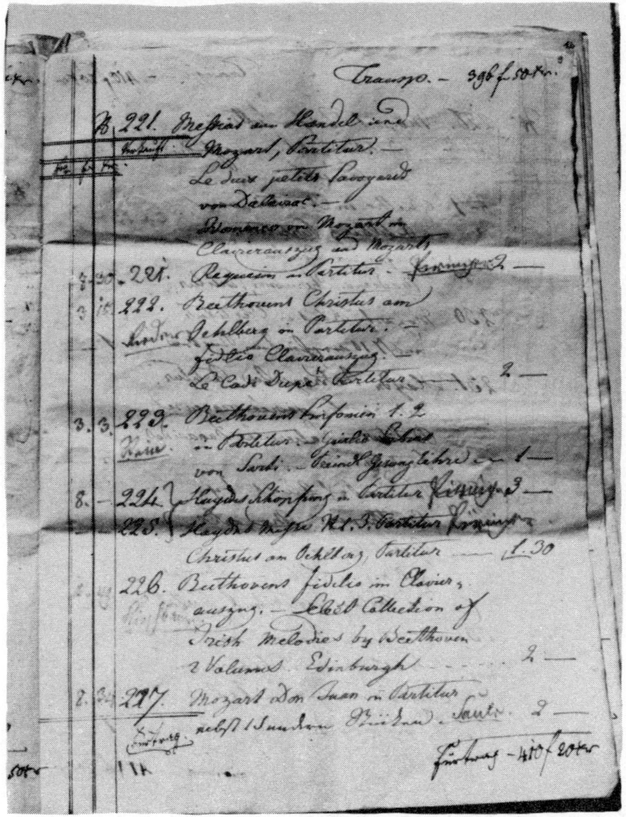

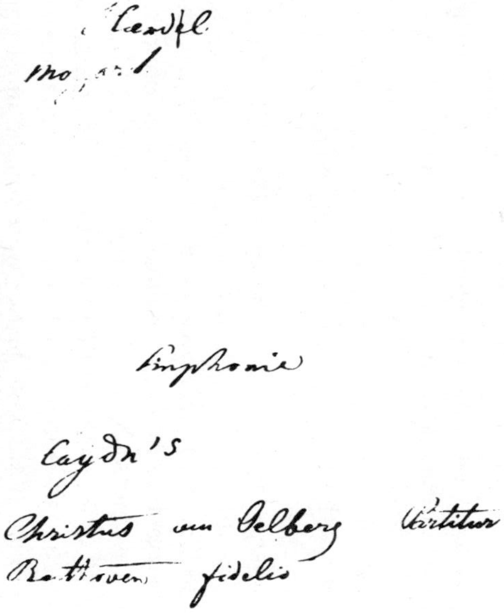

Plate V. Samples of Anton Gräffer's handwriting. (*left*) From a copy made by Gräffer of the *Nachlass* auction catalogue: Bonn, Beethovenhaus, NE 79. (*right*) From his copy of Beethoven's Tagebuch of 1812–1818: Iserlohn, Stadtarchiv

of words or phrases are either enclosed in square brackets or given in the commentary. Where Beethoven or the copyist omitted words, phrases, or question-marks in entries drawn from published literary texts, and these have been restored editorially, they have been enclosed in diamond brackets; however, square brackets are used for editorially restored punctuation other than question-marks. Clarifying punctuation has not been added to any entries other than those drawn from published texts. Where possible each extract from a published text has been compared with the edition that Beethoven is known or is likely to have used.

The text contains a large number of dashes (see Plate VI). Within the entries these are, in the main, Beethoven's usual substitutes for orthodox punctuation. Occasionally, however (as in Nos. 52, 60, and 162), they indicate the copyist's omission of illegible or indecipherable material; and in two instances (Nos. 20 and 28) Beethoven himself apparently chose not to enter material that he did not wish others to read. Dashes often serve to fill out lines of the text and to separate the entries; it may be assumed that these dashes were for the most part taken over from Beethoven's original manuscript.

As a general rule each paragraph of the Gräffer manuscript has been assigned a separate, consecutive number by the editor. There is some possibility of error in this procedure, for (as is usual in German manuscripts) most new paragraphs are not indented, so that where an entry extends to the very end of a line one cannot be certain whether the following line is a new paragraph or a continuation of the same paragraph. Such 'possible' new paragraphs are identified in the footnotes and are printed as new paragraphs in the English translation. Occasionally (for example, Nos. 60 and 94) two or more separate paragraphs of closely related materials are grouped under a single number. In several instances, where disparate materials appear in a single paragraph (for example, Nos. 63, 68, and 93), or where a sequence of separate quotations from published texts is run together in one paragraph (for example, Nos. 60 and 105), further subdivisions are sometimes made, designated by letters enclosed in square brackets ([a], [b], [c], etc.).

Each numbered entry is followed by an English translation. The English rendering has sought to find the middle ground between literalness and intelligibility. Orthodox punctuation has been employed where it clarifies the evident meaning of Beethoven's thought but not where it would result in an unwarranted 'interpretation' of the text. Nevertheless, the translation does attempt to suggest the meaning of obscure passages. The reader will, of course, want continually to consult the German transcription; he will find that lacunae, incoherent sentences, copying errors, and other difficulties often give rise to ambiguities in meaning. In the translation, editorially supplied punctuation is not identified. Square brackets may be used for alternative readings as well as for editorial emendations and additions; diamond brackets are used for some translations of words from published texts that have been editorially restored in the Tagebuch entries. Where an entry varies from a published text the translation will rely upon the text except where it seems clear that the divergence has a special significance.

As noted earlier, Nohl published, in *Die Beethoven-Feier und die Kunst der Gegenwart* (1871), an edition of the Tagebuch that was largely based upon the Gräffer/Gassner copy. He is to be credited for identifying many of the quotations and literary extracts in the Tagebuch, although his annotations in other respects are unreliable and fragmentary. Nohl omitted one entry (No. 146) by accident, and twelve entries (Nos. 7e and 55–65) because he had previously published them in his *Beethovens Brevier* (Leipzig, 1870) (there, however, they were printed according to the 'Fischhof' Manuscript). Besides its incompleteness, it is an unreliable edition, containing scores of significant errors – incorrect readings, word omissions or transpositions – and hundreds of deliberate emendations in spelling and punctuation. Modern spelling has been substituted for the original's often archaic spelling. To complicate matters, it is abundantly clear that Nohl, although he claimed that his edition was based solely on Gräffer/Gassner, actually used the Fischhof copy as well. Where the texts of the two copies varied he tacitly chose the reading that he preferred.

Though it did not achieve its goal, Nohl's transcription aimed at being a faithful rendering of the Tagebuch – it even included the numerous dashes. As a text it is greatly preferable to Leitzmann's publication, which was based primarily on the 'Fischhof' Manuscript. Leitzmann's edition is avowedly not a diplomatic transcription;[22] but it cannot be recommended even on its own terms, for apart from its modernisation of punctuation and spelling and a generous sprinkling of exclamation-marks for dramatic emphasis, it lacks eight entries (Nos. 32, 33, 46, 76, 135, 146, 147, and 161), includes material drawn from non-Tagebuch sources (Leitzmann Nos. 1–6, 69, 78, and 181–4), and is untrustworthy insofar as many words have been silently changed to 'clarify' obscure passages.

---

[22] Leitzmann, ed., *Beethoven: Berichte der Zeitgenossen*, vol. ii, pp. 385–6.

It must be emphasised that the present edition derives from a secondary source, one that contains a variety of faults. Of course in many instances one cannot tell whether the defects are faithful transcriptions of Beethoven's own errors or whether they are to be ascribed to the copyist's inadequacies. Occasionally one may observe Gräffer struggling to find a correct reading, as in No. 60, where he renders the word 'straft' as 'strebt? strahlt?'. Elsewhere, as in No. 106[a], errors appear to result from hasty, or even unthinking, workmanship. Several entries have been rendered opaque or even meaningless. Moreover it is not certain that Gräffer's copy represents the complete text as Beethoven left it. As Brenneis observes,[23] it cannot be ruled out that details that might have embarrassed or compromised various individuals were suppressed, perhaps by Hotschevar as executor of the estate. It should be added, however, that there is no evidence of such suppression, although one cannot help wondering why several pagan terms are omitted in Nos. 61, 64, and 65.

The manuscript, which measures 22.5 × 33 cm, consists of one gathering containing 24 bifolia (= 48 pages, of which the last five are blank). The ink is light grey except for the marginal notations, which are entered in black pencil. The paper carries a watermark: that of Mould A depicts an eagle over the letters 'GFA', and three hats arranged in a triangle, while that of Mould B is the same in reverse. The entire manuscript is in Anton Gräffer's hand except for the marginal notations, a few underlinings, and several internal corrections and glosses. Virtually all the marginal notations are by Nohl, made in preparation for his edition. In the footnotes to the entries I have specified those underlinings and internal corrections that I believe were made by Nohl in order to emphasise the discrepancies between the Gräffer and Fischhof copies.

The fate of Beethoven's original Tagebuch is unknown. Based on the existence of three leaves in Beethoven's hand which duplicate certain material in No. 60 and Nos. 61–2/93,[24] Nohl concluded that the Tagebuch had been partly or wholly dismembered and its leaves dispersed.[25] However, the leaf corresponding to Nos. 61–2/93 is significantly different in content and in arrangement of the material; the present entries could not have been copied from it. Nor could the two leaves corresponding to No. 60 have been Gräffer's source: the words 'den Saiten wühlen; Allein' could not be deciphered by Gräffer (he

[23] Personal communication.
[24] See commentary on Nos. 62 and 93.
[25] Nohl, *Die Beethoven-Feier*, p. 52. It seems likely that many more leaves would have come to light if Nohl's hypothesis were correct.

indicated the lacuna by several dashes), but they are perfectly legible in Beethoven's hand.

Brenneis has the impression that the Tagebuch is an assemblage of jottings and memoranda recorded in various calendars and notebooks.[26] However, a close study of the content and chronology of the entries demonstrates that Gräffer's copy was made from a unified, probably bound, diary rather than a miscellaneous assemblage of loose sheets. There is no reason to suppose that individual pages or entries have been inserted into the original sequence or that the sequence itself has been disturbed in any way. While it is not possible to establish the precise date for every entry in the Tagebuch, the many dated or clearly datable entries make it certain that Beethoven wrote the entries chronologically and that Gräffer copied them in the order in which they appeared in the original manuscript. The following is an outline of the approximate chronology of the entries:

> 1812: 1 or 1 and 2
> 1813: 2 or 3 to 16 or 17
> 1814: 17 or 18 to 33–37
> 1815: 34–38 to 70
> 1816: 71 to 110 or 111
> 1817: 111 or 112 to 141
> 1818: 141 to 171

III

The Tagebuch is one of the major source documents for Beethoven's biography during the personal and stylistic crisis that extended from the composition of the Seventh and Eighth Symphonies in 1812 to the completion of the 'Hammerklavier' Sonata in 1818, the years spanning the transition between his middle and late styles. No comparable document survives from any other period of Beethoven's life. The notebook that he kept between the end of 1792 and the beginning of 1794 (dubbed his 'Jugendtagebuch' in a recent edition)[27] is a log rather than a diary and, despite several entries of a subjective character, is primarily useful as a record of events and expenses. From time to time – even during the years of the Tagebuch's composition – Beethoven

---

[26] Brenneis, 'Das Fischhof-Manuskript', p. 112, note 3; this speculation is based on a misreading of Thayer i (1866), p. ix, which refers not to the Tagebuch, but to the 'Fischhof' Manuscript as a whole.

[27] Dagmar von Busch-Weise, ed., 'Beethovens Jugendtagebuch', *Studien zur Musikwissenschaft*, xxv (1962), 68–88.

made diary-like, prose entries on his sketches and autographs,[28] and, more rarely, on individual leaves of paper. Subsequently such entries appeared occasionally in the conversation books. In later years, too, he recorded items pertaining to household affairs and finances on calendars.[29] But there is no sign that Beethoven kept a diary on any other occasion, and, in view of his propensity for saving personal documents, it is doubtful that he did.

It seems probable that a personal crisis provided not only the background but the motive for beginning the Tagebuch. Of course Beethoven was scarcely a stranger to crisis. But throughout his earlier life it was characteristic of him that he could confide the details of his inner struggles to intimate friends: to such men as Franz Wegeler, Karl Amenda, Stephan von Breuning, Ignaz von Gleichenstein, and to such women as Helene von Breuning, Christiane von Lichnowsky, Josephine Deym, Marie Erdödy, and Antonie Brentano. A man who could write to a beloved friend 'As soon as we are together again with no one to disturb us, you shall hear all about my real sorrows and the struggle within myself between life and death'[30] surely had little need for the catharsis provided by a diary. For such confessional diaries often arise in the absence of alternative outlets for the sharing of private feelings. But by the autumn of 1812, with the departure from Vienna of the Brentano family and his estrangement or withdrawal from Gleichenstein, Breuning, Erdödy, and other close friends, Beethoven found himself in a state of heightened isolation. This isolation, along with the painful aftermath of the 'Immortal Beloved' love affair, may have provided a stimulus for the Tagebuch, with its pathetic opening entries. Apparently the commitment of his feelings to paper helped Beethoven to secure some perspective on the critical events that had overtaken him, for he continued to make entries in the Tagebuch from time to time during the next six years, especially at moments of great inner turmoil and self-doubt.

The Tagebuch served several simultaneous functions: it was at once Beeethoven's 'journal intime' and his commonplace book. In the latter capacity it records events in its author's life, documents details of his productivity and musical projects, serves as a reminder of things done and to be done, and is a repository of citations and extracts from various writings, both classical and contemporary. The specialist will find unique and valuable data on a wide variety of subjects, from the

---

[28] See, for example, N II, pp. 89, 132, 163, 319–20, 346, 353.
[29] Berlin, DSB, Autograph 35, 87a–c (calendars for 1819, 1822 (not 1820, as Schindler wrote), and 1823).
[30] Letter of [spring 1805] to Josephine Deym, Anderson no. 110.

cost of music paper to the date of the final revision of *Fidelio*, from minutiae of Beethoven's fees and finances to his exploration of older religious music in preparation for the *Missa solemnis*, from descriptions of his hearing aids to specifications of the string forces for his concerts of early 1814.

But it is largely as a 'journal intime' that the Tagebuch has fascinated Beethoven's biographers, for such a document is the quintessential record of subjective feelings. Unlike letters, the interpretation of which must take account of the recipient's personality, the relationship between writer and addressee, and the writer's personal interest, the 'journal intime' is free from self-consciousness, if not always from self-deception. And unlike the consciously crafted memoir or autobiography, with its artifices and simplifications, the intimate diary contains raw responses to immediate experience, registering in this instance its author's uninhibited reactions to intensifying deafness, to the termination of his marriage project, to his brother Caspar Carl's death, and to his assumption of the guardianship of his nephew Karl. On a less fateful plane it also records his frustrations over the trivialities of his financial and household affairs, his illnesses and medical treatments, his dissatisfactions with his servants, and other thorny details of his everyday life.

Such documents, of course, must be used with caution and supplemented by materials on the author's personality from more 'objective' sources. For, as is typical of diaries, Beethoven's Tagebuch has little to say about his moments of happiness, his periods of good health, his sense of kinship with his community. Nor does it adequately reflect the wide variety of Beethoven's activities or the extent of his productivity during these years. Wholly omitted, too, are historical and political references; reading it, one would scarcely imagine that it was composed during a period that embraced the closing months of the Napoleonic Wars, the Congress of Vienna, and the onset of the age of Metternich in Austrian history.

The Tagebuch is unsurpassed as a record of Beethoven's intellectual interests; it superbly documents the intermingling of classical, Enlightenment, and Romantic threads among his literary influences. His devotion to Homer, Plutarch, Schiller, and Christian Sturm's *Betrachtungen* is known from other sources, but it is only from the Tagebuch that one learns the extent (and in some instances even the existence) of Beethoven's attraction to Indian philosophy and literature, to the poetry of Herder, the *Fiabe* of Gozzi, the dramas of Alfieri, the 'Fate tragedies' of Zacharias Werner and Adolf Müllner, and the cosmological speculations of the young Kant. In the Tagebuch is ample confirmation of Beethoven's famous assertion: 'From my childhood I have striven to grasp the meaning of the better and wiser people of every age.'[31] This is not to imply that he possessed either unusual erudition or esoteric preferences. His intellectual inclinations were firmly in the mainstream of contemporary taste, and all his enthusiasms were shared by many educated men and women of his time. Predictably, there are many quotations from the ancients, and several other entries that appear to be quotations but that may be Beethoven's own formulations of commonplace or proverbial ideas. The presence here of an extract from a given author does not necessarily imply that Beethoven regarded it as a confession of his own faith, for certain of the texts – for instance, those by Müllner, Werner, Homer, Herder, and Schiller – were probably copied with a view to possible musical setting. However, Beethoven usually set only those texts that reflected his own sentiments.

The Tagebuch is equally important for its documentation of Beethoven's religious faith, which apparently was greatly reinforced during these years. It contains several direct appeals, even prayers, to a personal God and exemplifies Beethoven's undogmatic adherence to a wide variety of non-Christian religious forms. His even-handed acceptance of Christian, Eastern, and Graeco-Roman religious conceptions is typical of both Romantic and Enlightenment viewpoints, which rejected the authority of the Church while postulating that religious truth is independent of its formal manifestations.

Beethoven appears here to be particularly drawn to Eastern and Rosicrucian ideas of purification, asceticism, sacrifice, and the suppression of libidinal interest in the outer world. Perhaps these notions helped to enhance his ability to absorb the shocks of mortality, increasing infirmity, deafness, guilt, and disappointment. Throughout, the Tagebuch testifies to the resiliency of Beethoven's personality. For in it he not only gave vent to his feelings and set down those problems that deeply troubled him, he also weighed alternatives, considered consequences, and determined upon courses of action. The Tagebuch gives evidence of Beethoven's ability to counter adversity by renewed creative activity and by devotion to a stringent, if often misguided, standard of ethical action. Indeed creativity and morality may be regarded as the underlying themes of the Tagebuch, which in some sense is Beethoven's guide to *Tugend* and proper conduct. It serves to justify his actions to himself (or to an imaginary 'better' or 'future' self), to

---

[31] Letter of 2 November 1809 to Breitkopf & Härtel, Anderson no. 228 (trans. revised by the author).

assuage his guilt, to redeem those faults to which he so freely confesses. And virtue, in turn, is only a means to a higher purpose – the safeguarding and furtherance of Beethoven's creativity.

Beethoven's central conflict – between his longings for human contact and his devotion to his art – is writ large in the Tagebuch. The opening entry laments: 'for you there is no longer any happiness except within yourself, in your art', and as the years pass Beethoven explicitly calls for the subordination of his personal happiness to his creative work: 'Everything that is called life should be sacrificed to the sublime and be a sanctuary of art' (No. 40); 'Sacrifice once and for all the trivialities of social life to your art' (No. 169). Repeatedly Beethoven exhorts himself to break his isolation: he expresses his desire to take meals with friends, to share his griefs with others, to hold fast to the threads of social and familial kinship. But his yearnings for friendship, warmth, and love are not quite compatible with his equally strong yearnings for conflict-free surroundings in which to develop his artistic gifts. 'Live only in your art . . . This is . . . the *only existence* for you' (No. 88). In the last analysis Beethoven came to believe – however ambivalently and painfully – that he must follow a sacrificial path to artistic fulfilment.

A NOTE ON MONEY VALUES

1 florin (or gulden) = 60 kreuzer
1 silver florin = 2½ paper florins
1 gold ducat = 4½ silver florins = 11¼ paper florins

Paper florins were termed 'Wiener Währung' (abbreviated 'W.W.'), while silver florins were termed 'Conventions Münze' ('C.M.'). The rates were subject to wide fluctuations and are therefore only approximate. The following abbreviations, used by Beethoven in the Tagebuch, were in common usage: # = Dukaten; f = Florin; x = Kreuzer.

ACKNOWLEDGMENTS

I am grateful for assistance, corrections, advice, new information, and suggestions to Ingrid Scheib-Rothbart (Goethe House, New York), Clemens Brenneis (Berlin), Martin Staehelin (Beethoven-Archiv, Bonn), Joseph Kerman (University of California at Berkeley), Eric A. Blackall (Cornell University), Robert Winter (University of California at Los Angeles), Peter Riethus (Gesellschaft der Musikfreunde, Vienna), Rosemary Dooley and Rosemary Roberts (Cambridge University Press), Frederick Crane (University of Iowa), Douglas Johnson (University of Virginia), and especially to Sieghard Brandenburg (Beethoven-Archiv, Bonn) and the editor of this volume. Grateful acknowledgment is also due to the New York Public Library, Columbia University Libraries, Library of Congress, Deutsche Staatsbibliothek, Staatsbibliothek Preussischer Kulturbesitz, Österreichische Nationalbibliothek, British Library, Royal College of Music, Union Theological Seminary, New York Society Library, Yale University Libraries, Beethoven-Archiv, Stadt- und Universitätsbibliothek Frankfurt, Universitätsbibliothek Heidelberg, and Universitätsbibliothek Bonn. And to the libraries of the University of Virginia, University of Illinois, University of California at Los Angeles, Iowa University, Harvard University, University of Massachusetts, and State University of New York at Buffalo. The transcription of the Gräffer Tagebuch is made by kind permission of the Stadtarchiv, Iserlohn.

‖fol. 1r‖[1]Beylage I[?][2]
Beethovens Tagebuch
1812

[1] The words 'Ohne Zweifel von der Hand Gaßners', which are initialled 'L.N.' (that is, Ludwig Nohl), appear at the upper left margin. At the right, in three different, unidentified hands, appears: 'Nachlass von Gaßner', 'einzig', and 'KN Nr. 30'.
[2] The 'I' is crossed out with two vertical lines.

Supplement I
Beethoven's Diary
1812

Concerning 'Beylage', a transcription of the Tagebuch presumably was to have constituted one of the appendices to the 'Viennese biography' projected for publication in early 1828 (see above, pp. 194–6). In his *Beethoven nach den Schilderungen seiner Zeitgenossen* (Stuttgart, 1877), p. 146, Nohl also mistook Gräffer's hand for Gassner's.

1 Ergebenheit, innigste Ergebenheit in dein Schicksal, nur diese kann dir die Opfer— — —zu dem Dienstgeschäft geben — o harter Kampf! — Alles anwenden was noch zu thun ist um das Nöthige zu der weiten Reise zu entwerfen — alles mußt du — — finden was dein seligster Wunsch gewährt, so mußt du es doch abtrotzen. — absolut die stette Gesinnung beobachten.[1] Du darfst nicht <u>Mensch</u> seyn, <u>für dich nicht</u>, <u>nur für andre</u>, für dich gibts kein Glück mehr als in dir selbst in deiner Kunst — o Gott! gib mir Kraft, mich zu besiegen, mich darf ja nichts an das Leben fesseln. — Auf diese Art mit A geht alles zu Grunde   — —

[1] The following may be a separate paragraph.

Submission, deepest submission to your fate, only this can give you the sacrifices — — — for this matter of service. O hard struggle! — Do everything that still has to be done to arrange what is necessary for the long journey. You must — — find everything that your most cherished wish can grant, yet you must bend it to your will. — Maintain an absolutely steady attitude.
You must not be a *human being, not for yourself, but only for others*: for you there is no longer any happiness except within yourself, in your art. O God! give me strength to conquer myself, nothing at all must fetter me to life. — In this manner with A everything goes to ruin.

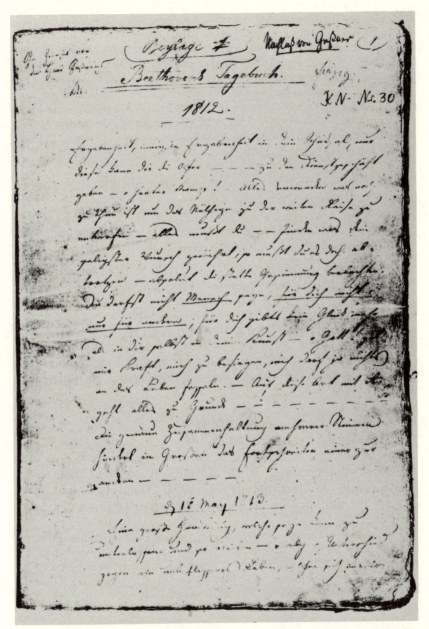

Plate VI. Anton Gräffer's copy of Beethoven's Tagebuch of 1812–1818, fol. 1r: Iserlohn, Stadtarchiv

This entry and No. 3 are usually considered to express Beethoven's reactions to the 'Immortal Beloved' love affair of mid-1812. 'A' may be the initial of the name of the addressee (Antonie Brentano?) of Beethoven's letter to the 'Immortal Beloved' (6–7 July [1812], Anderson no. 373). Unlike the 'A' at this point in the 'Fischhof' Manuscript, the 'A' in Gräffer's copy cannot be taken for any other letter. The words 'long journey' – if they are not a poetical reference to death – may refer to Beethoven's travels to or from the Bohemian spas in the summer of 1812, his journey to Linz in October, or his resolve to leave Vienna expressed in the 'Immortal Beloved' letter.

2 Die genaue Zusammenhaltung mehrerer Stimmen hindert im Großen das Fortschreiten einer zur andern — — — — —

    The precise coinciding of several musical voices generally hinders the progression from one to the other.

3   den 13 May 1813
Eine große Handlung, welche seyn kann zu unterlassen und so bleiben — o welcher Unterschied gegen ein unbeflissenes Leben, welches sich in mir ‖fol. 1v‖ so oft abbildete — o schreckliche Umstände, die mein Gefühl für Häuslichkeit nicht unterdrücken, aber deren Ausübung o Gott, Gott sieh auf den unglücklichen B. herab laß es nicht länger so dauern —

                    13 May 1813
    To forgo what could be a great deed and to stay like this. O how different from a shiftless life, which I often pictured to myself. O terrible circumstances, which do not suppress my longing for domesticity, but [prevent] its realisation. O God, God, look down upon the unhappy B., do not let it continue like this any longer.

This is apparently a further reference to the termination of the 'Immortal Beloved' love affair and to the dissolution of Beethoven's long-postponed marriage plans. Although a letter to Matthäus Andreas Stein bespeaks his intention to arrive in Baden on 13 May (letter of [early May 1813], Anderson no. 420), Beethoven remained in Vienna on that day.

4   alle Abends durchsehn.

    Look through them all in the evening.

5 Lerne Schweigen[,] o Freund. Dem Silber gleichet die Rede[,] aber zu rechter Zeit Schweigen ist lauteres Gold.

> Learn to keep silent, O friend. Speech is like silver, but to be silent at the right moment is pure gold.

Johann Gottfried Herder, 'Das Schweigen', from *Blumen aus morgenländischen Dichtern gesammlet*, which consists mainly of Herder's free renderings of didactic, aphoristic poetry from the *Būstān* and *Gulistān* by the Persian poet Sa'dī (c. 1184–1291); first published in *Zerstreute Blätter, vierte Sammlung* (Gotha, 1792), p. 11; reprinted in *Herders poetische Werke*, ed. Carl Redlich, Sämmtliche Werke, vol. xxvi/2 (Berlin, 1882), p. 374. Beethoven's canon on this text, WoO 168 No. 1, was entered in Charles Neate's *Stammbuch* on 24 January 1816; there is also a reference to the canon in the letter to Tobias Haslinger of [January 1816] (Anderson no. 600). According to Fanny Giannatasio del Rio's reminiscences, Beethoven wrote a canon on the same text for her family: see Friedrich Kerst, ed., *Die Erinnerungen an Beethoven* (Stuttgart, 1913), vol. i, p. 213. Six more Herder poems are copied into the Tagebuch: see Nos. 6, 55–9. A large folio sheet in Beethoven's hand contains copies of five further poems from the same collection: 'Die laute Klage', 'Morgengesang der Nachtigall', 'Die Perle', 'Anmuth des Gesanges', and 'Macht des Gesanges'. It was originally in the Artaria Collection, and is at present on loan from the Heirs of Stefan Zweig to London, BL, Department of Manuscripts: see *Führer durch die Beethoven Zentenar-Austellung der Stadt Wien 1927* (Vienna, 1927), no. 529. Beethoven set 'Die laute Klage' in 1814 or 1815 (WoO 135), and 'Der Gesang der Nachtigall' on 3 June (not May) 1813 (WoO 141). Eleonore von Breuning inscribed an aphorism of Herder's in Beethoven's 1792 *Stammbuch*. Two brief sketches for a setting of Herder's 'Die Schwestern des Schicksals' appear in the 'Kafka' Miscellany (London, BL, Add. MS 29801), fol. 100. For a further reference to Herder, see Kerst, ed., *Die Erinnerungen an Beethoven*, vol. i, p. 235.

6 Und regneten die Wolken Lebensbäche, nie wird der Weidenbaum dir Datteln tragen[.] verschwende nicht die Zeit mit schlechten Menschen,[;] gemeines Rohr wird nie dir Zucker geben. Kannst du ein gutes Schwerdt aus weichem Tohn [Thone] dir schmieden, ⟨?⟩ aendert[,] von Menschen gepflegt [gehegt,] je sich des Wolfes Natur, ⟨?⟩ ists nicht einerley dem[1] ⟨Regen,⟩ der hier auf salzigem Boden Distel und Dornen erzieht, Blumen der [den] Garten [Gärten] verleiht? Also verschwende du dir nicht Saamen und köstliche Wartung.[:] Böses dem [den] Guten[,] und Gutes [Guts] dem[1] Bösen erzeigen[,] ist Eins.— — — —

---

[1] The word 'dem' is not in Herder's text.

And even if the clouds were to rain rivers of life
Never will the willow tree bear dates.
Don't waste time with bad people;
Ordinary cane will never give sugar.
Can you forge a good sword out of soft clay?
Does the wolf's nature change when it is nursed by Man?
Is it not one and the same ⟨rain⟩ that makes thistles and thorns
grow here on salty ground and gives flowers to the gardens?
So, waste not seed and precious cultivation:
It is all one to show bad to the good and good to the bad.

Herder, 'Verschwendete Mühe', *Zerstreute Blätter, vierte Sammlung*, p. 27; reprinted in Sämmtliche Werke, vol. xxvi/2, p. 380 (see commentary on No. 5).

7 [a] Das beste an dein Uibel nicht zu denken ist Beschäftigung. —
[b] Seht ⟨ihr wohl,⟩ so ist der ‖fol. 2r‖ Mensch,[!] denn [D'rum,] wenn einer ist gefallen, mag der andere weinen; aber nicht zu richten sich erkühnen.

_____

[c] Leben gleicht der Töne Beben
Und der Mensch dem Saitenspiel[:]
Wenn es hart zu Boden fiel[,]
Ist der rechte Klang verschwunden
Und es kann nicht mehr gesunden
dann [?kann] allein nur Unlust geben
Darf mit andern nicht mehr klingen
Soll es Einigung dem Ohr
Zu dem rein gestimmten Chor
Störend nicht den mißlaut bringen[.]

_____

[d] Fragst du nach der Ursach wenn ~~Sterne au~~
Sterne auf ~~unter~~ und unter gehn?
Hier ist das geschieht nur klar [Was geschieht ist hier nur
  klar:]
Das Warum wird offenbar[,]
Wenn die Todten auferstehn! —

_____

[e] (Elvire allein, die Harfe im Arm, das Spiel mit immer leiseren, sanft verschwebenden Tönen endend [endigend].)
Wie der letzte Hauch [Laut] verklinget[,]
Der sich unter leiser Hand
Aus der Harfen[1] Saiten schwinget[;]

Beethoven's Tagebuch of 1812–1818

Wie's auf klaren Teich Kristallen [Teichkrystalle]
Sich von einem [eines] Tropfenfalle
Weiter stets und schwächer ringet[,]
||fol. 2v|| Bis es fern am Blumenstrand
Still verschwand.
So auch möcht' ich einst entschweben [verschweben]
Und verklingen in das bessre Leben! —
Wird mich[,] fern vom Vaterland[,]
In der Stürme rauher Wiege[,]
Wo ich angefesselt liege
Von der Liebe starkem Band —
Wird mich einst des Schicksals Strand [Hand]
Sanft empor zur Heimath heben.⟨?⟩

(Das Haupt auf die Harfe geneigt[,] bleibt sie eine Weile ruhn. Eine Saite springt, Elvire fährt erschrocken auf, die Harfe fällt ⟨dröhnend⟩ zu Boden.)
— — — — — Der Schall[,] die
           Welle —
Wohl sind sie des Lebens Bild,[;]
Doch die Wooge[,] die am Felsen
Sich in grauser Brandung bricht
Eine Well' ist's wie die andre[,]
Die im weißen Mondeslicht
Auf des Teiches Spiegel schwindet[:]
Und der Riß gespannter Saiten
Wie der Klang[,] der sanft verhallet[,]
Ist ein <u>Schall</u>
der den Fall
Eines Menschen kann bedeuten. —

[1] The 'n' is crossed out.

[a] The best way not to think of your woes is to keep busy.
 [b] Mark you well, such is Man!
   Thus, when one has fallen
   Another may *weep*;
   But must not *dare to judge.*
 [c] Life resembles the trembling tones
   And Man the lute:
   When it falls hard to the ground
   The true sound disappears
   And it cannot become whole again;

>   It can only give displeasure.
>   It may no longer sound together with *others*;
>   May it not disturb the ear's harmony
>   And bring discord to the pure-sounding choir.
> [d] Dost thou ask the *cause* when
>   Stars rise and set?
>   Only *what* happens is clear
>   The *why* will become apparent
>   When the dead arise!
> [e] *Elvira* (alone, harp in her arm, ending the music with ever quieter and softly disappearing tones):
>   As the last tone dies away,
>   That sounds under a soft hand
>   From the harp's strings
>   Like a drop fallen
>   On the clear crystal pond,
>   The rings become steadily weaker
>   Until they disappear quietly
>   In the distance on the pond's flowery banks,
>   So would I, one day, like to soar on high
>   And fade away into the better life! —
>   Far from the fatherland,
>   In the rough cradle of storms,
>   Where I lie bound
>   By love's strong bond,
>   Shall, one day, the hand of fate
>   Carry me softly upward to my home?
> (Her head bent over the harp, she rests awhile. A string breaks, Elvira starts up in fright, the harp falls ⟨echoingly⟩ to the ground.)
>   — — — — — The sound, the wave,
>   They are surely the image of life;
>   But the wave, that breaks on the rock
>   In a fearsome surge,
>   Is like the wave that
>   Disappears on the mirror of the pond
>   In the white moonlight;
>   And the rupture of the taut strings,
>   As the sound softly dies away,
>   Is a *sound*
>   Which portends
>   The downfall of a man.

7[b]–[e] are extracts from *Die Schuld*, a popular 'Schicksalstragödie' (Fate tragedy) by the German dramatist, editor, and critic Amandus Gottfried Adolf Müllner (1774–1829), which Beethoven considered for musical setting. *Die Schuld* was first produced on 27 April 1813 at Vienna's Burgtheater. No. 7[b] = Act iv, Sc. 7; No. 7[c] = Act iv, Sc. 8; No. 7[d] = Act iv, Sc. 11 – the closing words of the drama; No. 7[e] = Act i, Sc. 1 – the opening of the drama. Beethoven had access to the text before its publication in book form, *Die Schuld: Trauerspiel in vier Akten* (Vienna, 1816); the extracts quoted appear on pp. 130, 135, 146, 11–13. In No. 7[c], lines 4–10, and No. 7[e], lines 25–6 ('Doch die Wooge . . .'), Beethoven's text varies significantly from the published text.

8 Trochäen mit Daktilen zuweilen der –⌣⌣ ||fol. 3r|| nicht mehr gilt als der –⌣ lassen sich gut in dem Stücke von Dr Müllner sind meistens 4 füssige –⌣– diese lassen sich auch gut zur Musik. — — —

In trochaic [lines] with occasional dactyls the –⌣⌣ counts for no more than –⌣. They work out well in Dr Müllner's play, most of which is in [trochaic] tetrameters. These also are well suited to musical setting.

The reference is to Adolf Müllner's *Die Schuld* (see commentary on No. 7). Beethoven often marked out the metre of the texts in his sketches for vocal compositions: see Arnold Schmitz, *Das romantische Beethovenbild* (Bonn, 1927), pp. 76–7, and compare No. 49. The text is clearly corrupt.

9 Uiber mehrere Zweifel in der deutschen Poesie![1] Die Ouverture kann füglich darauf berechnet werden, daß sie mit einem Pizzicato endet welches Elvire auf der Harfe noch einige Sekunden fortzusetzen scheint.

[1] The following may be a new paragraph.

Concerning several doubts in German poetry!
The overture can be well laid out in such a way that it ends with a *pizzicato*, which Elvira appears to sustain on the harp for a few seconds.

The prefatory stage directions for Müllner's *Die Schuld* (see commentary on No. 7) specify: 'Die Ouvertüre muß mit einem Pianissimo endigen, welches Elvire einige Sekunden lang auf der Harfe fortzusetzen scheint.'

10 Wie muß das Eleison im Griechischen ausgesprochen werden? E – lei
e – le – ison ist recht.

      How should Eleison be pronounced in Greek? E – le – ison is correct.

11   Scher la a'mando la Rondinella
      scherzet liebet [liebend] die Schwalbe
      lieto gode la tortorella
      fröhlich freut sich Turteltäubchen
      io sola misera non io [?so] goder

      The little swallow jokes and loves.
      The little turtle-dove is merrily happy.
      I alone am wretched and unhappy.

(See commentary on No. 12.)

12 immer im Italienischen übersetzen und bloß wegen Zweifel hie und da die Woche ein zweymal den Universitätslehrer der italienischen Sprache fragen.

      Always translate the Italian and only if you have doubts here and there ask the Italian instructor at the University once or twice a week.

Beethoven was practising German–Italian translation, probably German into Italian because the lines contain several rudimentary grammatical and spelling errors. (The first line should be 'Scherz'amando la Rondinella'.) However, the Italian text may have been corrupted in copying; in that case, Beethoven was translating from Italian into German. The Italian instructor has not been identified. Beethoven's *Nachlass* contained a packet of Italian grammars as well as a copy of a German–Italian dictionary; the latter is now Berlin, DSB, Autograph 40,9.

13 Die Schärpe und die Blume
Der standhafte Prinz von Calderon

      The Sash and the Flower.
      The Steadfast Prince by Calderón.

Two dramas by Pedro Calderón de la Barca (1600–81): *La banda y la flor* and *El principe constante* appeared in August Wilhelm von Schlegel's translation in *Spanisches Theater: Schauspiele von Don Pedro Calderon de la Barca*, 2 vols. (Berlin, 1803, 1809; reprinted Vienna, 1813; 2nd edn, Leipzig, 1845), vol. i, pp. 155–306, vol. ii, pp. 123–252. Several of Beethoven's contemporaries, including E. T. A. Hoffmann and Bernhard Romberg, composed operas to German translations of Calderón's plays.

14 Ost Morgen — West Abend — Süd Mittag — Nord Mitternacht — —

East morning — West evening — South noon — North midnight.

In German poetic diction the parts of the day signify the four points of the compass.

15 ||fol. 3v|| Alles in Vorrath kaufen um den Betruegereyen des x x zu steuern — frage den x wegen Lichter an x geschrieben wegen der x.

Stock up on everything in order to control the cheating of x x. Ask x about lights; wrote to x about x.

Beethoven often thought that he was being cheated by his servants: see also Nos. 110 and 137. The missing names were probably not entered by Beethoven.

16 Ich muß den Engländern ein Wenig zeigen was in dem God seave[1] the King für ein Segen ist. — 1 f 12 x kostet ein Buch Notenpapier. — Das man gewiß schöner schreibt sobald man für das Publikum schreibt ist gewiß eben so wenn man geschwind schreibt.

[1] Spelled thus and corrected.

I have to show the English a little of what a blessing 'God save the King' is. A book of music paper costs 1 florin 12 kreuzer. That one certainly writes nicer music as soon as one writes for the public is certain, even when one writes rapidly.

Beethoven composed *Wellingtons Sieg oder die Schlacht bei Vittoria* Op. 91, which includes an orchestration of 'God save the King', between August and November 1813. He dedicated it to the Prince Regent of England. In 1803 Beethoven composed a set of variations for piano, WoO 78, on the British national anthem, and in *c*. 1814–15 an arrangement of it for chorus and piano trio, WoO

157 No. 1. In 1813 he hoped to obtain an invitation to visit England. For a 'book' of music paper, see No. 157. Beethoven rapidly composed many occasional works in celebration of the Allied victories over Napoleon.

17 Nb[1] immer zwey Linien zu den b[?] — genommen.[2] Zeig mir die Laufbahn, wo an dem fernen Ziel die Palme steht! — Meinen erhabensten Gedanken leihe Hoheit, führe ihnen Wahrheiten zu, die es ewig bleiben!

[1] 'Nb' is crossed out and 'K' written by Nohl in the left margin; 'K' is also crossed out.
[2] The following may be a new paragraph.

N.B. Always use two staves for the b —.
Show me the course where at the distant goal stands the Palm! — Lend grandeur to my most exalted thoughts, add to them the truths that shall endure for ever.

The letter 'b' may mean 'Bassi' (cellos and double basses) or 'Bläser' (wind instruments). The second sentence, in iambic metre, is apparently a quotation (source unknown).

18 Bey meiner letzten Musik im großen Redoutensaal hatten sie
18 Violin prim
18 " secund
14 Violen
12 Violoncelle
7 Contrabässe
2 Contrafagotte

At my last concert in the Large Redoutensaal there were 18 first violins, 18 second violins, 14 violas, 12 cellos, 7 double basses, 2 double bassoons.

Beethoven gave concerts in the Large Redoutensaal on 2 January and 27 February 1814; the first concert featured *Wellingtons Sieg* Op. 91, and the Seventh Symphony Op. 92; at the second these works were repeated and the Eighth Symphony Op. 93 was added. The orchestra was greatly augmented by *dilettanti* to almost three times its normal size. For the size of contemporary orchestras, see letter to Vincenz Hauschka of [1816] (Anderson no. 716); Heinz Becker, 'Orchester', *Die Musik in Geschichte und Gegenwart*, ed. Friedrich Blume, vol. x (Kassel, 1962), table following col. 192; and especially, Otto Biba, 'Concert Life in Beethoven's Vienna', *Beethoven, Performers, and Critics*, ed. Robert Winter and Bruce Carr (Detroit, 1980), pp. 87–91. The enlarged orchestra for Beethoven's concert of 7 May 1824 consisted of 24 violins, 10 violas, and 12 cellos and double basses.

19 Schuhbürsten zum Abputzen, wenn Jemand kommt. —

    Shoe-brushes for polishing when somebody visits.

20 [1]Zb. Bestimmung der Aerzte über mein Leben — — ist keine Rettung mehr — so muß ich — — — — — brauchen — ???[2] ||fol. 4r|| Es gehört um noch geschwinder zu vollenden was früher unmöglich — — Concilium mit x x x — — —

[1] In the margin, in addition: 'Zi' or 'Zb', apparently in Gräffer's hand.
[2] The following may be a new paragraph.

    For example, the diagnosis of the doctors about my life — — If recovery is no longer possible, then I must use — ???
    To accomplish even more rapidly what was impossible earlier it is necessary to —
    Consultation with x x x —

Little is known about Beethoven's serious illness early in 1814. The only reference in the correspondence of this period to such an illness is in a letter to the Archduke Rudolph of [September 1814]: 'Unfortunately my health some time ago suffered a severe blow owing to *an inflammation of my intestines*, which brought me almost to death's door. But I am *now much better'* (Anderson no. 493). Whether that letter and this entry refer to Beethoven's rumoured (and undocumented) venereal disease, or merely to another in his long series of digestive disorders, is unclear. Romain Rolland takes the suppressed words as a reference to suicide: see his *Beethoven: Les grandes époques créatrices (édition définitive*, Paris, 1966), p. 1459. Beethoven's physicians in 1814 included Andreas Bertolini, Jakob Staudenheim, and Johann Malfatti.

21 Rosamunde von Alfieri Ausgabe von Gozzi — Pertossi welche die Theres Malfatti von mir hat, zurück fordern.— — —

    Ask for the return of *Rosmunda* by Alfieri, Gozzi edition — Pertossi, which Therese Malfatti received from me.

Rosmunda is a tragedy in five acts by Count Vittorio Alfieri (1749–1803), Italian anti-tyrannical dramatist. It was written in 1778–80 and first published in *Tragedie di Vittorio Alfieri*, vol. ii (Siena, 1783); it appeared in numerous reprints and translations. Carlo Gozzi (1722–1806) is the influential Italian dramatist and librettist. 'Gozzi edition' may be *Le dieci fiabe teatrali del Conte Carlo Gozzi*, 3 vols. (Berlin, 1808). Schiller's version of Gozzi's *Turandot* was produced at the Theater-an-der-Wien in 1807; productions of works by Gozzi were undertaken by Treitschke, Schreyvogel, Reichardt, and others in Beethoven's circle: see Hedwig Hoffmann Rusack, *Gozzi in Germany: a Survey of the Rise and Decline of the Gozzi Vogue in Germany and Austria* (New York, 1930; reprinted New York, 1966), pp. 72–103. 'Pertossi' is probably a misreading; it may = Gozzi's *I pitocchi fortunati*. Beethoven proposed marriage to Therese Malfatti (1792–1851) in 1810; he lent books to her: see his letter to her of [May 1810] (Anderson no. 258). For Beethoven's study of Italian, see commentary on No. 12.

22 Die Oper Fidelio 1814 statt März bis 15ten May neu geschrieben und verbessert. —

The opera *Fidelio* 1814, instead of March, newly written and improved by 15 May.

The final version of the opera *Fidelio* was first performed on 23 May 1814. The revision had been begun by mid-February: 'My opera is also going to be staged, but I am revising it a good deal' (letter to Count Franz Brunsvik of 13 February 1814, Anderson no. 462). The extent of the work in February is described in a letter to Georg Friedrich Treitschke of [April 1814]: 'Before my concert [of 27 February 1814] I had just made a few sketches here and there, both in the first and in the second acts' (Anderson no. 479). See also N II, p. 296, note.

23 Beim Quartier den alten Ofen wegräumen, — auf den Boden tragen. —

Have the old stove cleared out of the lodgings and put in the attic.

Beethoven took lodgings in Baden towards late summer 1814.

24 Daß die Sache mit K[?] sich so verhält bin ich bereit mit einem Eid zu beschwören an K und B — G —

That the affair with K is so I am prepared to swear under oath to K and B — G —.

This entry probably relates to the progress, in the summer of 1814, of Beethoven's litigation against Prince Ferdinand Kinsky's estate to restore the full value of his annuity payments: see Thayer–Deiters–Riemann iii, pp. 440–2; Thayer–Forbes, pp. 590–1. If so, the first 'K' is Kinsky and the second is the curator of Kinsky's estate, Johann Kanka, who helped to negotiate a settlement agreeable to Beethoven, or Franz Anton von Kolowrat, a Bohemian count who, at Archduke Rudolph's urging, intervened on Beethoven's behalf: see letters to Kanka of 22 August 1814 to 24 February 1815, Anderson nos. 486, 497, 502, 520–2, 530; letter to Archduke Rudolph of late [1814], Anderson no. 513. 'B — G —' is obscure but may possibly refer to 'Böhmen Graf' Kolowrat. The matter was settled on 18 January 1815 (Thayer–Deiters–Riemann iii, pp. 489–91). For a synopsis of the Kinsky litigation, see V. Kratochvil, 'Beethoven und Fürst Kinsky', *Beethovenjahrbuch*, ed. Theodor von Frimmel, vol. ii (Munich and Leipzig, 1909), pp. 13–18.

25 Vieles ist auf Erden zu thun, thue es bald![1] Nicht mein jetziges Alltagsleben fortsetzen, die Kunst fordert auch dieses Opfer— — in der Zerstreuung ruhn um desto kräftiger in der Kunst zu wirken —

[1] The following may be a new paragraph.

> There is much to be done on earth, do it soon!
> I must not continue my present everyday life; art demands this sacrifice too. — Rest and find diversion only in order to act all the more forcefully in art.

26 Den [Denn] ausduldenden Muth verlieh den Menschen das Schiksal[.] —

> For Fate gave Man the courage to endure to the end.

The Iliad, Book xxiv, line 49. *Homers Ilias*, trans. Johann Heinrich Voss (Hamburg, 1793); Beethoven cites the Vienna reprint of 1814, vol. ii, p. 424. The Tagebuch contains another citation from *The Iliad* (No. 49) and three from *The Odyssey* (Nos. 74, 169, 170). There are frequent references to Homer in the conversation books and occasional references in the correspondence. Prosodic studies of hexameters from Homer appear in entry No. 49 and in the 'Scheide' Sketchbook of 1815–16 (SV 364; see N II, p. 328), and a draft canon on a text from *The Odyssey* occurs in a pocket sketchbook in the British Library (SV 189: London, BL, Egerton 2795): see Hans Boettcher, 'Beethovens Homer-Studien', *Die Musik*, xix (1926–7), 478–85.

27 1812 im October war ich in Linz wegen B — [1] Die Ohrenmaschine könnte so seyn, daß Sterne der Oeffnung den Eingang des Schalls sich der Schall rund um das Ohr fortpflanzte, um auf diese Weise gegen alle Oeffnungen hören könnte.

[1] The following may be a new paragraph.

> In October 1812 I was in Linz because of B.
> An ear-trumpet could be such that stars of the opening [?amplify] the entrance of the sound and the sound would be transmitted around the ear and in this way could be heard towards all openings.

On 5 October 1812 Beethoven arrived in Linz, where he stayed with his brother ('B') Nikolaus Johann (1776–1848), owner of an apothecary's shop in that city. The text of the second sentence is defective. According to Nohl (*Die Beethoven-Feier und die Kunst der Gegenwart* (Vienna, 1871), p. 57, note 1), one of Beethoven's ear-trumpets had stars near the opening. Ear-trumpets were made for Beethoven by Johann Nepomuk Mälzel (1772–1838) during 1814: see letters to Nikolaus Zmeskall von Domanovecz of [11 January 1814], and Dr Carl of [July 1814] (Anderson nos. 459, 485).

28 ‖fol. 4v‖ Von heute an nie in das Haus —— ohne Schande über dich von einem solchen — — — etwas zu verlangen. — — —

> From today on never go into that house — — without shame at craving something from such a person.

Possibly a reference to a brothel. See also Nos. 122 and 138.

29 Ein gutes Wort findet gut statt.

> A good word will come true.

A German proverb: see Franz von Lipperheide, ed., *Spruchwörterbuch* (Berlin, 1907), p. 1033, col. 2.

30 Der Haß dehnt [?lenkt] sich selbst zurück auf diejenigen, die ihn hegen.

> Hatred recoils upon those who harbour it.

Another proverb, commonplace with 'evil' for 'hatred', but not located in this precise form. Beethoven once said that 'he had been educated with proverbs': Ludwig Nohl, *Eine stille Liebe zu Beethoven* (2nd edn, Leipzig, 1902), p. 63.

31 <u>Gesetz</u>. Nach keiner abgeschriebenen Partitur Kopien zulassen, die mir wichtig ist. — und immer 20 und 24 liniges Papier.[1] — Deine [?Keine] Zeit vergeht geschwinder, rollt schneller um, als die wo wir unsern Geist oder ich mich mit meiner Muse beschäftige. —

[1] The following may be a new paragraph.

Rule. Don't allow copies to be made from a copied score of a work that is important to me. — And they must always be on paper with 20 and 24 staves. —
No time passes more quickly, rolls by faster, than when our mind is occupied or when I spend it with my Muse.

Beethoven probably means that all copies of his important works should be made from the original autograph rather than from second-generation copies. This entry may relate to the unauthorised copy of the *Fidelio* score that was used in a production at Mainz in the summer of 1814: see letter to Treitschke of [summer 1814] (Anderson no. 488). For discussions of the number of staves in Beethoven's autographs, see Alan Tyson, 'Sketches and Autographs', *The Beethoven Companion*, ed. Denis Arnold and Nigel Fortune (London, 1971), pp. 452–3; Lewis Lockwood, 'The Autograph of the First Movement of Beethoven's Sonata . . . Op. 69', *The Music Forum*, vol. ii, ed. William J. Mitchell and Felix Salzer (New York and London, 1970), pp. 22–3.

32 7 paar Stiefeln.

7 pairs of boots.

33 2300 f bin ich der [?den ?dem] F.A.B. schuldig, einmal 1100 und 60#[1]

[1] The passage has been crossed out with a single line.

I owe F.A.B. 2300 florins, once 1100 florins and 60 ducats.

Beethoven accepted loans from his intimate friends, the merchant Franz Brentano (1765–1844) and his wife Antonie Brentano (1780–1869). He never fully repaid the loans: see Maynard Solomon, 'Antonie Brentano and Beethoven', *Music & Letters*, lviii (1977), 165–7, with further references; see also letter to Antonie Brentano of (?1814) (Anderson no. 659, incorrectly dated [29 September 1816]), which probably refers to one of the loans that is the subject of this entry.

34 Gegen alle Menschen äußerlich nie die Verachtung merken lassen, die sie verdienen denn man kann nicht wissen wo man sie braucht — —
— Die Schottischen Lieder zeigen als ungezwungen die unordentlichste Melodie vermöge die [der] Harmonie behandelt werden kann.

Never *outwardly* show people the contempt they deserve, because one cannot know when one may need them.— — The Scottish songs show how unconstrainedly the most unstructured melody can be treated by harmonic means.

228   Maynard Solomon

Like Haydn, Pleyel, Weber, and Hummel, Beethoven prepared numerous arrangements of Scottish, Irish, and Welsh songs for the Edinburgh publisher George Thomson: see Op. 108 and WoO 152–7. For his work on arrangements of Scottish songs during late 1814 and early 1815, see letters to Thomson of 15 September 1814, October 1814, and 7 February 1815 (Anderson nos. 496, 503, 529); see also Kinsky-Halm, pp. 624–6, 657; Willy Hess, 'Handschriftensammelbände zu Beethovens Volksliederbearbeitungen', *Beiträge zur Beethoven-Bibliographie*, ed. Kurt Dorfmüller (Munich, 1978), pp. 96, 98.

35 Nie wird eine Partitur so richtig ab-‖fol. 5r‖geschrieben, als sie der Autor selbst schreibt. —

   No copy of a score is as correct as the score the composer himself writes.

36 Jeden Tag Jemanden zum Essen, wie Musici, wo man dann dieses und jenes abhandelt, von Instrumenten ect Violin, Violoncell ect —

   Every day share a meal with someone, such as musicians, where one can discuss this and that, instruments etc., violins, cellos, etc.

37 Den ersten besten Satz in Canons¹ erfunden auf Harmonie gebaut.

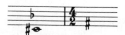

¹ The words 'in Canons' are crossed out, with dots underneath to signify 'stet'. In the margin, in Nohl's hand: 'N.B. steht nicht in der Berliner Hdschr.' Evidently Nohl understood that the omission of 'in Canons' in the Fischhof copy is evidence of the priority of the Gräffer copy.

   The best opening phrases in canons are built around harmonies.

38 34 Flaschen von der Gräfin Erdödy — —

   34 bottles from Countess Erdödy.

After a long estrangement, Beethoven and Countess Marie Erdödy (1789–1837) were reconciled early in 1815: see his letter of 29 [sic] February 1815 (Anderson no. 531). A gift of wine seems to have accompanied their reconciliation.

39 Überall wird Cortez, die Vestalinn aufgeführt.[1]

---

[1] In the margin, in Nohl's hand: 'Oct. 1814 Festvorstellung in Wien'.

Cortez and *La Vestale* are performed everywhere.

The operas *Fernand Cortez ou La conquête du Mexique* (first version 1809) and *La vestale* (1807) were composed by Gaspare Spontini (1774–1851). Very frequent references to productions of these operas in Vienna, Berlin, Dresden, Breslau, and Mannheim appeared in the musical press between October 1814 and April 1815: see the *Allgemeine musikalische Zeitung*, xvi (1814), cols. 706–7, 755, 788, 800–4, 866; xvii (1815), cols. 22–7, 59–60, 167, 225. One may deduce that this entry was written in late January or February 1815. Nohl's marginal date refers to the 'grand festival production' in Vienna of 1 October 1814: see Thayer–Deiters–Riemann iii, p. 451. See also the *Allgemeine musikalische Zeitung*, xvi (1814), col. 655; xvii (1815), cols. 51, 191, 256, 277, for references to performances of excerpts from the operas and to Spontini's appointment to the post of Berlin court Kapellmeister. Beethoven praised Spontini to Freudenberg (Friedrich Kerst, ed., *Die Erinnerungen an Beethoven* (Stuttgart, 1913), vol. ii, p. 114), and regarded *La vestale* as having an exemplary libretto: see Thayer–Deiters–Riemann iv, p. 465; Thayer–Forbes, p. 874.

40 Alles was Leben heißt sey der Erhabenen geopfert und ein Heiligthum der Kunst, laß mich leben, sey es auch mit Hilfsmitteln wenn sie sich nur finden! — — — — — — — — — — — — — — —

Everything that is called life should be sacrificed to the sublime and be a sanctuary of art. Let me live, even if by artificial means, if only they can be found!

41 ¹Die Ohrenmaschinen wo möglich zur Reife bringen, als dann lesen² [?reisen] — dieses bist du dir, den Menschen und ihm dem Allmächtigen schuldig, nur so kannst du noch einmal alles entwickeln was in dir alles verschlossen bleiben muß — — — und ein kleiner Hof — — eine kleine Kapelle — — — von mir in ihr den Gesang geschrieben angeführt, zur Ehre des Allmächtigen — des Ewigen Unendlichen — — —

---

[1] In the margin, in Nohl's hand: 'N.B.'
[2] The word 'lesen' is partly underlined, probably by Nohl.

If possible, bring the ear-trumpets to perfection and then travel.

This you owe to yourself, to Mankind and to Him, the Almighty. Only thus can you once again develop everything that has to remain locked within you. — — And a small court [?farmhouse] — — a small chapel [?church] — — in it the hymn written by me, performed for the glory of the Almighty, the Eternal, the Infinite.

Re 'ein kleiner Hof' (? = a small court): it was reported in 1809 by Johann Friedrich Reichardt that Beethoven hoped to receive an appointment as Kapellmeister to Archduke Rudolph after Rudolph's enthronement as cardinal: see Reichardt, *Vertraute Briefe* (Amsterdam, 1810), vol. ii, pp. 75–6; Thayer–Deiters–Riemann iii, pp. 188–9. But it seems more likely that 'Hof' = farmhouse, in which case this entry connects with Nos. 66 and 86.

42 So mögen die letzten Tage verfließen — — und ‖fol. 5v‖ der künftigen Menschheit. —

Thus may the [?my] last days flow by — — and [those] of future Mankind. —

43 Haendel,[1] Bach, Gluck, Mozart, Haydn's Portraite in meinem Zimmer — — —Sie können mir auf Duldung Anspruch machen helfen — —

[1] The second 'e' has been crossed out.

Portraits of Handel, Bach, Gluck, Mozart, and Haydn in my room. — — They can promote my capacity for endurance.

J. S. Bach, Handel, Mozart, and Haydn had long formed Beethoven's musical pantheon. Although this is the earliest documentary evidence of his high regard for Gluck, there is little doubt that he had long admired him as well: see letter to Heinrich Joseph von Collin of [February 1808] (Anderson no. 163); Czerny's memoranda to Otto Jahn (Friedrich Kerst, ed., *Die Erinnerungen an Beethoven* (Stuttgart, 1913), vol. i, pp. 57, 60); Kerst, ed., vol. i, p. 45. There is no record that Beethoven owned portraits of any composers.

44 Um nur nächst [?nichts] vom vergangenen man was werden wollte, so hat das Vergangene doch das Gegenwärtige hervorgebracht — Sie wurden irdisch — — erschreckliche Weissagungen und durch die Dichtungen, durch ihre —[1] Bedeutenheit — gerettet —

[1] The dash has been crossed out.

If only one wanted to separate oneself from the past, still the past has created the present. They became terrestrial — — terrible prophecies and through the poems, through their significance — rescued —

Perhaps a reference to the myths of a polytheistic religion. The text may be defective.

45 indem sie in großen Irrthümern lebten über <u>Sich</u> selbst, halte ich es für nöthig hier einen Standpunkt anzunehmen Da es schon öfters geschehen ist, daß sie nachdem sie ihre Tücke an mir ausgelassen, sie dann mit einiger Freundlichkeit wieder gut zu machen suchen — losgesprochen wurden sie nicht von ihrer Strafe — eine Ordnung geziemt zur Wichtigkeit in Ansehung ihrer Manen — und meiner.
— —

Because you lived under a great delusion about *yourself*, I deem it necessary to take a stand on this. For it has already often happened that after you have vented your spite on me, you then tried to make it up with some friendliness. You were not absolved of your punishment; an order is appropriate for the importance in recognition of your departed spirits — and mine.

Although the entry as transcribed is in the third person, it may be assumed that Beethoven's original was in the second person and was the opening of a draft letter – continued in No. 47 – probably to Johanna van Beethoven, wife of Beethoven's brother Caspar Carl: see *Ludwig van Beethovens sämtliche Briefe*, ed. Emerich Kastner (Leipzig, 1910), 2nd edn, rev. Julius Kapp (Leipzig, 1923), p. 314. MacArdle and Misch point out that 'Manen' is probably a misreading and they suggest as possible alternatives: 'in Ansehung Ihres Mannes — und meiner' (regarding your husband and me); or 'in Ansehung Ihres Namens — und meines' (regarding your reputation and mine): see Donald W. MacArdle and Ludwig Misch, eds., *New Beethoven Letters* (Norman, 1957), p. 165.

46 15 Buteillen im Zimmer der Dienstmagd
18 Hemden —

15 bottles in the maid's room.
18 shirts.

47 ||fol. 6r|| Wahrscheinlich glauben sie daß ich alles dieses nicht bemerkte allein — um sie nur [?nie] aus diesem Irrthum zu ziehn so will ich ihnen nur bemerken daß wenn ihnen vielleicht daran gelegen ist, einen besseren Eindruck auf mich zu machen dieses gerade die entgegengesetzte Methode ist — eben dadurch ich ungern wieder bedauern muß, daß mein Bruder sie ihrer verdienten Strafe entrissen hat, daß ich allein nicht so ihre Handlungen —

You probably believe that I did not notice all this; but to disabuse you of this error I will merely mention to you that if perhaps you care to make a better impression on me this is precisely the opposite method. That is why I must again reluctantly regret that my brother has rescued you from your deserved punishment, that I alone not so your actions —

Part of a draft letter (the last sentence is incomplete), apparently addressed to Johanna van Beethoven, wife of Beethoven's brother Caspar Carl; see also No. 45. In 1811 she had been sentenced to a month's house arrest on a charge of embezzling household funds from her husband: Thayer–Deiters–Riemann iv, p. 563.

48 immer von halb 6 bis zum Frühstück studirt —

Always study from half-past five until breakfast.

49 Illiade 22^r Gesang Seite 356

[1]$-\cup-\cup\cup-$ nun aber erhascht mich das Schicksal[!]
daß nicht arbeitslos in den Staub ich sinke[,] noch ruhmlos[,]
Nein erst großes vollendet [vollendend,] wovon auch Künftige hören[!]

[1] This line is preceded by an oblique stroke.

The Iliad, Book 22, page 356
But now Fate catches me!
Let me not sink into the dust unresisting and inglorious,
But first accomplish great things, of which future generations too shall hear!

The Iliad, Book xxii, lines 303–5. Homers Ilias, trans. Voss, p. 262; Beethoven cites the Vienna reprint of 1814, vol. ii, p. 357 (not p. 356) (see commentary on No. 26). The scansion marks were evidently for a projected musical setting.

50 Brühl beim Lamm, wie schön, meine vaterländischen Gegenden zu sehn, nach England ¹müssen² [?reisen] dann daselbst vier Wochen zugebracht.

¹ In the margin, in Nohl's hand: 'N.B.'
² The word 'müssen' is partly underlined, apparently by Nohl.

> At the Lamb in Brühl. How nice to see the regions of my fatherland; then I must go to England and spend four weeks there.

Theodor von Frimmel, *Beethoven-Handbuch* (Leipzig, 1926), vol. i, pp. 78, 422, suggests that this entry was written at Zum Lamm, an inn at Mödling adjoining the picturesque Brühl region beloved by Beethoven: see also Theodor von Frimmel, 'Beethoven und die Mödlinger Brühl', *Beethoven-Forschung*, v (1915), 1–32; Oscar G. Sonneck, *Beethoven Letters in America* (New York, 1927), pp. 3–6; N II, p. 132. Alternatively it may express Beethoven's wish to revisit the Brühl north of Bonn ('my fatherland') where Electors Joseph Clemens and Clemens August had built a splendid summer palace well known to Bonn's musicians. Beethoven spent the latter part of the summer of 1815 at Mödling and nearby Baden. His desire to visit England was of long standing (there is a possible reference in his 1792 *Stammbuch* – see N I, p. 143 and note), and his first dealings with the Philharmonic Society of London, in mid-1815, raised the possibility of an early visit. Perhaps he hoped to stay in Bonn on the way to England.

51 Zwei Eintheilungen meiner Musikalien ‖fol. 6v‖ meiner Skizzen Bücher — meiner Studien — meiner Partituren — meiner ausgeschriebenen. —

> Two divisions of my musical material: my sketchbooks [and] studies; my scores [and] fair copies.

In 1815 Beethoven was particularly concerned about organising his voluminous musical papers: see letters to Johann Baptist Rupprecht of [summer 1815], and to the Archduke Rudolph of [1815] (Anderson nos. 553, 592).

52 Die Mälzlische W.M. ist die stärkste nächst dem die — — — Man müste verschiedene im Zimmer für die Musik, Sprechen und noch die Größe des Saals haben.

> Next to the — —, the Mälzel ear-trumpet is the strongest. One should have different ones in the room for music, speech, and also for halls of various sizes.

'W.M.' is a misreading for 'G.M.' (= 'Gehörmaschine') or 'O.M.' (= 'Ohrenmaschine').

53 Bey Staudenheimer gefragt, was die dermaligen M gemacht, mich wegen einem guten

>   Asked Staudenheimer what the former ear-trumpet did, me concerning a good

Jakob Staudenheim (1764–1830) was one of Beethoven's physicians from 1811 or 1812 until *c.* 1824, and again, as consultant, in December 1826. 'M' = 'Maschine'. The sentence is incomplete.

54 Chladnik [Chladnis] Akustik Buch vom Klang nachgeschlagen. —

>   Consulted Chladni's *Die Akustik* — book on sound. —

Ernst Florens Friedrich Chladni (1756–1827) was an authority on acoustics and an inventor of several musical instruments. His writings include *Entdeckungen über die Theorie des Klanges* (Leipzig, 1787), *Die Akustik* (Leipzig, 1802), and *Neue Beyträge zur Akustik* (Leipzig, 1817), the last two published by Breitkopf & Härtel. An article on acoustics by Chladni appeared in the *Allgemeine musikalische Zeitung*, xvii (1815), cols. 14–15. In a letter of 10 March 1815 (Anderson no. 533) Beethoven asked Härtel for Chladni's address. In 1819 he hoped to (and perhaps did) attend one of Chladni's lectures: see *Ludwig van Beethovens Konversationshefte*, vol. i, ed. Karl-Heinz Köhler and Grita Herre (Leipzig, 1972), pp. 42, 247. Beethoven hoped to obtain advice concerning hearing aids: *Konversationshefte*, vol. i, p. 32.

55
>   Unter des Tigers Zahn hört' ich den Leidenden beten.[:]
>   "Dank dir[,] höchster, im Schmerz sterb ich, doch nicht in der Schuld["].

>   Under the tiger's tooth I heard the sufferer pray:
>   'Thanks to you, sublime one, I die in pain but free of guilt.'

Herder, 'Dank des Sterbenden', *Zerstreute Blätter, vierte Sammlung*, p. 103; reprinted in *Sämmtliche Werke*, vol. xxvi/2, p. 404 (see commentary on No. 5).

56
>   Willt du den Honig kosten[,] und Bienenstiche nicht ausstehen?
>   Wünschest Kränze des Siegs[,] ohne Gefahren der Schlacht?
>   Und [Wird] der Taucher die Perle vom Meeresgrund⟨e⟩ gewinnen[,]

O Mensch,¹ ⟨Wenn er,⟩ den Krokodill scheuend, am Ufer
  verziehte⟨?⟩
‖fol. 7r‖ Also wage! Was Gott dir beschied, wird Niemand dir
  rauben,[;]
Doch er beschied es dir, dir dem beherzten Mann.

¹'O Mensch' is not in Herder's text.

Do you want to taste honey without suffering bee-stings?
Do you desire the wreaths of victory without the danger of
  battle?
Shall the diver win the pearl from the ocean bottom if, fearing
  the crocodile, he tarries on the shore?
Risk everything, then! What God has granted to you, nobody
  can rob you of.
Indeed, he granted it to you, to you, brave man.

Herder, 'Müh' und Belohnung', Zerstreute Blätter, vierte Sammlung, p. 103; reprinted in Sämmtliche Werke, vol. xxvi/2, pp. 404–5 (see commentary on No. 5).

57   Wer Gott liebet[,] der achtet die Welt nicht über Verdienst
  hoch[;]
Denn er weiß es, sie gibt keinen gesicherten Tritt[.]
Pflege der Wissenschaft,[;] kein Pfad ist sicherer dem Men-
  schen[,]
Als den lange der Fuß weiserer Menschen betrat.
Meide den Schmerz⟨, je⟩ einen der Freunde gekränket zu
  haben,
Aber vor allen den Freund, welchem kein anderer gleicht.

He who loves God does not esteem the world more highly
  than it deserves,
Because he knows that it does not offer a sure footing.
Cultivate learning; no path is more secure for a man
Than that which has been trodden by wiser men.
Always avoid the pain of offending a friend.
But, above all, that friend who is like no other.

Herder, 'Das Leben der Menschen', lines 21–2, 25–6, 29–30, Zerstreute Blätter, vierte Sammlung, pp. 98–101; reprinted in Sämmtliche Werke, vol. xxvi/2, pp. 403–4 (see commentary on No. 5).

58   Trost des Lebens.
Im Ungemach verzage nicht den Tag zu sehn[,]
Der Freude dir für Sorgen bringt[,] und Lust für Gram[,]
Wie oft begann ein giftger Wind[,] und schnell darauf
Erfüllete der lieblichste Geruch die Luft!
Oft drohte dir ein schwarz Gewolk,[:] und ward verweht[,]
Eh' es den Strom [Sturm] ausschüttete aus dunklem [dunkelm] Schoos[,]
Wie mancher Rauch[,] der sich erhob, war Feuer nicht!
Sey also stets[,] im Unfall auch[,] voll guten Muths[.]
Die Zeit bringt Wunder an den Tag,[;] unzählbar sind
||fol. 7v|| Die Güter, die du hoffen kannst[,] vom großen Gott. —

'Life's Solace'
In adversity do not despair of seeing that day
Which will bring you joy rather than sorrow and pleasure rather than grief.
How often a poisonous wind arose, but soon after
The air was filled with the loveliest of scents.
Often a black cloud menaced you and was blown away
Before the storm emptied from the dark womb.
How often smoke ascended but there was no fire!
Therefore be of good heart even when accidents befall.
Time brings miracles to light; numberless are
The graces you can hope for from the great God.

Herder, 'Trost des Lebens', *Zerstreute Blätter, vierte Sammlung*, p. 102; reprinted in Sämmtliche Werke, vol. xxvi/2, p. 404 (see commentary on No. 5).

59   Auch den vertrautesten Freund verschone mit deinem Geheimniß!
Forderst [Foderst] du Treue von ihm, die du dir selber versagst?

Spare even the closest friend your secrets;
How can you ask fidelity of him, when you deny it to yourself?

Herder, 'Verschweigenheit', from *Vermischte Stucke aus verschiedenen morgenländischen Dichtern*, in Sämmtliche Werke: Zur schönen Literatur und Kunst, vol. ix, ed. Johann von Müller (Tübingen, 1807), p. 196; reprinted in Sämmtliche Werke, vol. xxvi/2, p. 428 (see commentary on No. 5).

60 [a] ⟨*Robert:*⟩ Nicht <u>Fragen</u>, Thaten sollst du spenden,[;] dich selber opfern[,] ohne Ruhm und Lohn?[!] — Erst übe[1] Wunder, willst du sie

enthüllen; und [nur] so kannst du dein Daseyn nur [ganz] erfüllen —
[b] ⟨Robert:⟩ Er hat mich ja entsagen und entbehren gelehrt, im
heiligen Gefühl der Pflicht — und [mir] seinen Himmel ja zurückgelassen.[!] [c] ⟨Robert:⟩ Und sey's auch wirklich Weisheit [—] o[,] so
schwebet vor meinem Innern doch ein ander [andres] Ziel. Sey dieß
ein Wahn — ich glaubs; [glaub',] es ist nichts bessers. Und dennoch
geb ich ihn um eine [Eure] Wahrheit, um einen [Euren] freudenlosen
Himmel nicht[.] — hat auch der Meister sich umsonst geopfert.[;]
Doch brenn ich lieber in dem schönen Wahn[,] um nicht in eurer
Wahrheit zu erfrieren. [d] ⟨Robert:⟩ Kampf für das Rechte und für des
Rechtes Tochter[,] die durch's Gesetz verklärte ewige Freyheit[;] Ergebung in den ungebeugten[2] ‖fol. 8r‖ Willen des eisernen Geschicks.[;]
Gehorsam und Entsagung[,] und wandellose Treue bis ins Grab! —
[. . .] ⟨Molay:⟩ starker Robert[!] du wirst [wirst du] die[3] Ergebung üben
und die[3] Entsagung? — [. . .]
Du bist ein Held — du bist[,] was zehnmal mehr ist, ein echter Mensch!
[. . .] nur des Schwächlings E̶i̶s̶e̶n̶f̶i̶n̶g̶e̶r̶ ̶d̶e̶s̶ ̶G̶e̶ Saiten zerreißt der
Eisenfinger des Geschicks.[;] Der Heldenmüthige bietet kühn die
Harfe[,] die ihn [ihm] der Schöpfer in den Busen legte[,] dem Schicksal
dar — Mags in — — — ⟨den Saiten wühlen; Allein⟩ den innern
herrlichen Akkord kanns nicht zerstören[,] und die Dissonanzen verschmelzen bald in reine Harmonie[,] weil Gottes Friede durch die Saiten
lächelt [säuselt.] mein starker Robert [! —] muß der starke Mensch
erliegen oder auferstehen vom Staube!⟨?⟩ — [. . .]
Ist der echte wahre Mensch ein Sklave der Umgebung oder frey?
Reißt er aus allen Stürmen, und,[4] was mehr ist, aus allen — — —
⟨Wonnen⟩ dieses Lebens nicht sein Besseres [beß'res] Ich? — Die Welt
in seiner Brust ist sie ein Theil der Elementen-Masse[;] — und kann[,]
was oft in dieser wogt und gährt [gähret,] auf jene wirken? Mensch!
kannst ‖fol. 8v‖ du erliegen? —
⟨Robert:⟩ Doch gibts [giebt's] Momente! Molay[:] ja[,—] die gibt es
freylich —
Doch [—] Gott sey Dank[!—] auch nur Momente — wo der Mensch[,]
von mächtiger Natur bezwungen[,] sein höheres Selbst ein Spiel der
Wogen wähnt![.] in solchen Augenblicken zeigt die[5] — — — — —
Abstand zwischen ihr und der Gottheit einst; sie strebt? strahlt? [straft]
des Menschen räthselhafte [frevelhafte] Kühnheit[,] ihr gleich zu seyn,
und wie oft [wirft] ihn in sein Nichts — — — — in solchen Augenblicken [solchem Augenblick] sinkt selbst der Weise zum Staub hinab
— auch er ist Sohn des Staubs[;] — doch er erhebt sich bald, gereinigt
geht er aus dem Verhängniß auf[,] und dadurch kündet der heilige
Wille seine Allmacht an —
Auch du wirst dich erheben[,] starker ⟨Robert!⟩ ⟨Robert:⟩ was kann

ihm [ich thun?] ⟨*Molay:*⟩ mehr als dein Schicksal seyn, denn Hasser, Lieben [den Hasser lieben] und das hohe Gut ~~im Erschaffen suchen~~ der Selbstvollendung im Erschaffen suchen.[!]

‖fol. 9r‖ Du bist das Ebenbild des Ewigen[:]
Wenn ihm die Menschen fluchen, lächelt er — Und schafft um ihre Hütten Paradiese[, — —]
Willst du noch selbstisch in die Wüste ziehn? — ⟨*Robert:*⟩ So[3] erröthend beuge ich mich vor deiner Größe[!] ⟨*Molay:*⟩ das solltest [sollst] du nicht[!] — du sollst mich übertreffen [. . .] sey[6] — — vorher den Menschen die unter dir sind [. . .] der Mann[,] der Einzelne[,] kann öfters mehr[,] als im Verein mit Tausend[;] denn schwer zu lenken sind der Menschen Willen[,] und selten siegt der bessere Verstand.

[1] Written 'über' and corrected.
[2] A marginal note on fol. 7v, in Nohl's hand, reads:
'aus Zacharias Werner's Theaterstücken
A.M.Z. 1811 S. 242 aus Breslau: Werners Weihe der Kraft mit Chören & Ouvertüre von Musikd.[irektor] Bierey. Libussa 1847 S. 416. C. Pichler Memoiren II & III, 64. — Schneller III 119. — Wiener "Samler" S. 192 (März 1813) Werners Theater in 5 Bänden bei Wallishäuser, der 1. Bd. die Templer auf Cypern. Febr. 1814 beendigt.' This may be translated and expanded as follows: 'From Zacharias Werner's *Plays*. The *Allgemeine musikalische Zeitung*, xiii (1811), cols. [241–]242, reported from Breslau that music director Gottlob-Benedikt Bierey composed a chorus and an overture to Werner's *Weihe der Kraft*. [See also the journal] *Libussa* (1847), p. 416. Caroline Pichler, *Denkwürdigkeiten aus meinem Leben*, 4 vols. in 2 (Vienna, 1844), vol. iii, p. 64. Julius Franz Schneller, *Ideen über Litteratur und Kunst*, ed. Ernst Münch, Hinterlassene Werke, vol. iii (Stuttgart and Leipzig, 1834), p. 119. *Der Sammler*, Vienna (March 1813), p. 192. [The Viennese publisher] J. B. Wallishausser published Werner's *Theater* in 5 volumes, completed by February 1814; the 1st volume is *Die Templer auf Cypern*.'
[3] The words 'die' and 'so' are not in Werner's text.
[4] Two crossed-out words follow.
[5] The following, to 'einst', should read: 'Gottheit, Uns jenen Abstand zwischen ihr und uns'.
[6] The following, to 'sind', should read: 'ein Herr von Menschen! Auch sie sind Herren, weil sie Menschen sind!'.

> [a] [*Robert:*] You shall dispense not questions but deeds,
> Sacrifice yourself without fame and reward!
> If you wish to unveil miracles, first practise them;
> Only thus can you fulfil your existence.
>
> [b] [*Robert:*] In holy consciousness of duty,
> He has taught me abstinence and renunciation,
> And left his heaven to me!

[c] [*Robert*:] And if this is *really wisdom* – there still
Hovers another goal before my inner eye.
Though it be only an illusion, I believe in it, there is nothing better.
Nevertheless I do not offer it against your truth,
Against your joyless heaven.
The master, too, has sacrificed himself in vain,
But I would rather *burn* in the beautiful illusion
In order not to freeze in your truth.

[d] [*Robert*:] Battle for right and for the daughter of right,
Eternal freedom that is transfigured through law,
Resignation under the unbending will
Of *iron fate*; obedience and renunciation,
And unswerving fidelity until the grave! — . . .
[*Molay*:] Strong Robert!
Will you practise resignation and renunciation? — . . .
You are a hero — you are what is ten times more,
A real man! . . .
Only the strings of the *weakling* are torn
By the *iron finger* of Fate;
The hero bravely presents to Fate the harp
Which the Creator placed in his bosom.
It might ⟨rage through the strings⟩;
But it cannot destroy the marvellous inner accord
And the dissonances soon dissolve into pure harmony,
Because God's peace rustles through the strings.
My strong Robert! — must the strong man
Succumb or be resurrected from the dust? — . . .
Is the real true man
A slave of his environment or is he free?
Does he not seize from all storms, and, what is more, from all
⟨raptures⟩ of this life
His better self? — The world in his bosom,
It is a part of the elemental substance;
And cannot it have an effect on what often
Surges and ferments within it? *Man*! can you succumb? —
[*Robert*:] But there are moments!
Molay: Yes, they surely exist,
But, thank God! only moments, when
Man, conquered by mighty nature,
Fancies that his higher self is in the play of waves.

> At such moments the ⟨Godhead reveals
> The distance between Him and us⟩;
> He punishes man's sacrilegious audacity
> In trying to emulate Him, and casts him into the void.
> At such moments even the wise man
> Sinks down into the dust — he too is the son of dust;
> But he soon rises, he goes forth cleansed
> Of the calamity, and through it
> The holy will pronounces His omnipotence.
> You too shall rise, strong Robert!
> [*Robert*:] What can I do?
> [*Molay*:] To be more than your fate,
> To love the one who hates and to seek
> The great good of self completion in creating!
> You are the mirror image of the Eternal:
> When men curse Him, He smiles,
> And creates paradise around their huts.— —
> Do you selfishly want to go into the desert? —
> [*Robert*:] Blushing, I bow before your greatness!
> [*Molay*:] You should not do that! You shall surpass me . . .
> Be ⟨a lord of men!
> They too are lords, because they are men!⟩ . . .
> Man, the individual, can often [see] more by himself
> Than when he is in the company of thousands;
> For the wills of men are difficult to guide,
> And seldom does the superior mind triumph.

Excerpts from Zacharias Werner, *Die Söhne des Thals, I. Theil: Die Templer auf Cypern* (Berlin, 1802). [a], [b], and [c] = Act iv, Sc. 1; [d] = Act iv, Sc. 2: see Werner, *Theater*, vol. i (Vienna, 1813), pp. 134, 136–7, 141, 153–7. The play is written in iambic pentameter. The italicised passages are not emphasised in the published text. Friedrich Ludwig Zacharias Werner (1768–1823) was a poet, Freemason, and pioneer of 'Schicksalstragödie' (see commentary on No. 7) who was converted to Catholicism in 1810 and became, for several years after 1814, a priest with a large Viennese following. His name appears occasionally in the conversation books; in December 1819 Karl Bernard asked Beethoven: 'With regard to Werner, when are you going to set him to music?' (*Ludwig van Beethovens Konversationshefte*, vol. i, ed. Karl-Heinz Köhler and Grita Herre, (Leipzig, 1972), p. 172). Among Beethoven documents referring to Werner, see letters to the Archduke Rudolph of [spring 1812] and to Haslinger of 10 September 1821 (Anderson nos. 367, 1056), and Theodor von Frimmel, *Beethoven-Handbuch* (Leipzig, 1926), vol. i, p. 197; see also Arnold Schmitz, *Das romantische Beethovenbild* (Bonn, 1927), pp. 31–2. The Werner passages also exist on two pages in Beethoven's hand. The first, from the beginning to 'oder

Beethoven's Tagebuch of 1812–1818

auferstehn vom Staube?', is in the Wegeler Collection, Koblenz: see the facsimile in Stephan Ley, ed., *Beethoven als Freund der Familie Wegeler-v. Breuning* (Bonn, 1927), p. 99. The second, from 'Ist der echte wahre Mensch' to the end, is in the Beethovenhaus, Bonn (SBH 514). It does not appear that these pages formed part of the original Tagebuch: see above pp. 204–5. Schubert's 'Morgenlied' (D 685) is from *Die Söhne des Thals*.

61 [a] Was frey ist[1] von aller Lust und Begier ⟨ist,⟩ das ist der Mächtige[.] Er allein. Kein Größerer ist, als Er,[.] ⟨Brahm,⟩[2] sein Geist[,] ist verschlungen in sich selbst. Er der Mächtige ist in jedem Theile des Raumes gegenwärtig.[. . .] Seine Allwissenheit ist von eig⟨e⟩ner Eingebung[,] und sein Begriff ⟨begreift⟩[2] jeden andren [. —] von allen viel begreifenden [vielbegreifenden] Eigenschaften ist die Allwissenheit die Größte[. . .] — für sie gi⟨e⟩bt es keine andre[1] ⟨dreyfache Zeit, keine dreyfache⟩[2] Art des Seyns. [. . .] Sie ist von allen [ist sie von Allem] unabhängig[.] [b] O Gottheit [Gott . . .] du bist das wahre[,] ewig selige[,] unwandelbare Licht aller Zeiten und Räume. Deine Weisheit erkennt tausend und mehrere [mehr als] tausend Gesetze[,] und doch handelst du allezeit frey und zu Deiner Ehre[.] Du ragst vor allen [warst vor Allem,] was ‖fol. 9v‖ wir vernehmen [verehren.] dir als [Dir sey] Lob und Anbethung.[!] Du allein bist der wahrhaft⟨e Bhagavan⟩[2] Seelige[,] die [du] das Lesen [Wesen] aller Gesetze, das Bild aller Weisheit [—] der ganzen Welt gegenwärtig [—] trägst Du alle Dinge. ⟨Sonne, Aether, Brahma⟩[2]

[1]The words 'ist' and 'andre' are not in Kleuker's text.
[2]The words 'Brahm', 'begreift', 'dreyfache', 'Bhagavan', and 'Sonne, Aether, Brahma', are in Kleuker's printed text as well as in the Royal College of Music copy (see commentary on No. 62 below).

[a] *Free from all passion and desire, that is the Mighty One. He alone. No one is greater* than He. ⟨Brahm,⟩ His spirit, is enwrapped in Himself. He, the Mighty One, is present in every part of space. His omniscience is self-inspired and His conception ⟨comprehends⟩ every other. Of all comprehensive attributes omniscience is the greatest . . . For it there is no ⟨threefold time, no threefold⟩ type of existence . . . . It is independent of everything. [b] O God . . . You are the true, eternally blessed, unchangeable light of all times and spaces. Your wisdom discovers a thousand and more than a thousand laws, and still You act ever freely and to Your honour. You existed prior to all that we revere. To You, praise and adoration! You alone are the true ⟨Bhagavan — the⟩ blessed one, the essence of all laws, the image of all wisdom of the whole present world — You sustain all things. ⟨Sun, ether, Brahma . . .⟩

[a] A commentary on chapter 1 of the *Rig-Veda*, quoted by Beethoven from Johann Friedrich Kleuker, *Das brahmanische Religionssystem im Zusammenhange dargestellt* (Riga, 1797), pp. 34–5. (This volume was published as a supplement to the German translation by Kleuker and Johann Georg Fick (as *Abhandlungen über die Geschichte und Alterthümer, die Künste, Wissenschaften und Literatur Asiens*, 3 vols. (Riga, 1795–7)) of Sir William Jones and others, *Dissertations and Miscellaneous Pieces Relating to the History and Antiquities, the Arts, Sciences, and Literature, of Asia*, 2 vols. (London, 1792)). The passage had appeared earlier in Nathaniel Brassey Halhed, *A Code of Gentoo Laws* (London, 1776; reprinted London, 1781), pp. xxxiii–xxxiv; Kleuker's translation appears to be a revision of the translation of Halhed by Rudolph E. Raspe, *Gesetzbuch der Gentoos* (Hamburg, 1778), pp. 27–8, later reprinted in Friedrich Majer, *Allgemeines mythologisches Lexicon*, vol. i (Weimar, 1803), p. 245. Halhed and Kleuker attribute the passage to 'Visischta Mahamuni', or the Bengali equivalent 'Bisesht Mahamoonee', presumably the sage and law-giver Vasishtha. (For problems relating to his identity, see F. Max Müller, ed., *The Sacred Books of the East*, vol. xiv (Oxford, 1882), pp. 11–15.) The underlined words are not emphasised in the published text. [b] A hymn in praise of the attributes of the divinity, Parabrahma, recounted to Paulinus in 1779 by a Brahman, Ciangra [sic] Govinda (not further identified). Again, Beethoven's source is Kleuker (*Das brahmanische Religionssystem*, p. 37), where the passage is cited from the Latin: Paulinus a Sancto Bartholomaeo, *Systema Brahmanicum* (Rome, 1791), p. 65. Beethoven did not use the translation in Paulinus, *Darstellung der Brahmanisch-Indischen Götterlehre* (Gotha, 1797), pp. 85–6.

The details of Beethoven's extensive interest in Eastern literature are as yet sparsely documented. Walter Schubring presents an inaccurate survey in 'Beethovens indische Aufzeichnungen', *Die Musikforschung*, vi (1953), 207–14, and in his identically titled (but somewhat different) paper in Hans Otto Günther, ed., *Indien und Deutschland* (Frankfurt-am-Main, 1956), pp. 11–15. For the literary and philosophical background, with comprehensive bibliography, see A. Leslie Willson, *A Mythical Image: the Ideal of India in German Romanticism* (Durham, N.C., 1964); see also René Gérard, *L'Orient et la pensée romantique allemande* (Paris, 1963).

62 Geist der Geister ⟨der⟩ die [du] durch jeden Raum ⟨und⟩ durch die endlose Zeit dich verbreitend.[,][1] über [Ueber] die Schranken[2] des emporkämpfenden [mit sich kämpfenden] Gedankens erhaben.[,] Dem [Den] Aufruhr befiehlst [befahlst] Du[3] zur schönen Ordnung zu werden.[,] Ehe Himmel waren [war], warst du. [Du:] Ehe Sphären[4] unter und über uns rollten, ehe die Erde im himmlischen [in himmlischem] Aether schwamm[,] warst Du Allein[;] bis durch deine ⟨geheime⟩ Liebe das was nicht war zum Werden[5] sprang[,] und dankvoll Lob Dir Sang![.] Was trieb Dich an zu äußern Deine Macht? Güte ohne Grenzen! Welch glänzend' Licht lenkte Deine Kraft? Weisheit ohne Maaß! Was zeigte sie zuerst? —O! Leite meinen Geist[,] o hebe

ihn aus dieser schweren Tiefe durch Deine Kraft entzückt[,] damit er furchtlos streb'[6] aufwärts in feurigem Schwunge.[;] Denn Du, Du weist allein, Du kannst allein begeistern. —

[1]In the margin, in Nohl's hand: 'N.B.'
[2]'Schranken' is crossed out and 'Gedanken' written in above, in Nohl's hand. The 'Fischhof' Manuscript reads 'Gedanken'.
[3]'Du' is not in Kleuker's published text.
[4]Written thus and corrected to read 'Spähren', as in the 'Fischhof' Manuscript.
[5]'Werden' is crossed out and 'Werke' written in above, in Nohl's hand. The 'Fischhof' Manuscript reads 'Werke'.
[6]The following should read: 'empor auf feurigen Schwingen'.

> Spirit of Spirits, who, through ev'ry part
> Of space expanded and of endless time,
> Beyond the stretch of lab'ring thought sublime,
> Badst uproar into beauteous order start,
> Before Heaven was, Thou art:
> Ere spheres beneath us roll'd or spheres above,
> Ere earth in firmamental ether hung,
> Thou sat'st alone; till, through thy ⟨mystick⟩ Love,
> Things unexisting to existence sprung,
> And grateful descant sung.
> What first impell'd thee to exert thy might?
> Goodness unlimited. What glorious light
> Thy pow'r directed? Wisdom without bound.
> What prov'd it first? Oh! guide my fancy right,
> Oh! raise from cumbrous ground
> My soul in rapture drown'd,
> That fearless it may soar on wings of fire;
> For Thou, who only know'st, Thou only canst inspire.

A German translation of the first verse of the *Veda*-like 'Hymn to Narayena' by Sir William Jones (1746–94); the stanza, he wrote, pictures 'the sublimest attributes of the Supreme Being': Sir William Jones and others, *The Asiatic Miscellany, Consisting of Translations, Imitations, Fugitive Pieces* (Calcutta, 1785), pp. 7–14; reprinted in Sir William Jones and others, *Dissertations and Miscellaneous Pieces Relating to the History and Antiquities, the Arts, Sciences, and Literature, of Asia* (London, 1792), vol. ii, pp. 351–6; German translation by Johann Friedrich Kleuker in the translation of Jones and others, *Dissertations and Miscellaneous Pieces*, by Kleuker and Johann Georg Fick as *Abhandlungen über die Geschichte und Alterthümer, die Künste, Wissenschaften und Literatur Asiens*, vol. iii (Riga, 1797), pp. 412–15. Thayer's and Schubring's identifications are to be disregarded: see Thayer–Deiters–Riemann iii, pp. 193–4; Schubring (see No. 61), pp. 212–13. Another, variant copy of this and the preceding entry in

Beethoven's hand is in London, Royal College of Music, 2176, facsimile in Alfred Christlieb Kalischer, ed., *The Letters of Ludwig van Beethoven*, ed. and trans. J. S. Shedlock (London, 1909), vol. ii, facing p. 124; the document first came to public notice when it was put up for auction in Leipzig on 26 October 1857: see *Berlin Musik-Zeitung Echo*, 4 October 1857, p. 311. In this copy, which covers both sides of a single leaf, the material of Nos. 61–2 is introduced without a break by that of No. 93[b], beginning 'Gott ist immateriel', and, along with other significant textual variations, contains the additions noted in note 2 to No. 61 as well as the heading 'Hymn' preceding this entry. A letter to Beethoven of late 1815 or early 1816 (Berlin, DSB, Autograph 35,41; until now misdated 1808 or 1809) from the orientalist Joseph Hammer-Purgstall refers to Beethoven's intention 'to set to music an Indian chorus of religious character'; presumably the Royal College of Music document was prepared by Beethoven for this purpose.

63 [a] ||fol. 10r|| Aus Gott floß alles rein und lauter aus. Werd' ich nochmals durch Leidenschaft zum Bösen verdunkelt kehrte ich nach vielfacher Büßung und Reinigung zum ersten[1] erhabenen reinen Quelle, zur Gottheit zurück. — — und — zu Deiner Kunst. [b] Kein Eigennutz beseelte dich dabey, so sey es jede Zeit, die Bäume beugen sich unter dem Uiberfluße der Früchte; die Wolken senken sich wenn heilsamer Regen sie füllt; und die Wohlthäter des Menschengeschlechtes blähen sich nicht in ihrem Reichthum. [c] Wenn unter der schönen Wimper die schwellende Thräne lauert, widersetze dich mit festem Muthe ihrem ersten Bemühen, hervorzubrechen. Auf Deiner Wanderschaft über die Erde, wo die Pfade bald hoch bald niedrig gehen und der ächte selten kenntlich ist, wird allerdings die Spur deiner Tritte nicht immer gleichförmig seyn; aber die Tugend wird dich in gerader Richtung tr vorwärts treiben.

[1] Written 'erstern' and corrected, probably by Nohl.

[a] All things flowed clear and pure from God. If afterwards I become darkened through passion for evil, I returned, after manifold repentance and purification, to the elevated and pure source, to the Godhead. — And, to your art. [b] [. . .] we have no private interest in the business. It is ever thus: trees are bent by the abundance of their fruit; clouds are brought low when they teem with salubrious rain; and the real benefactors of Mankind are not elated by riches. [c] When the big tear lurks beneath thy beautiful eyelashes, let thy resolution check its first efforts to disengage itself. In thy passage over this earth, where the paths are now high, now low, and the true path seldom distinguished, the traces of thy feet must needs be unequal; but *virtue* will press thee right onward.

[a] Appears to be Beethoven's formulation, perhaps inspired by phrases in Johann Friedrich Kleuker, *Das brahmanische Religionssystem*, (Riga, 1797), pp. 35, 174ff and/or the *Bhagavad-Gita*. [b] is from Georg Forster's translation (as *Sakontala; oder, Der entscheidende Ring, ein indisches Schauspiel* (Mainz and Leipzig, 1791; reprinted Vienna, 1800), Act v, p. 142) of *Sacontala: or The Fatal Ring: an Indian Drama*, translated by Sir William Jones (London, 1789; numerous reprints). Jones's work is a translation 'from original Sanscrit and Pracrit' of a play by Kalidasa, the foremost Sanskrit poet and dramatist, who flourished probably in the 5th century. [c] = *Sakontala*, Act IV, p. 123. The first sentence, the words 'and the true path seldom distinguished', and the closing phrase are additions to the Sanskrit original by Jones, whose translation has been used here. Kalidasa's play aroused great enthusiasm among Beethoven's contemporaries, including Herder, Schiller, and Goethe. Herder's 'Vorrede zur Sakontala' first appeared in the second edition of Forster's translation (Frankfurt-am-Main, 1803); his letters 'Ueber ein morgenländisches Drama', widely reprinted, first appeared in *Zerstreute Blätter, vierte Sammlung*, pp. 263–312 reprinted in Sämmtliche Werke, vol. xxvi/2 (see commentary on No. 5). In 1820 Schubert sketched two acts of *Sakuntala* (D 701).

64 [a] Selig [Gepriesen] ist ⟨der Mann⟩, der alle ⟨seine⟩ Leidenschaften unterdrückt hat[,] und dann mit seiner Thatkraft alle ‖fol. 10v‖ Angelegenheiten des Lebens[,] unbesorgt um den Erfolg verrichtet! [.] [b] Laß den Beweggrund in der That[,] und nicht im Ausgang seyn. Sey nicht einer von denen[,] deren Triebfeder zum Handeln die Hoffnung des Lohn⟨e⟩s ist. Laß dein Leben nicht in Unthätigkeit vorüber gehen. Sey betriebsam, erfülle deine Pflicht, verbanne alle Gedanken an die Folge[,] und den [der] Ausgang ⟨sey dir gleich,⟩ er möge [möge er] gut oder übel seyn,[;] denn ⟨eine⟩ solche Gleichmüthigkeit heißt ⟨Yog— —⟩ Aufmerksamkeit auf das Geistige. [. . .] Suche dann allein in der Weisheit eine Freystatt,[;] denn der Elende und Unglückliche ist dieß [dies] nur durch den Erfolg der Dinge. Der wahre Weise kümmert sich nicht ums [um das] Gute oder ⟨das⟩ Böse [Uebel] in dieser Welt. Befleissige dich also[,] diesen Gebrauch deiner Vernunft zu erhalten,[;] denn solcher Gebrauch ist im Leben eine köstliche Kunst. —

[a] Blessed [Praised] is ⟨the man⟩, who, having subdued all his passions, performeth with his active faculties all the functions of life, unconcerned about the event. [b] Let the motive be in the deed, and not in the event. Be not one whose motive for action is the hope of reward. Let not thy life be spent in inaction. Depend upon application, perform thy duty, abandon all thought of the consequence, and make the event equal, whether it terminate in good or evil; for such an equality is called ⟨Yōg— —⟩ attention to what is

spiritual . . . Seek an asylum then in wisdom alone; for the miserable and unhappy are so on account of the event of things. Men who are endued with true wisdom are unmindful of good or evil in this world. Study then to obtain this application of thy understanding, for such application in business is a precious art.

[a] *Bhagavad-Gita*, chapter iii, line 7. [b] *Bhagavad-Gita*, chapter ii, lines 47–50, with part of line 49 omitted. This precise conflation of [a] and [b], and the omission, occurs in William Robertson, *An Historical Disquisition Concerning the Knowledge which the Ancients had of India* (Dublin, 1791), pp. 286–7; Beethoven used Georg Forster's translation: *Robertson's historische Untersuchung über die Kenntnisse der Alten von Indien* (Berlin, 1792), p. 307. Robertson cited Wilkins's translation (used here): *The Bhăgvăt-gēēta, or Dialogues of Krĕĕshna and Ărjŏŏn*, trans. Charles Wilkins (London, 1785), pp. 45, 40.

65 Gehüllt in Schatten ewiger Einsamkeit[,] ‖fol. 11r‖ ein undurchdringliches [schimmerndes] Dunkel des Dickichts [dichtesten Lichts], ~~und~~ undurchdringlich, unzugänglich[,] unermeßlich[,]¹ gestaltet ausgebreitet. Ehe Geister waren eingehaucht[,] war nur sein Geist. Wie sterbliche Augen (um endliches zu vergleichen mit unendlichem,[)] in lichte Spiegel schauen. —

¹The following, to 'Geist', should read: 'Eh' Geister waren eingehaucht, Gestalten ausgebreitet, Sah' Brahm nur seinen Geist.'

> Wrapt in eternal solitary shade,
> Th' impenetrable gloom of light intense,
> Impervious, inaccessible, immense,
> Ere spirits were infus'd or forms display'd,
> Brehm his own mind survey'd,
> As mortal eyes (thus finite we compare
> With infinite) in smoothest mirrors gaze.

Verse 2, lines 1–6, of Sir William Jones's 'Hymn to Narayena', from Jones and others, *The Asiatic Miscellany*, pp. 7–14, reprinted in Jones and others, *Dissertations and Miscellaneous Pieces*, vol. ii, pp. 351–6, trans. Kleuker in *Abhandlungen*, vol. iii, p. 415 (see commentary on No. 62). According to Jones, the stanza 'comprises the *Indian* and *Egyptian* doctrine of the Divine Essence and Archetypal *Ideas*'.

66 Ein Bauerngut, dann entfliehst du deinem Elend! —

A farm, then you escape your misery!

A contemporary, diary-like passage on a large folio sheet containing transcriptions of five poems by Herder (see commentary on No. 5) expresses similar sentiments: 'If all else fails, even in winter, the country itself remains, like Baden, Lower Brühl, etc. It would be easy to rent a lodging from a peasant.' The full text is in Ludwig Nohl, ed., *Beethovens Brevier* (Leipzig, 1870), p. 104, note.

67 "Ihr haltet die Beschwerlichkeiten für Wegweiserinnen zu einem angenehmen Leben" Nichts ist wirksamer andere in Gehorsam zu erhalten, als wenn sie glauben, daß man weit mehr Klugheit besitze als sie — — ohne Thränen können weder die Väter ihren Kindern die Tugend einprägen noch die Lehrer ihren Schülern nützliche Dienste[1] in Wissenschaften beybringen auch die Gesetze nöthigen dadurch die Bürger, daß sie ihnen Thränen erregen der Gerechtigkeit nachzustreben.

[1]'Dienste' is underlined, evidently by Nohl.

'You take the hardships as signposts in an agreeable life.' Nothing is more effective to maintain the obedience of others than their belief that you are far wiser than they. — Without tears fathers cannot instil virtue in their children, or teachers the beneficial services of learning in their students; likewise the laws, by provoking tears from the citizens, cause them to strive for justice.

Evidently a quotation (source unknown). 'Dienste' was probably 'Dinge' (things) in the original.

68 [a] Tapfere und vortreffliche Leute führen zu edlen und rühmlichen Thaten, feige und schlechte zu unwürdigen Geschäften. [b] Denn das Laster geht durch Wege voll gegenwärtiger Lüste und beredet dadurch viele, ||fol. 11v|| ihm zu folgen. Die Tugend aber führt auf einen steilen Pfad und kann dabey nicht so leicht und geschwind die Menschen an sich ziehn, vornämlich wenn an einem andern Orte noch welche sind, welche sie auf einen abhängigen und angenehmen Weg abrufen. —[1] [c] Es ist an mehresten hinderlich von andern zu erlangen, wenn man als ein Lügner erscheint.[2] —

[1]The dash has been crossed out.
[2]Two parallel vertical strokes in the margin at the close of [c].

[a] Noble and glorious deeds are performed by brave and excel-

lent people, ignoble affairs by bad and cowardly ones. [b] For vice walks many paths full of present sinful desires and thereby induces many to follow it. But virtue leads on to a steep path and cannot attract men as easily and swiftly, especially if elsewhere there are those who call them to a sloping and pleasant road. [c] It is most troublesome to obtain anything from others if one appears to be a liar.

[a] A quotation (source unknown). [b] A gloss on Hesiod's 'hill of virtue' passage (*Works and Days*, lines 287–92). The most famous lines in Hesiod, they are frequently cited, glossed, or imitated by the classical authors. For details see Heber Michel Hays, *Notes on the Works and Days of Hesiod* (Chicago, 1918), pp. 122–3. Beethoven's source is not known. [c] Possibly a quotation (source unknown). 'Lügner' may be a misreading, perhaps for 'Leiher' (borrower).

69 — — — o sieh' herab Bruder, ja ich habe dich beweint und beweine dich noch, o warum warst du nicht aufrichtiger gegen mich, du lebtest noch und wärst gewiß so elendiglich nicht umgekommen, hättest du dich früher — — —[1] entfernt und mir ganz genaht. —

[1]The first of the three dashes has been crossed out.

O look down, brother, yes I have wept for you and still weep for you, O why were you not more open with me? you would still be alive and certainly would not have perished so miserably, had you earlier distanced yourself — — — and come wholly to me.

Beethoven's brother Caspar Carl, born 1774, died on 15 November 1815. The Sterbas surmise that the missing words refer to Caspar Carl's wife: see Richard and Editha Sterba, *Beethoven and His Nephew* (New York, 1954), p. 51.

70 Wegen einer Bibliotheck — große Bücher müssen aufrechtstehen und so daß man sie gemächlich nehmen kann.— — — — — — — — —
— —
||fol. 12r|| — — — — — — — — — — — — — — — — — —
— —
— —
— —

About a library: large books must stand upright and so that one can easily grasp them.

(See commentary on No. 51.)

71 Unsere Weltgeschichte wird 5816.

Our world history has now lasted for 5816 years.

This was presumably written at the beginning of 1816. According to popular belief, the Creation took place in 4000 B.C. See also No. 145.

72 Der mit einem Uibel behaftet wird, welches er nicht ändern kann, sondern welches nach und nach ihn dem Tode näher bringt und ohne welches sein Leben länger gedauert hätte, muß denken, daß er auch so durch Mord oder andere Ursachen hätte noch geschwinder umkommen können o glücklich wer nur für — — — — — — — — —

He who is afflicted with a malady which he not only cannot change, but which little by little brings him closer to death and without which his life would have lasted longer, ought to consider that he could have perished even more quickly through assassination or other causes. O happy, who only for —

Beethoven was often troubled by thoughts of his mortality. He was severely ill in the spring of 1816; on 13 May 1816 he wrote to Marie Erdödy: 'For the last six weeks I have been in very poor health, so much so that frequently I have thought of my death.' (Anderson no. 633)

73 Zeige deine Gewalt Schicksal! Wir sind nicht Herrn über uns selbst; was beschlossen ist, muß seyn, und so sey es dann [?denn]! — —

Show your power, Fate! We are not masters of ourselves; what has been decided must be, and so be it!

Possibly a quotation (source unknown).

74 Canon aus der Ode Odissée 5ter Gesang.
  Und die rosige Frühe entstieg des
                steigt
      edlen Thitanos Lager[,] und brachte das Licht
                          bringt
      den Göttern und sterblichen Menschen[.]

Canon from *The Odyssey*, Book 5.
And the rosy dawn arose from the noble bed of Tithonus
                                arises
And brought light to the gods and mortal men.
    brings

The Odyssey, Book v, lines 1–2. *Homers Odüssee*, trans. Johann Heinrich Voss (Hamburg, 1781), p. 95. The words 'steigt' and 'bringt' were added by Beethoven with a view to changing the metre. Beethoven's marked copy of Voss's edition is Berlin, DSB, Autograph 40,3. The marked passages are given in Ludwig Nohl, ed., *Beethovens Brevier* (Leipzig, 1870), pp. 15–31. A passage from *The Odyssey* is printed on the reverse of the title-page of *Meeresstille und glückliche Fahrt* Op. 112: see Kinsky-Halm, p. 323; the same passage is cited in Berlin, DSB, Mus. ep. varia 6 (= Grasnick 35,1). (See also commentary on No. 26.)

75 Alle Abends und frühe im Verein mit R [?K].

Every evening and early morning together with R [?K].

'R' is doubtless a misreading of 'K' (= Karl). Beethoven was appointed guardian of his late brother's son, Karl (1806–58), on 19 January 1816. He spent a good deal of time with him at the beginning of 1816: see, for example, the letter to Cajetan Giannatasio del Rio of [late February 1816] (Anderson no. 614).

76 Trotz meinem armen n — —

In spite of my poor n —

The letter 'n' may stand for 'Neffen' (nephew), that is, Karl.

77 ¹Alle Werke die [?wie] jetzt mit der <u>Violonzell Sonat</u> behältst du dir vor, dem Verleger ‖fol. 12v‖ den Tag der Herausgabe zu bestimmen ohne daß die Verleger in London und in Deutschland so zu sagen, keiner vom andern weiß, weil sie sonst weniger geben, es auch nicht nöthig ist du kannst zum Vorwand geben daß jemand anderer diese Composition bey dir bestellt hat. —

¹A horizontal stroke at the left of the first line.

With all of your works, as now with the *cello sonata*, you will reserve the right to specify to the publisher the day of publication, without, so to speak, the publishers in London and in Germany knowing about each other. Because otherwise they pay less. It is also not necessary. You can pretend that someone else has ordered this composition from you.

The cello sonata is one of those from Op. 102. Beginning as early as 1802 or 1803, Beethoven attempted to negotiate simultaneous publication of various works in different countries so that he could assure several publishers that each was obtaining first publication: see Alan Tyson, *The Authentic English Editions of Beethoven* (London, 1963), pp. 17–21. In 1815 Beethoven arranged for simultaneous publication by Steiner in Vienna and Robert Birchall in London of Op. 91 (piano arrangement), Op. 92 (piano arrangement), Op. 96, and Op. 97. The Op. 102 Cello Sonatas were published by Simrock of Bonn in March 1817; despite Beethoven's efforts, no English publisher could be found for them.

78 Ertragung — Ergebung — Ergebung so gewinnen wir noch beym höchsten Elend und machen uns würdig, daß Gott unsere Fehler — —

> Endurance. Resignation. Resignation. Thus we profit even by the deepest misery and make ourselves worthy, so that God our mistakes —

Beethoven's habitual advocacy of a stoical response to life's vicissitudes is repeatedly evidenced in the Tagebuch, as in Nos. 1, 26, 43, 60, 64, 67, 73, and 93[a]; see also his letter to Marie Erdödy of 13 May 1816 (Anderson no. 633).

79 Malheureusement les gentils médiocres sont condamne condamné à imiter les defauts des grands maîtres sans les aprecier les beautés: De là le mal que Michel Ange fait à la peinture.[,] Shakespeare à l'art dramatique et que Beethoven fait de nos jours à la musique. —

> Unfortunately, mediocre talents are condemned to imitate the faults of the great masters without appreciating their beauties: from thence comes the harm that Michelangelo does to painting, Shakespeare to drama and, in our day, Beethoven to music.

Quotation (source unknown). Beethoven's name was also linked with Michelangelo's by Johann Friedrich Reichardt (*Vertraute Briefe* (Amsterdam, 1810), vol. i, p. 232, letter of 16 December 1808) and with Shakespeare's by Amadeus Wendt (*Allgemeine musikalische Zeitung*, xvii (1815), col. 351).

80 [1]K betrachtest du als dein eignes Kind, alle Schwätzereyen, alle Kleinigkeiten achte nicht über diesen heiligen Zweck. Hart ist der Zustand jetzt für dich, doch der droben o er ist, ohne ihn ||fol. 13r|| ist nichts. —

[1]'K' is repeated in the margin, in Nohl's hand.

> Regard K as your own child, disregard all idle talk, all pettiness for the sake of this holy cause. Your present condition is hard for you, but the one above, O He is, without Him is nothing.

'K' is Karl van Beethoven. From the time that Beethoven assumed the guardianship of his nephew, he came to regard himself as Karl's father: see, for example, the letters to Marie Erdödy of 13 May 1816 (Anderson no. 633), to Kanka of 6 September 1816 (Anderson no. 654), and numerous letters to Karl signed 'your father'.

81 Das ~~Kenntz~~ Kennzeichen ist ohnedem Einmal[1] angenomhen —

[1]The 'E' is changed to lower case by Nohl.

> In any event the sign has been accepted. —

A continuation of No. 80.

82 Diabelli hat die Partitur der drey Quartetten Rasumovsky N. 5 Partitur aus dem [1]Prometheus Hr. Gebauer geliehen auf der Wieden— — — — Weinlese[?] und alle Musik im letzten Zimmer geht auf einen kleinen Platz —

[1]In the margin: '#'. The sign was perhaps made by Gräffer possibly to remind himself to pursue missing portions of a score that belonged to his employer, Artaria & Co.

> Diabelli has the score of the three 'Razumovsky' Quartets. No. [Nos. 4 and] 5 from the score of *Prometheus* lent to Herr Gebauer [who lives] in the Wieden. — — — Wine harvest and all music in the last room, [which] opens upon a small square.

Antonio Diabelli (1781–1858) was a Viennese pianist, composer, and music publisher. In 1816 he was an assistant at the firm of Sigmund Anton Steiner, who may have considered a reissue of the 'Razumovsky' Quartets Op. 59. Franz Xaver Gebauer (1784–1822) was choral director at the Augustinerkirche in Vienna and a leading member of the Gesellschaft der Musikfreunde. A partial copy of the score of *Die Geschöpfe des Prometheus* Op. 43 survives, with corrections by Beethoven: see Kinsky–Halm, p. 102. It still lacks Nos. 4 and 5, which Beethoven lent to Gebauer. Beethoven threatened Gebauer with legal action if he failed to return the missing portions of the score: see his letter to Gebauer of 26 July 1817 (Anderson no. 791). The text of the closing sentence is obviously defective.

83 Entschluß zu bleiben, mit H. ist es nichts. Es ist aus dem Hause, sondern mit einem Hofmeister im Hause alles gibt sich mit Festigkeit.

Decision to stay; it doesn't work out with H. It is outside the house, but with a tutor in the house everything will be settled.

Soon after assuming the guardianship of his nephew, Beethoven made plans to remove him from the Giannatasio Institute and educate him at home: see, for example, the letter to Marie Erdödy of 13 May 1816 (Anderson no. 633) and the diary of Fanny Giannatasio del Rio, entries of 4 May to 16 August 1816 (Thayer–Deiters–Reimann iv, pp. 529–32). However, Karl remained at the Institute until 24 January 1818. 'H.' may be a misreading for 'G.' (Cajetan Giannatasio del Rio).

84 Opern und alles seyn lassen nur für deine Weise schreiben — und dann eine Kutte wo du das unglückliche Leben beschließest. —

Leave aside operas and everything else; write only in your manner. And then a cowl to end this unhappy life.

85 [1]1814 am 22. Dezember ist das Lied auf Merkenstein geschrieben.

[1]In the margin, in Nohl's hand: 'erschien 16 Sept. 1816' (published 16 September 1816).

The song 'Merkenstein' was written on 22 December 1814.

Beethoven set 'Merkenstein' (text by Johann Baptist Rupprecht) for two voices and piano Op. 100, and for single voice and piano WoO 144. Both versions were sketched in November 1814: see N II, pp. 308–9, 316. WoO 144 was completed first and published late in 1815; Op. 100 was worked out in early 1815 and published in September 1816: see letter to Rupprecht of [summer 1815] (Anderson no. 553).

86 Zum Leben und aushalten ein Haus in der Vorstadt, auf dem Lande gehts nicht mit Karl. —

For living and working, a house in the suburbs; in the country it doesn't work out with Karl.

(See commentary on No. 83.)

87 Wie der Staat eine Constitution haben muß, so der einzelne Mensch für sich selber eine!

Just as the state must have a constitution, so must the individual have one of his own!

88 Nur in deinem Kunstleben [deiner Kunst leben,] so beschränkt du auch jetzt deiner Sinne halber bist, ‖fol. 13v‖ so ist dieses doch das ~~Einzige D~~ Einzige Daseyn für dich. —

Live only in your art, for you are so limited by your senses. This is nevertheless the *only existence* for you.

89 In tausend Fällen kann die [?dir] K. Helfer seyn im gemeinen Leben x x x —

In a thousand ways K. can be of help to you in daily life.

If 'die', 'K' = 'Kunst' (art); if 'dir', 'K' = Karl.

90 Staudenheimer sprechen wegen B. Beeilung mit dem Trio an Seine K.H. wegen 400 fl alles eiligst — im Nothfall schießt Er auch vor. — Zmeskall, Czerny, fragen wegen der Operation falls sie nicht bey G, — welches jedoch das Beste, — nicht nach P — t, sondern mit P. — abreden, wie es am besten zu machen sey —

Talk to Staudenheimer about B. Make haste with the trio for his Imperial Highness for 400 florins. Everything most urgent. At a pinch he also will pay an advance. — Ask Zmeskall and Czerny concerning the operation in case it is not at G's — which is nevertheless the best. — Not by [?at] P — t, better with P. — Arrange how it can best be done.

'Staudenheimer' is Jakob Staudenheim (see commentary on No. 53). The trio is the 'Archduke' Trio Op. 97, which, upon its publication by Steiner in September 1816, was dedicated to the Archduke Rudolph: see letters to Steiner of 4 September [1816] and 6 September [1816], and to the Archduke Rudolph of [c. 12 November 1816] (Anderson nos. 651, 655, 671). Karl underwent a hernia operation on 18 September 1816. 'B' may be 'Bruch' (operation). The operation was performed at the Giannatasio Institute ('G'). 'P — t' and 'P' have not been identified. Beethoven sought advice from Nikolaus Zmeskall von Domanovecz (1759–1833) and the composer Carl Czerny (1791–1857).

91 Die Reisekosten alles dieses ist nichts. — Ar — a vorschießen kann die Sonate im [und] Trio endigen bey Karl Medizin.

The travel costs, all this is nothing. — Ar[tari]a can pay an advance. Finish the sonata and the trio. Medicine at Karl's.

It is unclear what journey was being planned; it may have been related to Karl's operation (see No. 90). 'Ar — a' is the music publisher Artaria & Co., of which Domenico Artaria (1775–1842) was proprietor. The sonata is Op. 101, completed November 1816: see Kinsky–Halm, p. 279; N II, p. 344. The trio is probably an unfinished Trio in F minor, for piano, violin, and cello, which was being sketched at the time: see N II, p. 345.

92 Samstag oder Sonntags die Pillen wieder nehmen.

Take the pills again on Saturday or Sunday.

See also No. 130.

93 [a] Die große Auszeichnung eines vorzüglichen Mannes. Beharrlichkeit in widrigen harten Zufällen — [b] ⟨Da⟩ <u>Gott ist immateriel[,] deßwegen [so] geht er über jeden Begriff; da er unsichtbar ist, so kann er keine Gestalt haben. Aber aus dem, was wir von seinen</u> ‖fol. 14r‖ <u>Werken gewahr werden, können wir schließen, daß er ewig, allmächtig, allwissend,</u> ⟨und⟩ <u>allgegenwärtig ist</u>.

[a] The chief characteristic of a distinguished man: endurance in adverse and harsh circumstances. [b] ⟨As⟩ *God is immaterial, He is above all conception; as He is invisible, He can have no form; but from what we behold of His works, we may conclude that He is eternal, omnipotent, knowing all things,* ⟨and⟩ *present everywhere.*

[a] Evidently a quotation (source unknown). The thought was proverbial among the ancients. [b] is the German translation of Alexander Dow's rendering of a *sastra* of the *Vedas* recounted to him by a Brahman: 'Dissertation Concerning the Customs &c of the Hindoos', introduction to *The History of Hindostan*, trans. 'from the Persian of [Muhammad Kāsim] Ferishtah' by Alexander Dow (London, 1768), vol. i, p. xl. Dow's passage, slightly altered, was reprinted in William Robertson, *An Historical Disquisition Concerning the Knowledge which the Ancients had of India* (Dublin, 1791), p. 314, which was translated by Georg Forster as *Robertson's historische Untersuchung über die Kenntnisse der Alten von Indien* (Berlin, 1792), p. 337. Beethoven used Forster's translation. The passage exists also in a copy in Beethoven's hand, where it introduces the material in Nos. 61–2 (see commentary on No. 62).

94 (Aus der indischen Literatur)
[a] Man hat Werke der Baukunst die Pagoden aus umgeschaffenen Steingebirg in Indien— — —deren Alter man auf 9000 Jahre schätzt.
[b] Indische Tonleiter und Töne: Sa, ri, ya [ga], ma, na, da, ni, scha. [c] 5 jähriges Stillschweigen sind den künftigen Braminen im Kloster aufgelegt.
[d] Zeit findet durchaus bey Gott nicht statt. —
[e] ~~Nein~~ Einem dem die Vorstellung des lingams Aergerniß gab äußerte der Bramine ob derselbe Gott, welcher das Auge geschaffen hätte, nicht auch der Urheber der übrigen menschlichen Glieder sey? —
[f] Bei den Hindus einen ihrer Stämme herrscht Vielmännerey. —

(From Indian literature)
[a] There are works of architecture, the pagodas from unhewn stone mountains in India, the age of which are *estimated* at 9000 years.
[b] Indian scales and notes: *sa, ri, ga, ma, na, da, ni, scha*. [c] Five years of silence is required of future Brahmans in the monastery.
[d] For God, time absolutely does not exist. —
[e] To someone who was offended by the idea of the lingam, the Brahman uttered, 'Did not the same God who has created the eye also create the other human members?' —
[f] There is one tribe among the Hindus that practises polyandry.

These and similar 'marvels of the East' were widely reported in contemporary European writings about India. [a] The 'rock-cut' and cave temples of India actually date from *c.* 200 B.C. to *c.* A.D. 900, but eighteenth-century travellers speculated that they were of much greater antiquity. [b] The Indian scale is actually *sa ri ga ma pa dha ni* (= C D E F G A♯ B). [c] 'Youth destined to be Brahmans . . . are obliged also to observe the strictest silence, which continues five years': Paulinus a Sancto Bartholomaeo, *Viaggio alle Indae Orientali* (Rome, 1796); Ger. trans. by Johann Reinhold Forster as *Reise nach Ostindien* (Berlin, 1798), p. 268, note; Eng. trans. by William Johnston as *A Voyage to the East Indies* (London, 1800), p. 265, note. See also Johann Friedrich Kleuker, *Das brahmanische Religionssystem im Zusammenhange dargestellt* (Riga, 1797), p. 212. However, the ritual austerities required of candidates for instruction in Vedanta do not include so extended a period of silence. [d] *'Time, they say, exists not at all with God'*: Sir William Jones, 'On the Chronology of the Hindus', *Asiatick Researches; or, Transactions of the Society Instituted in Bengal, for Inquiring into the History and Antiquities, the Arts, Sciences, and Literature, of Asia*, ii (1790), p. 115. Compare 'The name time . . . does not exist in eternal substances and exists in non-eternal substances': *Vaiśesika*, Book ii, chapter 2, line 9, in *A Source Book in Indian Philosophy*, ed. Sarvepalli Radhakrishnan and Charles A. Moore (Princeton, 1957), p. 390. [e] The 'lingam' (phallus) is a procreative symbol of the god Siva. The quotation has not been located. [f] Perhaps a reference to the 'five-brother marriage' of the Pandu princes to Princess Draupadi described in the *Mahābhārata* (chapter ii, lines 12–13). Visitors to India reported contemporary instances of polyandry: see Nathaniel Brassey Halhed, *A Code of Gentoo Laws* (London, 1776; reprinted London, 1781), p. liv.

95 Jagd und Ackerbau macht den Körper behende und stark.

Hunting and agriculture make the body agile and strong.

This entry perhaps belongs with the preceding group. Paulinus describes how Indian youth are instructed 'in agriculture . . . and the military arts', among other subjects: Paulinus a Sancto Bartholomaeo, *Viaggio alle Indae Orientali* (Rome, 1796); Ger. trans. by Johann Reinhold Forster as *Reise nach Ostindien* (Berlin, 1798), p. 270; Eng. trans. by William Johnston as *A Voyage to the East Indies* (London, 1800), p. 267.

96 Also gesungen auch vortreffliche Worte ausdrücken:
Bey den Nemeischen Spielen [bey der Feyer der Nemeischen Spiele . . .] ⟨so traf es sich, daß eben⟩ sang der Sänger Pilades die Worte aus dem Stücke — — ⟨des Timotheus⟩ titulirt die Perser [welches den Titel hat, *die Perser*,] ⟨zu singen anfieng: —⟩ "Ich gebe Griechenlands ||fol. 14v|| Söhnen den herrlichen Schmuck der Freyheit" — und indem er mit seiner vortrefflichen Stimme die ganze Würde dieser Worte ausdrückte, so richteten alle Zuhörer ⟨auf dem ganzen Schauplatze

ihre Augen auf den Philopömen, und erhoben ein frohes Händeklatschen⟩.
Aus dem Plutarch

Sung this way, excellent words also are expressed.

At the Nemean Games . . . the singer Pylades sang the words from the play ⟨by Timotheus⟩ entitled *The Persians*: 'I give the sons of Greece the glorious jewel of freedom'. And while he expressed all the nobility of these words with his excellent voice, the eyes of all listeners ⟨in the theatre turned to Philopoemen and joyous applause was heard⟩.

From Plutarch.

Plutarch, *Philopoemen*, par. xi, lines 2–3. *Biographien des Plutarchs*, trans. Gottlob Benedict von Schirach, vol. iii (Berlin and Leipzig, 1777), p. 484. The heading is by Beethoven, who abridges and partly paraphrases the passage. Beethoven ranked Plutarch with Homer, Schiller, and Goethe: see [Johann Reinhold Schultz], 'A Day with Beethoven', *Harmonicon*, ii (1824), 11. He frequently cited Plutarch, as in letters to Wegeler of 29 June [1801], Nanette Streicher of [1818], the publisher Bernhard Schotts Söhne of 17 December 1824, and Karl van Beethoven of [shortly after 11 July 1825] (Anderson nos. 51, 930, 1325, 1396), and the report To the Magistrat der Stadt Wien of 1 February 1819 (Anderson Appendix C, no. 9).

97 Du mußt ein Kapital haben, das ist nichts anders als — — — — — zu verschaffen.

You must have capital; in other words, acquire —

Apart from his annuity (see commentary on No. 119), Beethoven had a capital of 4000 florins C.M. (= 10,000 fl. W.W.), which he deposited with the publisher Steiner in July 1816 at 8% interest; on 13 July 1819 he used this money to purchase eight National Bank shares: see Max Reinitz, *Beethoven im Kampf mit dem Schicksal* (Vienna, 1924), p. 110; letter to Steiner of [November 1816] (Anderson no. 677); Theodor von Frimmel, *Beethoven-Studien*, vol. ii (Munich, 1906), pp. 176–7. Beethoven was much concerned about mounting expenses connected with the guardianship of his nephew (see especially the letter to Ferdinand Ries of 8 May 1816, Anderson no. 632) and he was slow or remiss in meeting obligations to Steiner, Giannatasio, Dr Smetana, and others. He also sought advances from several sources: see Nos. 90–1.

98 Das Concert soll aus zwey Theilen bestehn, erster Theil eine neue Sinphonie zweyter Theil eine Cantate. —

> The concert should consist of two parts, the first part a new [?recent] symphony, the second a cantata.

This perhaps has to do with the benefit concert Beethoven hoped to obtain from the Philharmonic Society of London in the 1816–17 season: see especially letters to Charles Neate of 18 May 1816, and to Sir George Smart of [c. 11 October 1816] (Anderson nos. 636, 664). Later in the year, Beethoven wrote to Neate (letter of 18 December 1816) offering to write some new works for the Philharmonic Society – 'Symphonies, an Oratorio, or Cantatas etc.' (Anderson no. 683). The entry may refer, however, to a possible charity concert in Vienna that Beethoven was then considering (see No. 101), or even to the programme of the forthcoming concerts of 30 and 31 March 1817 at which the Eighth Symphony and the oratorio *Christus am Oelberge* were performed: see the *Allgemeine musikalische Zeitung*, xvii (1817), col. 306.

99 nur in den seltensten Fällen anderer Menschen Rath folgen, in einer Sache die schon überdacht ist wem können alle Umstände so gegenwärtig seyn, als Jemanden selbst?! —

> Follow the advice of others only in the rarest cases; in a matter which has already been thought through, who knows all the present circumstances as well as oneself?!

100 Diese Lacedamonier starben nicht ~~Todes nicht~~ Tod nicht Leben für Ehre achtend — — Sondern Tod und Leben mit Ehre bekrönt zu haben.

> These Lacedaemonians died ready to risk death or life for honour; — rather, they crowned death and life with honour.

Possibly a quotation (source unknown). Lacedaemonians were the inhabitants of ancient Sparta.

101 Im Falle einer Akademie für die Invaliden ist die Wiener Zeitung vom 26 August 1816 nachzulesen. —

> In the event of a benefit concert for the disabled soldiers look up the *Wiener Zeitung* of 26 August 1816.

260   Maynard Solomon

The *Wiener Zeitung*, 1816, no. 239, 26 August 1816, p. 1, reports that 'two Hungarian brothers' made an anonymous gift of 4000 florins W.W. for the aid of wounded veterans and their children, which the Ministry of War gratefully accepted and brought to the attention of the Emperor Franz.

102 Nur wie vorhin wieder auf dem Clavier ||fol. 15r|| in eigenen Phantasien — trotz allem Gehör

> Just as some time ago [I am] again at the piano in my own improvisations, despite my hearing [deficiency].

103 Man muß nicht durch die Wehmuth[1] sich wider den Verlust[2] Reichthums schützen noch durch den Mangel an Freundschaft wider den Verlust der Freunde noch durch die Enthaltung vom Kinderzeugen wider den Tod der Kinder, sondern durch die Vernunft wider alles. —

[1] 'Wehmuth' is partly underlined, apparently by Nohl.
[2] There follows a single letter, illegible and blotted.

> One should not seek refuge in melancholy against the loss of riches, nor in friendlessness against the loss of friends, nor in abstention from procreation against the death of children, but in Reason against everything.

Probably a quotation (source unknown).

104 Wegen T. ist nichts anders als Gott es anheim zu stellen, nie dort hin zu gehn, wo man Unrecht aus Schwachheit begehen könnte nur ihm ihm allein dem Alleswissenden Gott sey dieses überlassen! —

> With regard to T. there is nothing else but to leave it to God, never to go there where one could do wrong out of weakness; only leave this totally to Him, to Him alone, the all-knowing God!

Most Beethoven biographers link this passage (and No. 107) with the emergence in 1816 of apparent references to the 'Immortal Beloved': in the letter to Ries of 8 May 1816 (Anderson no. 632) and in the memoirs of Fanny Giannatasio del Rio (Thayer–Deiters–Riemann iii, p. 564; Thayer–Forbes, p. 646). If this is accepted, 'T.' may be Antonie ('Toni') Brentano, as suggested in Maynard Solomon, *Beethoven* (New York, 1977), p. 174.

105 [a] Nicht der ohngefähre Zusammenlauf der Atomen des Akkords[1][,] ⟨Lucrez⟩ hat die Welt gebildet; eingepflanzte Kräfte und Gesetze[,] die den weisesten Verstand zur Quelle haben, sind ein unwandelbarer Ursprung derjenigen Ordnung gewesen, die aus ihnen nicht von ohngefähr[,] sondern nothwendig fließen müssen, [musste.] [b] wenn in der Verfassung der Welt[,] Ordnung in [und] Schönheit Wetterleuchten [hervorleuchten]; so ist ein Gott. Allein[,] das [der] andere ist nicht weniger gegründet[:] wenn diese Ordnung aus allgemeinen Naturgesetzen hat herfließen können,[;] ||fol. 15v|| so ist die ganze Natur nothwendig eine Wirkung der höchsten Weisheit[.] —

[1]'Akkords' is not in Kant's text.

[a] It is not the chance confluence of the ⟨Lucretian⟩ atoms that has formed the world; innate powers and laws that have their source in wisest Reason are the unchangeable basis of that order that flows from them not by chance but inevitably. [b] When in the state of the world order and beauty shine forth, there is a God. But the other is not less well founded. When this order has been able to flow from universal laws of Nature, so the whole of Nature is inevitably a result of the highest wisdom.

[a] Immanuel Kant, *Allgemeine Naturgeschichte und Theorie des Himmels* (Königsberg and Leipzig, 1755; reprinted Zeitz, 1798), p. 108; reprinted in *Gesammelte Schriften*, ed. Königlich Preussische Akademie der Wissenschaften, vol. i (Berlin, 1902), p. 334. The 1798 edition was in Beethoven's *Nachlass*. [b] *Ibid.*, pp. 121–2; reprinted in *Gesammelte Schriften*, vol. i, p. 346. The passage is printed in bold type in the 1798 edition. For Beethoven and Kant, see Ludwig Schiedermair, *Der junge Beethoven* (Berlin and Leipzig, 1925), pp. 316–35; *Ludwig van Beethovens Konversationshefte*, vol. i, ed. Karl-Heinz Köhler and Grita Herre (Leipzig, 1972), pp. 235, 308.

106 [a] Der Stoff[,] woraus die Einwohner verschiedener Planeten[,] ja so gar die Thiere ⟨und⟩ Gewächse auf denselben[,] gebildet sind[,] muß überhaupt um desto leichter und feiner dort [leichtrer und feinerer Art,] in [und] die Elastizität der Wesen [Fasern] sammt der vortheilhaften Anlage ihres Baues[,] um desto willkommener [vollkommner] seyn, nach dem Maaße, als sie weiter von der Sonne abstehen. — [b] "daß die Trefflichkeit der denkenden Naturen[,] die Hastigkeit [Hurtigkeit] in ihren Vorstellungen, die Deutlichkeit und Lebhaftigkeit der Begriffe, die sie durch äußerlichen Eindruck bekommen, sammt dem Vermögen sie zusammen zu setzen, endlich auch die Behendigkeit in der wirklichen Ausübung, kurz[,] der ganze Umfang ihrer Vollkommenheit unter einer gewissen Regel stehen, nach welche⟨r⟩ dieselben[,] nach dem Verhältnisse des Abstands ihrer Wohnplätze von der Sonne immer trefflicher und vollkommener werden"[.] [c] daß die Vollkommenheit der Geisterwelt sowohl[,] als des [der] Materialischen in den Planeten[,] von dem Mercur an bis zum Uranus, oder vielleicht ‖fol. 16r‖ noch über ihm (wofern noch andere Planeten sind) in einer richtigen geraden Folge [Gradenfolge,] nach der Proportion ihrer Entfernungen ⟨von der Sonne,⟩ wachse und fortschreite.

[a] The matter from which the inhabitants of different planets, even animals and plants, are made has to be of a much lighter and finer kind, and the elasticity of the fibres along with the advantageous design of their structure all the more perfect to the extent that they are further from the sun. [b] That the excellence of thinking creatures, the swiftness of their imaginations, their exact and vivid grasp of concepts perceived through external impressions, together with the capacity for putting them together, finally also their agility in actual practice, in short, the sum total of their perfection stands under a certain rule according to which they become ever more excellent and perfect according to the distance of their habitat from the sun. [c] That, on the planets from Mercury to Uranus and even beyond (provided there are other planets), the perfection of the spiritual as well as material worlds grows and proceeds in a graduated sequence according to the proportions of their distances ⟨from the sun⟩.

Kant, *Allgemeine Naturgeschichte und Theorie des Himmels*. [a] = p. 133, [b] = pp. 133–4, [c] = p. 135; reprinted in *Gesammelte Schriften*, vol. i, pp. 358, 359, 360 (see commentary on No. 105). These passages are printed in bold type in the 1798 edition.

107 Jedoch gegen T so gut als möglich ihre Anhänglichkeit verdient immer nie vergessen zu werden — wenn auch leider nie davon vortheilhafte Folgen für dich entstehen könnten. —

Nevertheless be as good as possible towards T; her devotion deserves never to be forgotten, although unfortunately advantageous consequences could never accrue to you.

See No. 104 and commentary.

108 Zwar [Zwei] Kräfte[,] welche beyde gleich gewiß, gleich einfach und zugleich gleich ursprünglich im [und] Allgemeinen [allgemein] sind, nämlich die Anziehungs- und Zurückstossungskraft

> Two forces, which are both equally certain, equally unitary and at the same time equally original and universal, namely the forces of attraction and repulsion.

Kant, *Allgemeine Naturgeschichte und Theorie des Himmels*, Foreword, pp. [xv–xvi]; reprinted in *Gesammelte Schriften*, vol. i, p. 234 (see commentary on No. 105). Beethoven alters the order of the phrases and adds the word 'nämlich'.

109 Nie mit einem Bedienten mehr allein leben, es ist und bleibt das Misliche, setzten wir nur den Fall, der Herr wird krank und der Diener vielleicht auch. —

> Never again live alone with one servant, it is and remains hazardous; just imagine the situation where the master falls ill and the servant perhaps does so too.

Beethoven kept one servant (with whom he was very dissatisfied) from 25 April till the end of October or beginning of November 1816. He was ill and bedridden from 14 October for some weeks: see letter to Zmeskall of [3 November 1816] (Anderson no. 669). In November he engaged two new servants, one of whom was Wenzel Braun.

110 Das kürzeste ein bestimmtes Bierhaus anzuweisen um den Betrügereyen auszuweichen.

> The shortest way to avoid the cheating is to order from a particular restaurant.

In the autumn of 1816 Beethoven several times expressed his fears that he was being cheated by his servants: see his letters to Zmeskall of [3 September] and [3 November 1816] (Anderson nos. 650, 669). See also No. 15.

111 Der [Wer] Thränen aerndten [ernten] will[,] muß Liebe säen.

> He who will reap tears must sow love.

Friedrich Schiller, *Wilhelm Tell*, Act v, Sc. 1. Beethoven cited the passage from *Sämmtliche Werke*, vol. vi (Vienna, 1810), p. 343; Beethoven's copy is Berlin, DSB, Autograph 40,6. Schiller was one of Beethoven's favourite contemporary authors; there are two further Schiller citations in the Tagebuch (Nos. 112, 118) and frequent references to him in the letters, conversation books, and reminiscences of contemporaries: see Maynard Solomon, 'Beethoven and Schiller', *Beethoven, Performers, and Critics*, ed. Robert Winter and Bruce Carr (Detroit, 1980), pp. 162–75. Apart from 'An die Freude', Beethoven set only a few minor texts by Schiller; in 1809 he hoped to compose incidental music to *Wilhelm Tell* but he was assigned Goethe's *Egmont* instead. His *Nachlass* included 21 volumes of the so-called 'Grätzer Taschenausgabe' of Schiller's works published in 1824.

112 Barmherzige Brüder im Tell. —
schließen einen Halbkreis um den Todten und singen im [in] tiefen [tiefem] Ton:
  ‖fol. 16v‖ Rasch tritt der Tod den Menschen an[,]
  es ist ihm keine Frist gegeben[,]
  Es stürzt ihn mitten in der Bahn[,]
  Es reißt ihn fort vom vollen Leben[,]
  Bereitet oder nicht[,] zu gehn![,] —
  Er muß vor seinem Richter steh⟨e⟩n!

  The Monks Hospitallers in *Tell*.
They form a semi-circle around the dead man and sing in a deep tone:
  Death hurries on with hasty stride,
  No respite Man from him may gain,
  He cuts him down, when life's full tide
  Is throbbing strong in every vein.
  Prepared or not the call to hear,
  He must before his Judge appear.

Schiller, 'Gesang der Mönche', from *Wilhelm Tell*, Act iv, Sc. 3, cited from *Sämmtliche Werke*, vol. vi, p. 330 (see commentary on No. 111). Beethoven's setting of these lines, for two tenors and bass WoO 104, was written in the *Stammbuch* of Franz Sales Kandler on 3 May 1817, in memory of the sudden death of the violinist Wenzel Krumpholz (c. 1750–1817) on the previous day. Krumpholz was one of Beethoven's earliest friends in Vienna. The translation used here is that of Sir Theodore Martin in Schiller's *Works, Histories and Dramas* (London, 1846–9), vol. ii, as quoted in *The Works of Friedrich Schiller*, ed. Nathan Haskell Dole, 10 vols. in 5 (New York, 1901–2), unnumbered vol., p. 345.

113 (Vedi [Dedi] malum et accepi)
(Plinius)

> I behaved badly and I was treated badly.
> (Pliny)

Pliny, *Epistulae*, Book iii, letter 9, lines 3–4.

114 Tum ¹etsi [Tametsi] quid homini potest dari majus quam gloria et laus et a⟨e⟩ternitas⟨?⟩
(Plinius)
Wiewohl was kann man einem Menschen größeres geben, als Ruhm und Lob und Unsterblichkeit?

¹Originally written differently and thoroughly crossed out.

> Nevertheless, what greater gift can be conferred on a man than fame and praise and eternal life?
> (Pliny)

Pliny, *Epistulae*, Book iii, letter 21, line 6.

115 Audi multa, loquere pauca

> Listen to much, but speak only a little.

Latin proverb: 'Audito multa, sed loquere pauca': see Alfred Henderson, ed., *Latin Proverbs and Quotations* (London, 1869), p. 32.

116 Etwas muß geschehen — entweder eine Reise und zu dieser die nöthigen Werke schreiben oder eine Oper — solltest du den künftigen Sommer noch hier bleiben so wäre die Oper vorzuziehn, im Falle nur leidlicher Bedingnisse — ist der Sommeraufenthalt hier, so muß jetzt schon beschlossen werden wie, wo? —

> Something must come to pass — either a journey and for this to write the necessary works or an opera. Should you still remain here during the coming summer the opera would be preferable, assuming only passable conditions. If you stay here for the summer, then you must now decide how, where?

Beethoven had numerous opportunities to travel in 1817. Ries invited him to London, Marie Erdödy to Munich, and Karl Pachler to Graz: see letters to Ries of 9 July 1817, to Marie Erdödy of 19 June 1817, and to Pachler of [September 1817] (Anderson nos. 786, 783, 823). He also considered journeys to Switzerland and Italy: see letter to Xaver Schnyder von Wartensee of 19 August 1817 (Anderson no. 803), and No. 120; and he consulted his attorney about the validity of his baptismal certificate in the event of his leaving Austria: see letter to Kanka of [late March 1817] (Anderson no. 772). Nevertheless, he remained in Austria, spending the summer in Heiligenstadt and Nussdorf.

117 Gott helfe du siehst mich von der ganzen Menschheit verlassen, denn Unrechtes will ich nichts begehen, erhöre mein ||fol. 17r|| Flehen doch für die Zukunft nur, mit meinem Karl zusammen zu seyn, da nirgends jetzt sich eine Möglichkeit dahin zeigt o hartes Geschick o grausames Verhängniß, nein, nein, mein unglücklicher Zustand endet nie. — —

> God help me, Thou seest me forsaken by all Mankind, because I do not want to commit an injustice; hear my plea to be together with my Karl, but only in the future, as there does not appear to be any possibility of that now. O harsh Fate, O cruel destiny, no, no, my miserable state will never end.

Presumably the 'injustice' is the separation of Beethoven's nephew Karl from his mother, Johanna van Beethoven. For Beethoven's desire to live with Karl, see commentary on No. 83.

118 Dieß Eine fühl' ich und erkenn' es klar:
Das Leben ist der Güter höchstes nicht,
Der Uibel größtes aber ist die Schuld.

This one thing I feel and clearly perceive:
Life is not the sovereign good,
But the greatest evil is guilt.

Schiller, *Die Braut von Messina*, closing lines.

119 Dich zu retten ist kein anderes Mittel als von hier, nur dadurch kannst du wieder ~~zu den~~ so zu den Höhen deiner Kunst entschweben, wo du hier im Gemeinheit versinkst nur eine Sinfonie — — — — — und dann fort fort — fort — derweilen die [den] Gehalt aufgenommen, welches selbst auf Jahre geschehen kann. —

There is no other way to save yourself except to leave here, only through this can you again lift yourself to the heights of your art, whereas here you are submerged in vulgarity. Only a symphony — and then away, away, away. Meanwhile collect the salary, which can still be done for years.

A reference to a projected journey in 1817. Evidently Beethoven wished to escape from the unaccustomed strains of the guardianship of Karl. The 'salary' is the lifetime annuity granted to Beethoven as of 1 March 1809 by the Archduke Rudolph and the Princes Lobkowitz and Kinsky. The annuity was liable to be cancelled if Beethoven moved his domicile from Austrian territory: see Thayer–Deiters–Riemann iii, pp. 125–6; Thayer–Forbes, p. 457.

120 Uiber den Sommer arbeiten zum Reisen, dadurch nur kannst du das große Werk für deinen armen Neffen vollführen später Italien Sizilien durchwandern mit einigen Künstlern — mache Pläne und sey getrost für L. —¹ — — — — — — — — — — — — — —
— — — — — — — — — — — — — — — —
— — — — — — — — — — — — — — — —
— — — — — — — — — — — — — — — —

¹ 'C' in the right margin, in Nohl's hand.

Work during the summer in order to travel; only thus can you accomplish the great work for your poor nephew; later, wander through Italy, Sicily, with some artists. Make plans and be consoled for L.

Beethoven's letters of this period are silent concerning a trip to Italy. For a projected earlier visit, see letter to Breitkopf & Härtel of 19 February 1811 (Anderson no. 297). Nohl takes the 'L' as a misreading of 'C' (Karl).

121 ‖fol. 17v‖ Meines Erachtens zuerst die Salzwasserbäder wie Wiesbaden etc.[?] alsdann die Schwefelbäder wie Aachen (warm) unendlich (kalt)

In my opinion first the salt-water baths like Wiesbaden, etc.; then the sulphur baths like Aachen (warm) and Landeck (cold) —

This is another indication of Beethoven's travel plans for the summer of 1817, which were never implemented. 'Unendlich' ('unending') is a misreading, probably of 'und Landeck' ('and Landeck', a spa in Germany). For data on the medicinal and chemical properties of these spas, and the temperatures of their waters, Beethoven consulted Christoph Wilhelm Hufeland, *Praktische Uebersicht der vorzüglichsten Heilquellen Teutschlands* (Berlin, 1815), esp. pp. 173–5, 213–18, 309–14.

122 Abends und Mittags in Gesellschaft seyn es erhebt und ermüdet nicht so daher ein anderes Leben dieses im Hause zu führen. —[1] Sinnlicher Genuß ohne Vereinigung der Seelen ist und bleibt viehisch, nach selben hat man keine Spur einer edlen Empfindung vielmehr Reue —
— — — — — — — — — — — — — — — — —
— — — — — — — — — — — — — — — — —
— — — — — — — — — — — — — — — — —

[1]The following may be a new paragraph.

To be in company evenings and middays is uplifting and is not tiring. Therefore lead a different life at home. —
Sensual gratification without a spiritual union is and remains bestial, afterwards one has no trace of noble feeling but rather remorse.

There is evidence that Beethoven patronised prostitutes from c. 1811 onwards: see Maynard Solomon, *Beethoven* (New York, 1977), pp. 220–1, 262; see also Nos. 28 and 138.

123 Vor einigen Tagen einen Brief ohne Recipisse auf die Post gegeben nach Frankfurt — wieder am 22 April Brief nach F — — t ohne R. Auf die Post gegeben — eben so am 26 — eben so am 29 mit einem Lied —

A few days ago posted a letter without a receipt.
To Frankfurt. On 22 April another letter to Frankfurt without R. Sent by post. The same on the 26th. The same on the 29th, with a song.

Beethoven's friends in Frankfurt-am-Main were Franz and Antonie Brentano (see commentary on No. 33). None of the eight letters to them listed here and in Nos. 133, 139, and 141 has survived. The 'Lied' was possibly the second (revised) version of 'An die Geliebte' WoO 140, which was published, with 'Das Geheimnis' WoO 145, by Simrock early in 1817: see Kinsky–Halm, p. 610. Another possibility is the song 'So oder so' WoO 148, published 15 February 1817, of which a copy inscribed to Frau Brentano survives (Bonn, Beethovenhaus, SBH 752). 'R.' = 'Recipisse' (receipt).

124 Es muß sich auf einem Stück Papier schriftlich finden, daß ich 15 f auf die Wohnung auf der Landstrasse darangegeben habe. —

There must be a record in writing that I have given a deposit of 15 florins for the apartment in the Landstrasse.

In late April 1817 Beethoven took lodgings in the Landstrasse, No. 268, second floor, so as to be near the Giannatasio Institute, attended by his nephew Karl.

125 [a] verum gutta cavat lapidem.
(Wirklich in Wahrheit) ein Tropfen höhlet einen Stein aus [b] tausend[1] schöne Augenblicke verschwinden, wenn Kinder in hölzernen ‖fol. 18r‖ Instituten sind, wo sie bey guten Eltern die die[2] seelenvollsten Eindrücke welche bis ins späteste Alter fortdauern, empfangen können. —

[1]The word 'tausend' is preceded by an open bracket.
[2]The first 'die' is covered by an ink-blot.

[a] A drop of water hollows a genuine stone.
(Really, in truth) a drop of water hollows a stone. [b] A thousand beautiful moments vanish when children are in wooden institutions, whereas at home with good parents they could receive the most soulful impressions that endure into the most extreme old age.

[a] Ovid, *Epistulae ex Ponto*, Book iv, letter 10, line 5 (but lacking 'verum'), followed by Beethoven's inaccurate translation. [b] Perhaps a quotation (source unknown). The entry relates to Beethoven's plan to remove his nephew Karl from the Giannatasio Institute.

126 Ruhe und Freyheit sind die größten Güter. —

Tranquillity and freedom are the greatest treasures.

Apparently Beethoven's commentary on No. 118.

127 [1]Wahre Freundschaft kann nur[2] beruhen auf der Verbindung ähnlicher Naturen —

[1]In the margin, in Nohl's hand: 'nie' (never).
[2]The word 'nur' is underlined, probably by Nohl. The 'Fischhof' Manuscript reads 'nie'.

True friendship can only be founded on the connection of similar natures.

Probably a quotation (source unknown). Compare 'Similarity is the mother of friendship' (Greek proverb); and 'For binding friendships, a similarity of manners is the surest tie' (Pliny). Beethoven expressed a similar sentiment in a letter to Ries of 24 July 1804: 'The foundation of friendship demands the greatest similarity in the souls and hearts of men.' (Anderson no. 94)

128 Eibischholz —

— — — — — — — — — — — — — — — — — — — —
— — — — — — — — — — — — — — — — — — — —

Althaea root.

A medication: althaea is a marshmallow root used as a demulcent or emollient to soothe irritated mucous membrane.

129 Gall bemerkt, dem wachsenden Körper sey das kalte Bad nicht zuträglich er will sogar man soll junge Leute zwischen dem 14 und 21 Jahre noch nicht kalt baden lassen, sondern nur dann erst wenn der Körper völlig ausgewachsen sey. —

Gall observes that a cold bath is not beneficial to the growing body; he even recommends that one should not allow young people between the ages of 14 and 21 to take cold baths, but only when the body is fully grown.

Franz Joseph Gall (1758–1828), Austrian anatomist, author, and founder of the immensely popular pseudo-science of phrenology. He lectured in Vienna until 1802; after 1807 he made his home in Paris. His major work is *Untersuchungen über die Anatomie des Nervenssystems überhaupt, und des Gehirns inbesondere* (Paris and Strasbourg, 1809); he published further volumes and the work appeared in numerous translations. Beethoven's concern is for his nephew Karl.

130 Am 2 May die Pulver genommen und die Brust einschmieren —

On 2 May took the powders and rubbed my chest.

Beethoven had a lingering cold from mid-October 1816 until mid-1817. Starting 15 April his doctor prescribed a powder to be taken six times daily and a volatile ointment to be applied to the chest three times daily: see letter to Marie Erdödy of 19 June 1817 (Anderson no. 783).

131 ein Zimmer vermiethen und eine Wohnung auf dem Lande sogleich[1] nehmen —

[1]The prefix 'so-' is crossed out, with dots underneath to signify 'stet'. The word is 'gleich' in the 'Fischhof' Manuscript.

> Rent a room and take a lodging in the country.

In June Beethoven took temporary lodgings in Heiligenstadt.

132 Mein letzt ausgetrettener Bedienter heißt Wenzel Braun ist am 17 May 1817 ausgetretten.[1] —

[1]The third 't' is crossed out.

> My recently retired servant is called Wenzel Braun; he left my service on 17 May 1817. —

Wenzel Braun entered Beethoven's service in late October or early November 1816 (see commentary on No. 109).

133 Am 21 May nach Frankfurt.

> On 21 May to Frankfurt.

The reference is to a letter to Franz and/or Antonie Brentano (see commentary on No. 123).

134 Karl hat dort 2 Stunden Latein, des Tags — eine Stunde Geographie, Geschichte, Naturgeschichte, Religion — Karl ist ein ganz anderes Kind wenn er einige Stunden bey dir ist — ‖fol. 18v‖ daher bleibe bey dem Plan ihn zu dir zu nehmen — auch hast du weniger Sorgen für dein Gemüth — welche Albernheiten sind dort in diesen?! — ! —[1]

[1]The first dash is crossed out.

> Karl has 2 hours of Latin there every day — one hour of geography, history, natural history, religion. Karl is a totally different child when he is with you for several hours. Therefore stick to the plan to take him in with you. Your state of mind will be less uneasy, too. What absurdities there are in these things?!!

Beethoven was deeply interested in guiding his nephew Karl's education. This entry describes Karl's course of study at the Giannatasio Institute, where he was a boarder.

135 am 9 May 203 #
hingegen hievon am 1 Juny 28 genommen
bleiben 172 übrig

> On 9 May 203 ducats
> but 28 taken from them on 1 June
> remaining: 172

On 10 May 1817 Johanna van Beethoven paid Beethoven 2000 florins W.W. as her contribution to the cost of Karl's upbringing: see the contract between Johanna van Beethoven and Beethoven of 10 May 1817 (Anderson Appendix C, no. 6). To this Beethoven added 200 florins W.W.: report To the Magistrat der Stadt Wien of 1 February 1819 (Anderson Appendix C, no. 9); the total was equivalent to approximately 203 ducats. The Giannatasio Institute's annual fee of 1100 florins W.W. (see letter to Ries of 8 May 1816, Anderson no. 632) was payable in quarterly instalments (see letter to Giannatasio of [1817] (Anderson no. 872)), each equivalent to 28 ducats. Beethoven often made errors in simple calculations, as in the above.

136 alles Uibel ist geheimnißvoll und für sich allein nur größer ja [?je] populärer jemehr man sich mit andern bespricht, viel erträglicher und dadurch, daß das was wir fürchten völlig bekannt wird ist es, als hätte man irgend ein großes Uibel überwunden.

> All evil is mysterious and appears greater when viewed alone; [it is] all the more ordinary, the more one talks about it with others; it is easier to endure because that which we fear becomes totally known; it seems as if one has overcome some great evil.

Probably Beethoven's own words. Compare 'Speech concerning a fatal evil is some mitigation of it' (Ovid, *Tristia*, Book v, letter 1, line 59).

137 Das Alleinleben ist wie Gift für dich bey deinem Gehörlosen Zustande, Argwohn muß bey einem niederen Menschen um dich stets gehegt werden.

> To live alone is like poison for you in your deaf condition; you always have to be suspicious with an inferior person around you.

Beethoven often suffered from morbid suspicions about his servants, and tended to view them as 'inferior' persons. For example, he wrote to Zmeskall on [23 July 1817]: 'it drives me to despair to think that owing to my poor hearing I am condemned to spend the great part of my life with *this* class of people, the most infamous of all, and partly to depend upon them —' (Anderson no. 790). See also No. 15.

138 Die Schwachheiten der Natur sind durch die Natur selbst gegeben und die Herrscherin Vernunft soll sie durch ihre Stärke zu leiten und zu vermindern suchen. —

The frailties of nature are given by nature herself and sovereign Reason shall seek to guide and diminish them through her strength.

Perhaps a quotation (source unknown). Possibly another reference (see No. 122) to Beethoven's remorse after contact with a prostitute. In early December 1817 he wrote in the 'Boldrini' Sketchbook (SV 71) '34 xr am Lusthaus' (34 kreuzer at the brothel): see N II, p. 353.

139 am 6 December nach F — t geschrieben

Wrote to Frankfurt on 6 December.

Beethoven continued to note the dates of his letters to Franz and/or Antonie Brentano (see commentary on No. 123).

140 man würde vielleicht besser mit einem Bedienten und Frau auskommen —

Perhaps one would fare better with a servant and his wife.

Beethoven's conflicts with a succession of servants intensified during this period. He did not engage a servant couple.

141 ||fol. 19r|| den 27 December nach F — t geschrieben den 3 Jenner[1] — — — 10 —

[1] In the margin, in Nohl's hand: '1818'.

Wrote to Frankfurt on 27 December. On 3 January — 10 [January] —

Dates of letters to Franz and/or Antonie Brentano (see commentary on No. 123).

142 Das Küchenmädchen erhält 60 f Lohn jährlich und 12 x Brodtgeld täglich. —

The kitchenmaid receives 60 florins salary per annum and 12 kreuzer bread money daily

The kitchenmaid was either 'Baberl', who left Beethoven's service on 12 January 1818, or her replacement, who arrived on the same day: see letters to Nanette Streicher of [28 December 1817] and [early January 1818] (Anderson nos. 839, 885). For the cost of maintaining servants, see letter to Ries of 8 May 1816, and letters to Streicher of 2 October [1817] and [c. 7 January 1818] (Anderson nos. 632, 824, 884).

143 ich muß mich bey dem Superintendenten der Reformirten erkundigen wegen B der das Trio aus D von mir hatte, das einzige Wichtige[1] Schlemmer hat noch eine Partitur von Christus am Oelberg von mir. — Ich habe Bretter genug für noch einen Fensterladen — was kosten Kotzen ? — außen und innen für die Thüre die Strohmatten —

[1] The following may be a separate paragraph.

I have to ask the superintendent of the Reformed [Church] about B, who had the Trio in D from me, the only important one.
Schlemmer still has a score of mine of *Christus am Oelberge*. — I have enough boards for one more window shutter. What do blankets cost? — Straw mats for the outer and inner doors.

The superintendent of the Reformed (that is, Calvinist) Church has not been identified; 'B' is possibly J. X. Brauchle. The 'Trio in D' is probably the Piano Trio Op. 70 No. 1. Wenzel Schlemmer (1760–1823) was Beethoven's most reliable copyist from as early as the late 1790s until his death: see Alan Tyson, 'Notes on Five of Beethoven's Copyists', *Journal of the American Musicological Society*, xxiii (1970), 440–4. In preparation for his nephew Karl's arrival (see commentary on No. 144), Beethoven purchased household items and had a carpenter in to make repairs: see letter to Nanette Streicher of [23 January 1818] (Anderson no. 886).

144 [1]Karls Zeugnisse vom G zu verlangen ich habe nie das letzte

[1]In the margin: vertical stroke followed by 'G'.

> Ask for Karl's report card from G. I have never had the last one.

Beethoven withdrew his nephew Karl from the Giannatasio Institute on 24 January 1818 and began to educate him at home. 'G' = Giannatasio.

145 5818 rechnet man unser Bewußtseyn auf unserm Planeten

> Our consciousness on our planet is calculated as 5818 years.

The reference is to the year 1818 (see commentary on No. 71).

146 Der Heurathskontrakt zwischen meinem Bruder Kaspar und dessen Frau wurde 1806 am 25 May geschlossen.

> The marriage contract between my brother Caspar and his wife was concluded in 1806 on 25 May.

Other memoranda by Beethoven concerning this marriage contract are Berlin, DSB, Autograph 35,18.

147 Schulden von ihr und meinem Bruder auf dem Hause Summa 16852 f 20 x[1]
Der Susanna [Johanna] Beethoven ihr Sohn Karl ist Universalerbe da die beyden Slamatschen [Lamatschen] ‖fol. 19v‖ Schuldschein oder Sätz von 7000 f gehören, Gänzlich aus der Disposition des Großvaters meinem Neffen Karl zu und liegen auf dem Haus der Mutter — — diese jedoch den lebenslänglichen Fruchtgenuß hat. —
Das Haus der Mutter K wurde um 16400 f geschätzt, also den vierten Theil für Karl das Haus der Mutter K trägt 1930 f Zins jährlich ohne Inbegrif der Wohnung der Wittwe des Gatten [Garten], diese beyden letzten sammt Keller können füglich jährlich auf 600 f beym Haus angenommen werden, die Mutter hat ebenfalls den Fruchtgenuß der obigen 1000 [7000] f welche Karl gehören — alsdann die Hälfte der Pension — — — — — — — — — — — — — — — — —
— — — — — — — — — — — — — — — — — — — —
— — — — — — — — — — — — — — — — — — — —

[1]Underlined, apparently by Nohl.

Debts from her and my brother on the house. Grand total *16,852 florins, 20 kreuzer.*

Her son Karl is Susanna [Johanna] Beethoven's sole heir, for the two Lamatsch's notes or agreed-upon sum of 7000 florins belong, totally according to the arrangement of his grandfather, to my nephew Karl and are deposited in his mother's house — — although she has the lifelong usufruct thereof. —

K's mother's house was valued at about 16,400 florins, therefore one fourth for Karl. K's mother's house yields 1930 florins in rent yearly, not counting the widow's apartment and the garden [?garden-house]. These last two, including the cellar, could be estimated at 600 florins yearly from the house. The mother again has the usufruct of the above 1000 [7000] florins which belong to Karl. Also half the pension.

Caspar Carl van Beethoven and his wife Johanna jointly owned and lived in the house in the Alservorstadt, No. 121, in Vienna. The inventory of Caspar Carl's estate valued the house at 16,400 florins W.W., subject to various debts and mortgages: see Thayer–Deiters–Riemann iii, p. 633, where the liabilities are greatly understated. In the summer of 1818 the house was sold for 20,000 florins W.W., on which only a small gain was realised owing to the size of the liabilities: see *Neue Freie Presse*, 25 December 1907, p. 13; see also No. 163. The 'grandfather' is either Johanna's father, Anton Reiss, or grandfather, Paul Lamatsch. Beethoven's nephew Karl was the sole heir of Johanna's mother, Theresia Reiss (*née* Lamatsch), who died on 23 July 1813: see the Draft of a Memorandum to the Court of Appeal, Vienna, of 18 February 1820 (Anderson Appendix C, no. 15); Donald W. MacArdle and Ludwig Misch, eds., *New Beethoven Letters* (Norman, 1957), p. 332. She bequeathed 7000 florins W.W. to Karl, payable to him upon the death of Johanna, who had the lifelong usufruct of the bequest. The 7000 florins was invested in the house, perhaps as a down payment. According to the report To the Magistrat der Stadt Wien of 1 February 1819 (Anderson Appendix C, no. 9), Karl 'has 7000 gulden V.C. [that is, W.W.] as a mortgage on his mother's house . . . and the interest on which his mother enjoys'; see also letters to Johanna van Beethoven of 29 March 1818 and to Johann Baptist Bach of 27 October 1819 (Anderson nos. 897, 979); Draft of a Memorandum to the Court of Appeal, Vienna, of 18 February 1820 (Anderson Appendix C, no. 15); *Ludwig van Beethovens Konversationshefte*, vol. ii, ed. Karl-Heinz Köhler and Dagmar Beck (Leipzig, 1976), p. 80. Caspar Carl's will divided his property equally between Johanna and Karl; therefore Karl was entitled to one fourth of the net proceeds from the sale of the house.

148 Mittwoch den 15 Nov. 1815 starb mein unglücklicher Bruder Carl Van Beethoven geboren den 4 September 1807

On Wednesday 15 November 1815 my unhappy brother died. Karl van Beethoven was born on 4 September 1807.

Caspar Carl van Beethoven died on 15 November 1815, of tuberculosis. His son, Karl, was born on 4 September 1806 (not 1807).

149 191§ des neuen Gesetzbuches

Paragraph 191 of the new Civil Code.

Paragraph 191 of the *Allgemeine bürgerliche Gesetzbuch für die gesammten Deutschen Erbländer der Oesterreichischen Monarchie* (Vienna, 1814) (p. 41) reads in part:
Untauglich zur Vormundschaft sind diejenigen, . . . die eines Verbrechens schuldig erkannt worden sind, oder von denen eine anständige Erziehung des Waisen oder nützliche Verwaltung des Vermögens nicht zu erwarten ist.
(Those persons are unsuitable for guardianship . . . who are known to be guilty of a crime, or from whom a respectable upbringing of the orphan or an advantageous management of the estate cannot be expected.)
For Beethoven's reliance upon this clause in his attempt to exclude Johanna van Beethoven from the guardianship of her son Karl, see his letter to the Imperial and Royal Landrechte of Lower Austria, of 25 September 1818 (Anderson Appendix C, no. 7); Draft of a Memorandum to the Court of Appeal, Vienna, of 18 February 1820 (Anderson Appendix C, no. 15); see also Beethoven's reference to it in a conversation book of January 1820: *Ludwig van Beethovens Konversationshefte*, vol. i, ed. Karl-Heinz Köhler and Grita Herre (Leipzig, 1972), p. 191.

150 Das kostbarste für einen Mann.
Sertorius achtete auf den Schein des Schimpfes[,] der dabey war [,] nicht, und ‖fol. 20r‖ behauptete[,] er kaufe nur die Zeit, die das kostbarste für [vor] einen Mann sey, der wichtige Dinge ausführen wolle.

A Man's Most Precious Possession
Sertorius did not mind the *appearance of dishonour that occurred, and he maintained that he would merely buy time, which is the most precious thing for a man who wants to accomplish important things.*

Plutarch, *Sertorius*, par. vi, line 3. *Biographien des Plutarchs*, trans. Schirach, vol. v (Berlin and Leipzig, 1778), p. 193 (see commentary on No. 96). The heading and the underlinings are Beethoven's.

151 Den 16 Jenner 1818, 25# zum Kurs v 399 gewechselt für 3 — 3 f WW am selbigen Tag wieder 10# noch 10# Dukaten gewechselt in allem in diesen von Gott verliehenen Fond — —

> On 16 January 1818, 25 ducats at an exchange rate of 399 exchanged for 3 — 3 florins W.W. On the same day again 10 ducats another 10 ducats exchanged in all into this God-bestowed fund.

Beethoven's savings were deposited in a fund with his publisher Steiner at 8% interest (see commentary on No. 97). According to a receipt dated 17 January 1818 (Anderson Appendix G, no. 9), he deposited 25 gold ducats with Steiner on that day. The source of the money is unclear. The text is defective making it difficult to reconcile the mathematics of the transaction.

152 Wie Dummheit und Elend auf immer gepaart bleiben.

> How stupidity and misery remain for ever paired.

153 Auf den Leipzig October ein Nationallied schreiben und dieses alle Jahre aufführen.[1] In B jedes Volk mit seinem Marsch und dem Te Deum Laudamus. —

[1]The following may be a separate paragraph.

> To write a national hymn on the Leipzig October and perform this every year.
> N.B. each nation with its own march and the *Te Deum laudamus*.

Very probably refers to the Battle of Leipzig, 16–19 October 1813, in which Napoleon's forces were decisively defeated by Austria, Prussia, and Russia. The work was never composed. 'In B' should be 'N.B.'

154 Solche Einsätze — zu Schriften wie Pasqualati in [?] einem Q gehabt.

> Such deposits, along with written acknowledgments such as Pasqualati had for [?in] his lodgings.

Baron Johann Pasqualati (1777–1830) was a friend of Beethoven and owner of the house in the Mölkerbastei, No. 1239, where Beethoven lived, on and off, between 1804 and 1815. He remained Beethoven's loyal friend and adviser until the composer's death; he received the dedication of the *Elegischer Gesang* Op. 118. 'Q' = 'Quartier' (lodgings). The text is defective.

155 [a] Bach's Litaneyen nicht zu vergessen — [b] Frau Baumgarten vom ersten und zweiten Ludwig

> [a] Don't forget Bach's Litanies. [b] Frau Baumgarten of the first and second Ludwig.

[a] Beethoven explored liturgical music in 1818: see No. 168. 'Bach's Litanies' are C. P. E. Bach, *Zwey Litaneyen aus dem Schleswig-Holsteinischen Gesangbuch* for two choruses (Copenhagen, 1786). Beethoven had copied several passages from this work into his 'Eroica' Sketchbook (N 1880, p. 55), and as a young man had treasured his father's copy of Bach's *Morgengesang am Schöpfungstage* (Bonn, Beethovenhaus, SBH 745). [b] Beethoven was uncertain of the date of his birth and believed that his baptismal certificate of 17 December 1770 actually designated his older brother Ludwig Maria (baptised 2 April 1769, died 9 April 1769): see Maynard Solomon, 'Beethoven's Birth Year', *Musical Quarterly*, lvi (1970), 702–10. He wrote on a copy of the certificate that Wegeler procured for him: 'The baptismal certificate seems to be incorrect, since there was a Ludwig born before me. A Baumgarten was my sponsor, I believe.' (Bonn, Beethovenhaus, SBH 493); and in a conversation book of 1820: 'Bongard must have been the name of my godmother, or Baumgarten' (*Ludwig van Beethovens Konversationshefte*, vol. i, ed. Karl-Heinz Köhler and Grita Herre (Leipzig, 1972), p. 237; see also p. 225). See also the letter to Wegeler of 2 May 1810 (Anderson no. 256). Beethoven's godmother was Gertrud Baum.

156 für Haendel ein eigenes Gestelle —
Dies Gestelle muß bey jeder Lücke eine Leiste haben, welche leicht beweglich zu machen so für größere und kleinere Bücher. —

> A separate rack for business papers.
> This rack has to have a strip at each opening, which can be easily moved. Thus for larger and smaller books.

'Haendel' here probably designates materials pertaining to business and legal affairs rather than the name of the composer. In any event, Beethoven owned only a few volumes of works by Handel in 1818.

157 Das Notenpapier wird bey der Stadt Nürnberg gekauft und das Buch kostet 2 Gulden von[?] 10 bis 16 Linien ist immer dasselbe gewiß. — —
— — — — — — — — — — — — — — — — — —
— — — — — — — — — — — — — — — — — —

Music paper is bought at Stadt Nürnberg and a book costs 2 gulden. Anything from 10 to 16 staves is always the same [price].

Theyer's Stadt Nürnberg was a Viennese retail shop in the Kärntnerstrasse, No. 961, carrying a variety of goods, including paper. A 'book' of music paper normally contained 24 'Bogen' (sheets or bifolia). For the number of staves in Beethoven's autographs, see references in the commentary on No. 31.

158 ||fol. 20v|| Die Mutter Karls suchte selbst den Vergleich, allein die Basis davon war, daß das Haus verkauft werden sollte, wo man rechnen konnte, daß alle Schulden bezahlt würden, und nebst der Hälfte Wittwengehalts nebst der übrig bleibende Theil vom verkauften Hause nebst der Mitgenießung als für Karls Wünschen sie einst alle anständig, sondern sehr wohl leben könnte, da aber das Haus nicht verkauft wird! welches die Hauptbedingung war, worauf der Vergleich geschlossen wurde, da man vorgab, daß schon die Execution hierauf lastete so müssen meine Skrupel nun aufhören und ich kann wohl denken daß sich die Wittwe nicht schlecht bedacht, welches ich ihr von Herzen wünsche, das Meinige o Herr hab ich erfüllt,

Karl's mother herself wanted to come to terms, but the basis of this was that the house would be sold, from which one could assume that all debts would be paid and, along with half of the widow's pension, along with what remained from the sale of the house, along with the joint usufruct for Karl's needs she could live not just decently but very well; but inasmuch as the house is not going to be sold! which was the main condition on which the settlement was reached, because one asserted that execution had already been levied against it, so I now have to set aside my scruples and I can indeed suppose that the widow hasn't situated herself badly, which I wish her from my heart. I have fulfilled my part, O Lord.

(See commentary on No. 160.)

159 es sei möglich gewesen ohne Kränkung die Wittwe[1] war aber nicht andem und du Allmächtiger siehst in mein Herz, weißt daß ich mein eigenes Beste um meines theuren Karls Willen zurückgesetzt habe, segne mein Werk, segne die Wittwe warum kann ich nicht ganz meinem Herzen folgen und sie die Wittwe fürder — — — — —

[1]Followed by a word (?'Es') which has been crossed out.

It would have been possible without hurting the widow's feelings but it was not to be. And Thou, almighty God, seest into my heart, know that I have disregarded my own welfare for my dear Karl's sake, bless my work, bless the widow, why cannot I entirely follow my heart and henceforth — the widow —

(See commentary on No. 160.)

160 Gott Gott mein Hort mein Fels o mein ‖fol. 21r‖ Alles du siehst mein Inneres und weißt wie wehe mir es thut Jemanden leiden machen müssen bey meinem guten Werke für meinen theuren Karl!!! o höre stets Unaussprechlicher höre mich — deinen unglücklichen unglücklichsten aller Sterblichen. — —

God, God, my refuge, my rock, O my all, Thou seest my innermost heart and knowest how it pains me to have to make somebody suffer through my good works for my dear Karl!!! O hear, ever ineffable One, hear me, your unhappy, most unhappy of all mortals.

Beethoven was deeply unsettled about the fairness and consequences of the contract entered into between him and Johanna van Beethoven on 10 May 1817, which provided that she cede to her son Karl one half of her widow's annual pension of 333 florins 20 kreuzer W.W., and the flat sum of 2000 florins W.W. (Anderson Appendix C, no. 6; Thayer–Deiters–Riemann iii, p. 635; iv, p. 550). The house was Alservorstadt, No. 121, owned three fourths by Johanna and one fourth by Karl: see No. 147. By late March 1818 Johanna was actively attempting to sell the house (see letter to Johanna van Beethoven of 29 March 1818 (Anderson no. 897)), perhaps in order to pay her own and Caspar Carl's debts: see No. 163. Albert Leitzmann observes (ed., *Ludwig van Beethoven: Berichte der Zeitgenossen, Breife und persönliche Aufzeichnungen* (Leipzig, 1921), vol. ii, p. 373) that 'mein Hort mein Fels' is an apparently unconscious quotation from Gellert's 'Bitten', which Beethoven set to music in 1801–2 (Op. 48 No. 1).

161 Am 20 Februar 1818, 12 Stück Dukaten gewechselt für elendes Papier 156 f zum Kurs von 202, eben so von — — —

On 20 February 1818 I exchanged 12 ducats for wretched paper: 156 florins at a rate of 202, also from —

In February 1818, Beethoven received 12 ducats from the publisher George

162 Seit 10 August sah die Mutter Karl nicht. —¹ ein — geschrieben worin auch melodramatisches vorkommt, kurzum Cantate mit Chor — Schauspiel so daß man sich in allem zeigen kann — — — — — —
— — — — — — — — — — — — — — — — — —
— — — — — — — — — — — — — — — — — —

¹The following may be a separate paragraph.

> Since 10 August Karl's mother has not seen him.
> Write a — in which there is also a melodrama. To sum up, cantata with choir — spectacle so that one can show oneself in everything.

Following a quarrel between Beethoven and Johanna van Beethoven in August 1817, he and Giannatasio agreed to restrict her access to Karl at the Giannatasio Institute to two visits per year: see letter to Giannatasio of 14 August 1817 (Anderson no. 800). The planned composition was never written; it is perhaps related to the projected 'Adagio Cantique' of 1818 (N II, p. 163).

163 Nach dem letzten Ausweis scheinen die Schulden der Wittwe 23100 — — — — — — — — — — — — — — —
— — — — 925 — — — — — — — — — — — — — —
— — — 24025 und 145# zu betragen sie scheinen freylich noch nach meines Bruders Tod vermehrt worden zu seyn¹ — — — — —

¹The entire passage is crossed out, with dots under the first line, up to 'Schulden', signifying 'stet'. In the margin, probably in Gräffer's hand: '5 Zeilen Pausen' (5-line space); this is followed by a note in Nohl's hand: 'Nb. nicht durchstreichen' (N.B. do not cross out).

> According to the latest financial statement the widow's debts seem to amount to 23,100 florins
> $\underline{925}$
> 24,025 and 145 ducats, they actually seem to have increased after my brother's death.

The 'widow' is Johanna van Beethoven. The debts include those of her husband and the liabilities on her house (see No. 147 and note, and No. 158). The total exceeded by more than 4600 florins W.W. the amount realised from the sale of the house in mid-1818. The sale was apparently forced by her creditors.

The income from the house did not cover the interest on the debts, assuming a rate of 8%. Johanna's known income thereafter consisted of one half of her widow's pension (which she refused to draw for several years after 1818) and the interest on her son's 7000-florin inheritance: see No. 147.

164 Beklagenswerthes Schicksal warum kann ich euch[1] nicht helfen

[1]Followed by '(auch)', apparently in Nohl's hand.

> Lamentable Fate, why can I not help you?

The reference is apparently to Johanna van Beethoven.

165 Den 19 May 1818. hier in Mödling eingetroffen gebadet vom 21 May an das erstemal

> Arrived here in Mödling on 19 May 1818. Bathed for the first time on 21 May.

Beethoven, together with Karl, a housekeeper ('Frau D.'), and a kitchen maid ('Peppi'), stayed in Mödling at the 'Hafnerhaus' in the Herrengasse (see commentary on No. 166).

166 Den 8 Juny 1818 in Mödling ist die neue Haushälterin eingetretten[1]

[1]The third 't' is crossed out, probably by Nohl. The word is spelled 'eingetreten' in the 'Fischhof' Manuscript.

> In Mödling the new housekeeper started on 8 June 1818.

'Frau D.' and 'Peppi' were discharged before 8 June. A new cook, whose name is not known, was hired on that day: see letter to Nanette Streicher of 18 June 1818 (Anderson no. 904).

167 ||fol. 21v|| Trogloditen Höhlenbewohner.

> Troglodytes [means] cave-dwellers.

168 Um wahre Kirchenmusik zu schreiben alle Kirchenchoräle der Mönche etc.[?] durchgehen wo [?so] auch zu suchen wie die Absätze in richtigsten Uibersetzungen nebst vollkommener Prosodie aller christkatholischen Psalmen und Gesänge überhaupt.

In order to write true church music go through all the Gregorian chants etc. Also look there for the stanzas in the most correct translations along with the most perfect prosody of all Christian-Catholic psalms and hymns in general.

Although the earliest surviving sketches for the *Missa solemnis* date from 1819, Beethoven apparently decided during 1818 to compose it. With the help of Friedrich August Kanne, Karl Peters, and Joseph Czerny, and with access to the libraries of the Archduke Rudolph and Prince Lobkowitz, he examined sacred music from Gregorian chant to Palestrina and the Bachs. He also worked to improve his imperfect command of Latin prosody: see Berlin, DSB, Autograph 35,25; Thayer–Deiters–Riemann iv, p. 334, note 1. See Warren Kirkendale, 'New Roads to Old Ideas in Beethoven's *Missa solemnis*', *Musical Quarterly*, lvi (1970), 676–7, 699–700.

169 Opfere noch einmal alle Kleinigkeiten des gesellschaftlichen Lebens deiner Kunst, o Gott über alles! denn die [dessen] ewige Vorsicht lenkt allwissend das Glück oder [und] Unglück sterblicher Menschen.[!]

Sacrifice once and for all the trivialities of social life to your art, O God above all! For eternal Providence in its omniscience and wisdom directs the happiness and unhappiness of mortal men.

The second sentence is from *The Odyssey*, Book xx, lines 75–6. *Homers Odüssee*, trans. Voss, p. 387 (see commentary on No. 74, see also commentary on No. 26).

170   Es sind ja den Menschen nur wenige Tage beschieden[.]
Wer nun grausam denkt[,] und grausame Handlungen ausübt[;]
Diesem wünschen alle, so lang' er lebet[,] nur Unglück![,]
Und noch selbst im Tode wird sein Gedächtniß verabscheut[.]
Aber wer edel denkt[,] und edle Handlungen ausübt[;]
Dessen würdigen Ruhm verbreiten die Fremdlinge weithin —
Unter die Menschen auf Erden[,] und ‖fol. 22r‖ jeder segnet den Guten[.]

Homer

To men are allotted but a few days.
Now he who is cruel in thought and deed
Everyone wishes him lifelong misfortune,
And even in death his memory is abominated.

Beethoven's Tagebuch of 1812–1818

But he who is noble in thought and deed,
His worthy fame is spread abroad by strangers
To all Mankind, and everyone blesses the righteous man.
>   Homer

The Odyssey, Book xix, lines 328–34. *Homers Odüssee*, trans. Voss, p. 373 (see commentary on No. 74; see also commentary on No. 26).

171 Gelassen will ich mich also allen Veränderungen unterwerfen[,] und nur auf deine unwandelbare Güte[,] o Gott! mein ganzes Vertrauen setzen.¹ Dein[,] Unwandelbarer,[!] Deiner [dein] soll sich meine Seele freuen. Sey mein Fels, ⟨Gott! sey⟩ mein Licht, ewig meine Zuversicht!

¹The following may be a new paragraph.

Therefore, calmly will I submit myself to all inconstancy and will place all my trust in Thy unchangeable goodness, O God!
My soul shall rejoice in Thee, immutable Being. Be my rock, ⟨God, be⟩ my light, my trust for ever!

Christoph Christian Sturm, *Betrachtungen über die Werke Gottes im Reiche der Natur und der Vorsehung auf alle Tage des Jahres* (Reuttlingen, 1811), vol. ii, p. 565 (closing lines and quatrain, entry for 29 December). Beethoven's marked copy of this edition is Berlin, DSB, Autograph 40,2; the marked passages are given in Nohl, ed., *Beethovens Brevier* (Leipzig, 1870), pp. 33–72. Sturm (1740–86) was a Lutheran clergyman whose writings attempt to formulate a reconciliation between science, Enlightenment, and religion. Beethoven's deep attachment to Sturm is asserted by Schindler (1860), *passim*, esp. vol. ii, p. 161; Eng. trans. p. 365. See Arnold Schmitz, *Das romantische Beethovenbild* (Berlin and Bonn, 1927), pp. 91–3.

Index of Tagebuch Entries

The figures in this index refer to the numbering of the Tagebuch entries.

annuity, 119
art, Beethoven's attitude to his, 1, 16, 25, 31, 40, 41, 84, 88, 119, 169
Artaria, ?91
Bach, Carl Philipp Emanuel, 155a
Bach, Johann Sebastian, 43
baptismal certificate, 155b
'Baumgarten, Frau' [Baum, Gertrud] (godmother), 155b
Beethoven, (Caspar) Carl van (brother), 45, 47, 69, 146, 147, 148, 163
Beethoven, Johanna van (sister-in-law), 45, 47, 146, 147, 149, 158, 159, 162, 163, ?164
Beethoven, Karl van (nephew), 75, 76, 80, 81, 83, 86, 89, 91, 117, 120, 134, 144, 147, 148, 158, 159, 160, 162
    Beethoven's desire to live with, 86, 117, 134
Beethoven, Ludwig Maria van (brother), 155b
Beethoven, (Nikolaus) Johann van (brother), ?27
Braun, Wenzel, 132
Brentano, Franz and Antonie
    correspondence with, 123, 133, 139, 141
    financial dealings with, 33
    (*see also* 'Immortal Beloved')
compositions
    Op. 43, 82
    Op. 59, 82
    Op. 70 No. 1, ?143
    Op. 72, 22
    Op. 85, 143
    Op. 91, ?16
    Op. 97, 90
    Op. 100, ?85
    Op. 101, 91
    Op. 102, 77
    WoO 144, 85
    Scottish songs, 34
    Piano Trio in F minor (unfinished), 91
    (for further details *see* Index of Beethoven's Compositions, Sketches, Letters, and Other Documents, below)
compositions, planned or projected
    'Adagio Cantique', ?162
    cantatas, ?98, 162
    church music, 168
    'National Hymn', 153
    operas, ?84, 116
    symphonies, ?98, 119
concerts, 18, 98, 101
confessions, prayers, moral exhortations and general precepts, 1, 3, 7a, 28, 34, 41, 42, 69, 78, 80, 87, 99, 104, ?110, 117, 126, 136, 152, 158, 159, 160, 164, 169, 171
    (*see also* religious outlook; stoicism)
countryside, Beethoven's desire to live in, 41, 66, 86, 131
Czerny, Carl, 90
death, thoughts on, 20, ?40, 72, 112, 170
deafness, 102, 137
    (*see also* hearing aids)
Diabelli, Antonio, 82
domestic matters, 15, 19, 23, 32, 38, 46, 122, 137, 143
    (*see also* servants)
education, 67, 83, 125b, 134, ?144
financial matters, ?16, 24, 33, 90, 91, 97, 119, 124, 135, 142, 147, 151, 154, 157, 158, ?159, ?160, 161, 163
Gall, Franz Joseph, 129

Index of Tagebuch entries

Gebauer, Franz Xaver, 82
Giannatasio del Rio, Cajetan, ?90, ?144
Gluck, Christoph Willibald, 43
Handel, George Frideric, 43
harmony and counterpoint, 2, 34, 37
Haydn, Franz Joseph, 43
hearing aids, 27, 41, 52, 53, ?54
illness, health, medical treatments, 20, 40, 90, 91, 92, 109, 121, 128, 129, 130, ?165
(see also death, thoughts on)
'Immortal Beloved', 1, 3, 104, 107
improvisation, 102
Italian, study of, 11, 12, 21
Lacedaemonians, 100
Lamatsch, Paul, ?147
library, organisation of Beethoven's, 51, 70, 156
literary quotations
  Bhagavad-Gita, ?63a, 64a, 64b
  Govinda, Ciangra, hymn to Parabrahma, 61b
  Herder, Johann Gottfried, Blumen aus morgenländischen Dichtern, 5, 6, 55, 56, 57, 58
  Herder, Vermischte Stücke aus verschiedenen morgenländischen Dichtern, 59
  Hesiod, Works and Days, 68b
  Homer, The Iliad, 26, 49
  Homer, The Odyssey, 74, 169, 170
  Jones, Sir William, 'Hymn to Narayena', 62, 65
  Kalidasa, Sakuntala, 63b, 63c
  Kant, Immanuel, Allgemeine Naturgeschichte und Theorie des Himmels, 105, 106, 108
  Müllner, Amandus Gottfried Adolf, Die Schuld, 7b, 7c, 7d, 7e
  Ovid, Epistulae ex Ponto, 125a
  Pliny, Epistulae, 113, 114
  Plutarch, Philopoemen, 96
  Plutarch, Sertorius, 150
  proverbs, German, 29, 30
  proverbs, Latin, 115
  Rig-Veda, 61a
  Sa'dī, see Herder, Johann Gottfried
  Schiller, Friedrich von, Die Braut von Messina, 118, 126
  Schiller, Wilhelm Tell, 111, 112
  Sturm, Christoph Christian, Betrachtungen, 171
  Vedas, sastra from, 93b
  Werner, Friedrich Ludwig Zacharias, Die Söhne des Tals, 60

unknown sources, 11, 17, 44, 67, 68a, 68c, 73, 79, 93a, 100, 103, 125b, 127, 138
literary references
  Alfieri, Count Vittorio, Rosmunda, 21
  Calderón de la Barca, Pedro, La banda y la flor, 13
  Calderón, El principe constante, 13
  Chladni, Ernst Florens Friedrich, Die Akustik, 54
  Gall, Franz Joseph, 129
  Gozzi, Carlo, 21
  Müllner, Amandus Gottfried Adolf, Die Schuld, 8, 9
  Shakespeare, William, 79
lodgings, 23, 86, 124, 131, 154, 165
Mälzel, Johann Nepomuk, 52
Malfatti, Therese, 21
Michelangelo Buonarroti, 79
Mozart, Wolfgang Amadeus, 43
orchestral forces, 18
orientalism, 5, 6, 56, 57, 58, 59, 61, 62, 63, 64, 65, 93, 94, ?95
Pasqualati, Baron Johann, 154
prosody, 8, 10, 49, 168
publishers, 77, 91
Reiss, Anton, ?147
religious music, 41, 153, 168
religious outlook, 41, 61, 62, 63, 64, 65, 93, 94, 104, 117, 159, 169, 171
(see also confessions . . .)
Rudolph, Archduke, 90
Schlemmer, Wenzel, 143
scores, 31, 35, 51, 82, 143, 157
servants, 15, 46, 109, ?110, 132, 137, 140, 142, 166
(see also domestic matters)
sexual references (possible), 28, 122, 138
sketchbooks, 51
Spontini, Gaspare, 39
Stadt Nürnberg, Theyer's, 157
Staudenheim, Jakob, 90
stoicism, 1, 26, 43, 60, 64, 67, 73, 78, 93a
times of day/points of the compass, 14
travel plans, 1, 41, 91, 116, 119, 120
  to England, 50
  to German spas, 121
  to the Rhineland, ?50
  to Italy, 120
  to Sicily, 120
travels
  to Brühl, 50
  to Linz, 27
  to Mödling, 165
troglodytes, 167

working materials, **16**, **31**, **51**, **70**, **156**, **157**
(*see also* library, organisation of Beethoven's; scores)

working methods, **2**, ?**4**, **8**, **9**, **16**, **17**, **31**, **35**, **36**, **37**, **48**
world chronology, **71**, **145**
Zmeskall von Domanovecz, Baron Nikolaus, **90**

Index of Beethoven's Compositions, Sketches, Letters, and Other Documents

COMPOSITIONS

Op. 1: three Piano Trios, 18, 22–3
  No. 1 in Eb, 22, 24–5, 147
  No. 2 in G, 1–2, 15–16, 18, 22–3, 25–6
  No. 3 in C minor, 1–2, 14–15, 18–23, 25–6, 147
Op. 2: three Piano Sonatas, 18, 25
  No. 1 in F minor, 2, 15, 24–5
  No. 2 in A, 1–2, 12, 15, 23
  No. 3 in C, 1–2, 12, 15, 23–6, 147, 154
Op. 3: String Trio, 15, 22
Op. 4: String Quintet, 1–3, 5, 7, 9, 11, 13–17, 26
Op. 5: two Cello Sonatas, 23
  No. 1 in F, 154
  No. 2 in G minor, 96–7, 145
Op. 7: Piano Sonata in Eb, 155–6
Op. 9: three String Trios
  No. 1 in G, 23, 26
  No. 3 in C minor, 26, 145
Op. 10: three Piano Sonatas
  No. 1 in C minor, 143, 155–6
  No. 3 in D, 27, 151
Op. 11: Clarinet Trio, 96
Op. 13: Piano Sonata in C minor ('Pathétique'), 143, 145
Op. 15: First Piano Concerto, 1, 15–16, 18, 23, 25, 155
Op. 16: Quintet for Piano and Wind, 23, 96–7, 154
Op. 18: six String Quartets, 107
  No. 1 in F, 35
  No. 2 in G, 35–6, 159
  No. 5 in A, 143
  No. 6 in Bb, 29–46 passim, 56
Op. 19: Second Piano Concerto, 2, 14–15, 25, 27, 155
Op. 20: Septet, 96
Op. 21: First Symphony, 23, 157
Op. 22: Piano Sonata in Bb, 35
Op. 23: Violin Sonata in A minor, 35
Op. 27 No. 2: Piano Sonata in C# minor ('Moonlight'), 156
Op. 29: String Quintet, 147–9
Op. 30: three Violin Sonatas, 71
  No. 2 in C minor, 143
Op. 31: three Piano Sonatas, 49, 69, 71–2
  No. 1 in G, 69, 154
  No. 3 in Eb, 69, 72
Op. 34: Piano Variations in F, 48–9, 69, 71–3
Op. 35: Piano Variations in Eb, 47–84 passim, 102
Op. 36: Second Symphony, 23, 27, 101, 149
Op. 37: Third Piano Concerto, 143, 155
Op. 43: ballet *Die Geschöpfe des Prometheus*, 49, 86, 102, 252–3
Op. 44: Variations for piano trio in Eb, 25
Op. 46: song 'Adelaide', 23
Op. 47: Violin Sonata in A minor ('Kreutzer'), 150
Op. 48 No. 1: song 'Bitten', 281
Op. 52 No. 2: song 'Feuerfarb'', 2
Op. 53: Piano Sonata in C ('Waldstein'), 27, 150, 154–5
Op. 54: Piano Sonata in F, 107
Op. 55: Third Symphony ('Eroica'), 27, 49, 56, 72, 85–105 passim, 132, 150, 152
Op. 56: Triple Concerto, 107
Op. 57: Piano Sonata in F minor ('Appassionata'), 14, 27, 101, 107, 129, 145, 153, 157
Op. 58: Fourth Piano Concerto, 107–9, 134–6, 155
Op. 59: three String Quartets ('Razumovsky'), 107–40 passim, 252
  No. 1 in F, 108–9, 112, 114, 117, 120–1, 129, 131–4, 138, 150

Op. 59 – cont.
  No. 2 in E minor, 108–9, 112, 114, 117, 120–1, 128–31, 134, 139, 145
  No. 3 in C, 109, 112–14, 117–32, 140, 151
Op. 60: Fourth Symphony, 108–9, 134–6, 150
Op. 61: Violin Concerto, 108–9, 134–5, 137
Op. 62: Overture to *Coriolan*, 108–9, 134–5, 137
Op. 67: Fifth Symphony, 14, 85, 88, 91, 108, 116, 135, 150–1, 154
Op. 68: Sixth Symphony ('Pastoral'), 135, 150–1
Op. 69: Cello Sonata in A, 150
Op. 70 No. 1: Piano Trio in D ('Ghost'), 101, 150, 274
Op. 71: Wind Sextet, 23
Op. 72: *Leonore* (1805, 1806), 86, 107, 109
  Fidelio (1814), 105, 116, 207, 227
  Overture to *Fidelio*, 151
  (see also Op. 138)
Op. 73: Fifth Piano Concerto, 155
Op. 74: String Quartet in E♭, 151
Op. 81a: Piano Sonata in E♭, 151
Op. 84: music for *Egmont*, 264
Op. 85: oratorio *Christus am Oelberge*, 86, 259, 274
Op. 87: Trio for two oboes and cor anglais, 15
Op. 88: song 'Das Glück von Freundschaft', 196
Op. 91: *Wellingtons Sieg* ('Battle' Symphony), 221–2, 251
Op. 92: Seventh Symphony, 14, 126–7, 157–8, 205, 222, 251
Op. 93: Eighth Symphony, 27, 152, 157–9, 205, 222, 259
Op. 95: String Quartet in F minor, 116, 145
Op. 96: Violin Sonata in G, 151, 251
Op. 97: Piano Trio in B♭ ('Archduke'), 116, 150, 251, 255
Op. 98: song cycle *An die ferne Geliebte*, 155
Op. 100: song (for two voices) 'Merkenstein', 253
Op. 101: Piano Sonata in A, 255
Op. 102: two Cello Sonatas, 250–1
  No. 2 in D, 150
Op. 103: Wind Octet, 2–4, 6, 8, 10, 12, 14–15, 26
Op. 106: Piano Sonata in B♭ ('Hammerklavier'), 116, 205
Op. 108: twenty-five Scottish songs, 228

Op. 111: Piano Sonata in C minor, 145
Op. 112: cantata *Meeresstille und glückliche Fahrt*, 250
Op. 113: music for *Die Ruinen von Athen*, 116
Op. 117: music for *König Stephan*, 116
Op. 118: *Elegischer Gesang*, for four voices and string quartet, 279
Op. 120: Variations on a Waltz by Diabelli, for piano, 54
Op. 123: Mass in D (*Missa solemnis*), 162, 167, 207, 284
Op. 125: Ninth Symphony, 14, 85, 91, 264
Op. 127: String Quartet in E♭, 158
Op. 130: String Quartet in B♭, 153, 158
Op. 131: String Quartet in C♯ minor, 145
Op. 132: String Quartet in A minor, 158, 161–91 *passim*
Op. 135: String Quartet in F, 101, 158
Op. 138: Overture *Leonore* No. 1, 124
WoO 5: Violin Concerto in C, 23–4
WoO 14 No. 7: Contratanz in E♭, 49
WoO 36: three Piano Quartets, 14, 27
  No. 1 in E♭, 15
  No. 2 in D, 14–15
  No. 3 in C, 2, 13, 15, 24, 26
WoO 37: Trio for piano, flute, and bassoon, 15
WoO 38: Piano Trio in E♭, 15
WoO 47: three Piano Sonatas, 196
  No. 1 in E, 15
  No. 2 in F minor, 15
  No. 3 in D, 15
WoO 58: cadenzas to Mozart's Piano Concerto in D minor K 466, 155
WoO 63: Variations on a march by Dressler, for piano, 196
WoO 77: Variations in G for piano, 35
WoO 78: Variations on 'God save the King' for piano, 221
WoO 80: Variations in C minor for piano, 113
WoO 87: Cantata on the death of Joseph II, 23
WoO 88: Cantata on the elevation of Leopold II, 23
WoO 92: concert aria 'Primo amore', 23
WoO 104: song (for male voices) 'Gesang der Mönche', 264
WoO 118: song 'Seufzer eines Ungeliebten', 1, 23
WoO 135: song 'Die laute Klage', 215
WoO 140: song 'An die Geliebte', 268

Index of Sketches

WoO 141: song 'Der Gesang der Nachtigall', 215
WoO 144: song (for single voice) 'Merkenstein', 253
WoO 145: song 'Das Geheimnis', 268
WoO 146: song 'Sehnsucht', 49
WoO 148: song 'So oder so', 268
WoO 152–157: Irish, Welsh, Scottish, and other songs, 228
WoO 157 No. 1: 'God save the King' for chorus and piano trio, 221–2
WoO 168 No. 1: canon 'Das Schweigen', 215
WoO 203: canon 'Das Schöne zu dem Guten', 164

UNFINISHED OR FRAGMENTARY WORKS
accompaniments to the *Lamentations of Jeremiah*, 53–5, 175–6

Fantasia and Variations in C minor/major for piano, 131
Oboe Concerto in F Hess 12, 2
Piano Trio in F minor, 255
Symphony in C (1795–6), 22, 27, 147–8

COPIES MADE BY BEETHOVEN OF MUSIC BY OTHER COMPOSERS
Fux, Johann Joseph
    two fugues from *Gradus ad Parnassum*, 184
Haydn, Franz Joseph
    String Quartet Op. 20 No. 1, 17
Mozart, Wolfgang Amadeus
    String Quartet K 387, 30
Palestrina, Giovanni Pierluigi da
    Gloria, 163
    motet *Pueri Hebraeorum* (attrib. Palestrina), 163

SKETCHES

Numbering of the sketches is in accordance with Hans Schmidt, 'Verzeichnis der Skizzen Beethovens' (SV)

BERLIN
SV 17: Artaria 205, bundle 7 (DSB), 163
SV 22: Artaria 213, Parts 1 and 2 (SPK), 164, 173
SV 28: Autograph 11, Part 2 (SPK), 164
SV 29: Autograph 19e (SPK), 35–46 *passim*, 108
SV 31: Autograph 28, 'Fischhof' Miscellany (SPK), 2, 22, 25–6, 115, 147
SV 46: Grasnick 2 (SPK), 36
SV 54: Grasnick 20b (DSB), 114, 117
SV 60: Landsberg 6, *see* Other locations
SV 61: Landsberg 7 (SPK), 50, 115, 117
SV 63: Landsberg 9 (DSB), 116
SV 64: Landsberg 10 (SPK), 108–9, 114, 117, 120, 128–9, 131, 151
SV 67: Mendelssohn 15 (SPK), 114, 120
SV 71: 'Boldrini' Sketchbook (lost), 273
SV —: Sketch in Conversation Book no. 85 (DSB), 184

BONN, BEETHOVENHAUS
SV 75: BH 100 (SBH 616), 113, 117, 121, 125–9
SV 104: NE 47, 'de Roda' Sketchbook (SBH 680), 163–70, 174, 178, 183, 188–9
SV 110: Mh 63 (SBH 606), 2

SV 119: Mh 72 (SBH 617), 113, 117, 121, 125–9
SV 129: Mh 81 (SBH 657), 116
SV 130: Mh 82 (SBH 658), 116
SV 131: Mh 83 (SBH 659), 116
SV 132: Mh 84 (SBH 656), 116
SV 136: Mh 88 (SBH 623), 116
SV 155: BSk 2 (SBH 660), 116
SV 156: BSk 3 (SBH 661), 116
SV 157: BSk 4 (SBH 662), 116
SV 161: BSk 8 (SBH 652), 169
SV 173: BSk 18 (SBH 646), 116

LONDON, BRITISH LIBRARY
SV 185: Add. MS 29801, fols. 39–162, 'Kafka' Miscellany, 14, 22, 25, 37, 54, 73, 115, 175, 215
SV 188: Add. MS 31766, 'Pastoral' Symphony Sketchbook, 151, 197
SV 189: Egerton 2795, 225

PARIS, BIBLIOTHÈQUE NATIONALE
SV 208: Ms. 58, no. 2, 54
SV 213: Ms. 60, no. 2, Mass in C Sketchbook, 115
SV 238: Ms. 86, 116
SV 240: Ms. 88, 116
SV 243: Ms. 91, 116
SV 244: Ms. 92, 116

Index of Beethoven's Compositions, Sketches, Letters, etc.

VIENNA, GESELLSCHAFT DER
MUSIKFREUNDE
SV 259: A 11, 25
SV 262: A 33, 131
SV 263: A 34, 'Kessler' Sketchbook,
   47–84 passim
SV 265: A 36, 113, 117–21, 126–31
SV 288: A 58, 164
SV 290: A 60, 113

OTHER LOCATIONS
SV 315: Cambridge, Fitzwilliam
   Museum, Mus. ms. 287, 116
SV —: Koblenz, Wegeler Collection, 164
SV 60: Kraków, Biblioteka Jagiellońska
   (formerly Berlin), Landsberg 6,
   'Eroica' Sketchbook, 101–5, 108, 279
SV 336: London, Royal College of
   Music, MS 2175, 113

SV 342: Moscow, Central (Glinka)
   Museum for Music Culture,
   'Moscow' Pocket Sketchbook,
   163
SV 343: Moscow, Central (Glinka)
   Museum for Music Culture,
   'Wielhorsky' Sketchbook, 47–84
   passim, 101
SV 344: Moscow, Central (Glinka)
   Museum for Music Culture, 24
SV 350: New York, collection of Mrs
   Rebecca Friskin, 108
SV —: New York, Pierpont Morgan
   Library, 116
SV 358: New York, Public Library, JOD
   71–2, 116
SV 364: Princeton, New Jersey, Library
   of William Scheide, 'Scheide'
   Sketchbook, 181, 225

LETTERS

Numbering and dates of the letters are in accordance with Anderson. Dates that Anderson has supplied are in square brackets; some suggested changes are in round brackets.

no. 51: 29 June [1801], 258
no. 58: [22 April 1802], 71
no. 62: [18 October 1802], 48, 70–1
no. 79: [June 1803], 102
no. 94: 24 July 1804, 270
no. 110: [spring 1805], 206
no. 132: 5 July 1806, 108
no. 134: 3 September 1806, 108
no. 136: 1 November 1806, 130
no. 145: 16 June [1807], 135
no. 146: [23 June 1807], 135
no. 148: [soon after 23 June 1807], 135
no. 149: [soon after 23 June 1807], 135
no. 163: [February 1808], 230
no. 228: 2 November 1809, 208
no. 256: 2 May 1810, 279
no. 258: [May 1810], 224
no. 297: 19 February 1811, 267
no. 367: [spring 1812], 240
no. 373: 6–7 July [1812], 214
no. 420: [early May 1813], 214
no. 459: 11 January 1814, 226
no. 462: 13 February 1814, 224
no. 479: [April] (?March) [1814], 105, 224
no. 485: [July 1814], 226
no. 486: 22 August 1814, 225
no. 488: [summer 1814], 227
no. 493: [September 1814], 223
no. 496: 15 September 1814, 228
no. 497: 19 September 1814, 225
no. 502: [autumn 1814], 225

no. 503: October 1814, 228
no. 513: [1814], 225
no. 520: 11 January 1815, 225
no. 521: 14 January 1815, 225
no. 522: [14 January 1815], 225
no. 529: 7 February 1815, 228
no. 530: 24 February 1815, 225
no. 531: 29 February 1815, 228
no. 533: 10 March 1815, 234
no. 553: [summer 1815], 233, 253
no. 592: [1815], 233
no. 600: [January 1816], 215
no. 614: [late February 1816], 250
no. 632: 8 May 1816, 258, 260, 272, 274
no. 633: 13 May 1816, 249, 251–3
no. 636: 18 May 1816, 259
no. 650: [3 September 1816], 263
no. 651: 4 September [1816], 255
no. 654: 6 September 1816, 252
no. 655: 6 September [1816], 255
no. 659: [29 September 1816] (?1814), 227
no. 664: [c. 11 October 1816], 259
no. 669: [3 November 1816], 263
no. 671: [c. 12 November 1816], 255
no. 677: [November 1816], 258
no. 683: 18 December 1816, 259
no. 716: [1816], 232
no. 772: [end of March 1817], 266
no. 783: 19 June 1817, 266, 270
no. 786: 9 July 1817, 266
no. 790: [23 July 1817], 273

Index of Other Documents

no. 791: 26 July 1817, 253
no. 800: 14 August 1817, 282
no. 803: 19 August 1817, 266
no. 823: [September 1817], 266
no. 824: 2 October [1817], 274
no. 839: [28 December 1817], 274
no. 872: [1817], 272
no. 884: [c. 7 January 1818], 274
no. 885: [early January 1818], 274
no. 886: [23 January 1818], 274
no. 897: 29 March 1818, 276, 281
no. 904: 18 June 1818, 283
no. 930: [1818] (? 13 January 1818), 258
no. 979: 27 October 1819, 276
no. 1056: 10 September 1821, 240
no. 1290: 20 May 1824, 171
no. 1325: 17 December 1824, 258
no. 1366b: 3 May 1825, 164
no. 1372: 17 May 1825, 169
no. 1396: [shortly after 11 July 1825], 258
Appendix A: 6–10 October 1802 (the 'Heiligenstadt Testament'), 193–4, 196

Appendix C, no. 6: 10 May 1817 (contract), 272, 281
Appendix C, no. 7: 25 September 1818, 277
Appendix C, no. 9: 1 February 1819, 258, 272, 276
Appendix C, no. 15: 18 February 1820 (Draft of a Memorandum to the Court of Appeal), 276–7
Appendix G, no. 8: [c. August 1817] (? February 1818), 282
Appendix G, no. 9: 17 January 1818 (receipt), 278

LETTERS OF (CASPAR) CARL VAN BEETHOVEN
to Härtel, 10 October 1804, 107
to Härtel, 24 November 1804, 107
to Breitkopf & Härtel, 12 February 1805, 96
to Hoffmeister & Kühnel, 27 March 1806, 108

OTHER DOCUMENTS

'Fischhof' Manuscript (Berlin, DSB), 194–5, 197–200, 203, 205, 214, 243, 269, 271, 283
'Heiligenstadt Testament', see Index of Letters, Anderson Appendix A
Jugendtagebuch, 1792–4 (London, Heirs of Stefan Zweig), 205
Nachlass auction catalogue, copies of, 195, 201
Stammbuch, 1792 (Vienna, Österreichische Nationalbibliothek), 193–6, 215, 233

Tagebuch, 1812–18, copies of
Anton Gräffer's (Iserlohn, Stadtarchiv), 194, 198–200, 202–5, 228
Joseph Fischhof's (Berlin, DSB), 194, 198–200, 203–4, 214, 228, 243, 269, 271, 283
Andreas Velten's (Bonn, Universitätsbibliothek), 194, 200
Otto Jahn's (Berlin, DSB), 194, 200

General Index

Citations of the standard works by Thayer, Nottebohm, and Kinsky–Halm are not usually indexed.

Adlung, Jakob, 184
Albrechtsberger, Johann Georg, 10, 56–8, 176, 184, 190
Alfieri, Count Vittorio, 207, 223
Amenda, Karl, 206
André, Johann, 170
Arnold, Denis, 227
Artaria & Co., 56, 193, 195–6, 198, 215, 252, 255
Artaria, Domenico, 255

Babbitt, Milton, 92
'Baberl' (servant), 274
Bach, Carl Philipp Emanuel, 61, 172, 279, 284
Bach, Johann Baptist, 196, 276
Bach, Johann Sebastian, 230, 284
Bäuerle, Adolf B., 195
Baum, Gertrud, 279
Beach, David, 92
Beck, Dagmar, 276
Becker, Heinz, 222
Beethoven, Caroline van (nephew Karl's wife), 193–4
Beethoven, (Caspar) Carl van (brother), 96, 107–8, 170, 207, 231–2, 248, 250, 275–7, 281–2
Beethoven, Johann van (father), 279
Beethoven, Johanna van (sister-in-law), 193–4, 231–2, 248, 266, 272, 275–7, 280–3
Beethoven, Karl van (nephew), 193–5, 207, 250, 252–4, 258, 266–7, 269–72, 274–7, 280–3
Beethoven, Ludwig Maria van (brother), 279
Beethoven, (Nikolaus) Johann van (brother), 225–6
Bekker, Paul, 86
Bente, Martin, 197

Berlioz, Hector, 86
Bernard, Karl, 240
Bertolini, Dr Andreas, 196, 223
Bhagavad-Gita, 245
Biba, Otto, 222
Bierey, Gottlob-Benedikt, 238
Bigot, Marie, 129
Bigot, Paul, 129
Birchall, Robert, 251
Blume, Friedrich, 90, 174, 197, 222
Boettcher, Hans, 225
Bonham's (auction rooms), London, 114
Brandenburg, Sieghard, 36, 47–8, 55, 60–1, 63, 71–2, 200
Brauchle, Joseph X., 274
Braun, Wenzel (servant), 263, 271
Breitkopf & Härtel, 48, 70–1, 102, 108, 208, 234, 267
  see also Härtel, Gottfried Christoph
Brenneis, Clemens, 195–8, 204–5
Brentano, Antonie, 206, 214, 227, 260, 262, 268, 271, 273–4
Brentano, Clemens, 162
Brentano, Franz, 206, 227, 268, 271, 273–4
Breuning, Eleonore von, 215
Breuning, Helene von, 206
Breuning, Julie von, 134
Breuning, Stephan von, 130, 134, 193–4, 206
Brockhaus, Heinz Alfred, 142
Brunsvik, Count Franz, 224
Brunsvik, Josephine, *see* Deym, Countess Josephine
Bureau des Arts et d'Industrie, 134–5
Busch-Weise, Dagmar von, *see* Weise, Dagmar

Calderón de la Barca, Pedro, 220–1

General Index

Carl, Dr, Edler von Adlersberg, 226
Carr, Bruce, 222, 264
Cassiodorus, Magnus Aurelianus, 167
Cassirer, Fritz, 87
Chapman, Roger E., 30
Chladni, Ernst Florens Friedrich, 234
Chodkowski, Andrzej, 141–2, 157
Chopin, Frédéric, 146
Clemens August, Elector of Cologne, 233
Clementi, Muzio, 49, 134
Coleridge, Samuel Taylor, 91
Collin, Heinrich Joseph von, 134, 230
Cooper, Martin, 162
Cramer, John Baptist, 114, 143
Czerny, Carl, 230, 254–5
Czerny, Joseph, 284
Czikann, J. J. H., 195

Dahlhaus, Carl, 47–8, 61, 89, 101
Derr, Ellwood, 61
Deym, Countess Josephine, 206
Diabelli, Antonio, 252
Döring, Johann Friedrich Samuel, 172, 186, 188
Dole, Nathan Haskell, 264
Dorfmüller, Kurt, 228
Dow, Alexander, 256
Downs, Philip, 95, 100
Draeseke, Felix, 89
Drouot Rive Gauche (auction rooms), Paris, 116

Earp, Lawrence, 105
Emerich, G. A., 109–10
Engelsmann, Walter, 88–91
Epstein, David, 93
Erdödy, Countess Marie, 206, 228, 249, 251–3, 266, 270

Feder, Georg, 173–4
Ferishtah, Muhammad Kāsim, 256
Fick, Johann Georg, 242–3
Finscher, Ludwig, 131
Fischer, Kurt von, 47
Fischhof, Joseph, 197–200
Fishman, Natan L., 47–9, 60, 72, 101
Fiske, Roger, 162
Floros, Constantin, 102
Forbes, Elliot, 88, 91
Forkel, Johann Nikolaus, 173
Forster, Georg, 245–6, 256
Forster, Johann Reinhold, 257
Fortune, Nigel, 227
'Frau D.' (servant), 283
Freudenberg, Karl Gottlieb, 169, 229
Frimmel, Theodor von, 225, 233, 240, 258

Friskin, Rebecca, 108
Fröhlich, C. W., 171
Fuchs, Aloys, 196–7
Fux, Johann Joseph, 56, 58, 92, 184

Gall, Franz Joseph, 270
Gassner, Ferdinand Simon, 197–9, 203, 212
Gassner, Frau, 199
Gebauer, Franz Xaver, 252–3
Geiringer, Karl, 30
Gellert, Christian Fürchtegott, 281
George, Prince Regent of England, 221
Gérard, René, 242
Gerber, Ernst Ludwig, 176
Gerstinger, Hans, 194
Gestalt psychology, 87
Giannatasio del Rio, Cajetan, 250, 253, 258, 272, 275, 282
Giannatasio del Rio, Fanny, 215, 253, 260
Glarean, Heinrich, 162
Gleichenstein, Baron Ignaz von, 134–5, 206
Gluck, Christoph Willibald, 230
Goethe, Johann Wolfgang von, 90–1, 245, 258, 264
Goldschmidt, Harry, 163, 195
Govinda, Ciangra, 241–2
Gozzi, Carlo, 207, 223–4
Gräffer, Anton, 194–200, 202–5, 212, 214, 223, 228, 252
Gräffer, Franz, 194–5
Grätz (near Troppau), 109, 129–30, 135
Grasnick, Friedrich August, 196
Graun, Carl Heinrich, 172
Grove, Sir George, 87, 90
Günther, Hans Otto, 242
Guhr, Carl, 179

Härtel, Gottfried Christoph, 107, 234
(see also Breitkopf & Härtel)
Häuser, Johann Ernst, 174
Halhed, Nathaniel Brassey, 242, 257
Halm, August, 88, 94
Hammer-Purgstall, Joseph, 244
Handel, George Frideric, 230, 279
Haslinger, Tobias, 215, 240
Hauschka, Vincenz, 222
Haydn, Franz Joseph, 1–2, 15–19, 21–4, 26, 28, 55–7, 142, 146–8, 152, 154, 158–9, 228, 230
  String Quartet Op. 20 No. 1 in Eb, 17
  String Quartet Op. 76 No. 3 in C, 56
  String Quartet Op. 76 No. 6 in Eb, 56

Haydn, Franz Joseph – cont.
  Symphony No. 94 in G ('Surprise'),
    17, 22
  Symphony No. 95 in C minor, 18–19,
    21–2
  Symphony No. 97 in C major, 22,
    147–8
  'London' Symphonies, 17, 23, 147
Hays, Heber Michel, 248
Henderson, Alfred, 265
Herder, Johann Gottfried, 207–8, 215–16,
    234–6, 245, 247
Herre, Grita, 184, 234, 240, 261, 277, 279
Hesiod, 247–8
Hess, Willy, 157, 228
Heydt, Johann Daniel von der, 174
Hiller, Johann Adam, 172
Hoffmann, E. T. A., 88, 171, 221
Hoffmeister & Kühnel, 108
Holz, Karl, 167, 195, 197
Homer, 207–8, 225, 232, 249–50, 258,
    284–5
Hotschevar, Jacob, 193, 195, 204
Hüffer, Eduard, 198
Hufeland, Christoph Wilhelm, 268
Hummel, Johann Nepomuk, 228

'Immortal Beloved', 206, 214, 260, 262
Indy, Vincent d', 152–3

Jahn, Otto, 194–5, 200, 230
Johnson, Douglas, 56, 114, 147, 195, 198
Johnston, William, 257
Jonas, Oswald, 91
Jones, Sir William, 242–3, 245–6, 257
Joseph Clemens, Elector of Cologne, 233

Kalidasa, 244–5
Kalischer, Alfred C., 197, 244
Kandler, Franz Sales, 264
Kanka, Johann Nepomuk, 224–5, 252,
    266
Kanne, Friedrich August, 284
Kant, Immanuel, 207, 261–3
Kapp, Julius, 85, 90, 231
Kastner, Emerich, 231
Kauder, Hugo, 101
Keats, John, 100
Kerman, Joseph, 29–30, 37, 49, 54, 132,
    143, 155, 159, 162, 164, 175, 181–2
Kerst, Friedrich, 215, 229–30
Kinsky, Prince Ferdinand, 224–5, 267
Kinsky, Georg, 27, 195–7
Kirkendale, Warren, 57, 162, 167, 170,
    181, 190, 284
Kirnberger, Johann Philipp, 58–9, 171–2,
    182

Klein, Hans-Günter, 35, 114, 196
Kleuker, Johann Friedrich, 241–6, 257
Klimowitsky, Abraham, 163
Kloiber, Rudolf, 153
Klopstock, Friedrich Gottlieb, 114
Knecht, Justin Heinrich, 170–9, 182, 185
Koch, Heinrich Christoph, 171
Köhler, Karl-Heinz, 163, 184, 195, 234,
    240, 261, 276–7, 279
Kolowrat, Count Anton von, 224–5
Kramer, Richard, 54, 72, 130–1, 175
Kratochvil, V., 225
Kross, Siegfried, 35
Krumpholz, Wenzel, 264
Kühn, Hellmut, 167
Kühnau, Johann Christoph, 172
Kunze, Stefan, 48

Lam, Basil, 162
Lamatsch, Paul, 276
Landon, H. C. Robbins, 17, 30
Lang, Paul Henry, 95, 100
Leitzmann, Albert, 198–9, 203, 281
Ley, Stephan, 241
Lichnowsky, Princess Christiane von,
    206
Lichnowsky, Prince Karl von, 109, 129,
    130, 134–5
Lipperheide, Franz von, 226
Linke, Joseph, 167
Lobkowitz, Prince Franz Joseph, 135,
    162, 267, 284
Lockwood, Lewis, 49, 105, 227
Lorenz, Alfred, 87–8
Lowinsky, Edward, 101
Luther, Martin, 177

MacArdle, Donald W., 231, 276, 282
Mälzel, Johann Nepomuk, 226, 233
Mahābhārata, 257
Majer, Friedrich, 242
Malfatti, Dr Johann, 223
Malfatti, Therese, 223–4
Marek, George R., 85
Martin, Sir Theodore, 264
Marx, Adolph Bernhard, 86, 94, 191
Mason, Daniel Gregory, 161
Mattheson, Johann, 184
Michelangelo Buonarroti, 251
Mies, Paul, 47–8, 55–6, 66
Mikulicz, Karl Lothar, 50
Mila, Massimo, 161–2
Misch, Ludwig, 231, 276, 282
Mitchell, William J., 29, 92, 227
Mizler, Lorenz Christoph, 184
Moore, Charles A., 257
Mortimer, Peter, 176

General Index

Moscheles, Charlotte, 194
Moscheles, Ignaz, 194
Mosel, Ignaz Franz, Edler von, 196
Mozart, Wolfgang Amadeus, 2, 14–16, 22, 30, 121, 124–5, 132, 142–7, 152–5, 158, 230
   K 380 Violin Sonata in Eb, 14
   K 387 String Quartet in G, 30
   K 425 'Linz' Symphony, 142
   K 457 Piano Sonata in C minor, 145
   K 458 String Quartet in Bb ('Hunt'), 142
   K 464 String Quartet in A, 143
   K 465 String Quartet in C, 121, 124–5, 132
   K 478 Piano Quartet in G minor, 146
   K 491 Piano Concerto in C minor, 143–5
   K 493 Piano Quartet in Eb, 142
   K 515 String Quintet in C, 147
   K 516 String Quintet in G minor, 142
   K 522 *Ein musikalischer Spass*, 146
   K 551 'Jupiter' Symphony, 142, 146
   K 575 String Quartet in D, 121
   K 581 Clarinet Quintet, 121
   K 590 String Quartet in F, 142
Müller, F. Max, 242
Müller, Johann von, 236
Müller-Blattau, Joseph, 47
Müllner, Amandus Gottfried Adolf, 207–8, 216–19
Münch, Ernst, 238

Napoleon, 85, 222, 278
Naue, Friedrich, 172
Nedden, Otto zur, 89
Neate, Charles, 215, 259
Newman, William S., 141
Niemann, Konrad, 142, 163, 195
Nisbet, Hugh Barr, 90
Nitsche, Peter, 167
Nohl, Ludwig, 113, 194, 197–9, 203–4, 212, 222, 226, 228–9, 233, 238, 243–4, 247, 250, 252–3, 260, 267, 269, 273, 275, 283, 285
Nottebohm, Gustav, 47–8, 57, 59, 70–1, 87, 94, 102, 112–14, 120–1, 127, 130, 169, 194
Novalis (pseudonym of Friedrich von Hardenburg), 162

Oppersdorff, Count Franz von, 134
Orel, Alfred, 2
Orsini, G. N. Giordano, 90
Oser, Ernst, 91
Oulibicheff, Alexandre, 86
Ovid, 269, 272

Pachler, Karl, 266
Palestrina, Giovanni Pierluigi da, 162–3, 169, 182, 284
Pasqualati, Baron Johann, 278
Paulinus a Sancto Bartholomaeo, 242, 257
'Peppi' (servant), 283
Peters, Karl, 284
Philharmonic Society of London, 233, 259
Pichler, Caroline, 238
Pleyel, Ignaz, 228
Pliny, 265, 270
Plutarch, 207, 257–8, 277
Poelchau, Georg, 173
Prach, Ivan, 132
Prod'homme, J. G., 24

Radhakrishnan, Sarvepalli, 257
Raspe, Rudolph E., 242
Razumovsky, Count Andreas Kirillovich, 107, 134–5
Reckow, Fritz, 89
Redlich, Carl, 215
Reichardt, Johann Friedrich, 224, 230, 251
Reinitz, Max, 258
Reiss, Anton, 275–6
Reiss, Theresia, 275–6
Rellstab, Ludwig, 164
Réti, Rudolph, 91
Riemann, Hugo, 47, 91
Riepel, Joseph, 184
Ries, Ferdinand, 17–18, 85, 258, 260, 266, 270, 272, 274
Riezler, Walter, 88, 95
Rig-Veda, 241–2
Rinck, Johann Christian Heinrich, 177
Ringer, Alexander, 49
Ritterbush, Philip C., 90
Robertson, William, 246, 256
Roeder, Erich, 89
Rolland, Romain, 223
Romberg, Bernhard, 221
Rosen, Charles, 95, 141, 146–7, 149, 152–3
Rousseau, G. S., 90
Rudolph, Archduke, 134, 223, 225, 230, 233, 240, 254–5, 267, 284
Rupprecht, Johann Baptist, 233, 253
Rusack, Hedwig Hoffmann, 224

Sa'dī, 215–16, 234–6
Salm, Peter, 90
Salzer, Felix, 29, 92, 227
Schaal, Richard, 197
Scheide, William, 181

Schenk, Johann Baptist, 56
Schiedermair, Ludwig, 27, 261
Schilling, Gustav, 197
Schiller, Friedrich von, 207–8, 224, 245, 258, 263–4, 266
Schindler, Anton, 85, 134, 193–4, 196–8, 206, 285
Schirach, Gottlob Benedict von, 258, 277
Schlegel, August Wilhelm von, 221
Schlemmer, Wenzel, 274
Schlösser, Louis, 72
Schlosser, Johann Aloys, 194–5
Schmidt, Hans, 35
Schmidt-Görg, Joseph, 54
Schmitz, Arnold, 219, 240, 285
Schneider, Hans, 114
Schneller, Julius Franz, 238
Schnyder von Wartensee, Xaver, 266
Schott (Bernard Schotts Söhne), 171, 258
Schreyvogel, Joseph, 224
Schubert, Franz, 241, 245
Schubring, Walter, 242–3
Schuhmacher, Gerhard, 131
Schultz, Johann Reinhold, 258
Schuppanzigh, Ignaz, 107
Shakespeare, William, 251
Shedlock, J. S., 197, 244
Siegel, Hedi, 92
Simpson, Robert, 153
Simrock, Nikolaus, 196, 251, 268
Smart, Sir George, 259
Smetana, Dr Carl von, 258
Solomon, Maynard, 1, 85, 227, 260, 264, 268, 279
Somfai, László, 30
Sonneck, Oscar G., 233
Spector, Stephen, 114
Spitzer, Leo, 100
Spontini, Gaspare, 229
Stadt Nürnberg, Theyer's, 279–80
Staehelin, Martin, 197, 199
Staudenheim, Dr Jakob, 223, 234, 254–5
Stein, Matthäus Andreas, 214
Steiner, Sigmund Anton, 251–2, 255, 258, 278
Sterba, Richard and Editha, 248
Streicher, Nanette, 258, 274, 283
Sturm, Christoph Christian, 207, 285

Thayer, Alexander Wheelock, 27, 85, 113, 193–4, 198, 205, 243

Thibaut, A. F. J., 163
Thomson, George, 130, 228, 281–2
Tovey, Donald Francis, 87, 97, 102, 146–7, 150, 152–5
Treitschke, Georg Friedrich, 105, 224, 227
Truscott, Harold, 161
Tucher, Gottlieb von, 163
Türk, Daniel Gottlob, 170–8, 184–7, 190
Tyson, Alan, 48, 53, 85–6, 109, 113–14, 274 135, 155, 195, 197, 227, 251,

Vaišesika, 257
Vasishtha, 242
Vedas, 255–6
  (see also Rig-Veda)
Velten, Andreas, 194, 200
'Viennese biography' of Beethoven, 194–7, 212
Virneisel, Wilhelm, 35–6
Vivaldi, Antonio, 162
Vogler, Georg Joseph, 170, 172–3, 175–7, 179–80
Voss, Johann Heinrich, 225, 232, 250, 284–5

Wagenseil, Georg Christoph, 56
Wagner, Richard, 16, 85–7, 89–90
Waldstein, Count Ferdinand, 142, 194
Wallishausser, J. B., 238
Watermarks and paper-types, 109–12, 114–18, 204
Weber, Carl Maria von, 228
Webster, James, 56
Wegeler, Franz Gerhard, 130, 206, 258, 279
Weise, Dagmar, 197, 205
Wendt, Amadeus, 251
Werner, Friedrich Ludwig Zacharias, 207–8, 237–41
Wilkins, Charles, 246
Willson, A. Leslie, 242
Wimsatt, William K., 90
Winter, Robert, 222, 264

Zahn, Johannes, 163
Zarlino, Gioseffo, 162, 167, 182
Zmeskall von Domanovecz, Baron Nikolaus, 196, 226, 254–5, 263, 273
Zweig, Stefan, Heirs of, 215

Addenda and Corrigenda to *Beethoven Studies* [1] (New York, 1973; London, 1974) and *Beethoven Studies 2* (London and New York, 1977)

BEETHOVEN STUDIES [1]

p. 7: For 'Beethoven' read 'Beethowen'. A discussion of this point will be found in *Beethoven Studies 2*, pp. 13–14.

pp. 85, 93. The missing leaf referred to as 'D' has recently come to light; it is now in the Beethovenhaus, Bonn.

BEETHOVEN STUDIES 2

pp. 11–12. Further instances of the 'Peter Zöh' watermark are to be found in a letter to Prince Nikolas Galitzin of 25 January 1823 (Anderson no. 1123) and two letters to Schindler, both undated (Anderson nos. 1126, 1138).

pp. 20, 23 (bottom), 24. The date of the letter to Adolf Martin Schlesinger should be 28 June 1820 (it is given correctly at the top of p. 23).

pp. 26–9. The autograph of Beethoven's letter to Probst of 26 July 1824 has come to light; it is now in a private collection in the U.S.A.

pp. 29–32. At the sale of Johann Andreas Stumpff's *Nachlass* by Puttick & Simpson, London, on 30 March 1847, lots 67–73 consisted of manuscript copies of the same seven scores by Beethoven that are listed in this letter. This is strong confirmation that Stumpff was Johann van Beethoven's unnamed correspondent.